THE GAMBIT

Allen Longstreet

Surbhi!
Sorry this took so long.
It was a pleasure meeting you
at YALcon 2016, and keep being
the witty badass you are! :)
I hope you enjoy this wild ride
of a novel. Definitely anti-government
and anti-corruption. Take care!
♡ - Allen
10/14/2016

THE GAMBIT

ISBN-13: 978-1512284539
ISBN-10: 151228453X

Cover design by Aaron Tallman and Colton Lidey

Acknowledgements

First and foremost, I would like to thank Mr. Campbell for taking the time to meet me at Starbucks in July of 2014 to discuss the idea I had for this book. I had a rough impression of what would take place in the novel, but our conversation was the foundation for this epic thriller. I had thought of the first spark, but you fanned the flame. I appreciate all the brainstorming we have done in the past and I look forward to whatever we talk about next. You are consistently an inspiration in my life.

Ryan, I cannot express my thanks enough for your help with creating the character of Grey. He would have been one shitty hacker if it wasn't for you. Your intellect is unrivaled, and very few people I know can even touch your level of thought. Thank you for your excitement and encouragement with this project, and I appreciated your willingness to let me read you the scenes that you helped create. This book would not have been the same without your contribution.

Thank you, Daniela Jewell, for your explanation on the effects of radiation on dividing cells and how to properly use an electron microscope. Your knowledge of biology and the lab environment was a great assistance in creating the scenes at MIT.

Melanie Gill, thank you for your tidbit of advice on a certain scene that I will not mention. Let's just say I had to have your womanly advice.

Lastly, I would like thank the brave seven who made this story what it is. Owen, Grey, Rachel, Stefan, Ian, Lucas, and Brody—you all will forever be in my heart and mind. I can only hope that you impact the reader the same way you did me. Thank you for speaking to me the times my words fell short. You helped me make an exhilarating story.

Dedication

To the many men and women who have been delivered injustice by the hands of the unknown. May the truth always reign supreme.

To my mother, my father, and my brother. I love you all dearly.

"In the name of the best within you, do not sacrifice this world to those who are its worst. In the name of the values that keep you alive, do not let your vision of man be distorted by the ugly, the cowardly, the mindless in those who have never achieved his title. Do not lose your knowledge that man's proper estate is an upright posture, an intransigent mind and a step that travels unlimited roads. Do not let your fire go out, spark by irreplaceable spark, in the hopeless swamps of the approximate, the not-quite, the not-yet, the not-at-all. Do not let the hero in your soul perish, in lonely frustration for the life you deserved, but have never been able to reach. Check your road and the nature of your battle. The world you desired can be won, it exists, it is real, it is possible, it's yours."

– Ayn Rand

PREFACE

My heart pounded relentlessly in my chest. I stood behind the double doors of the emergency exit in complete darkness, engulfed in the smell of my own sweat. I could hear the muffled voices of the anchors delivering the daily headlines just a few feet in front of me. I began to wonder—*is this even reality? Can I wake up from this nightmare?* With everything that had occurred, I knew that was not the case. My ultimatum had already been decided for me. It was unfathomable in my mind to think that I was even in the cross-hair to begin with, let alone being the most wanted criminal in the United States. Thoughts of what I was about to do bombarded my mind and caused a nauseating pit in my stomach to form. My greatest wish was that there was another option, but this was the only way. I knew this was my last stand, a final leap of faith to ensure my struggle was not in vain. My hands perspired and trembled wildly as I held the cold metal push-bar of the double doors. I breathed rapidly and closed my eyes, seeing the images of everything that has happened within the past two weeks. I swallowed hard and remembered the words of a person who I love. Justice is like fire; if you cover it with a veil, it still burns. They are the veil, and I am the fire. I will watch their lies burn, not in vengeance, but in preservation of the only thing that is real in this world—the *truth.*

Convergence HQ – Washington, D.C.

09:24 **10-07-2016**

Dear Mr. Owen Marina,

You are cordially invited to the 2016 presidential debate for recognition as the co-founder of the Convergence Party and the outstanding contributions your office has made to Senator Paul Goodman, Convergence Party nominee. Congratulations, due to your effort the Convergence Party has claimed fifty-nine percent of the benchmark polls. All three nominees in each party will debate and give their closing statements per status quo. Dress requirement is formal attire; men must wear suit and tie. Women must wear a dress or business attire. The debate will be held at the Georgetown University Amphitheater.

3700 O St. NW, Washington, D.C 20057

October 11th, 2016

Doors open at 6 PM EST – 9 PM EST air time.

The ticket in this envelope is VIP access marked with the Great Seal of the United States, allowing you seating in the front three rows. These seats are reserved for the families of the candidates, and the democratic, republican, and convergence campaign leaders. The federal government rate is available at the Ritz-Carlton Spa Georgetown for the evening of the event. This ticket allows for one extra admission of a spouse. Join us on this historic night in American History.

I grinned as I held the firm letterhead beneath my fingers. What an honor it was to be given VIP access to such an event. I was thrilled.

"What is it, boss?" my colleague Alexis asked. I tried suppressing my smile before answering.

"It's an invitation to the final debate next week."

"No way!" she shouted, "Congratulations, Owen!"

"Hey, everyone, look what Owen got!"

Her voice trailed off as she bounced around the office informing more of my coworkers. She was a petite woman with bleach-blonde hair—one of those people who knew what was going on in the lives of others the moment it happened.

I felt a heavy hand grasp my shoulder.

"My boy! You're going to the debate?" I spun around in my desk chair to see the chairman of the party looking down at me with an overjoyed expression.

"Well, I guess I am now, Cole."

"He would get it," one of our temps Barbara announced. "He has the most passion! He's the reason we are ahead in the polls."

I shook my head side to side humbly, laughing under my breath at her comment. For reasons we were all aware of, I did not want recognition for the effort I had put into this campaign. My passion was fueled by much deeper reasons.

Within moments I had half of the office surrounding my desk, the rest were busy at work. Being less than a month away from the most important election in American History, it was incredibly hectic, the sounds of phones ringing filled my ears long after I left work daily.

"Speech! Speech! Speech!" Alexis chanted amongst the circle of our coworkers.

"No, no, I'd rather not." I politely declined.

"Aw, come on!" she insisted, "You earned it! Say something, Owen! You worked so hard on this campaign and we all know it."

I reluctantly stood up out of my desk chair in front of the crowd encircling me.

"Guys, I know I was invited, but with all honesty, you deserve this ticket. Without the help of everyone, this office would be nothing. Barbara, Alexis, Joseph, Nicolas, there are countless others whose names I don't need to mention because you guys are all important. I accept this ticket humbly. I feel honored to be the leader of this campaign, and if you all know a shred about me you know I am not here for the money or the title. I am here for the security and knowledge that there will never be another Confinement again."

Half of the faces in the audience became contorted, and a few grimaced from my words.

"Those three months of Hell we all spent in this capital will never occur again. *That* is the reason why I am so passionate. I have said it many times. In my opinion, it is the prime reason our campaign is invincible. The people do not trust the leaders of our past, it is time for a new America. The atrocity they committed will never be forgotten. We will not grant them power any longer."

The office applauded in reaction to my speech. A couple of my coworkers stood up and gave me a standing ovation.

"That's the damn truth if I've ever heard it!" Cole shouted while giving me a rough pat on the back. "Everyone stay put, I've got a treat and another announcement," he said, circumventing the crowd and heading to the break room. Knowing Cole, it would involve alcohol. He was a walking testament to the saying *work hard, play hard.*

When he reemerged, he had two bottles of champagne in his hands, and he weaved his way back beside me.

"Owen, would you help me do the honors?"

As he asked I could smell the alcohol on his breath. Perhaps he had taken a shot when he was in the break room. If there was any alcohol in our building, it would have come from his office and his office only. Spending over three decades in politics was more than enough to wind up in an asylum, and I wasn't surprised he was an alcoholic.

"My pleasure," I said.

He handed me the bottle, and I held its weighty glass with the cork facing outward. Cole used his free hand to brush his thin, gray hair out of his eyes. The sweat beaded along his hairline. He always seemed to sweat like a swine when he drank.

"Ahem," Cole cleared his throat. "Whether you are a volunteer, an intern, or employee in this office, remember the contribution that was made here, in the past year. The Convergence Campaign wouldn't be where it is today if it wasn't for your dedication and unwavering belief of what this party stands for. Each and every one of us wakes up every day fueled by the same motivation. Truth in government, removing the corporate ties from the political equation, and civil liberties for every American. Like Owen said, we will *not* allow another Confinement to happen again! Their reign is *over!*"

"Yeah!" the crowd shouted in unison.

"In light of our efforts, and with the triumph of Senator Goodman over the other candidates in the last debate, we have claimed over fifty-nine percent of the benchmark polls!"

The entire office erupted into an uproar—cheering, whistling, I could feel myself beginning to grin in the heat of the moment.

"It is time to celebrate!" Cole hollered rambunctiously.

We shook the champagne bottles violently and popped off the corks together, our office scrambling to grab a glass to fill with the effervescent liquid. I saw a few people using their empty coffee cups as a substitution.

I pictured what it would be like if the press were to come in and request a quote from Cole or me on our continued success. They had been popping in and out quite often, and we were always in the headlines of the news. I could see it now—*Convergence Headquarters celebrating with drinks before noon.* Some might have remarked that we were unconventional, but that was precisely what we intended to be. The American People were championing us. Every day that passed their support only grew stronger. Senator Goodman had a surefire spot in the White House. The only groups which were opposing this political awakening were the democrats and republicans. Valiant were their efforts—if you could call it that—but their attempts to hamper our campaign were futile because their lies were nothing short of slander.

The boisterous voices of my colleagues had turned to a soft chatter. Cole began to raise his glass to make a toast.

"I'd like to make a proposition with all of you in this office. If Goodman takes the polls by a landslide in the election, we are all going to Smith Commons to celebrate on my tab! Free booze on me!"

The combined cheers and hoots were deafening. Once the ruckus settled down, silence reclaimed the office.

"I love that bar," Alexis whispered to the woman next to her.

"With all of that being said," Cole began, "I have no doubts whatsoever that the Convergence Party will produce the first independent candidate to take the White House. *Nothing* will stand in our way. Thank you all for your hard work and carry on with your day."

Within moments, the phones resumed with their incessant ringing. The chaos of office life was equivalent to watching a colony of ants work together to carry a piece of bread back to the queen. Except this was politics, and ensuring Senator Goodman's election was our metaphorical queen.

As I sat back down at my desk I felt Cole's firm hand once again.

"This final debate is the pith of our campaign. Once Goodman hits on the points that caused the Confinement, it'll be a straight shot to home plate. You've done an excellent job running this campaign, Owen. You should be proud of yourself. If you want to come out for some drinks after work they are on me."

"It has been an honor, Cole. Thanks for funding most of it."

"Funding? Hell, I'd rather go bankrupt funding this than rot in that prison of a Camp we lived in."

"No shit, you got that right," I agreed.

"Well, my boy, I'll see you Tuesday at the debate. Save my wife and I a seat, will ya?"

"Absolutely," I responded with a grin as he shook my shoulder roughly and walked back to his office.

I spun around in my chair and faced the desktop screen. My to-do list was always growing—like a pesky weed I would uproot that came back bigger every time. Emails, inquiries from newspapers and magazines for interviews on the recent benchmark polls. I was one man stretched very thin, but I knew that in a month this would all be over. All the coffee, long hours, and little to no sleep would be worthwhile. Goodman's election would be the beginning of a new America. A memory I could look back on when I was an old man and remember that I took part in history.

I walked out of the office building to see the weather hadn't changed a bit from this morning. The sky was overcast, painting the world shades of gray. I felt a light drizzle falling. The air was cold and humid. As I breathed in the moisture coated my nose. A soft breeze crept into my button-up and torso, so I zipped up my motorcycle jacket.

"See you later, boss," I heard from behind me.

When I turned around I saw Alexis ducking into her Volkswagen Beetle with a flirtatious smirk.

"See you," I responded with an awkward smile before putting on my helmet. I didn't feed her flirting by returning the action. She was attractive, but I wasn't going to get involved in interoffice relations. I had already been down that road, and although it was an exhilarating ride, I wasn't fond of making the same mistake twice. I was quite certain Alexis had a fetish for the boss-and-intern scenario. I could see the lust in her eyes when she looked at me and the fantasies played out in her mind like a porno. The promiscuous intern in skimpy clothing, the boss telling her he needed to see her in his office. The scene played out in my mind was enough to give me a chubby, and get Alexis more worked up than she ought to be. In a month from now, after the election, I'd most likely never see her again. For those reasons, I chose not to pursue her.

There was one *other* reason, though. I was straddling it. I turned the key and hit the ignition switch, holding in the clutch and revving the engine. The shrill, metallic growl of the 998 cubic centimeters beneath me were just brimming with raw power, ready to devour the asphalt in front of it.

My YZF-R1 was my baby—my everything. I had an R6 for years, and then I bought this model in 2012, dumping the majority of my money into it in the years before the Confinement. Some people used drugs for a high, but my drug was the speed, the adrenaline that pumped through my veins when I was tucked into the body of a bike, accelerating faster than anything else on the road.

I let the clutch slip slowly and made my way onto New Jersey

Avenue. I took it easy because the street was congested, and I wasn't on my main route yet. I then turned onto Massachusetts Avenue where I hit the daily rush-hour. Traffic in D.C. was a nightmare. The roads were too narrow for a city of this size. We were on some list for worst traffic in the US. Luckily for me, I wasn't stuck behind this line of cars. If I was it would have made the fifteen-minute trip into half an hour or longer.

I weaved in and out of the traffic. It was like an intricate dance, a pattern. There was something seductive about being exposed, zipping down the street on two wheels, passing all the people stuck...*confined* in their cars.

When I blinked I saw a flashback—a mother and daughter holding hands. The mother whispered with her voice trembling, "*Thank you.*"

I whipped around a curve, speeding with anger, and purposely over-blinking to phase back into the present. The word *confined* drew me back to that memory. It was a memory from a time I wished I could forget.

Shifting into a higher gear, I slalomed between the traffic with finesse. This was innate for me. My motion was fluid. The high-pitched sounds coming from the engine were soothing, they canceled out all other noise that lingered from work, thoughts, and all the bullshit I fought so hard to keep out. Riding was my solace—the peace in my being.

I cut right hard, my knee just barely scraping the ground as I whipped around the corner onto Wisconsin Avenue. I passed a cop in the opposite lane, and as I glanced in my mirror he didn't turn around. Smart move on his part, for if he did *attempt* to pull me over I'd be going over 150 miles per hour before he could even U-turn back into my lane. Let's say I did give the officer the satisfaction of stopping me, I could have almost guaranteed that I would get out of it. I was somewhat of a local celebrity, as was Cole and the majority of the party. Although they still worked under direct legislation from the laws that were already in place, the cops, teachers, and firefighters were all ready for our party to take the White House. Sometimes out in public I recognized a face, someone I recalled having a conversation with. It hurled me back in time to the Confinement. A simple face could be the trigger that catapulted the memories forward. The planning, the ideas...it was where it *all* began.

I crossed the state line into Maryland. I had called Bethesda home since the beginning of 2012, about eight months after I graduated from university. I pulled in behind the Bethesda Theater and opened my garage to park the bike. I took off my helmet and made my way to the entrance of the Whitney. Living in the D.C. metro area, life could be extremely hectic, but when I came back home, I felt like it was *home.*

The automatic doors opened, and I was surrounded by the amber glow from chandeliers that filled the lobby. The soft browns and beiges were always welcoming.

"Owen! How was work?" the concierge Ricardo asked.

"Just another day in paradise, my friend."

"I'm sure, it should be smooth sailing after the polls came back."

"I won't celebrate until the eighth, just to be sure," I answered, smirking.

"You know you guys have my vote," he said as I neared the elevator.

"Ah, Ricardo, you're a good man. Have a good night."

He grinned from my compliment. "Goodnight."

The smooth hum from the elevator always was accompanied with a deep exhalation. It was a precursor to privacy—a rare occurrence in the time after the Confinement. Everyone knew my face, which made me feel so connected to the cause, but yet so *exposed.*

I walked down the hallway and opened my apartment door. Mine was the last one on the left, a corner unit. It was only one bedroom, but I chose this one because it had more room than the other models. The crisp whites gave everything a clean look. I left the walls the way they were when I moved in, I didn't have the time to decorate. I sat down on the couch and turned on the flat-screen.

"...Tonight's special report, the Union of Concerned Scientists is filing a lawsuit against the Nuclear Regulatory Commission, with an offer of dropping the charges in exchange for the commission to be willing to re-investigate the nuclear material collected from the scene outside of Wall Street on Black Monday. The commission has made no comment regarding the lawsuit, but their lawyer has given us a quote saying that the commission followed strict protocol in the testing of the nuclear materials recovered..."

Yeah, sure. I thought.

"...The Union's report tells a different series of events that followed Black Monday. When the EPA finished their clean-up, the NRC's final report claimed that the Strontium-90 came from a Russian source with the help of the infamous Viktor Ivankov—American-born Russian who worked at the Port of New York for almost a decade. In his later years, he was one of the lead operators for the X-Ray Radiography machine used to intercept potential anomalies shipped into the US through cargo containers. This report by the NRC poses many questions in the minds of the rest of the country and the world for that matter. Russia has made no comment on their involvement with being the source for the Strontium-90. Nevertheless, the tension between the US and Russia has been at an all-time high. Experts say if anything further were to occur we'd be at war overnight. What the Union is demanding is that the NRC and the federal government answer the hard-hitting questions that remain unanswered to the American public. Why, when questioned, does the Port of New York's staff all reply with the same answer? That Viktor Ivankov was the mastermind behind this and the case is closed, and when the Chief of Staff for the Port is requested the images of the container which encased the Strontium-90, he says those images are classified. Why is it that the only labs the nuclear material have been tested in are those of the EPA and the federal government? But, the biggest question that has been on the minds of Americans since Black Monday is the whereabouts of Viktor Ivankov. Where was he during the Confinement? Who is helping him elude the feds? To this day he hasn't been arrested or killed, failing to be found on any of the registries from the Camps. The closest the FBI came to apprehending him was six months ago, when they received a tip stating he had been seen at a convenient store in remote Cashiers, North Carolina—deep in the Nantahala National Forest. Upon the FBI's arrival and inquisition of employees and patrons of the store, they were informed he had been hiding out in a small cabin nearby. When the agents stormed the residence it was vacant. There wasn't a trace that anyone had been living there. What they did find, though, would turn out to be the most baffling piece of the case since Ivankov disappeared. It was a note left on a wooden desk, only five words long. It has been shared by millions on social media, revered by conspiracy theorists, and has only spawned more questions in our minds. Here is that note once again…

THE LAND OF
THE ~~FREE~~

A chill raced across my skin. I turned off the TV as the sensation swept over me. I'd seen that same image hundreds of times on the news, and I still had the same reaction. The erratic, scribbled handwriting in all caps. Then, the deliberate, heavy-handed strikes through the word *free*. I shuddered once more. To some, his message might have suggested that we would no longer be free if he or the Russians committed more terrorist acts. I, on the other hand, interpreted the message to find a different meaning. That for whatever reason, and for whichever motives—Viktor Ivankov sent his five-word message blaring to the American public. *We* were no longer the land of the *free*…

The Ellipse – Washington, D.C.
11:17 02-05-2015

The sounds of horns resonated through the air, signaling our second meal of the day. A light flurry fell from the sky, and a bitter breeze accompanied it. The lines to get our lunch stretched out for a football field in distance or more—there were three—all of them converged into the main line where we were served the meal.

This was the 'Nourishment Zone' I had been assigned to, and I absolutely loathed it. The direction of our lines faced the White House, and it made me nauseated to think our president was less than a quarter of a mile away, enclosed in warmth and luxury. I pondered that if he were out here with all of us, in the frigid mid-Atlantic winter, waiting for a sad excuse of a meal, perhaps he would have hesitated before signing the executive order which initiated the Confinement.

The smell of shit was intermingled with ground beef. If it was anything like the meat we have been served for the past three weeks, then it wasn't meat at all. This was of a lesser quality than the meat at Taco Bell, or the canned chili that had been sitting out for hours at a family cookout. Maybe it *was* scraped from a can, but it tasted as if it had sat out in the sun for a day or two. There it was again, that awful shit stench—always intermittent. It was from the hundreds of port-a-johns which lined the sidewalks.

Our line was probably one of two dozen or more in our District.

The D.C. Confinement Camp was comprised of five districts. I was assigned District 1 during sorting which was surprising to me because Bethesda was closer to District 2 and 3, which were Northwest and Northeast Washington. Districts 4 and 5 were Arlington and Alexandria, and within those five districts housed the nearly six million people of the Washington Metro Area. I wondered if the other cities were in Confinement too, we haven't been told anything at all. I glanced down at the only information I had. I was wearing it—my identification wristband.

Marina, Owen 12/7/1988
District 1 – Nourishment Zone 11

*Screw this...*I turned the wristband back around. As my line grew closer to the converging point, I sighed with frustration. I fucking worked for the government and I was still behind these fences. Were these the 'comprehensive benefits' the EPA offered? What I would do just to ride my bike, or to sit at a bar and have a drink. Fuck.

From behind me, a bald, burly man walked past. The skin on his arms had turned red from the cold. He was wearing a cut up t-shirt. He looked like the kind of guy who might ride a Harley, and judging by his size he enjoyed a diet of steak and potatoes. The scent of cigarette smoke filled my nose. He must have smuggled some in when he was sorted, or the guards had sold him some. A couple feet in front of me, where the line began to converge, he cut in front of a woman and her young daughter. My eyebrows furrowed at the sight.

I looked to my left, and then my right. The armed guards lined the rows of port-a-johns, waiting for the smallest disruption in behavior. If I brought attention to myself who knows what could happen.

I saw the woman gently reach for the man's shoulder.

"Excuse me, sir. You just cut in front of me and my daughter."

He didn't even react, like he hadn't heard her. The soft-spoken woman then moved to his side, and that was when I saw she was also pregnant.

What kind of asshole passes a pregnant mother?

"Sir," her voice now a little firmer. "You jumped in front of me."

"No shit, lady. Now let it go and keep to yourself."

Her expression turned harsh instantly. That was when I left my place in line and began approaching them.

"Keep to myself? We all have to wait for our food, so you have to too—just like everybody else. Go to the back of the line!"

He turned around with a smirk, like this was all some joke.

"Well, you don't look like you're in any condition to *make me*," he said, glancing down at her stomach. He drew in his cigarette and exaggerated the exhale as he blew the smoke at the mother's face. She started coughing. Anger surged through me.

"But I am, asshole."

He laughed when he saw me and puffed up his chest to flaunt his size. In the corner of my eye, I saw the daughter pulling at her mother's wrist. "Mommy," she whimpered.

"What the hell are you gonna do about it?"

I punched him square in the face with all my strength and he staggered and fell onto one leg. The line around us opened up as people turned to watch. I lunged at him on the ground and began wailing punches, trying my best not to allow him to retaliate. His nose and lip were bleeding, then with his fist he deflected one of my punches and nailed me in the chin. I fell backward and he punched me once more—knocking my head back onto the grass. He slammed my left arm against the grass and suddenly with his right hand I saw him grab his cigarette, and he smashed it against the inside of my forearm.

"Ahhh!" I groaned from the singeing pain.

With the adrenaline, I used my free hand to clip him in his temple, knocking him sideways. In a quick turn, I kneed him in his groin, and then I was free. I kicked him once in the teeth and a couple more times in the stomach.

I breathed heavily as I ceased fighting, and suddenly I heard a noise. I clutched my side in agony as the rubber bullet hit my ribs, then another on my hip.

"Disturbance!" the guards shouted as they closed in on me. The alarms began to sound. If my fight led to a riot or upheaval, the bullets would no longer be rubber.

The guards tackled me to the ground, and then violently pulled me up. Half of which were surrounding the man on the ground doing the same to him. They held my arms firmly and dragged me away. I craned my neck backward to find the mother and daughter. They stood facing me, holding hands as the snow swirled delicately around them. There were tears in the mother's eyes, and the daughter waved goodbye.

"Thank you…" Her voice trembled. "*Thank you…*"

The Whitney – Bethesda, MD
07:52 10-11-2016

I sat straight up in bed, gasping for air, and drenched in a cold sweat. As I calmed down, realizing I was in my room, I rubbed the inside of my left forearm. In the pale morning light the dark scar was just a dot, and always a reminder of my time in the Confinement.

"*Thank you…*" I heard the woman's voice whisper.

I shook my head to rid myself of the flashback.

Out of all the things that occurred during my three months in Confinement, that memory haunted me the most. There was not a week that went by where I didn't dream about it. I looked forward to the winter and wearing long sleeves. People loved to ask how I got the scar, and I hated retelling it. I threw my arm around and it hit the pillow next to me. It had been a long time since I had a woman in my bed. After the Confinement, I got to enjoy somewhat of a burst of stardom.

"Aren't you Owen Marina? One of the founders of the Convergence Party? I saw your interview with the Huffington Post. You are *so hot…*"

It always went along those lines. Don't kid yourself, the fruit was ripe and ready, so I picked it. Many times. Although, the flings only filled a gap, a part of me that had been empty so long. I thought I *had* something more at one point, a relationship with substance, but that didn't end well. So now at twenty-seven I was alone. No wife, no kids, not even a dog—just my bike. At this stage, it felt like I was engaged to my party for Christ's sake. Then again, I imagined the wedding being a sweet one and having a blowout of a reception. I set the date for November 8th. Perhaps Goodman and Cole would walk me down the aisle.

Ha. I stood up out of bed, laughing at myself for personifying our party. I was so backed up on sleep, I would either end up drinking more often than Cole, or wind up in a psych ward. Tonight though, tonight would be the moment that sealed the deal for our party. Perhaps, it would mean I could relax, work a little less, and answer fewer emails…because within less than a month, Senator Goodman would be President-Elect of the United States. I grinned, knowing that I had been a part of this monumental political awakening in our history. Even a year and a half later, I still remained shocked when people called me a 'founder'. Who would have thought, me—a booze drinking post-grad working in Washington became a founder of something. I hope you're proud, Mom…

Georgetown University – Washington, D.C.
18:31 10-11-2016

I cruised down Canal Road, weaving around cars that were in my path. This was the long way around, but due to less traffic, it was a lot faster for me on my bike. Anytime I revisited Georgetown or anything along the Potomac, I always took this route; it was very green. I could smell the water from the canal on my right, with trees surrounding me on both sides. It reminded me of where I grew up in Virginia.

Within minutes, I was approaching the bend which looped around and revealed the university. Cars lined 37th St. NW as far as I could see in front of the Copley and Healy lawns. I had already passed the parking garage, and I was sure when the workers saw who I was they would offer to valet, and there wasn't a chance in Hell I'd let anyone park my bike. I parked in a spot along the street, locking my bike once I stopped. I slid my helmet off and set it on the seat while I made sure my tie was straight.

Walking down the sidewalk, I had my helmet in one hand and slipped my keys in my pocket with the other. I was a block away, and I could already see the reporters lining the entrance. I was glad I wore my favorite suit. Paparazzi tend to capture the most horrifying angles. I figured that out one night when I left a bar and saw my drunken grin on a tabloid the next morning.

As I approached the entrance to the circle driveway, I heard a wave of chatter rise amongst the reporters. I was still a length away when the first camera flash went off.

"Sporting the royal colors tonight I see," a familiar reporter said.

"Always, always."

"Mr. Marina! What are your thoughts on tonight's debate? Will Goodman trample the other candidates a third time?"

"Mr. Marina, what is your response to the accusation from the democrats and the republicans stating that your party has no real platform, it's just fueled by the hype of the American People."

"Mr. Marina, Mr. Marina…"

My name blended in with the electric snaps from their cameras—it was always dizzying.

I turned around to deliver my statement.

"It doesn't matter anymore what they think. A sore loser's 'statement' is nothing more than an insult. Those same democrats and republicans were safe and comfortable whether they lived within or outside of the boundaries during the Confinement. They had immunity, and *we* didn't. Remember that…"

The reporters erupted with more questions as I turned my back to them. I looked up at the castle-like design of the buildings. Gray brick blended in with the sky. I approached Gaston Hall, where the debate was being held, and in all my years here at Georgetown I could have counted the times I'd been in the hall on one hand.

I approached the old, wooden doors, and I spread my arms and legs out, for there were security guards who used the wand to check me for weapons. They also patted me down before letting me in. Once I entered, things were more tranquil. All the people in the finest business attire, holding conversations at just above a whisper. The stage was draped with fabrics and the podium in lights, embellished with the Great Seal. The back wall of the hall was lined with dozens of news networks that would broadcast the debate.

As important of a member as I was in the political community, I had a moment of awkwardness. I felt like I was walking into the lunchroom on the first day of high school, nervously scanning the crowd to find some of my peers to hang out with. I was the young gun, the 'kid' or 'boy' as Cole called me. Over half of the heads in the room were peppered with gray, or just all white. I had made such a quick emergence in the political world, and although I knew I had influence, I felt intimidated. It was as if I were playing a game, and the instructions were written decades ago by all the people in this room…and since the start I had been *breaking* the rules.

People don't like those who break the rules, especially when my rebellion threatened their title. I knew my cause was backed with purpose and value. I exhaled, trying to relax, then I spotted Cole along one of the aisles with his wife on his arm, talking to a man and a woman.

I adjusted my tie-clip and walked towards them. Immediately, Cole met my eyes and with his free hand he motioned for me.

"Owen! Come join us, my boy."

His voice was always somewhat of a shout.

"Owen, it's been long overdue, but this is my wife, Carla."

"So nice to meet you! My husband tells me you are quite the leader around the office."

I shook her hand gently.

"I try to fit the title," I laughed sheepishly. *Damn it. I should have said more.*

"You better watch yourself tonight, Carla, he's a lot better looking than I am, charming all the girls at work and doesn't know what he's got going for him."

I blushed and revealed a suppressed grin.

"Oh stop, he's turning red for God's sake. You better watch that mouth of yours, or I might just go home with him!"

We all laughed. *So…awkward…just bite your tongue.*

Carla and Cole looked like a couple that had similar interests. She seemed as if she had drunk too many glasses of wine and Cole probably paid off the guard to sneak in his flask. Her hair was dyed red, and Cole would rather buy a fifth than purchase something to mask the gray.

"Hell would have to freeze over before you left me, but anyway, while we're here I'd like to introduce you to the chairmen of the other parties. Owen, this is Marc—Chairman of the Republican Party."

"Marc Fleming, nice to meet you," he said as he shook my hand with a vice-grip grasp. I returned the strength equally. He had a red tie on, naturally.

"Same to you, Marc, Owen Marina."

"Owen this is Veronica Hall—Chairwoman of the Democratic Party."

"Veronica, it's a pleasure to finally meet you."

"Owen Marina, my pleasure," I said.

Her hand was as cold as ice. I could feel it transferring through my skin. Her eyes were cat-like and glacier blue. The color of her hair resembled sand when it was wet. The sensation her presence gave me almost made me pull my hand away…but that would have been rude.

"How couldn't I know who you are?" she quipped. "Bravo, Owen. You've managed to blend Hollywood and politics."

"Is that supposed to be a compliment?"

"Take it how you see fit. You're like a celebrity. I can't walk into a store without seeing your face on some tabloid."

I paused, thinking of a witty comeback.

"Well, Veronica, maybe I am the first 'celebrity' in politics who isn't just a puppet."

Her eyes turned into slits, and she pursed her lips in reaction to my statement. She looked at me as if I were an insect…an insect that needed to be squashed. I felt a tension in the air and no one else spoke. Her expression then changed quickly from scornful to a patronizing smile.

"Well then, I guess you are a rare breed in Washington. Am I right?" she asked, glancing at everyone.

Cole, Carla, and Marc all laughed to end the tension. I didn't laugh, I just smiled and stared back at Veronica. Beneath her ice-blue eyes, I sensed something hostile, like inside there was a pot of boiling water about to spill over. I didn't like her already…at *all.*

"He's a rare breed all right, just look at him! I wonder if his parents are as good looking as he is."

Cole's rough slap on my shoulder broke my stare with Veronica.

Smile. Act like nothing happened.

"Carla, you're going to have to tell your husband to stop hitting on me," I joked. Everyone laughed.

"You wish I was hitting on you, Marina! You're not my type anyway," he said, laughing, and grabbed the back of my neck, giving me a good shake.

In my adult life, I'd never met anyone as abrasive and loud as Cole. He just liked roughhousing all of his friends. It probably didn't help he was constantly buzzed.

"Well Cole, it was nice catching up with you and your wife. Also, pleasure meeting you, Owen," Marc said and shook my hand.

"Same to you, Marc."

"I'm going to head back and talk to the rest of my party," he announced, slipping out of our circle.

Veronica began to leave also.

"It was a pleasure to meet you all. Oh, and Owen…with your success at running a campaign at such a young age, I'm sure you will have a bright future ahead of you in Washington."

"Thank you," I replied.

Veronica didn't mean those words. I could tell by her tone.

They walked away and joined people in the other aisles.

"Well who pissed in her cheerios?" Carla said, leaning in toward us.

Cole and I laughed, but I wasn't looking at him or his wife. My eyes were locked on Veronica. I was watching her gestures, her demeanor. So prim and proper she appeared, but there was something about her that was cold and rigid. I knew who she was from being a part of the Convergence Party, but I had never met her in person until today.

She glanced up at me. Our eyes locked. I returned her stare, and in the depths of my being I suddenly sensed something *malicious*. Veronica then smiled and turned back to her colleagues.

"You done checking Veronica out, Marina?"

I phased back to reality.

"Hell no, she's far from my type."

"You know you like cougars!"

"Shut up, Cole. Carla, I think you need to take your husband's flask away from him. The debate hasn't even started and he's half-drunk."

"I would, but so am I!"

We all laughed, with Carla hanging on to Cole's arm to keep herself balanced.

"Well if you two need a taxi, I'll treat. I'd be the DD, but I doubt we all want to spoon on my bike."

"Maybe I do?" Carla quipped in a whimsical, feminine tone, and brushing my arm as she latched on her husband's.

"You guys are crazy," I replied, shaking my head.

"All right, well let's go talk to the other members," Cole suggested.

I glanced at my watch—8:47 p.m. The auditorium was engulfed in the dim glow from sconces that lined the walls. Spotlights shone brightly on the three podiums on the stage. It was about to begin. I could hear the soft conversations from the news networks that lined the back of the room. Cole was sitting to my left with his wife beside him.

"Now all we have to do is sit back and relax. Goodman is going to crush the other candidates," Cole whispered to me.

I nodded in agreement. He was right, Senator Goodman had dominated the previous debates. There were too many gaps of information in their rhetoric, and they had no credible answers to who was behind the Confinement and why it lasted for three months. The republican and democrat nominees had been attempting to use dying ideologies to support their plight. They used sayings such as, *"This was what our country was founded on."* It sickened me when I heard that said in the first debate. Our country was founded on freedom. We seceded from Great Britain because of taxation and forced war debt on the Colonies. The most disgusting truth was that they had the nerve to say things like that, and yet they imprisoned their own citizens. I felt the singeing flames of anger licking at my insides. I snuffed them quickly and exhaled to relieve the anxiety that accompanied thinking of the Confinement. November 8th would be the day I could finally breathe again, knowing that Senator Goodman would clean house in Washington and never allow another Confinement.

The moderator of the debate walked out, took his seat in front of the stage, and shuffled some papers in his hands. It was about to begin. I saw the security guards standing in front of the exits, securing them.

"Attention attendees and news crews, please remain silent throughout the duration of the event. All exits are secured, no one is permitted to go in or out until the debate has concluded and gone off-air. The debate lasts ninety minutes. We ask that you use the restrooms now if you need so."

"Senator Blanton, what are your plans for health care reform?" the moderator asked.

"The republican platform calls for more affordable health care premiums and prescriptions for Americans. We will tweak Obamacare to where the people who already had preexisting insurance will not have to lose coverage. We will not implement any kind of socialized medicine, due to higher taxes on the middle class, and more limited options of choices from the universal system. We have seen it many times where citizens of other countries come get care here because they aren't forced to wait because their procedure is not necessary. There is no reason to force people to pay for the care of everyone else. We need to lower taxes for business owners in order to get the economy back to how it was before the Confinement."

"Senator Goodman, rebuttal?"

"The Convergence Party calls for a single-payer universal system. A system where any man, woman, or child can walk into a doctor's office, or a hospital, and receive basic care free of charge. We have tried insurance reform before. Obamacare was a first step towards a change, a misguided step at that. We are going to leave behind the lies and misconceptions that have been handed down to us by previous generations, politicians, and the pharmaceutical industry. We have a mindset that we cannot afford it, or that taxes will become exorbitant in the process. We *can* afford it. If we can afford to spend billions of dollars on our defense budget every single year, we can afford to take care of our citizens."

Cole nudged me, and I smiled. Our party was the innovators, the game-changers. We wanted to keep what had always worked in America and get rid of what didn't. When Goodman took office the playing field would be level.

I looked around. I was surrounded by purple ties, vests, and pocket squares. "*Sporting the royal colors tonight I see.*" I flashed back to the words of the first reporter that saw me. That was wording many magazines and tabloids used to describe our party's colors—*royal.* During the Confinement, Cole and I would brainstorm about the details of the

Convergence. We wanted our colors to reflect our name as closely as possible, so we combined republican red and democrat blue to get purple.

Our party was seated in the middle of the auditorium and faced directly in front of the podiums. On my left were the democrats, and my right were the republicans. I caught sight of Veronica's sandy-brown hair. Her hands rested in her lap and her blue suit blended in with the others around her. I slowly turned to the right and spotted Marc's weathered skin and red tie. He was staring intently at the debate.

I sat smack-dab in the middle of my competition, and suddenly I felt unsettled. Was I the *sheep* between the *wolves*? Perhaps the event planners took into account that our ideas and colors were a blend of both parties. I felt a draft and a chill raced across my skin. It reminded me of when I shook Veronica's hand. Her cat-like eyes flashed again in my mind. The way she had looked at me was almost frightening.

My eyes continued to wander around the auditorium. I saw in front of me were many of the sponsors who funded our campaign since the beginning, with their wives or immediate family. As I scanned the familiar faces, in the row in front of me a few seats to my right, I halted.

There was a man who I didn't recognize. His hair was white-blond and so short you could see the skin of his scalp clearly. He had a stern, protruding jawline, and pale skin. His appearance made me infer that he was of European descent. Swedish? German? *Russian?*

I began to feel the tension growing in my gut. He was wearing *our* colors and I didn't recognize him at all. My brow creased as I attempted to draw his face from my memories…nothing. Who invited him? This was my party. I would have known someone that was involved in even the smallest positions. There wasn't anything that was done that wasn't cleared with Cole or me first. I craned my neck back to see the rest of our party sitting behind us. There wasn't one I didn't recognize—except him.

I nudged Cole with my elbow and leaned closer to him.

"Cole, who invited that guy?" I asked, whispering.

"Who?"

I nodded to my right and held my index finger low to point in his direction.

Cole didn't answer. He seemed to be confused, and the skin on his forehead was scrunched up.

"The blond?"

I nodded again.

"He's probably a sponsor."

I wasn't buying it. Cole and I were the founders. After my quick scan around the room, I had recognized every face. These were people we had held meetings with, organized fundraisers, and even shot the shit at the bar. These faces, these people, were our friends. This man was *not.*

"Turn around and look. We know everyone except him."

Still holding his wife's hand, he peered back for a moment, then turned to lean into me and whispered, "You're right…"

Who invited this guy? The thought bombarded my mind over and over again.

"Relax, he got through security."

Cole's words didn't help calm me the least bit. I looked over at the rogue man and scrutinized him for any traces of malevolence. He slightly raised his left hand and glanced down at his watch. He pressed a button on it, and I saw a digital timer begin to count up.

What the hell is he timing? This isn't a jogging track.

The debate still had forty-five minutes remaining. Him fiddling with his watch only made my suspicions multiply. How could I begin to trust a stranger who was wearing the colors of *my* party, and yet we had never met face-to-face? The man's expression hadn't changed from the moment I laid eyes on him. He stared outward, without reaction to anything the candidates were saying—almost stoic.

My curiosity was consuming me. I had to protect my party. My hands began to sweat as I acknowledged how preposterous my assumptions were of this man who sat peacefully in the crowd. What if I was wrong? Perhaps the press would presume I analyzed him in a discriminatory manner. If he did turn out to be Russian, it would be an even worse outcome for me.

No—my gut insisted. *Something isn't right.*

I stood up out of my seat. Instantly I felt dozens of eyes on me, and as I walked up the steps security was already meeting me.

"Sir, you need to sit back do—"

The deafening noise made my ears ring so loud that I could hardly hear the screams behind the buzzing drone. Heat and the smell of blood filled my nose. I clutched my side as something sharp pierced me. I heard another ear-splitting explosion. Smoke clouded my vision and I coughed violently as I choked on the fumes. My hand was moist from blood. Flashing lights and sirens were distorted in the background of screams.

People were scrambling over seats and running towards the exits, with blood staining their face and clothes. Where were Cole and his wife? My heart raced with adrenaline, and I fought my way through the crowd. The smoke was so thick my vision began to fade out.

No…I have to find Cole. My vision went black, and my body hit the ground.

GU Hospital – Washington, D.C.
10:14 10-12-2016

A heart-rate monitor was beeping, over and over—so smooth and rhythmic. The overly-sanitized smell that was distinct to hospitals filled my nose. I shivered beneath a thin sheet. The room was too chilly to be comfortable.

Sensations. Indications that I was, indeed, still alive.

"He's waking up," a female voice said.

"The sedatives are wearing off," a male answered her. "When he comes to his senses, inform him of what happened. Then we can discharge him. His wounds weren't nearly as severe as some of the others."

Wounds? I felt a sharp, stabbing pain in the right side of my abdomen. I clutched the area with my hand, and I felt the tug of my IV as I did so.

"Slow down there, Mr. Marina."

I blinked, opening my eyes to see a man, presumably the doctor, looking down at me with a half-hearted smile. Behind his eyes was emptiness. I could tell he had information that I did not.

"Where am I? Is Senator Goodman alive?" I asked, sounding frantic. The beeps of the heart-rate monitor sped up.

"Yes, all the candidates made it out with only minor lacerations. I was worried too. If something happened to Senator Goodman, who would I vote for?" the doctor asked me smiling and placed his hand on my shoulder. The moment I felt the weight of his hand on my shoulder, it reminded me of Cole.

"The Chairman," I sputtered. "Cole Pavich. Is he alive?"

His face turned solemn.

"He is in critical condition in the ICU."

My stomach sank. I felt nauseous, and my gut began to heave as if I was going to puke.

"I'll get the pan," the nurse said, darting off to the side.

"What happened to him?" I asked, my voice rising.

"I'm afraid that's confidential," he said.

"Confidential my ass! He is my partner for God's sake!"

He displayed a quick look of sympathy.

"Mr. Pavich sustained multiple injuries from shards of metal and nails that were used to create the pipe bombs."

"Pipe bombs?" I stared at him blankly with disbelief.

"Yes, Mr. Marina. I'm sorry to inform you, but there was an unknown terrorist attack on the debate last night. There are seventeen dead, and eighty-eight injured."

I noticed my ears were ringing and I felt a dull ache inside of them, almost like they had been damaged. It was then I remembered the deafening sounds of the bombs exploding, and the attendees' screams that followed.

"I have to see Cole. I can't just check out of here without seeing him."

"Unfortunately you can't see him because his condition is unstable. You can look through the glass, though, in the O.R.—I can get you in."

"Thank you for offering. Also, Doc, honestly, do you think Cole will pull through?"

He recomposed himself and changed back to being professional.

"Right now I can't say. If he wants any chance of living, he needs to become stable first. Diana, if you could please get his discharge papers."

The doctor walked out of my room and the nurse followed. She returned moments later by my side with papers on a clipboard.

"Mr. Marina, this first paper you have to sign is going over what we treated you for."

"Which was?" I asked.

"You received an impalement to your lower abdomen, from a two-inch nail that came from the pipe bomb. We administered a tetanus shot. We have sent over your prescriptions to the closest pharmacy for an antibiotic and a low-dose Vicodin for pain."

She handed me the clipboard and the pen. I signed.

"I probably won't need the Vicodin."

She gave me a smirk. "Just wait until you try to sit up. It'll feel like you've done a thousand crunches."

"Great…"

"These next couple pages are regarding your insurance, and the last one you are signing is for us to release you."

When I finished, I handed it back to her and she organized them neatly, putting them beneath the silver clamp.

"I'm going to get the doctor," the nurse began. Her eyes turned cold, and her expression troublesome. "Between us, you need to go see your friend, Cole, as soon as you can."

My stomach turned at her words. She was disconnecting the IV and heart-rate monitor, but before she did I heard my heart speed up.

"Hurry then, please."

She nodded, her lips pursed and tense. She hurriedly walked out of the room, and I sat up in the bed. As I did so, I felt the same sharp, stabbing pain I did when I awoke. The nurse wasn't joking. It felt as if someone had punched me in the gut with all of their strength. I stood up and stretched out, coughing as I did so. My throat and lungs felt dry and irritated every time I took a breath. I guess it was from the fumes of the bombs.

Bombs…

The word entered my mind like a strange foreign body would enter my blood. I wanted to rid myself of the thought.

I couldn't come to grasp with what happened last night. It played from my memory like a blur—the screams, the smoke, and the terror in people's faces. The *final* debate before the election and now this happened. Who could have done such a thing? How did pipe bombs get past security?

Questions manifested so rapidly it was almost dizzying. I inhaled deeply to calm myself down. I heard two quick raps on the door.

"Mr. Marina, are you ready?" asked the doctor.

"Yes."

"Please, follow me."

Sore and stiff, I trailed him down the corridor. His white gown flowed behind his legs like a cape.

I heard the *ding* from the elevator as the doctor pressed the button. When the doors opened, I stepped in behind him. Cole was on the fourth floor. The smooth hum, which I have heard so many times using the elevator at my apartment, didn't make me feel relaxed as it always did. This humming noise made me sick, as if behind the elevator doors there would be something waiting for me, something terrifying, when they opened. *Cole Pavich is in critical condition…*

I pushed air out of my nose and shook my head in an attempt to forget those words.

When the doors opened I followed the doctor. Within fifty feet, he stopped and turned to face a room on the left.

The top half of the wall was made of glass and allowed me to see inside. My heart fluttered, as I saw Cole with more tubing, gauze, and monitors than any person should have at one time. I clutched my mouth as I saw him and winced in pain as my forehead scrunched, fully-flexed. The only things that were recognizable above the disarray of equipment were his gray hair and his face. Doctors and surgeons surrounded him.

I imagined if he was awake, he would swat away at all of these prodding doctors and immediately demand his wife to bring him a drink.

His wife… "Doc, where is his wife Carla?"

"She is in a nearby room out of surgery. If everything remains stable, she will be removed from the ICU before noon."

I felt a slight wave of relief as he said that. If Cole woke up to his wife dead, I couldn't imagine how he would continue on. He had been with her since his college years.

"Mr. Marina," the doctor began hesitantly. "I know how much you don't want to hear this, but…don't get too attached to the idea that Mr. Pavich will make it through. He has lost a lot of blood and received lacerations to major arteries. Overnight, while you were still unconscious, he was undergoing cardiovascular surgery. We were surprised he made it this far. It didn't help that he had alcohol in his blood, which thinned it."

"I'm not surprised. The man loves to drink," I joked, trying to swallow the information I was just given. "He will make it through, I know it."

I heard a pager go off. The doctor looked down at his waistband.

"Well, I must go. I am needed on another floor. Mr. Marina, I'm not saying he won't pull through. I'm just saying you need to say a prayer…and also come to terms that this may be the last time you see him."

He patted me on the back and disappeared.

I felt like a small piece of me had been torn away as he said that.

That reality he spoke of, one in which Cole Pavich, the co-founder, my mentor, and most importantly my friend—didn't exist—was something I couldn't handle. A reality I couldn't face. If he died, that would leave me as the only founder of the Convergence Party left. We were a team. We *both* created the party. Neither one of us took the title as the creator. We were the two founders.

I neared the glass, and I put my hand up to it. I sniffled and tried my hardest to restrain tears from coming out, but regardless they became glassy. In that moment, I sent all the positive energy and thoughts within me through the glass to him.

Hang in there Cole. We both have to watch Goodman win. You still owe me those drinks at Smith Commons after too, you crazy bastard.

I took one last look at Cole and turned away. I reached the elevator and the doors opened. Inside, a younger, female nurse pressed the button for the third floor and glancing at me in my hospital gown, she pressed the lobby button for me.

"Thank you," I said.

She smiled, "You're welcome. It's an honor to be in the same elevator as you, Mr. Marina."

I shook my head smiling and turned to her. "Now, why is that?"

"Because you are brave. You and Cole both. I was in District 1, too. I remember seeing you and him sitting cross-legged in the grass during lunches. At the time, you were just strangers, but now, that memory is a fond one."

"Why didn't you come talk to us?" I asked playfully.

The elevator reached her floor, and as the door opened, she turned to face me.

"Because I knew I would be interrupting greatness. I will never forget the passion, the intensity, on both of your faces. I could tell you two weren't just complaining about how shitty the Confinement was, like everyone else. You were plotting a *solution*."

I was dumbfounded from her explanation. Such a sharp memory this nurse had. I didn't even recognize her face. The doors began to close, and I quickly stuck my hand in front of the sensor to stop them.

"Thank you for everything you have done, Mr. Marina. Everyone in this hospital is on edge, worrying about the health of Mr. Pavich. We will do our best, I promise you that."

"Thank you…" I said just as the doors closed, and I lost sight of the angel-faced nurse.

When I reached the ground floor, I smiled, thinking about the effect I have had on people I had never even met. That in itself was more valuable than any form of monetary wealth. It made me feel rich—richer in soul—a feeling no corporate billionaire has ever had the chance of knowing.

Baked & Wired – Washington, D.C.
11:57 10-12-2016

Chatter surrounded me. The bold, aromatic smell of coffee wafted in the air. I sat alone at a two-top table against the wall and fiddled with the remains of a spinach and feta quiche. I barely had an appetite. The pain pills were still wearing off. I clasped the ceramic handle gently and sipped my Café Au Lait. Its lukewarm contents helped revive me from the sluggish sedation I was in last night. Every few seconds I felt the same, shooting pain in my abdomen. The left side of my jaw was swollen and bruised. I assumed I received that when the smoke from the bombs caused me to black out.

When I drove my bike away from the hospital, just a short while ago, I felt empty, like I was leaving behind strands of myself, and all I was left with was a pile of loose ends in my lap. My mind was still so jumbled. I was trying to piece together the recollection of last night's events. The only things I could remember were the conversation with Veronica and Marc, and watching the debate. Then, I saw the unfamiliar man to my right. The bombs exploded before I could reach security and tell them. I wondered if he was the terrorist that planted the bombs.

The TV mounted in the corner of the shop was set to CNN. They were playing the same loop of footage from the cameras filming the debate when the bombs went off. I could barely stomach the sounds of the screams in sync with the explosions. It was horrifying to replay in my mind. I took another sip of coffee—my mug was empty.

I stood up and went to the counter. Today was definitely a two-cup kind of morning.

"How can I help you?" the barista asked.

"I'll have another Café Au Lait, please."

"Cold or steamed milk?"

"Cold, thank you."

She turned around and prepared my drink. I tried to focus on the sounds of the liquid and ignore the newscast playing behind me.

When she returned, she pushed the drink towards me.

"That will be $2.88, please."

I reached for my wallet and pulled out the money to hand her.

"You look familiar. I feel like I've seen you somewhere before," the barista mentioned and narrowed her eyes with a flirty grin.

"You have," I answered with a chuckle and returned her smile.

"It's on the tip of my tongue…"

"I'm Owen Marina, co-founder of the Convergence Party."

Her eyes widened and her smile vanished.

"Is that why you're all beat up?" she asked, pointing to the TV.

My smile disappeared too. "Yes, I was there."

"I'm glad you made it out all right," she said with concern.

"I am too. I just hope my friend pulls through."

"I hope he does too," she replied and nodded solemnly.

"Thank you again," I tipped the mug in her direction.

"Of course, it's my pleasure."

I returned to my seat. I had my iPhone plugged into the outlet. It was finally powered on from being dead most of the night. The little red bubbles read **67** messages and **11** voicemails.

Holy shit…

I began scrolling through and reading some of the messages. There were dozens from my colleagues, a couple friends, and some of the funders that had survived last night's attack. They all sent messages regarding prayers and thoughts to the situation. One of the first voicemails I had received only minutes after the attack was from my dad. I could tell by the time he had called.

I checked my email. There were already requests from the Washington Post, Huffington Post, and others to do an interview on my experience during the debate. I shook my head. I always disliked how quick they were to make a buck off of someone's story.

"…This just in…" I heard the sharp tone of a female anchor on the

TV. I glanced up with interest. "…The CIA has released the two suspects involved in last night's horrific terrorist attack at Georgetown University's Gaston Hall…"

I sipped my coffee and stared intently at the TV.

"…The first suspect, now deceased from his injuries, was Russian-born Alexei Malchikov. Authorities have mentioned the possibility of him being tied to Black Monday's Viktor Ivankov. This now brings into question further Russian involvement with the US. He was twenty-nine years old. Here is his picture entering last night's debate…"

I almost spit my coffee out. I coughed, choking on the hot liquid.

It was him. The blond, European-looking man who I was so suspicious of. He *was* the culprit. *He was wearing our colors.* Damn, that wouldn't look good to the press. Why the hell would a terrorist don our colors and then lose his life in the process?

"…The second suspect, who was deemed wanted by the CIA just minutes ago, was caught on camera standing and then climbing the steps just seconds before the explosives went off…"

My stomach dropped. My fingers clasped the ceramic handle so hard that I thought I might break it. I couldn't breathe.

"…Owen Marina, Convergence Party co-founder, is wanted for involvement in plotting of the attack. It is believed by officials that Alexei planted the bombs, and Owen helped create them. An alumni of Georgetown, in the years before he became the founder of the Convergence Party, he was a field chemist for the EPA and also had a bachelor's in chemistry. Were they trying to send the existing government a threat? A message? The feds are still gathering more informa…"

The anchor's words began to sound distorted. I felt my heart racing out of my chest, almost unbearable it was going so fast. Sweat dripped down my forehead, and I felt dizzy and sick.

The shop became silent. I looked around at all the faces, and they were staring back at me. No one said a word. They just stared. Their eyes frightened and nervous. They analyzed me as if I were some sort of monster. I saw a woman slowly pick up her cell phone and dial a number.

This isn't happening. This must be some sort of mistake.

I stood up, and a couple people gasped in fright from my sudden movement. My forehead was creased in stress and anger.

"Hello…I, uh, I'd like to report a wanted fugitive." I heard the woman on her phone struggling to whisper as if I wouldn't hear. I decided to ignore her. What use would it be trying to stop her? I was wanted, but yet I'd done nothing wrong. This was a fuck up.

"Ma'am," I asked the barista as I reached the counter. She flinched as if I was going to jump over the counter and hurt her.

"Seriously? You were just flirting with me a minute ago."

"That was before I knew you were a terrorist…and helped kill all of those innocent people," she whimpered.

"You really believe that bullshit? I had nothing to do with that attack. I hope everybody in here hears that too!" I said, raising my voice.

"What do you want from me?" she asked, with tears filling the corners of her eyes.

"Just give me a pen, or actually, give me a Sharpie. Do you have one?"

She tossed the Sharpie on the counter and turned away from me. I grabbed it angrily and turned around to walk out of the shop.

Amazing how people are so quick to believe the media. I shook my head in distaste and adrenaline began to surge as I realized the situation I was being thrown into. *What do I do?*

I pulled out my phone and began writing down phone numbers on the inside of my forearm. *Dad, Cole, my office, my ex.* As popular of a figure I was in Washington, I had only four numbers worth keeping. Life as a workaholic was a lonely one.

I had to call *someone.* God forbid they caught me before I could make a statement. Maybe I should call the press? I wondered if they would believe me, that this was all a false conclusion. *Alexei Malchikov was wearing our colors.* The pit in my gut began to grow and constrict with tension. *Why* would a terrorist be wearing our colors? The thought kept resurfacing over and over again.

I quickly dialed the number to my office.

Ring…Ring…Ring…Ring…

A month before the election and they didn't answer in three rings? They knew better than that.

"Convergence Party Headquarters, this is Nicolas."

"Damn it, Nic, it's about time you picked up! It's Owen."

"Owen! No shit, have you seen the news? There's no way anyone in this office believed that's true. Such bullshit, someone is out to get us. Are you all right?"

"Well, besides my injury, my second cup of coffee got interrupted by finding out I was a wanted criminal."

"Don't worry, Owen. We are going to find a way to figure out what happened. Cole is still in the ICU, by the way."

My heart sank from hearing his condition had not improved.

"I saw him through the glass, in the hospital this morning. It doesn't look too good."

"Yeah, it's absolute chaos in here right now. The phones are going off the hook. People are wanting to know about your involvement with the attack."

"What is your answer for that?" I pressed.

"That Owen Marina had nothing to do with the bombs. That this is some mistake."

"Good," I answered. "Stay strong, Nic."

"I will, boss."

The call disconnected. I suddenly saw three black Tahoes and two police Chargers screech around the corner of the street, maybe a half-mile away.

"No fucking way…" I murmured.

My fight-or-flight instincts kicked in. I put on my helmet and sprinted to my bike. I hit the ignition switch and skidded out in front of the shop.

The sirens grew louder behind me.

I have to outrun them.

I turned right onto M Street, then immediately onto 30th St. NW. I glanced in my mirrors, and the Chargers were getting closer.

Accelerating in second gear, I approached K Street with frightening speed. *Please don't let me get hit.* I whipped left onto K Street and an SUV blared their horn—I barely missed being clipped. I pulled the throttle. The torque threw me back into a wheelie and I balanced it all the way up the on-ramp onto Rock Creek Parkway. Glancing back again, I saw them merging on the Parkway.

Goodbye. I slammed back down on two wheels and shifted into higher gear. My speedometer quickly raced over one hundred, and I didn't let off. There was also plenty of room for me to weave in and out of traffic. One lane change from a vehicle without using their signal could have been the end of my life. Then again, dying on my street bike, to me, was a preferred route, compared to rotting in a prison for a crime I didn't commit.

4 mi

Once I get on I-95 I can really lose them. I continued to speed, slaloming between the vehicles. The benefits of having my bike equipped with a turbo were undoubtedly the added speed, but also, the distinct sound allowed other motorists to hear me coming. It helped keep me safe.

North to Baltimore? Or south to Richmond? My intuition took me south, back to my home state of Virginia. I had to see my dad. I could only imagine what was going through his mind after seeing his only son in the news. I bore right and accelerated up the on-ramp and merged onto the interstate. Sliding into the farthest left lane, I began to reach speeds well over 120 miles per hour. I glanced back in my mirrors and saw the Chargers becoming smaller and smaller. The passing cars were a blur as I approached 150 miles per hour. The only way I was going to outrun them, to have any chance of an escape, was by maintaining that speed.

Richmond 120 mi

If 95 remained empty, at this rate, I would be there in around forty-five minutes. I felt my iPhone vibrating in my pocket, and as I felt the sensation, I realized they would be tracking my location through it. I slipped it out and tossed it. Whoever told the media that I was the culprit, made a *big* mistake. *They picked the wrong fight, with the right guy.*

CIA Headquarters – Langley, VA
12:41 10-12-2016

"Ma'am, the last street camera caught him on I-95 South going well over 140 miles per hour. They've lost him."

The flames of anger licked my insides. My teeth were clenched as I watched the video recording of him zipping by on his motorcycle.

"Well, if he doesn't kill himself at that speed first, we need to find out where he is going. You said the father still lives in the house Owen grew up in, correct?"

"Correct. The father, Ted Marina, lives in a house in a small development in Midlothian, Virginia."

I watched the graphics populate the many screens that surrounded us. The birth certificates, documents, and addresses. All the information *I needed,* right at their fingertips. There was no way he was going to slip through our grasp again.

"What about his mother?" I asked.

"Mother is deceased. Died of a heart attack in 2007."

"Well, that eliminates the question of which parent he would go to first. Easy enough for us. Are we still triangulating his movements?"

"No ma'am, he destroyed his phone on the interstate just moments ago."

I paused, thinking.

"If he continues at the pace he is going, he will reach Richmond in a half-hour. Our guys won't be able to apprehend him in time. Contact the Midlothian Police Department. Inform them that Owen Marina is the most wanted fugitive in the United States. Have them intercept his arrival."

One of the men beside me picked up his phone and began to call.

"Ma'am, you do realize that if he happens to not go to his dad's house, if he deviates from the main roads onto back roads, with the capacity of his bike, we could lose him for good. We have all of his receipts pulled up for the YZF-R1 he is on. It is far from stock. It has over twenty grand of upgrades on it. That bike can go in excess of 200 miles per hour, and from our records this isn't his first bike. He has been riding close to a decade. This gives him an advantage over our guys on the ground."

I wanted to smack him so badly, but I restrained myself.

"That is nothing but an excuse. I want *every* camera, every pair of eyes we have, watching for that bike. Put an alert out to every police station in the Southeast, give them his tag number. We will catch him when he reaches Midlothian. That has to be his destination."

"Right on it, ma'am."

I stared at the video loop of Owen's bike—a black blur, shooting past the visible field of the camera on I-95. I smiled at the thought of us putting him in handcuffs, and the court case that would follow. Even the best lawyer wouldn't be able to get him out of his situation. Our evidence was foolproof.

"If Owen wants to take us on a chase, then we will chase him, and a *merry* chase it will be."

Midlothian Turnpike – Midlothian, VA
13:21 10-12-2016

The engine grumbled and sputtered as I slowed down to exit the turnpike. The skin beneath my jacket was unbearably icy. I wasn't in gear that would keep me warm during high-speed interstate travel. I never planned on having to flee Washington. On most days, after my coffee, I might have responded to some emails, or gotten on a conference call, but today *wasn't* most days.

I hurried down the back roads of my hometown and navigated them solely by memory. Autumn colors—burnt orange, cardinal red, and amber leaves blanketed the yards and the edges of the street. What a majestic display they put on, as if their change of color were a final performance before their death. The sun sneaked out from behind the clouds periodically. Although it was overcast, there was no rain, and many homeowners were taking advantage of the lack of precipitation to break out their riding lawn mowers. If you ever wondered what upper-middle class America looked like, Midlothian was it. Perfectly manicured lawns, a close-knit community, and just a short drive to the city.

Welcome to Suburbia.

I turned onto Oakengate Lane and the familiarity caused memories to flood my mind. Our street sat behind Salisbury Lake. Many of the families who lived here when I was growing up never left. I imagined the streets would be filled with children and their parents in a few weeks, trick-or-treating for Halloween. I smiled momentarily, and as I pulled into the driveway I thought I should conceal my bike in the backyard. I parked it, and as I took off my helmet I saw the glimmer of sunlight reflecting off the lake. I used to smoke weed with my buddies the summer before my senior year while kayaking, and then we would all get paranoid when someone forgot the eye-drops. I would cautiously walk into the kitchen in hopes of avoiding my parents, all for some munchies.

Only in America—first world problems. Now, after the Confinement, many of those lighthearted times had disappeared. They were cherished times. The *real* world, the world that I lived in, was no longer carefree. We lived in the wake of a tragedy, and the forceful imprisonment that followed haunted us all. Our reality was *darker*. That was something I was hell-bent on changing.

Before I took a step onto the back porch the door flew open.

"Owen," my father gasped.

"Dad…" I said as we embraced in a hug. I could feel him exhale as I held him. The fact that I was alive and in his arms was enough to comfort him. It was enough for me, even if that comfort was short-lived.

He glanced to his left and to his right at the neighbors' houses.

"Come inside."

I followed him through the door and was instantly enveloped in the warmth of the house. My skin was still numb from the ride over. After all the years, my old home hadn't changed a bit. There was the rustic walnut table in the dining room, with matching chairs, and the many picture frames that lined the walls. Our house was built in the twenties. My dad bought it when I was in my mom's womb. Back then, property in this area was one-fourth of what it was now. It was a smart investment. My mother, while she was still alive, was passionate about French antiques and design. Much of our furniture she chose and my dad never sold or changed any of it. They were pieces of her, fragments of who she was. It had almost been a decade and he still hadn't remarried. I doubted he ever would. He couldn't let go of her.

"What the hell is going on, Son?"

As he asked me that question, I had the realization that I was just as helpless as he was. What *did* I know?

"This must be some mistake. Just an hour ago I was in a coffee shop, and then I saw myself on the news. I just don't understand."

My dad looked towards the carpet in thought and then glanced back up at me.

"What you just said, Owen—say it again."

"That I just don't understand?" I questioned, confused.

"No, before that."

"That this must be some mistake."

"Yes! Yes, *that this must be some mistake*."

"What are you getting at, Dad?"

I saw a barren emptiness behind his eyes as if he was digesting the gravity of his thoughts.

"That this *wasn't* a mistake, Owen. Have you seen the news? You are *the* guy. Not just a potential suspect, or an accomplice. You are the one they want. The media is going berserk right now."

Ring...Ring...Ring...

Mine and my father's eyes locked. His home phone was ringing. It still had the classic, mid-nineties ring that was the standard sound for all phones at the time.

"The only calls I get on this phone are for the election," he mentioned nervously.

My dad picked up the phone and put it to his ear.

"Hello. Sheriff Aldridge, no, I—I'm not watching it right now. I had to shut it off. What? No, I haven't seen him. What do you mean?"

There was a long, *long* pause. I watched some of the color leave his face. My pulse began to increase. I felt flushed with heat.

"Yes sir, I understand. Thank you, tell the boys I said thank you, too."

He set the plastic phone on its base.

"We have ten minutes before the feds get here," he announced, expressionless.

"Ten minutes?! Are you serious?"

He had pressed a button on his watch moments ago.

"We probably have nine now, get up! You have to get out of here, fast."

Where the hell am I going to go?

"Dad, what did Sheriff Aldridge say?"

"He said the IT guys *accidentally* crossed up the wires, and they created a fake accident outside of town. A couple ambulances were all they needed. It backed up traffic on the turnpike for miles. They called me on a secured line. Apparently someone working for them is well-versed in cyber-security."

"They did it because of who you were to them…" I murmured.

"Yes, he said they gave us the window because of my tenure."

I felt grateful that my dad's title as retired Sheriff assisted me in my evasion.

"Get your shit together, Owen. You have to leave now! They will have our street blocked off in minutes."

He shuffled me towards the back door, and as we made it onto the porch, I turned to him.

"Dad, you can't stay here. You have to go somewhere! A hotel, or maybe your second cousin Bobby's place in Chester. He's not related, is he?"

He shook his head and dismissed my statement with his body language.

"I'm not worried about me, Owen. I'm worried about you."

"But Dad, if they can't have me, they will come for you. You're the only family I have."

He grabbed my shoulders and gave me a shake.

"That's exactly my point. You're the *only* family I have. I can't lose you, Son. Get out of here, now!"

He pushed me down towards my bike and walked with me. He glanced at his watch.

"Five minutes. Five minutes until they're here."

I turned around as we reached my bike.

"Dad, I…I don't know how I will get in contact with you, but I will find a way."

He wrapped his arms around me in a firm hug.

"I love you so much, Son. Take care of yourself, please. We will figure this out. Whoever created this lie will be exposed."

"I hope so," I added with uncertainty in my voice.

His brow furrowed from my statement.

"Owen, you can't just hope. You have to take action! You know that better than I do. Look what you and Cole have accomplished in Washington. You didn't get to where you are by *hoping*. You are where you are now because you didn't sit on the sidelines during the Confinement. You figured out a solution. Don't give up your dream just because of this, Son. Who knows what will happen with the polls because of the attacks."

The polls…

Hearing his comment was like running face-first into a wall. A fire began to burn inside me. The same fire I felt every time I saw my scar. My father's words had rekindled the fire.

"Thank you, Dad. Be careful. All right, old man?"

He laughed, "I might be old, but I can still kick your smart ass if I wanted to."

"I love you, Pops."

"I love you too, Owen. Stay in the backyards. Go now. If you circle around the lake you can bypass the streets and get back onto the turnpike. Go somewhere, some place that isn't family, or to someone you haven't talked to in a long time. Hurry!"

I hit the ignition switch and began to carefully maneuver through the edges of the neighbors' yards. I had to get around shrubs, speed up when dogs came hurtling towards me, and be careful not to slide down to the lake. This kind of riding, especially in the grass, was ten times as difficult as speeding down the interstate at 150 miles per hour.

I was halfway around the lake. I knew I would be coming up on the back road that would lead me away from my house, and also keep me from the direction where the feds would be coming from.

My dad's voice echoed in my mind. "*Go somewhere, some place that isn't family, or to someone you haven't talked to in a long time.*"

My thoughts hit a dead wall. Everyone I knew was in D.C. It'd been ten years since I graduated high school, since I'd lived here.

Who do I know? Someone who I was close with but hadn't talked to in a while.

That was it. As I made it back onto asphalt, I knew my destination. I knew I'd be safe there, at least for the evening. Only back roads would be used. No highways or interstates.

Grey's House – Chesterfield, VA 14:11 10-12-2016

I drove down the suburban street and glanced at the houses to the left. *Which one is Grey's?* I saw the maroon paneling and the color confirmed the house's familiarity in my mind. I pulled into the driveway and parked the bike on the side of the garage. Nervously, I glanced around at the surrounding houses to see if anyone was outside. Luckily, the coast was clear.

I banged on the door with my fist. *Come on, Grey. Come on.*

The door opened and Grey pushed open the glass storm door.

"Owen! What the fuck are you doing here?" he asked, with wide eyes.

"Well nice to see you too, Grey," I answered sarcastically.

"Get your ass in here. Did anyone see you?"

"No, not that I know of."

He shut the door behind me and quickly locked the deadbolt. Inside, not much had changed since the last time I had visited him. It was the typical bachelor pad living room. There was a flat-screen TV, a PlayStation 4, and a saggy old couch. There were minimal decorations and plain white walls. It was obvious it was a rental property. I could smell popcorn, like he had just popped a bag.

Grey stared at me like I was a ghost, as if I had just appeared out of thin air. He almost seemed *scared.*

"We need to put your bike in the garage," he announced. "I'll go open it, and you go through the backyard and pull it around."

I nodded my head and walked out the back door onto the deck. The grass was covered with dead maple leaves. I reached my bike, and when I hit the ignition switch I tried my best to let the engine idle. I was afraid the noise would draw attention to myself.

I pulled it around and quickly parked it in the garage. Before I could turn it off, the garage was already closed behind me. Grey didn't wait to let me in. He just closed the door and left me in the dark.

When I walked into the kitchen, I turned into the living room to see Grey sitting on the edge of an ottoman, anxiously tapping his foot on the ground with his fingers interlaced.

Perhaps he was praying I would disappear. Who in their right mind would want to be an *accomplice* to last night's attacks?

"What, do you think I did it?" I asked him nonchalantly.

He glanced up at me with his expression contorted. Maybe I should have seemed less relaxed when I posed the question.

"*Did* you?" he spat.

"Fuck no. I had nothing to do with the bombs."

My words didn't appear to placate Grey at all.

"Then why did you jump out of your seat and walk up the steps right before the bombs went off? Have you even seen the news?"

"Not since this morning. I was in a coffee shop having breakfast, and then the story came in."

Grey stood up and grabbed the remote from the old, weathered love seat across the room.

"Look—you need to see this shit."

I saw the image fade in on the flat-screen as he turned it on. He didn't even have to change the channel. I guess Grey had been watching it last. It was set on CNN.

"...The last time authorities caught him on video was just an hour ago, getting off I-95 onto the Midlothian Turnpike. We now know he went to his childhood home off of Oakengate Lane, behind Salisbury Lake. His father, who still resides there, has been taken into protective custody and is being questioned on Owen's whereabouts..."

Motherfuckers. They have my dad...

"Just wait," Grey said. "That is just the beginning of the shit they've been spewing on here."

"...Now, let's go over to Shanna, who is with body-language expert and renowned psychologist, Dr. Nina Grant..."

The camera switched views to a female reporter who sat across from the doctor. They were both sitting in powder-white stationary chairs.

"...So tell us, Dr. Grant, what do you interpret from the video footage of last night's attack at the final debate? What indicators are seen with the fugitive, Owen Marina?"

They had an interactive TV screen, perhaps a smart computer, behind them. The doctor stood up and began using her finger to point around the screen. The video was of me standing up out of my seat at the debate and walking up the steps. Then, the feed caught the bombs and black smoke filled the auditorium.

"…See, in the moments before he stands he keeps glancing around the auditorium, almost like he was waiting for something…"

I *could not* believe what I was hearing.

"…When he stands, the guards immediately attempt to intercept him as he began to climb up the steps. *Boom*…and then they go off. See, this area right here…" She used her index finger to draw a red circle around the front few rows of the Convergence Party. "…was the hardest hit. The front rows had the most casualties. Interestingly enough, Owen was sitting in those front rows, and just *happened* to get up at the perfect time to save himself from critical injuries."

"He was fleeing the bomb authorities presume he helped create."

"Yes, and you see here if we zoom in. That is sweat dripping from his hairline. We are all aware now that the other suspect, Alexei Malchikov is deceased, so the CIA has made a statement saying this was an attempted suicide bombing. *Attempted*, because Owen is still on the run. Maybe the weight of losing his own life was too much to bear?"

My jaw was slowly falling lower and remained agape.

"They are making you out as a coward," Grey interjected. "The media has gotten a taste for you and they want more."

"I can tell…" I mumbled, still flabbergasted from the picture the news was painting of me.

"Owen, w*hy* did you stand up?"

I turned to look at Grey. He stared at me with distrust behind his brown eyes, and he kept a cold, standoffish disposition. When he spoke, his mouth was hidden behind his scraggly, black beard.

"You have a DVR, right?"

"No. Of course dude, it's 2016."

"Rewind it back before I stood up."

He rewound the newscast to the right spot. He pressed play. I saw my head move to the right, toward Alexei.

"Stop," I said. "Look."

"What?" Grey asked, confused.

I stood up and pointed at the blond-headed Alexei.

"*He* is why I stood up. Minutes before the bombs, in the footage they *aren't* airing, I was looking around at my party and realized that I didn't recognize him. I even asked Cole if he had ever seen him before, at any of our fundraisers or meetings. Cole was at a loss for words, too. He was wearing our colors, Grey…and to top it off, sitting in our section, staring at the debate if he was some fucking emotionless robot!"

Grey seemed perplexed. Like he was piecing together information in his mind.

"Who let him in?" I asked, my voice rising. "That's the same question I asked Cole, and he replied with, "*Relax, he got through security.*" About a minute before I stood up, I saw Alexei press a button on his watch, and it was a timer. It started counting up. I had to say something to security because I knew Alexei was bad news. I knew he didn't belong."

There was a long pause. I was breathing heavily, and my jaw was clenched in frustration.

"You've given them the perfect story, Owen," Grey announced. "You've given them everything they need to make it believable. Your background in chemistry, your knowledge of the layout of Georgetown from having attended there. Those are exactly the kind of pieces the gullible American public would need pieced together for them by the media, in order to turn their political hero, into a terrorist."

I felt nauseous. His words pierced my mind. I could feel a headache coming on. He was *right.*

"Owen, you look lightheaded. Sit down, man," Grey demanded.

He stood up and sat me down on the sofa. The sickening, churning motion I felt in my stomach had not lessened—it was only growing stronger. I tried to exhale slowly to ease my racing heart.

"They have my dad…" I murmured.

Grey stared at me and remained silent.

"Do you think he is safe?"

"If he is being held by the people who created this lie, then no—not at all."

"…We ask for everyone in the greater Richmond area to let authorities know if they have any information regarding Owen Marina's whereabouts. He is riding a highly-modified, black Yamaha YZF-R1 with Maryland tags. His tag number is VRE-487. Please call the CIA's hotline toll-free at 1-888-FIND HIM…"

"Do your neighbors keep to themselves?" I asked.

"Typically, yes, I can have a couple people over, smoke weed on my back porch, and no one ever bothers me. Then again, I've never had a wanted fugitive over my house, either," he answered. Sarcasm riddled his words.

I recalled seeing only four houses, including Grey's, on the dead-end road he lived on. The street was less than a mile away from the Pocahontas State Park. The area was rural and wooded.

"Let's hope they keep to themselves today," I said.

Grey stood up and peeked through the split in the blinds. He turned back to me and slipped his cell phone out of his pocket.

"It's been fifteen minutes since you got here. If someone saw you and reported it, some form of law enforcement would be here. Fifteen more minutes and we should be in the clear…at least for tonight."

"You don't mind me staying?"

He shrugged his shoulders. "Well, you don't have anywhere else to go, do you?"

"No, I don't," I answered.

"What made you come here? Out of all places. I'm just curious. We haven't talked in almost two years."

His expression was cold as he stated that fact, like he was upset that I *hadn't* kept in touch.

"That's exactly the reason I came here. The last time I talked to you it was on an entirely different phone, and phone number. My dad told me to go somewhere they wouldn't know to look, to someone I hadn't talked to in a long time. You were the first person that came to mind."

He didn't respond. He just sat across from me and stared. Perhaps he was still absorbing my explanation.

"Well, despite the circumstances, it is nice to see you, Owen. I wish we would have kept in touch more, man. Then again, the Confinement kind of fucked that up. How was the D.C. Camp?"

"Shitty," I blurted. "How was the Richmond Camp?"

"The same. Sometimes I still have dreams of the groups of people who would riot, and wouldn't quit once the rubber bullets were used. Did the guards in your camp—"

"Yes," I said, cutting him short. "They did."

Grey nodded. His Adam's apple moved as he swallowed.

"So, I guess all the Camps were the same."

"Didn't you watch the news at all?" I asked, surprised from his statement.

"After we were released, I tried to avoid the news altogether."

I blinked, and I saw the image of the mother and daughter holding hands. My breath became shallow and rapid just from the small flashback of the memory. I felt a singeing sensation on my left forearm. Occasionally I would have ghost pain where the cigarette had left its mark.

"I know what you mean," I consoled.

Grey smiled, shook his head, and began to laugh. "You know, the only time I *would* watch the news was when you were on it."

"For real?" I laughed with him.

"Yeah man, I would tell my friends, 'I used to get in trouble with that guy. We used to cause mayhem back in Midlothian.'"

"Those were the good ole' days," I said.

"No shit man, you're telling me. It was hard enough being a working adult when a degree can't get you as much as it used to. My student loans kept piling up. Then, after the Confinement it made it twice as difficult. If the Supreme Court wouldn't have done what they did no one would have been able to return to their jobs. Too much stress in a poorly run world..."

Grey was referring to the kick-start mandate the Supreme Court implemented shortly after releasing the citizens from the Camps. It was a law that all business owners, suppliers, and anything far and few between had to lower costs of goods to the public. They forcefully lowered the inflation to the pre-2000 level. The Government paid the tab. They filled in the gaps wherever they could, in order to get people back into the swing of things. After all the Supreme Court did to help us, it raised the question—*who* was behind the Confinement?

"You nailed it man. Crime in the cities is just getting worse, and robbery is at the highest it has been in fifty years in Washington."

"I could imagine..." Grey mumbled.

"So, what do you do nowadays?" I asked. "I know that degree of yours has been serving you well, am I right?"

"Not at first it didn't. Surprisingly enough, though, after the Confinement I got a job with Wells Fargo working in Richmond."

"Very nice, man!" I raised my voice and grinned from his news. "What do you do for them?"

Grey revealed a sly smile as I asked my question.

"Network security. Apparently after the Confinement, the execs of the bank were redirecting money to their own offshore accounts. The financial instability of Post-Confinement America was the reason, or at least, that was their statement in court. The bank lost over one-hundred million dollars during that time. That's why I was hired. I closed the loop.

I created a secure network."

"Badass!" I said with enthusiasm.

"It pays the bills," he replied, staying humble. "I get to work from home most days. The only time I go to the bank is for meetings, or when there is something I can't look into remotely. It's still not as badass as what you do, though. A founder of the most famous political party in the twenty-first century."

"Are you kidding me, Grey? Look where that title has landed me."

Grey's face lost a shade of color as I mentioned that.

"Would you trade everything you've done to not be in this predicament anymore?"

"Of course not," I answered. "I would never."

"Exactly, your mark has already been made. What your party has done to unite this country is unprecedented, and I know you are aware of that, too. That's why I posed the question in the way that I did."

"Well, in reality I think it was the country that united itself. It was a commonly held distaste for the existing powers that chose to imprison us. Without the Confinement, mine and Cole's idea would have never resonated with people. We wouldn't have been able to make an impact, or our mark, as you worded it."

There was a pause. Grey's expression was worrisome, and he nodded in the direction of the TV.

"Well, whoever *they* are, the ones that are behind this lie…they are trying to *erase* your mark."

Grey's cold words swept over me like a frigid winter night. In his dark eyes, I saw that we both knew what he had said was the truth.

"You okay with chili?" Grey asked. "I don't recall you being a vegan, from what I can remember."

"Given that I've only had a quiche and some coffee all day, I'd eat just about anything at this point."

"On that note, dinner is served my friend," Grey announced as he set the steaming bowl in front of me. "It's been in the slow-cooker all day."

"Where are your roommates?" I asked.

Grey sat down in front of me. "They're out of town. Your timing couldn't have been better."

I blew air on the spoonful of chili in front of me. The blend of spices and hardy texture created a delicious meal. It was comforting to have at a time like this when I couldn't relax.

"Oh, nice," I said.

The clinking of our spoons against the ceramic bowls was the only sound I could hear. Grey kept looking up at me between bites. I was surprised with as bushy his beard was it didn't get messy.

"So, are you still with that girl? What was her name, Megan?"

I blinked. I didn't want to tell him the news.

"No, we broke up a little over a year and a half ago."

"What happened? I thought you both were going to get hitched one day. Weren't you guys together for like, five years or something?"

My gut twisted as he reminded me of that fact.

"Yes, Grey. Five years."

Grey's expression became sullen. His eyes were softer, and his mouth was closed. I think he caught on that *Megan* wasn't something I enjoyed talking about.

"Ah, shit man. I'm sorry I brought her up. We can drop it if you want to. Did she cheat on you or something?"

I swallowed. It was so hard for me to say it. It had been a year, and I still felt guilty about what happened.

"She broke up with me for what I became. She couldn't handle the person I had turned into. She wanted to spend time with me, and I wanted to be at the office. I couldn't balance the two."

"No way…" Grey murmured.

"Yes. She made me choose. She made me choose between my party and her. I was livid at the time, for being given that ultimatum, and for the fact that she couldn't wait until after the election…but back then, there was still a whole year left. She was fed up from being on the back burner while I became the most popular face in Washington. I chose the Convergence over her. I chose my passion over love."

"Damn dude, that's rough," Grey consoled.

"No shit, I thought I was going to marry her, too. You remember we met back while we were in Georgetown."

"Yep, I remember like it was yesterday. When I came to visit you during your junior year, and we all went out to the bar together, back when it was still a rush to be twenty-one."

I laughed at the memory. What good times he spoke of.

"I'm surprised my liver made it through those four years."

"And your GPA," Grey added.

"Ha, that was a little worse off than my liver was," I joked.

"We both made it, though, you know. The fact that we are both employed and not out in the streets after the Confinement is an accomplishment in and of itself."

"That's exactly what I want to change in Washington. There can't be another Confinement again. Perhaps when Goodman takes office we will finally get some answers."

"Aren't you worried about the polls? I mean, after what happened last night and then today, do you think it might hurt your party in the election?"

I felt the same, crushing feeling I felt at my dad's when he had mentioned that.

"It probably will…" I admitted.

There was a silence. I was finished with my chili and Grey was still working on his. He kept glancing up at me as he ate his food. Almost like he was afraid to break the tension in the air.

"So, how was the chili?" he asked awkwardly.

"It was great, man, I really appreciate the meal and everything else, too."

"Anytime, man. What are friends for?"

"I don't really know anymore. I work too much to have many of them."

"I find that hard to believe," Grey said.

"Why?"

"Because you are social, and one of the best flirts I've seen with women still to this day."

"Women are different, man. I'm almost tired of how many know my name in D.C. It's almost like, how am I supposed to build any kind of relationship when the press makes me out to be this good-looking hero whose shoes I can't even fill. If only they knew it was just an idea. It all began with an idea. I'm no hero. I'm just like everybody else."

"Have you been seeing anyone?"

"No, man, unfortunately no. Just one night stands with women I meet out at the bar. That I'll probably never see again."

Grey shook his head and laughed. "I wish that was my problem, you cold-hearted bastard."

"Well, maybe if you'd shave that possum off your face you could get some."

"You wish you could grow a beautiful beard like this," he mocked, dramatically caressing his scraggly beard.

"I've never tried. I would grow one if I didn't have to uphold an appearance and could work from home, you lucky shit."

"I'll trade places with you, pretty boy."

I stared at him with a deadpan expression.

The humorous smile faded away from his face.

"Actually. I take that back," he mumbled.

"I thought so."

In the background of our conversation, the TV was on low volume, still playing the repetitive stream of information they had been looping all day. A couple hours had passed. Part of me had relaxed, and the other part was worried sick that the CIA would come barging through the door.

"So, Owen…what is your plan?" Grey asked, staring at me from across the table.

"My plan?" I stammered.

"Did I stutter?" he laughed at my zoned-out response.

"I mean. No, I don't. I don't have the slightest idea of what to do, or where to go."

Hearing my verbal surrender to the situation I was in made me sick. It was against my nature to give up, to quit. It didn't feel *right.*

"Well," he said slowly, with a smirk growing on his face. "Maybe I can help you. Maybe we can *make* a plan."

"Elaborate."

"Owen, do you even realize the gravity of what is going on here?"

"Yes, Grey, I do. I'm the most wanted fugitive in the US. Thank you for pointing out the obvious."

He shook his head, dismissing me.

"What was the first thing you said to me when I asked you if you did it?"

"Fuck no—that was the first thing I said," I answered him.

"Then after, you told me how someone must have created this lie, that it wasn't just a mistake."

"Yes…"

"Do I really have to piece this together for you, Owen?"

"Oh, come on Grey, stop this storytelling shit and spit it out!"

He grabbed our bowls and put them in the sink, and when he came back he remained standing.

"Owen, think about it. Perhaps the people who were behind the Confinement are behind this lie, too. Why else would they frame an innocent man? You and Cole are the *leaders* of the party. Don't you see how your party's existence threatens the continuity of their own?"

"I'm following you," I said. Grey was getting worked up. He paced in the dining room and moved his hands around as he spoke.

"Here is the thing, Owen. *If* they win, if they convince the public long enough that you are the enemy, then you will *become* the enemy. If the truth never gets out, that it's all a sham, then your cause will be lost. Everything you worked for will disappear. They will get what they want. Goodman will lose the election."

I felt rage begin to bubble up inside of me. My heart rate increased.

"Then the question is," I began, "who is *they?*"

"*That* is what we have to find out. Come, follow me to my office."

"Remember what I told you I do?" Grey asked.

"Network security."

"Yes, now let me ask you a dumb question."

"You sound like my dad," I said, laughing.

He shook his head. "Anyway, since I am the head of network security at the bank, there is no one above me in terms of the job that I do. I am the lone wolf."

"Nicely put, you know, with the beard and all." I peppered in some sarcasm.

He chuckled at my remark.

"Now, the sole purpose of Wells Fargo hiring me was to prevent what happened with the old execs that ran the bank shortly after the Confinement. When I arrived, everything was as clean as a whistle. The execs were already gone. So I created a network that would allow me to monitor everything."

"Everything?"

"*Everything.* What they wanted me to do was to make a system that it was impossible to commit grand larceny or launder money. I could have easily done just that. What I thought, though, was that in this kind of job market, if I made everything so perfect that my network could be secure indefinitely—they might get rid of me. Especially when they pay me a high salary compared to the rest of their staff, and I work from home. I am essential *only* if I can maintain my network without them learning how it operates. Once they figure out how it works, they could train some pushover fresh out of college who would do it for half the pay."

"Continue."

"So, what I did instead was I created a node system in the existing network."

"A node as in, a sensor?"

"Precisely," he responded. Excitement burned behind his eyes. "Any time an employee in my bank were to manually edit a report, move money from one account to another, etcetera, it is flagged and sent to my inbox. Then I can view the event from my computer. The employees don't know this because I am the only person allowed to know. All I have to do is report to corporate if I see something suspicious."

"All right, so when you arrived it was as clean as a whistle…and *now?*"

He grinned.

"In the past three months, I've been getting more things flagged to my inbox than in my one and a half years at the bank combined. Ironically, it coincided with the arrival of the new vice-president. The odd thing, though, is it was like he had done this before…like this wasn't his first rodeo when it came to money laundering. The flags I received were mundane, similar to the things I would see an auditor mess up, or a teller screw up on a deposit. You see, what allows me to stay stealth is the district managers don't tell any of the execs that I exist. When I go into the building, they think I am just basic IT support. The employees don't realize I monitor the entire network and report to corporate. That was how they designed it to be, after losing one-hundred million dollars in a short period of time."

"So, what have you found?" I asked.

He grabbed a folder, filled with papers that made it as thick as a textbook.

"I knew this guy was up to no good. This was something I had to go into the building for because the events that were in my inbox just didn't add up. To me, it seemed like the VP had executed this well enough to where what the system *saw* was different from what was actually happening in day-to-day operations. So I scrounged the audit packs, the paperwork, it took me weeks. Then the truth began to reveal itself, and that was when I realized he wasn't the only one in on it, the auditors were too. The reason why this guy is still here is because apparently he is 'doing so much' to help business. The accountants have now been posting false profits, making it appear like the bank is making more money than it actually is. They are making it seem like more money is coming in so they can steal some of the *real* money that is. If the Government were to audit us, we'd be fucked. Our internal auditors are turning a blind eye to it. I just wonder how much of a cut he is giving them."

I was impressed by how extensive Grey's research was.

"Dude, have you not reported it yet to corporate? Won't you lose your job for not stopping it from occurring in the first place?"

His expression looked troubled as I said that. But, behind that veneer I sensed confidence. He had a plan.

"Yes, technically I would. It has taken me nearly a month to compile all of this evidence against him. I was going to report it to corporate on Friday, to give them the weekend to look over it. That is until you came to my door today."

My brow furrowed in confusion.

"What does any of this have to do with me?"

Grey smiled. "Let me finish, Owen. You of all people should know I have a plan."

He was right. In high school, I remembered the class discussions and debates. Grey was always a couple steps ahead of everybody. He was quiet…but his mind was loud.

"Enlighten me," I replied.

"Remember the senior prank I did in high school?"

"Ah, the infamous Grey Maxwell's gift. How could I forget?"

He laughed from me mentioning what it was called amongst our circle.

"I told you what I did to make that happen, right?"

"Well, at the time, you were more worried about being allowed to graduate than revealing your secret to your friends. You might have said something about it, but I forgot. I just remember being released from school shortly after we made it into homeroom."

"I used to take that advanced computers class our senior year, and part of our training was learning how to clean out the computers in the office and accessing the registry. So what I did was put a key log on one of the administrator's computers. All they had to do was enter their credentials, and all I had to do was open my email to retrieve it. So the night before the prank, I stayed at the school late to 'work on a project'. I used the credentials to log in, and then I did a system-wide hack which created a glitch that nullified every username and password that was presently used."

"And that's why we had the day off."

"Exactly," he grinned. "Then I realized that when my computer teacher was questioned, he would point out to the administration that I was the brightest in the class…and if *he* were to look into the right computer, he would see where I set up the key log. I figured out a way to turn myself in and giving the administration the data in exchange for me being able to walk at graduation. I gave them the forged data on how it was an experiment to show that the school's system was not secure. As upset as they were, they just gave me two weeks of suspension, as I'm sure you recall."

I smirked from his statement. "I remember it quite well. You spent the last two weeks of the school year smoking weed and playing World of Warcraft."

"The deed was well worth the punishment," he replied with a wink.

"You cocky bastard…"

"Anyway, back then in high school I was decent at hacking, and not very well-versed in what it takes to write script and execute it properly. During college, I learned quite a bit more about software engineering in general, and the group of friends I hung out with were into hacking too. We were white-hats though—good hackers. We hacked and then revealed the information to the people we hacked in order to make their information more secure. Black hats are the famous hackers, the ones who hack into government websites, retail stores, *banks…*"

I glanced up at him with curiosity.

"Grey, you aren't thinking of..."

"Yes, but just wait, it gets better. At Wells Fargo, my position gives me clearance to perform extensive background checks. Any kind of information I want, I can have. So I called the Wells Fargo in Baltimore and told the IT that I was doing some scheduled maintenance on their server. I faxed over my credentials, and I was in. Like I told you, I had a feeling the VP had done this before, because of the camouflaged flags I was getting to my inbox. Not just any thief can do that, it has to be a thief who has stolen *before*. I accessed a list that showed the accounts with the highest balances down to the lowest. After I scrolled past the multi-millionaires, *I found it*.

Grey paused. I held my hands out and shrugged, coaxing him to respond.

"Fourteen accounts. Fourteen accounts with identical balances, and the serial numbers associated with the accounts are sequential, but all the names on the accounts are different. They have to be squatter accounts, people who are involved that hold the account in their name. It was like these fourteen people never went to the bank to begin with. Someone on the inside opened up the accounts and got the paperwork signed outside of work. Once I isolated the accounts, I looked into the balance history of them. That was when I discovered that seven of the accounts each had one-hundred thousand dollars in them from the day they were opened. The *other* seven, one by one each had one-hundred thousand dollars wired into them. The time between the first deposit of 100K in the eighth account and the last deposit in the fourteenth account of the same amount was—guess…"

"Three months?" I blurted.

"Three months. Exactly the amount of time the VP has been in charge at my bank. The icing on the cake is what I found earlier this week when I went to the bank in person. After crunching the numbers and working around the false profits, the amount that had been stolen was seven-hundred thousand dollars. The same amount that was split and wired into the remaining seven accounts in Baltimore."

"No shit…" I mumbled. I was stunned at the level of corruption that was going on. His idea echoed in my mind like a bell being rung. "Grey, are you really thinking of *taking* it?"

He sat down on the edge of the bed beside me. He had his glasses on and many papers in his hands, it made him look like a professor. He was intelligent enough to be one.

"Owen, have you heard of Bitcoin?"

"Yes, I have. The feds hate it. It's essentially a currency they can't control. It's decentralized."

"You're correct. So, think about this. If I were to hack the main server in Baltimore and get the needed credentials to those fourteen accounts, I could write a script that wipes out the money in each of the accounts and combines it all together. But then, where would we be able to hide 1.4 million dollars? The answer is Bitcoin. We could trade the 1.4

million to a Chinese bank and in exchange get Bitcoin. The great thing about the Coin is essentially it can be stored anywhere…like a flash drive, for example. We could sell the Coin on the Darknet, in increments, and only when we needed the funds on the go."

"*On the go*?" I asked, confused. "I am the one on the run, not you."

"Dude! Do you not realize the magnitude of what's going on here?"

"Of course I do—"

"No, let me finish. *We* know the truth, Owen. We are right, and whoever created this lie is *wrong*. If we expose this and execute it properly, this is going to be the biggest government scandal in history. You are not going to make it on your own, not with just your street bike. They have too many eyes watching and too much power. I am going to help you, and if you don't take my help, I can promise you that you won't make it very far after you leave my house."

His words sank in. The truth he had just spoken of was undeniable.

"Well, once you take the money, won't they come after you too?"

"Not that it matters anyway, but *that* is the best part. Once those accounts are wiped out, what can the VP do? Nothing. He is a sitting duck. He can't report to corporate the money was taken, because if he does, the crime he committed will be visible. If he doesn't stay quiet, he will shoot himself in the foot. That is what will keep me off the radar. Plus, part of the script I'm going to write will make it seem like the money just vanished. I will leave no trace that I was ever there to begin with."

"Goddamn man, you're a fucking genius!"

He pushed his glasses up the bridge of his nose and stood up.

"Why thank you, Owen, for complimenting me with such eloquent wording."

"Smartass…" I mumbled.

"In the meantime, though, you're going to need some cash."

He walked around to the side of his bed and picked up the edge of the mattress. He pulled out a handgun and laid it in front of me. I stared at him in disbelief.

"You can't be kidding me," I said.

"Owen, you're already a terrorist. What's a little armed robbery gonna hurt?"

"My reputation! I'm not a *real* criminal, man."

"But, you're a politician," Grey retorted with a sly smirk.

"Good one," I quipped.

"Dude, regardless of what you do, you are the media's bitch right now. They are going to tarnish you any way they can. Whoever is feeding them this false information knows they have the power. We have to shake them up a little bit, and prove to them that you aren't just going to give up without a fight."

I shook my head in agreement.

"You're right, Grey. I think you've got a good plan."

"It's a damn good plan, at least for now. I know I can execute the script properly, too."

"What a résumé you have, you went from hacking the school computers to hacking banks."

"Progress is key," he said and winked.

Grey sat down and started opening programs on his desktop. I carefully picked up the handgun and held it in my hand. The weight of it alone was formidable, and thoughts about robbing a bank tomorrow with it were even more nerve-wracking.

"All right Owen, I put some fresh sheets and pillows in our guest bedroom. It's one door down."

I gave him a peculiar look. "Are you trying to get rid of me already?"

"No, but with the kind of stress you've been under today, you should probably get some rest. You'll need the energy for tomorrow."

I felt a wave of anxiety as I imagined what the coming days might bring.

"You're probably right," I admitted.

"Plus, I highly doubt you would want to stay up all night and watch me write script."

"You thought right," I agreed. "You aren't going to sleep? You're crazy man."

"Most people of my caliber would take a couple days to a week to encode a script as complex as this. We don't have that kind of time. So, it's not crazy, it's *necessary*."

"I'm glad you see it like that," I said.

He glanced at me with a serious expression. "Owen, if you don't want to rot in a federal prison for the rest of your life, every single thing you do from here on out *has* to be necessary."

I nodded and let his comment settle.

"Also, if you don't mind, can you make a pot of coffee before you hit the sack?"

I shot him a dramatic, exaggerated glare—as if his request was too difficult.

"Of course man, of course."

The Gambit

Grey's House – Chesterfield, VA
08:07 10-13-2016

I set my coffee on the faux wood of the table. Grey refilled my cup. The pouring sound, along with the bold aroma helped calm my nerves. Simple pleasures before a chaotic day. Grey sat down in front of me. I noticed he had dark circles under his eyes.

"Did you get any sleep?"

"No. I'll sleep when it's done."

"How did everything turn out?"

He pressed his lips together and appeared nervous.

"The script looks great, but there is no way of being sure it will work until I hit enter. Once I'm remotely in their server, one incorrectly written command could mean a rejection—a failure in the execution of the script."

It dawned on me *why* Grey had stayed up all night. This kind of hacking wasn't to be taken lightly.

"We'll see, I guess. I have faith in you, though. Any luck with the banks?"

He nodded.

"Since it was daytime there, I managed to find a Chinese bank willing to do the exchange into Bitcoin. They emailed me over the paperwork, and I signed it and sent it back. The account and routing numbers to the bank are embedded in the script. So the moment the money is taken from the VP's accounts, it is immediately diverted into the Chinese bank. I have instructed them to send me an encrypted file with the Bitcoin. If everything goes smooth with the script, the last few steps will be an easy ride."

"*Then* you can get some sleep."

"Exactly," Grey said with a smile.

"So, you're *sure* there are no undercover officers at your bank?"

"I'm sure. We have paid security that comes to check the property in the evenings, and the only time they come in the daytime is to bring the biggest deposits. That's why you need to leave soon—in the early morning activity is minimal."

"Okay," I answered, and took the final sip of my coffee.

He stood up and went upstairs. I looked at the empty mug in my hand and wished I didn't have to leave at all…didn't have to face my reality.

When Grey returned, I noticed he had something clenched in his fist. He walked around the dining room and went into the garage. He flicked on the light.

"Are you ready?" he asked.

"Hardly," I replied.

I followed him into the garage. In the dim, yellow lighting, the exhaustion on Grey's face was even more pronounced. I sat on my street bike and he stood beside me.

"Here you go, Owen," Grey said as he opened my hand. He placed a flash drive in my palm, and I shoved it in my jacket pocket. "That is a ghost drive. If anyone were to stick that in a computer and tried to see what was on it, it appears as if it is empty."

"Badass," I said.

"Indeed, it is. You need to put the flash drive in the tower, or laptop, while the computer is still off. Once it turns on, in around two seconds press F2. On some machines, it may be F12. When it gives you the option of how to boot up, choose USB. It will prompt you to put in a password. This ghost drive essentially is an operating system you can plug in and use when you need to. It is how we're going to communicate with each other."

"So, how *do* we communicate? It's not like I can login to Facebook and send you a message."

He laughed loudly at my statement.

"No, that is the last thing you would want to do. There is a

Bitmessage account already set up and accessible through this drive. Use the same password you used to get into the ghost drive to get into Bitmessage. It's encrypted email, it circumvents the normal pathways on the web to avoid being monitored. It's actually what Snowden used to leak some of his information."

"No shit. What is the password?" I asked.

"It's thirty characters long."

"What the fuck, Grey! You better write that down for me."

"Already have. Here," he said, handing me a folded up paper. "It's a random pattern of characters. It would take the fastest computer in the world over a million years to decode it."

"Damn, talk about secure."

"Right?" he said, grinning.

"So, Grey, where are you going after today?"

He glanced to the ground momentarily in thought.

"I have a friend in Virginia Beach I might go see…but mainly, I'm going to wait until you contact me through Bitmessage and tell me where to head next."

I put my hand on his shoulder and shook him.

"Grey, I have no words for you deciding to do this, to help me."

He shook his head. "There's no need to thank me. The way I see it is we have two options. We let them win, *or*, we put up the best damn fight we've got."

"Damn right, my friend!"

Grey paused and looked me up and down. "Did you forget something?" he asked.

I returned his question with a confused stare. He walked back into the house, and a few moments later he returned with the black handgun he had shown me last night.

"Remember, Owen. You are going to have to scare the shit out of them. I know it's not who you are, but remember—it's *necessary*. I'll be watching the security cameras. When you reach the vault, I will unlock it for you. If it *happens* not to work, there is a woman with red hair who is in one of the offices. She is the manager of the bank. Only she will have the code to access the vault."

"Got it," I said.

Grey patted my back roughly. He stepped back and pressed the button to open the garage.

"Only backroads to Richmond, all right?" he reminded me.

"Yes, that's how I got here. Backroads."

"Good," he nodded. "Just get in, get the money, and get out of there. The rest is up to me."

"How will I know you got the money?"

"You won't," Grey answered. "Not until we speak again. Use the flash drive, and whatever you do—*do not* lose that password."

"Anything else, Dad?" I asked in a childish voice, mocking him.

"Shut up," he pushed me. "Good luck out there."

"Thanks, I'll need it."

I hit the ignition switch and quietly pulled out of Grey's driveway. The air was crisp, and it was a clear blue sky. I inhaled the fresh air through my helmet and tried to enjoy my last half hour of peace. May God help me…

MIT – Cambridge, MA
08:13 10-13-2016

"Are we in the clear?" I asked.

"For now," she answered.

"Keep watch for me, please."

My assistant walked towards the glass door of the lab. I heard buttons being pressed and then a click. She had switched the settings to *Experiment in Progress*. Now, only staff could get in. We didn't want *any* interruptions.

"Where did you say you got this sample again?" she questioned from across the room.

"Manhattan," I responded while setting up the bone marrow sample on the slide.

"So how do you even know that cat was in the Danger Zone?"

"I don't…but it's worth a shot."

"But is it worth the risk, Stefan?"

I looked over my shoulder to her. "Emily, no one is keeping you here. You aren't being forced to help me with this experiment."

She huffed.

"I am aware of that. Although, you know just as well as I do that the EPA and FEMA killed all the exposed stray animals for a reason."

"And that, my dear friend, is exactly what we are trying to find out."

"Just get it done quickly, okay?" she pressed.

"We both have a task at hand here. You do yours, and I'll do mine."

"Bite me," she spat. "Well, at least if I go down you go down with me."

"Indeed, I will. Do you think Professor Trantham would rat us out to the feds and betray our research? I highly doubt it. Now relax, please. You're stressing me out."

"Oh, you think *you're* the stressed out one? Please…"

With the slide in the airlock of the electron microscope, I fired the beam. I waited for the image to process and began to examine the structure of the bone marrow. The nuclei looked hardly damaged. I had an additional sample from the same cat of more marrow, and I slid the transparency in the slot.

"What do you see?" Emily asked anxiously.

"Hold on," I said.

This slide was the same. The marrow cells looked relatively undamaged. The doctorate program I was in was for Nuclear Engineering, but my two bachelor's degrees were for Physics and Biology. I retained enough from my Biology days to know that this was *not* normal.

"Emily, last time I checked, Strontium-90 settles almost entirely in bones, correct?"

"Entirely in the bones, yes. Almost ninety-nine percent is deposited in the bones. It acts like calcium. *Why?* What did you find?"

With the cold metal desk in my hands, I felt my mind ignite. In my independent research since the dirty bombs outside of Wall Street almost two years ago, I have been playing the scientific lottery…and *today*, I hit the jackpot.

"Give me a scalpel, now," I demanded.

Emily darted away from her position by the lab entrance and in moments returned to my side with a scalpel. "Stefan, is it *not* in the bones?"

"No," I said, glancing at her. "It's not."

Astonishment filled her eyes.

"Your theory…that it might not be Strontium…"

"Yes. We need to look at the soft tissue—quickly."

She nodded as I began slicing beneath the fur of the cat's thigh. After a few moments, I removed the tiniest sliver of meat from the cat. I sliced that sliver in two and placed it beneath a new slide. If my theory was correct, when we stained the samples with a protein that isolated the microtubules, we would be able to view the cell division going on, or the lack thereof.

I looked at the new image that came on the screen.

What I saw was shocking. The cell nuclei were damaged, and as I focused the lens in on one section, I noticed what appeared to be the beginning of the process which causes cancer.

"Emily, slice off a piece from another limb—something different."

I could hear her fiddling with the scalpel. I reached for another slide and pushed it in her direction. She put the new slide underneath the microscope and I saw the image change.

As I focused the lens, the cells were *all* the same. The nuclei damaged, the cells stuck in a dysfunctional mitosis, and pre-cancerous growths.

I walked around from the image display. Emily stared at me wide-eyed.

"Look," I said quietly. I backed away from the table and let her see our discovery.

"It's not Strontium," Emily gasped. She stepped away from the image and faced me. "They lied. They *lied* about what it was."

"Then what is it?" I asked.

"Perhaps Cesium-137. It appears to be evenly distributed throughout the soft tissues. There are other isotopes that act in the same manner, but this is definitive evidence that this cat's radiation exposure was from something other than Strontium-90."

Behind Emily, there was more congestion in the hallway outside the lab. The day was beginning.

"We have to clean this up, take a few more samples from its soft tissues, and dispose of it properly. Like you said, it's not worth the risk of Professor finding out."

She nodded and began taking more samples, preserving them in vials as she did so.

"I can't believe your hunch was right…and to think, out of all the specimens you've brought in without radiation exposure and now this. How much did you spend on that cat?" she asked.

"I gave the homeless lady a hundred bucks. She put up a good fight, but I told her if the cat really *was* in the Danger Zone on Black Monday it wouldn't live much longer. She confirmed it had been ill, and I told her we might be able to heal it in the lab."

"You liar," she replied, shaking her head in disapproval.

I shrugged. "All in the name of science, Emily."

"That was probably her only friend."

"She had a dozen more surrounding her," I said. "I have a heart too, you know."

"Or so you claim," she responded with a smile and continued packing up the equipment.

I heard someone at the door, a student, trying to get in with their palm on the scanner. It was being denied.

"Shit, hurry!" I urged her. "Keep our samples locked away and get rid of the cat. I have to make a phone call."

In light of my discovery, I hadn't the slightest idea of what to do. How could I report something that the government had tried so hard to destroy? My dad potentially could help, but he would want more evidence before he made a claim that bold. He would need something peer-reviewed, something more. I took out my phone and dialed the number for the EPA. I had someone, someone on the inside who had kept quiet and lied to me about the very evidence I now had. Perhaps *she* could help…

Emily was running circles around me, and I could tell she had cleaned quickly enough for our experiment not to be revealed to the student trying to get into the lab.

"EPA, how may I direct your call?" said the voice on the other line.

"Can you please connect me to the office of Ms. Walling?"

Wells Fargo – Richmond, VA
08:28 10-13-2016

I had managed to make it into the city without any issues. The streets were filled with morning traffic, and I pulled up to the curb on the side of the bank. I saw a meter when I stepped off my bike. I wasn't going to be here long anyway, so I ignored it and began my walk to the entrance.

My heart pounded out of my chest. I could feel the cold metal of the gun in my right hand inside my jacket pocket. *What am I about to do right now?*

I was having a hard time preparing mentally to rob the bank, but as I neared the shiny revolving door, I swallowed hard. This was *necessary*.

I walked into the bank and pulled the gun out of my pocket. I aimed it toward the ceiling and fired two shots.

Screams filled the bank and the employees froze.

"Everybody listen up!" I yelled and walked towards the counter. My heart was in my throat. "If you make one wrong move I will blow you the fuck away. Don't try anything stupid! Stay down on the ground!" I commanded, waving my gun around at the people lying flat on the marble floor. I turned and pointed the gun at the employees who all had their hands up.

"I hate to put a damper in your day, I really do," I shouted, my voice echoing throughout the lobby. "But I'm going to have to step behind the counter and get into the vault."

As I stepped behind the counter a female employee was just a foot away. She was younger, short-haired, and she stared at me, shaking her head side to side with tears in her eyes.

"You can't," she whimpered. "It's locked."

Grey's House – Chesterfield, VA
08:30 10-13-2016

I sighed with relief as I watched the piece of script that contained the Chinese bank's routing numbers processing. The script executed seamlessly. I sipped my coffee, which wasn't helping my racing heart. Having stayed up for over twenty-four hours was beginning to make me delirious.

Suddenly, it hit me. I just became a millionaire.

I grinned and laughed, shaking my head, and thought of how hard I had worked my entire life…and to think, I just pressed enter and waited thirty seconds.

I opened the minimized window of the security cameras at my bank to see Owen approaching the vault door. I almost spit my coffee out.

Shit. I opened our network mainframe that I was booted into remotely and began searching for the correct scripts that were associated with monitoring the vault's lock. I knew from experience, the vault door sent out a ping every time it was opened or locked. What I needed to do was essentially send the lock a message wirelessly to unlock itself.

I found the right script. I reversed the code and sent it back to the lock.

Nothing.

My stomach sank. I saw Owen pulling at the vault's lock.

I tried again. **/Denied**.

Angrily, I hit the enter button over and over.

/Denied

/Denied

/Denied

/Denied

"Fuck!" I shouted and slammed my fist against the desk.

Owen continued pulling on the vault's lock. He wouldn't stop trying.

Remember what I told you, buddy. Remember…

I began searching for another route. I had to search the event log, to find the last time someone opened the vault. The password would have been manually entered into the keypad, and the ping would be encrypted to protect the numbers themselves.

Wells Fargo – Richmond, VA
08:33 10-13-2016

Whipping around, I waved my gun at the employees in front of me. I was beginning to sweat from the adrenaline. I glanced down at my watch. I had pressed the timer the moment I walked in. Three minutes had passed and my backpack was still empty—no money.

If it happens to not work, there is a woman with red hair who is in one of the offices. She is the manager of the bank. Only she will have the code to access the vault.

Grey's words echoed in my mind. I kept my gun aimed at the employees and left the vault door. There were four offices in my view, and I peered into the first one. A brunette—she was on the phone. "*Get off* the phone," I threatened, pointing the gun directly at her. She hung up and kept her hands in the air. I went to the office beside her, another brunette. The corner office, the fourth one, was the largest. My instincts were leading me there, and I followed. There she was, dressed in a black business suit and had *red* hair.

"Stand up," I said.

"I can't help you," she retorted.

I shook my head and walked around to her desk and pressed the gun against her back.

"Are you *sure* about that?" I whispered into her ear.

She stood out of her desk and walked out of the office into the lobby.

"To the vault, now!" I yelled. I shot another bullet into the ceiling.

"The cops are on their way here," she said calmly as we walked.

"Then hurry up!" I pushed her forward.

When we reached the vault, she didn't do anything.

"I'm not going to open it."

My time is running out…

I stood beside her and pressed the gun against her temple.

"I *will* fucking blow your brains out!" I screamed.

Tears filled her eyes and I saw her swallow. I would have never blown her brains out. I was not a killer…but everybody in this bank thought I was a terrorist who already *had* killed, and I was going to use that to my advantage.

She pressed six digits and the vault lock clicked open.

I turned the lock and pulled open the heavy, metal door. Inside was the most cash I had ever seen at one time. Shelves upon shelves of money. I immediately unzipped my backpack and started piling in bundles of hundred dollar bills. I kept my gun pointed at the bank manager, to keep her in the vault with me. If I was in here alone, all they would have to do is—

The vault door slammed shut, and I heard the mechanism lock.

My face turned blank. We were trapped.

The bank manager stared at me with a smile.

"Now you're just a sitting duck," she laughed.

Anger surged through my body. I knew there were other employees right outside the vault door.

"I will fucking kill her right here! Open this goddamn door! Do you all want her blood on your hands? Open the fucking door!" I screamed at the top of my lungs and pounded on the metal door with my free hand.

I started to panic. I searched around the vault for a way out, for anything…and in one of the top corners I saw it. It was a security camera. I stared at it, and in that moment I tried to plead with my facial expression, displaying how desperate I was.

I know you're watching Grey. Get me out of here, I know you can do it. Please find a way before it's too late.

Grey's House – Chesterfield, VA
08:36 10-13-2016

"I will fucking kill her! I swear to God I'll do it!" Owen screamed in a rage.

"Please Owen, don't blow her brains out…" I mumbled, watching the security camera video.

I looked at my script. It was cracking the encrypted digits from the last ping that the manager just punched in moments ago. My timer read twenty-nine seconds. Twenty-nine seconds until I could remotely enter the passcode to the vault.

Come on…come on…

On another screen, I was simultaneously opening up the emergency functions of the bank just in case the cops were closing in. It had been seven minutes. They couldn't have been far off now.

Eleven seconds. Ten. Nine. Eight.

I zoomed out to see all twenty security cameras. Scanning quickly through them, the cameras that faced down the street showed Richmond Police approaching at high speed.

"Oh fuck! Fuck!" I yelled.

One—the digits appeared.

378416. I punched them in immediately. Switching over to the emergency functions, I locked all the automatic doors from the outside and turned on all the fire sprinklers. The dozens of people that were lying on the floors were now standing up and scrambling towards the exits.

"It's all up to you now…" I said, covering my mouth from the intensity of what was unfolding at my work.

Wells Fargo – Richmond, VA
08:37 10-13-2016

I turned the vault lock open. All the employees and patrons were running out of the bank. The emergency sprinklers were spraying water everywhere.

God damn Grey. You saved me, you fucking genius.

The sound of sirens echoed from outside. I saw officers scrambling up the bank steps.

"Oh shit!" I yelled and began sprinting towards the exit on the side where I parked my bike. I *had* to get to my bike before they did. The police ran into the automatic doors and tried to pry them open. They appeared to be locked.

I heard gunshots and saw the glass door to my right shatter, I ran through the glass in an attempt to get out faster. I might have cut myself, but I couldn't tell.

With a backpack full of money, I hopped onto my bike as more cop cars whipped around the intersection. I heard bullets fly past.

I popped a wheelie, maneuvering myself around the cars. When I turned on the next street, I went back on two wheels and accelerated as quickly as I could. In my rearview I could still see the police. I-95 would be coming up any moment. I saw the sign and looped onto the on-ramp. My knee scraped the asphalt as I leaned into the curve. Without a destination, I sped up over 150 miles per hour on I-95 South.

CIA Headquarters – Langley, VA
08:41 10-13-2016

"How in the *fuck* did we lose him?" I shouted and slammed my hands against the metallic counter. I felt my left eyelid twitching and I had my teeth clenched.

The fifty-something people in the room stared at me. I couldn't wait to see which one of these mindless shits had the nerve to speak up first.

"Ma'am, those were the Richmond Police. The FBI and Homeland Security were shortly behind them. Something went wrong. Apparently someone had access to the bank's main server and assisted Owen in his robbery."

I pursed my lips and exhaled through my nose. I was *furious*. A tiny bead of sweat began to drip down the forehead of the man who had answered my question.

"You are the Central Intelligence Agency for Christ's sake! How in the hell are you going to let him slip by so easily? Everyone in this room is going to need to take their position more seriously, unless you want to end up decommissioned with a reputation so terrible you won't be able to land a job as a mall cop."

No one said a word.

"We just got word Owen is heading south on I-95," someone said in the crowd.

The security camera video populated the many screens in the room. It showed Owen tucked into his bike, zipping by like a little black blip.

"Get a chopper in the air," I demanded. "Call all the police stations along 95, give them his info. We are *not* going to let him get away again…"

Knightdale Bypass – Raleigh, NC
09:39 10-13-2016

I was headed west towards the city. Around thirty minutes ago I saw a helicopter flying behind me in the distance. Given the fact that I had already lost the police, if the helicopter were to stay with me I would have never been able to escape. I maintained a higher speed and took the exit to merge onto the less traveled Highway 64. Now, the highway had become I-495, and I knew within a few miles I would hit more congested roads from entering the city. It was time to *hide*.

I saw an exit sign.

Exit 420

New Hope Rd ↗

I smiled when I saw the name of the road, and took it as a message to get off the highway. When I came to the stoplight I turned left and went south. The road was windy and had very few cars on it. It was relieving to see that. I came to an intersection. The street sign read **Poole Road**. I recalled going over a bridge just moments ago on the highway and a river ran beneath it. Contemplating my orientation, I took another left.

Poole Road was just as barren as New Hope. The road curved gently, and it was enjoyable after the hour-long blur of racing down I-95. After a mile, in the distance I saw what looked to be a small bridge; murky water slipped beneath it.

As I approached, I saw a small wooden sign for **Poole Road Park**. There was a tiny dirt parking lot on my left and I was beaming as I pulled in. There were only two other cars parked. This was exactly what I needed. A park—no security cameras and minimal traffic.

I idled as I drove around the lot. When I saw the river, I followed the walking trail along its edge. I wanted to be as far away as I could. Stealth was *key.* A half-mile of wandering later, I found an open, flat part of the forest which would be ideal for me to ride through. I followed it, and ended up a few feet from the water and surrounded by trees. I stepped off my bike and glanced back through the trees to see if anyone was around—no one. I exhaled and sat on the ground facing the river, leaning against a tree trunk.

The exhaustion I felt was overpowering. The nerves in my hands and wrists felt numb, almost shocked. Vibration from the throttle at such a high speed was the culprit. I could barely hear the river running past. The shrill growl from my bike still rang in my ears.

I closed my eyes—resting them. The woods surrounded me, and for the first time since hearing the news yesterday, I felt *safe.*

The lumpiness of my backpack was causing me pain. I slid it off and set it in front of me. Opening the flap, I actually laughed to myself as I stared at the huge bundles of hundred-dollar bills.

I fucking *robbed* a bank. What a day.

Out of curiosity, I took out one of the bundles and removed the paper bands. I began counting…ninety-seven, ninety-eight, ninety-nine, one-hundred.

Ten thousand dollars. I shook my head in disbelief at the amount of money I was holding.

I guess this is what a big-time drug dealer feels like.

I dug around my backpack and pushed around the different bundles. I glanced back at the woods behind me again—no one.

I set the bundles of money out in front of me in a line. Soon, it became two lines. When I was finished counting, I had one-hundred and twenty thousand dollars. I could hardly think straight. There was no *way* I would ever need this much cash, even in my escape.

I wondered if Grey had wired the money successfully.

1.4 *million* dollars. I couldn't fathom that kind of wealth. Then again, facing the federal government, our 1.4 mil was a drop of water compared to their ocean of funds.

I rested my arm on top of my helmet and zipped my jacket up tight. I had to let the time slip by, perhaps rest until the sun began to set…

Days Inn South – Raleigh, NC
16:58 10-13-2016

The sun was gone and the twilight began fading away. After meandering around the outskirts of Raleigh for a while, I saw a small motel to my right. From the exterior, it appeared like it had seen its fair share of everything; it was a little run down. I was sure that anyone with a TV would recognize me, so I would have to approach check-in with caution. Maybe, just maybe, I could blend in for the night with the other locals who frequented this budget motel.

The parking lot was devoid of activity. As I pulled in, I noticed around the back there was a line of Leyland trees by the dumpsters. I hopped my bike onto the curb and tucked it behind the Leylands. There was a dark-colored fence a couple feet behind it, and as I walked away it was camouflaged perfectly.

I stuck my hands in my jacket pockets and walked towards registration. I kept my helmet on for anonymity, and I opened the entrance door. A bell jingled.

No one was at the counter. Even when I went to the desk, there wasn't the slightest indication that someone was on duty.

I calmly waited.

Finally, a weary-looking guy came to the desk in a blue polo shirt and some khakis. He had dark circles under his eyes, and I could smell the mix of cigarettes and cologne as he stood across from me. He appeared to be my age.

"Do you have a reservation?" he asked.

"No, I need a room for tonight."

My helmet muffled my words. He gave me a peculiar, contorted expression.

"I can't hear you, sir. Could you take off your helmet, please?"

I swallowed. I was exhausted from being on the run, and I really hoped I could have a place to lie my head down tonight. In the corner of the room there was a TV on the wall. I couldn't hear what channel it was on...but regardless, I still slid my helmet off.

His eyes grew wide as he saw my face. My heart sped up.

Fuck...

He reached down behind the desk and I quickly grabbed his wrist with my gloved hand. I held it firm, yet lightly, and he froze from the shock.

"Sir, you're going to have to let go of me, I'm going to call the cops."

"No, you're not," I replied calmly.

"Let go of me!" he said, raising his voice.

"Not until I know I can trust you."

"Trust me? You're wanted. They're going to find you anyway."

"But *not* tonight," I said firmly, looking him in the eyes.

"They're offering a reward to whoever turns you in. Fifty-thousand dollars."

I laughed. Beneath his sullen eyes, I caught the look of someone who was struggling, and maybe in his free time he used drugs. Perhaps pain pills or something similar. The reward was *alluring* to him. It was an easy way to get richer than he had ever been.

I tightened my grip on his wrist.

"Look..." I glanced at his nametag. "Larry, those people offering that reward? They won't give it to you. You would never see that money."

I could practically hear him in my head saying, "*Bullshit.*"

"How do you know?"

"Because they framed me. I am innocent. I didn't kill any of those people."

He didn't believe me.

"But, why though? Why frame *you*?"

"That's what I am trying to figure out. The *real* question though is, Larry, when their lie is exposed, what side do you want to be able to tell people you stood on? Helping the feds, the ones who allowed the Confinement, or helping me?"

He blinked and appeared more relaxed, but he didn't respond.

"Larry. I am going to let go of your hand, and you are *not* going to pick up the phone. You are *not* going to call the police. Do you understand?"

He nodded, and I let go of his hand. He stood there with straight posture, just waiting for what I was going to do next. I saw his Adam's apple move as he swallowed. Behind him, near the ceiling, I saw a security camera. My instincts almost caused me to sprint out of the lobby and run back to my bike.

"Larry, does that security camera work?"

He glanced backward at it.

"Oh, that? No, it's broken. Our owners are too cheap to fix it."

"You're serious?"

"Yes, it's been broken for about a month now."

I shook my head, still somewhat nervous to trust this stranger in front of me.

"So, what does a room run here a night?"

"Sixty-five dollars," he answered and began clicking on his computer.

"All right, I'll take it," I said.

"A king bed?" he proposed.

"Sure, whatever you have."

I saw in his facial expression he was nervous, and he was still hesitant to believe the truth I had told him—that I was framed.

"Can I see an ID, please?"

"I can't have my name in your system, it's too risky. I'm going to pay in cash, by the way."

"Well, then what do you want me to do?"

He sounded frustrated. Like I was demanding too much.

"I don't know. Get creative, for all I know I could be John Smith and live here in Raleigh."

He blinked, and I realized he was able to do what I had asked. Before I took out the money, I had an idea overtake me.

"Larry, can I ask you something personal?"

He cocked his head to the side, surprised at my question.

"What?"

"How much do you make here?"

He paused, and I saw some disappointment in his eyes.

"Minimum," he mumbled.

The new federal minimum wage was nine dollars an hour. It was upped to help boost economic activity and spending.

"So, what…in a year you make like, twenty-thousand dollars?" I ball-parked my estimate high for a reason.

"Less," he said.

I put my backpack on the ground and unzipped it. I took two

bundles out and slapped them on the counter. Looking around, there was still no one in the lobby.

Larry's jaw dropped.

"Take my room rate from this, and keep the change."

"Excuse me?" he asked, bewildered.

"This is yours. This is your *reward* for keeping quiet. I am trusting you to do just that."

He scratched the back of his shaggy, sandy-blonde hair.

"I can't just take that. You stole it. How much is that?" I heard curiosity in his voice.

"Well, apparently, it's more than you make in a year. Twenty-thousand dollars."

He began choking on air, or maybe saliva. He coughed until he regained composure.

"Larry, this is not blood money. No one died when I took this today. It is yours. Think of it as a thank you for helping me. Now, on the other hand, if you turn me in, and if they *were* to give you that money, which I highly doubt—*that* would be blood money."

I sensed some form of understanding from what I had just said. It made sense to him.

"Take it," I demanded and pushed the money closer to him.

He walked into the back and came back out with a laundry bag. He put the two bundles inside and quietly made my keys. He handed them to me and looked me straight in the eyes. This time, *without* fear.

"Breakfast starts at six and ends at ten. Our restaurant is limited. I could heat up a pizza for you later."

He was so calm it was almost disturbing. I wondered if he would betray me.

"Larry, you promise that you'll keep your word, only if it be for tonight? Tomorrow you can rat me out, I don't care. Just let me sleep tonight, please."

He blinked and pursed his lips. I saw a smile emerge, and he nodded.

"Checkout is at ten, Mr. Smith."

I took the keys and returned his nod. I walked out of registration and looked down at my key packet. Room 107. First floor. I wandered around the perimeter of the property and followed the numbers until I found mine.

As I opened the door, I smelled the faint smell of cigarette smoke.

The linens were outdated, and so was the room…but it was perfect. I plopped down on the king bed and put the money in the safe that was sitting in the closet. The black, blank screen of the TV faced me, and I could see my reflection in it. The irony was, that even if I were to turn it on—I would still be able to see myself…

I awoke, still bundled up in my riding jacket. The room was too warm, and I could feel sweat on my chest and back. I unzipped it and freed myself from the restricting clothes. I glanced down at my watch—7:46 p.m. I had passed out for a little over two hours. I needed the rest, though. Robbing the bank had drained all my energy.

My stomach growled. I hadn't eaten in twelve hours.

"Our restaurant is limited. I can heat up a pizza for you later."

I recalled Larry's earlier statement in the lobby.

Judging by the motel, the food would most likely be mediocre…but with my predicament, it would be safer not to go out in public.

I had no clothes besides what I was wearing. Only my riding gear, helmet, and 100K. I walked to the safe and knelt down. I took out twenty or so of the hundred dollar bills. After what happened during registration, I might need it for bribery again.

I left my room and shuddered at how cold it was outside. The sky was empty, and a breeze blew every few seconds. When I neared the lobby, I peered through the glass to see if anyone was inside—no one. The parking lot was barren. Everything seemed low-risk, which was what I was aiming for. It then struck me that Larry must have kept his promise. No feds. I sighed in relief.

I entered from the side door, and when I approached the counter, there was no one. I cleared my throat to signal my arrival. Larry walked out from the back office and came to the desk.

"How can I help you, Mr. Smith?" he asked, smiling.

I couldn't help but to return his grin.

"At check-in, you mentioned something about a pizza."

"Yes, are you hungry?"

"*Very*," I answered.

"I can do pepperoni or cheese. They are ten dollars each."

With all this cash, the price wasn't a factor.

"Here is a hundred," I put it on the counter and smirked. "Keep the change."

Larry shook his head in disbelief. "You're too kind."

"No, honestly, it's the least I can do to repay you."

"With everything you already have given me, now I feel like I'm the one who owes *you*."

I dismissed his statement. "No, of course not. Don't worry. It's well appreciated."

"So...about that pizza," he laughed.

"I'll take cheese."

He grabbed the hundred. "It'll be about fifteen minutes. I'll bring it out to you. The restaurant area is right around the corner." He pointed to my left.

I walked towards the restaurant, in the direction he indicated, and I saw the floral carpet begin. It was old, faded, and stained. The dining room was more like a hallway—shaped like a lowercase L. The chairs and tables were a stained faux-mahogany. A few of them had paint peeling off of the legs. I sat down in a two-top table, facing the doorway from which I had come.

A table across from me, an old Asian woman sat with her back against the wall at a four-top table. It was as if she was waiting for her family to join her for dinner...but by the looks of this motel, I doubted that was the case.

I sat in silence for minutes. I had the urge to pull out my phone, maybe go on Facebook or text someone. I had nothing but money. Which was useless, when all I felt was alone. The Asian woman had a plate in front of her, and there was nothing but pizza crust on it. She glanced over at me and smiled. I saw a few of her teeth were yellowish, and one was missing. I returned her smile. She was wearing nylon purple sweatpants and a vibrant green windbreaker. It looked like the eighties had regurgitated all of its worst fashion onto this woman. Then again, it might have been all she was able to afford. This *was* Post-Confinement America we were living in.

There was a TV in the corner of the restaurant. The channels were changing, and I noticed she was holding a small black remote in her left hand.

Suddenly, Larry came around the corner with a steaming pizza. He set it down in front of me and laid a roll of silverware beside the plate.

"Holler if you need me," he said.

I nodded at him with a smile.

Disregarding the silverware, I ate the pizza with my hands. I spent the past year and a half eating at formal dinner parties, with so much silverware on each side of the plate I had to have Cole help me distinguish which were to be used. It was reminiscent of college—pizza. With the first bite I realized Larry wasn't lying when he had offered to '*heat up*' a pizza for me. This was not made fresh, but rather popped into an oven. Regardless, it was enough to satiate my rumbling stomach.

The channel switched to a newscast. I glanced up and saw CNN. I slowed my eating.

"…Owen Marina was last seen by the police chopper getting off of I-95 and heading west on I-40, towards Raleigh. Authorities are saying he is most likely hiding out somewhere in that area. Please remember to call 1-888-FIND HIM. The FBI is offering a fifty-thousand dollar reward for his capture…"

I swallowed hard. The pizza slid down my throat.

The Asian lady turned to me, blinking, and then turned back to the TV. She turned to me *again*, and this time pointed at me. My heart raced, and then she moved her index finger towards the TV, and back to me again. A complete stranger now knew *who* I was. I couldn't just sit back and watch her have this realization without *saying* anything.

I stood up, left my half-eaten pizza, and sat down in the seat diagonal to her. She stared straight at me, expressionless. Being so close, I could now see her in detail. Her skin resembled a grape that had pruned out in the sun all day. She had full cheeks and olive-colored skin. She then pointed at the TV once more and nodded to me. As if she was silently saying, "*Look, it's you.*"

This time, *I* pointed at the TV, and then back at myself.

"I didn't do it," I said. "I am innocent."

She didn't respond. Just stared at me, blinking. Through her narrow eyes, I couldn't tell if she had even absorbed what I said.

"Do you understand me?" I asked her slowly, pronouncing every word individually.

She laughed. "Just because I Asian doesn't mean I don't know English. Dumb white boy."

I couldn't help but display a shocked look with her response. I felt bad.

"I'm sorry, I really shouldn't have assumed so quickly."

She cackled. Her old voice cracked with each laugh. She sounded like a long-time smoker. She didn't respond. Just looked back up at the TV for a moment, staring at the video of me on I-95 and the photo from my license in the corner of the screen.

She pointed at the screen again, then turned to me and suddenly placed her hand on top of mine on the table. I had an urge to pull back, but she leaned in towards me. With her free hand, she used her index finger to tap my chest, right around my heart.

"*God* has *eyes*," she whispered, stretching out the words.

I was speechless. She nodded behind her in the direction of the TV.

"They bad people. *Same* people who took us from our homes. You… *You* good."

I shook my head. I didn't understand.

"How? How do you know I'm good?"

She threw her hands up in a shrug, smiling.

"Because I know!" she cackled once again, her voice raspy.

"What does that mean? God has eyes…"

She came in closer to me again.

"When I was little girl, I live in California. My parents came with me from Laos. Father always say to me, *'God has eyes, Laura.'* I never understand. Then, one day, I come home from school and homeless man ask me for money. I have no money. I was ten, maybe. But, I have lunchbox with extra food from school. I give him my food."

I listened intently to her story. Through her broken English, I sensed a lifetime of wisdom behind her rough appearance.

She paused.

"I get home. My dad was on porch. He saw what I did. He saw I gave my food. Then, he point to homeless man eating on street. He smiled, and say, 'Now you understand, Laura? *God has eyes.* God *sees* through your eyes. When young, the soul pure. God does work through the young.'"

My mouth was agape. I had no words.

"What, am I that ugly?" she asked, laughing at my sudden stupor.

"No, no—what you said. It was so deep."

She rested her hand on top of mine again.

"The ocean deep, too. Remember, most people drown in water too deep. They scared to go away from shallow water. They see the horizon but will never know what lies past."

Confused from her riddle, my face contorted.

"What do those words mean to me?"

With her hand still on mine, she lifted her index finger to point at the TV.

"What they say on the news. That is shallow water. If someone were to shine a light, they would see under the surface is lies. Their water not deep enough to hide truth for long."

"With all due respect, Laura, I think their water is deep enough to sink me to the bottom of the ocean and I'd never be seen again."

She shook her head no.

"You don't get it. It may *seem* like they have lots of water. Like a whole ocean…but, it's all shallow. They spread their water too thin."

"Hmm…" I mumbled.

"Owen, right?" she asked.

"Shh—not so loud."

Her raspy voice cracked in laughter. "What, you worried about local hooker telling on you?" her smile was so wide it revealed her deteriorating teeth.

"No," I laughed, "I'm just trying to be careful."

Her eyes became softer.

"Owen…" This time, her voice was lower.

"Yes," I murmured back.

"I remember when you first came on TV. Your nice suit and excitement in eyes. Our country had many problem. You came on stage like you had answer—a secret you had to share."

I recalled the memory. My first big interview with NBC.

"I was so nervous," I said.

"You didn't look it," she encouraged. "After long while, Owen, you became next great leader. Creator of Convergence Party. I watch you often. One thing I notice is that your ideas good for people. Good for everyone. Everyone except *them*."

She pointed back to the TV. Her expression now tense.

"*They* will drown in water deep as yours, Owen. They fear what is on the other side of horizon, because they lose power if they go too deep. Your story, your water, is much deeper, much cleaner water than theirs. It scare them."

I just listened as her clench on my hand grew tighter.

"Yesterday, I see they make you terrorist. I know it a lie. What happen Owen, is *those* people, make shallow story in shallow water. You and I, we deep. We know better. What happen now is, those people try to drag everyone *back* to shore. Back to where it shallow. Where they have power."

This woman's simple, yet complex analogies were stunning me. Her statement sparked a question.

"Laura, what am I supposed to *do*?"

There was a long pause and she pursed her lips.

"You have to teach them how to *swim*. Those people are trying to take everybody back to shallow water. You must teach them to swim so they can see what beyond the horizon. Before it too late…"

There was so much truth behind her symbolic wording.

"I see…" I mumbled, still digesting her explanation.

"Why you sit down with me, anyway?" she asked, changing the subject.

"You were pointing at me," I said with a confused look.

She busted out laughing.

"Good! My plan work! I wanted you to talk to me. I know who you are when you first sit down."

"Why me?" I questioned.

"Because, you tall, handsome celebrity. Never thought I see you in place like this."

"I never thought I would be framed for the bombs. I never thought I would rob a bank, either."

"You rob bank?" she lit up in excitement.

"Yes, I needed cash. Everything I own is back at my apartment."

"Nice. Remind me of movie I once saw, *Bonnie & Clyde*. But where is Bonnie?"

I sighed. My heart sank from her comment, and all it took was this overly-frank woman to remind me that I was alone.

"I don't have a Bonnie. Right now I'm solo, I'm just Clyde." I mustered up the strength to finish my sentence.

"But how? Look at you." She waved her hand up and down as if she were displaying me to a crowd.

"That's a good question. Maybe it's because I chose my passion over my lover."

She creased her eyes from my statement.

"Owen, if your lover make you choose, she not *real* lover," she whispered.

"I wish those words were enough to stop feeling guilty about choosing."

"No. No guilt," she responded firmly. "Let go of guilt. One day, you find woman who see your passion, and she help you follow it. That is true lover."

"I agree," I said.

She looked at me playfully and revealed her haphazard, yellow teeth.

"I will be Bonnie."

I laughed and patted her hand.

"I appreciate the kind offer, Laura, but I will have to pass."

"Well, shit," she said jokingly. Her accent was so heavy I couldn't help but laugh when she cursed.

"So, Laura, what is your story? Why are you here?" I changed the subject.

She glanced at me. Her expression showed reluctance.

"Like I said, I was born in California. My parents come to North Carolina when I thirteen. Some family already here. I live here since. Ten year ago, my husband, father of my daughter, die of lung cancer. It was very hard for our family. Very hard to be alone."

"I'm sorry for your loss," I interjected.

"I sorry too. For me, every day since is a dark day."

Glancing at her hands, I noticed she had a ring on her wedding finger.

"Three year ago, I meet new man. I didn't feel alone for first time in *very* long time. He nice to my daughter, he work hard. The *only* thing was he like to drink. But, it never problem. New Year 2015 come and go. Couple days after, kaboom."

She paused, and I clenched my teeth from the memory.

"You remember…the riots…fire in streets. I never forget the bank they burn down in Los Angeles. My hometown."

"I remember," I confirmed.

"Then, Obama start Confinement. In days before, I remember big Army trucks pass by at night. When I wake up, I see equipment, tents, port-o-potty. I knew something no right…but where can I go? Nowhere. We stuck. Taken from our home. Three months sleep in cold tent, with too many people. No privacy."

I tried to keep my eyes open…because if I were to blink, the moment my eyelids closed I would see it all again. The anger that burned my soul was a wound that would never heal.

"When we finally go home. My husband's work lay him off. They need to save money after Confinement. He start drinking every night. He buy cheap liquor, and I smell it on his breath in bed. He was mad and sad. Angry at world. I don't blame him. In past six month, we argue a lot. He come home drunk from bar, or friends, and we fight. He beat me…"

Anxiety coursed through me as she uttered those words.

"I tried to hide bruises from my daughter when she come visit. But she smart. She know. I left him. I had no choice, my daughter make me live with her. She like her father, so smart. She have good job with Duke Energy. So now, I live with her. I am happy I left."

"I am happy you left too," I added. "Why aren't you at her house now?"

She smiled and brushed her thumb across my hand.

"Husband know where my daughter live, Owen. My daughter say it no safe to stay alone in house. So, when she go on business trip, she buy me hotel to stay in."

"Does your daughter think it is safe here?"

"It is all she can afford. I like it, Larry take good care of me."

All she can afford…

The words echoed. Her road had been extremely rough. Perhaps I could brighten her day.

"Laura, can you do me a favor?"

"Depends," she said, hesitantly.

"I promise, it's nothing bad, or difficult."

"Okay. Tell me."

"I need to change my appearance. If I give you the money to buy it, could you get me some things?"

She nodded. "What kind of things?"

"Hair dye. Find men's blond hair dye. Bleach blond. A set of new clothes. A pair of pants, a hooded jacket, and sunglasses."

There was a pause. Then she opened her palm.

"Money," she demanded.

I pulled out my wallet and kept it below the edge of the table, so she couldn't see it.

"There is a Walmart a few blocks away. I saw it when I rode in."

"I know where it is. I live here, remember?"

I laughed. "You don't mind walking, do you?"

"God gave me two feet, and they still work."

Smiling, I took my wallet out where she could see it. I pulled out and counted twenty-two hundred dollar bills. As I was counting, Laura's eyes grew wide.

"Very expensive hair dye," she said.

"No, Laura. This money is for you. Buy my things with it, and when you get back I'll give you more."

She stared at me as if I was crazy, like the words I had just said didn't process.

"What? No, I can't. That your money."

I pushed it towards her adamantly. "Laura, this is for helping me. Use it to help you and your daughter."

Her lip quivered. In the corners of her eyes, I saw tears form.

"That so kind of you…" She sniffled and stood up. She kept her eyes to the ground and I could hear her becoming more emotional. "Okay, I go now."

I stood up in front of her—towering over her small frame.

I opened up my arms, insinuating we should hug, and I waited for her confirmation.

She peered up at me with glassy eyes and wrapped her arms around my torso. I heard a hiccupped cry as she held me. Although she was not my blood, the fact that Laura was a *mother* was sentimental to me. It had been over eight years since I had held my own mother in my arms.

"Don't cry…" I said as I patted her back.

"I—I just never have a stranger be so nice to me…"

"You deserve it."

She looked up at me and tapped on my chest with her index finger.

"You are *good*, Owen. Remember, your water deep. You must teach the people to swim…keep them away from shallow water. Keep them away from their *lie*."

Her words resonated in my mind and I let go of her.

"I will, I'll remember," I said.

"Okay, *now* I go," she announced with a laugh and began walking towards the lobby.

"I'll wait here," I called back to her.

I saw her walk out of the door, but it wasn't a walk, more of a slow waddle. I gave her twenty-two hundred dollars with no promises, no guarantees…just a mutual trust from the conversation we had just had. She was right, though. We were both *deep*.

An hour passed. I had changed the TV station to AMC. They were playing reruns of *Breaking Bad,* which was the perfect way to pass the time. Plus, I was tired of hearing my name on the news. I had heard a few people check in, but luckily none of which came into the restaurant. Occasionally, doubt would seep into my mind. I wondered if Laura was coming back. I scolded myself for thinking that. It was natural to have been cautious, but I had put my trust in her, and I knew she wouldn't just take my money and leave.

I heard the bell ring to the lobby door. I watched through the arch of the restaurant and saw Laura with bags at her side. She hoisted them up and plopped them on the table.

"I'm back," she announced, her voice flat.

"I see that," I replied with a chuckle.

"It all here. You check."

I rummaged through the plastic bags and saw the hair dye, glasses, and clothes. Everything was there just like she said.

"Did anything happen to you? I was wondering what took so long."

"I went shopping, too," she informed me with a grin.

"What did you get?"

Her outfit hadn't changed, and I didn't see anything with her that resembled a purchase. She pulled out a small Nikon camera from her purse. She was beaming with joy.

"I set it up at Walmart. I love pictures. My husband pawn my camera three month ago. My daughter can't afford to get new one. Now I can make photo album again."

"I'm happy you could get one," I encouraged.

"Me too. Thank you so much."

"It's the least I could do, no problem."

She didn't respond. I noticed a childlike enthusiasm in her expression, like she had a grand idea that she was just itching to tell someone.

"Owen…" She mumbled.

"Yes…" I said, tilting my head towards her playfully.

"Can we take a picture? Me and you?"

"Oh…uh…Laura, I don't know. It probably isn't—"

"Please! It safe with me, it safe."

The thought of a photo surfacing with me in it was frightening. God forbid, if it were to get on social media before I left the hotel it could mean game over. Then again, I had yet to change my appearance, and I could tell this *meant* something to her.

"All right, you win," I conceded.

"It has timer. I set it, hold on." She said, fiddling with the camera. She set it on the edge of a windowsill along the dividing wall between the restaurant and lobby. "Ok, ten second!"

She scurried to my side and I put my arm around her. We both smiled, and after a few seconds the flash went off.

"Let me check!" she said and looked at the screen. "Look, Owen—it come out great!"

She was practically bouncing up and down from the photo, and when I held the camera I did see that the photo turned out great. We both smiled like we were long lost friends who posed for a picture.

"I like it, Laura. It's great. Just please, whatever you do, keep it to yourself."

"Yes, yes yes," she obliged. "I won't show to no one. Only my daughter."

Just the thought of her showing it to *anyone* else irked me, but it was out of my control.

"When does your daughter come back from her business trip?"

"Monday. I'm here rest of weekend."

Four days. I shouldn't worry so much.

"All right. Oh, and Laura, I have the rest of your money."

"Rest?" her eyes bulged. "I thought you kidding?"

I laughed. "No! I was serious. Here, this makes five-thousand total."

I handed it to her. She stared at the crisp bills in the palm of her hand in disbelief.

She wrapped her arms around me again.

"Thank you, thank you so much. You are a great man."

She squeezed me tight.

"I hope it helps you and your daughter."

"It help *a lot.* Very much. Your mother must be proud."

My mother…

"Thank you. I hope she is, too."

Laura inspected me. "Owen, you look tired. Go rest."

"I guess you're right," I admitted. "Thank you for all of this." I grabbed the bags and put them on my arms. I gave her one more hug goodbye.

"No, thank you. I pray for you, Owen. Take care."

"I will Laura, you do the same."

"Thank you," she said. "Remember, teach the people how to swim. Expose their shallow lie…"

"I will remember. Thank you for your advice. Goodnight!"

"Goodnight," she replied. I walked past the lobby and around the breezeway toward my room. As I neared it Laura's words echoed in my mind.

"*Remember, teach the people how to swim. Expose their shallow lie…*"

I rinsed my foamy hair under the hot shower. The chemical smell of the dye filled my nose. I even put some on my eyebrows. In a few minutes, I would no longer be the *most wanted* Owen Marina. I would be a blond, oddly-dressed version of myself. Hopefully, it would be enough not to get recognized out in the public. As I washed my body the longevity of the day was apparent. My muscles were exhausted and I was becoming sleepy.

I turned off the water and stepped out. I dried off and wrapped the towel around my waist. The mirror was covered in steam. I wiped it off and laughed at myself. I was bleach-blond. It reminded me of when my wrestler friends in high school would make bets if they won a certain match the whole team would have to go blond.

With the towel still around my waist, I walked to the bed where the plastic bags of clothes sat.

"…Breaking news coming in from Georgetown University Hospital tonight…"

I froze. The TV was still on from before my shower. I *couldn't* breathe.

"Cole Pavich, co-founder and Chairman of the Convergence Party was pronounced dead moments ago. Doctors say the extent of the damage done to major arteries was too great, and he succumbed to his wounds at 9:20 p.m.…"

A tremor arose within me. The hot tears blurred my vision and fell past my lips. I groaned and let out the loudest of guttural cries. I choked, and my lungs burned from coughing. I collapsed to the floor—sobbing violently—hiccupping cries without end. The skin on my forehead and cheeks hurt from being so scrunched up. I felt empty and nauseous inside. Part of me was gone…vanished…dead. I felt alone before today. I'd felt alone for a long time, but now, I was *truly* alone. That loneliness, that emptiness, was eroding. It dissolved the soul, it chipped away at it. The pain in my chest was unbearable. The tears were endless. With Cole's death, half of their battle was won. They *killed* my other half—my teacher, mentor, and closest friend. Half of our party *died* tonight. I sobbed harder from the thought. In the background of groaning cries the newscast continued.

"…This leaves Owen Marina as the sole founder of the Convergence Party. Although, given his recent terrorist activity, this might very well be the party's downfall. Analysts are already saying the polls will most likely reflect lower numbers in light of the bombings at Georgetown. What does this mean for the Convergence Party? We don't yet know. Senator Goodman will remain in the race, but the party's future looks bleak. Meanwhile, the manhunt for Owen still continues…"

I couldn't contain my pain. Hearing those words, *that* reality, was like being shot in the gut and left for dead—bleeding out. My spirit was being sapped from me, my energy, my willpower. I felt like the walls of the room were closing in, and I closed my eyes to avoid the sensation. In two days, they had transformed my party from the undoubted victor to the most questionable choice on the ballot. One founder dead, and the other a wanted terrorist. They had reduced me to this, hiding in a dumpy motel and lying naked on the worn carpet. Whoever *they* were…they were *winning*.

"Nothing is more powerful than an idea whose time has come."

– Victor Hugo

District 1 – Washington, D.C.
10:05 03-12-2015

"You and I aren't all that different, you know," he said, sitting across from me on his bunk.

I looked up at him. His statement was questionable.

"How do you figure that?" I asked. "You're a rich politician."

"Not anymore, I already told you. I was a representative for two terms back in Pennsylvania, and then I came here to lobby those bastards into doing the *right* thing."

"How did that turn out for you?"

"Bad. I've witnessed it countless times. Money is going from one hand to the other, nothing really gets done, it's all a big show. The lobbyist scratches the politician's back in the form of financial support, and the politician scratches the lobbyist's back by including their special interest in the back of some ridiculously long bill. It's not about the people anymore, it's about capital. I tried to change things when I was in the House. I tried as a lobbyist, and yet all I did was scratch the surface. How can you affect the direction of a machine that has been on the wrong path for years? How do you stop a train with that much speed, with enough fuel to keep it going for the next century, and with so many people riding it?"

"That's a damn good question…" I murmured.

"The answer is *right* in front of us!" he exclaimed, slapping the backside of his hand against his open palm. "*This*—the Confinement.

This is what we *needed* to be the catalyst for change, something this drastic. Imagine this as a wildfire. Once the ash settles, it will make the ground more fertile, and from that soot-covered ground *we* will emerge. Something entirely new, a new party, and a new direction for our country."

His enthusiasm made me crack a smile.

"Cole, with all due respect, I'm a chemist. I don't know the first thing about what it takes to create a political party."

"But you understand! You see the flaws in our system just like I do. We both work for the same people—"

"Half of the people who live in this area work for the government," I interjected.

He shook his head at my sardonic comment.

"Owen, you're *different* from them. I can tell."

"Why me?" I pressed. "What is it about me, Cole, which has you so fixated on the fact that I'm your guy? We've talked for weeks about this, and I'm still not sold on the idea that we could create something the whole country would latch on to. People have been bickering red versus blue since before my grandparents' time. Why should I believe for a *second* that we could accomplish a feat that ambitious?"

He blinked and remained expressionless.

"Well, if we don't do it, someone else will. Some group or organization will try to become the diamond in the rough. But, the problem is most people who gain influence and power abuse it. They become greedy and want more. On the contrary, if *we* were the first ones to rise from the ashes…the first ones with the bright idea…we would have the spotlight. Now here is the kicker. Once we have the spotlight, we focus on *the people*. We use all of our power and influence to dismantle the current system, and then rebuild it. That way, it keeps greed and corruption out of the equation."

My eyes darted across the floor. I pondered his statement.

"All right, I'll throw the ball back in your court. Let's say we did create a revolutionary political party, and it attracted a mass following. Who would be our candidate? What would be our platform? You saw the numbers after Black Monday. Our economy is toast, dozens of the biggest banks around the country were set afire, and now we are all trapped here for God knows how long. Don't you figure it will be just as stagnant after all of this is over?"

He revealed a small smile.

"Do you know who Senator Paul Goodman is?" he asked.

"No. I told you, I'm a chemist."

"Typical American citizen," he scoffed. "You know zilch about the people who make your laws."

"I don't care," I retorted.

"Aren't you mad about being stuck here, behind these fences? Aren't you tired of eating this shitty food and sleeping in the cold with a hundred other people?"

"*Yes*," I answered, shooting him an intense glare.

"Well then, *now* you care."

His logic resonated through my mind like a bell ringing.

"Okay. I see your point. This Goodman guy, who is he?"

"He is one of the two senators of Pennsylvania. He is a democrat, but his track record is solid—bipartisan and very independent. I know he must be losing his mind right now with the rest of those idiots on Capitol Hill. I hope they are writing a bill to veto Obama's executive order. Anyone with half a brain knows that this was a totalitarian move."

"What if they never let us go?" I asked.

My statement caused Cole to freeze. Behind his green eyes, I saw that my words struck a chord. In his mind, those words were *unspeakable*.

"You can't think like that, Owen. You can't."

I stayed quiet—just staring back at him.

"Anyway, back to what I was saying...Goodman is a democrat, *but*, if we gave him a new party to lead, to represent, we might have a ticket to the White House. Think about how angry everyone is. How everybody we've run into in the lunch lines says this was the *final* straw. We can use their anger to fuel the change. We will have the support we need."

His idea was alluring. I've listened to this gray-haired man with a type-A personality rant about this for the past few weeks. Since our bunk beds were side-by-side, I couldn't avoid him. He kept telling me that maybe we ran into each other for a reason. I remember at one point he called it *fate*. Regardless, I had nothing but time, and I lent him my ear. Something still didn't click with me, though, and I couldn't figure it out. I wasn't one to go outside of my field of expertise. Last time I checked, politics and chemistry didn't mix.

"Your idea makes sense," I acknowledged. "But, I still don't get it. Why me? I know nothing about politics. I don't even vote. Why out of the hundreds of thousands of people in our district have you chosen me?"

He shook his head at my persistence and pushed back his hair behind his ear. He started laughing and seemed to be very hesitant.

"Owen, don't take this the wrong way, but have you ever looked at yourself in a mirror?"

I stared at him dumbfounded.

"You can't be serious," I said.

"I am," he replied firmly. "You look like you belong in some Abercrombie catalog."

I tried to form words, but air just slipped out.

"You want me just because of my looks? What kind of bullshit is that?"

He leaned in and motioned for me to lower my voice, grabbing my shoulder.

"No, no, no. I told you not to take it the wrong way—"

"How else am I supposed to take it?" I spat. "So I'm useless to you, besides a handsome face."

"Owen, calm down," he begged, and his grip on my shoulder tightened. "You're more than that. That's what I told you earlier, remember? You've got the whole package. You're smart, witty, and just happen to have good looks, too."

I exhaled—trying to let his words sink in.

"Every successful organization needs a figurehead, someone the public can immediately recognize as the leader. You're it, Owen. You will be the face of our party."

"What if I don't want to be the face of your party," I countered.

"It's not my party, it's our party. We will be co-founders, fifty-fifty in everything we do."

I was still heated.

"I don't know. I'm just not fond of the idea of being known for my looks and earning my living off of that."

Cole slid his hands up his face, stretching the skin out. He let out an exasperated sigh.

"You said a while back ago you work for who, the EPA?"

"Yes. I'm a field chemist."

"Do you love it?"

"I like it. I'm good at it," I answered.

"I asked you if you *love* it," he repeated.

His question irritated me.

"I like it most days, and hate it others. I've never really *loved* working."

Cole grinned from my answer, which kind of freaked me out.

"How old are you?"

"Are we playing twenty questions?" I joked.

"Just answer the damn question."

"I'm twenty-six."

"And I am a couple years from sixty," he announced.

"You don't look like almost-sixty."

"Thank you, but anyway, take a lesson from me, kid. Time is going to fly by so fast you won't know what happened to it all. Look at me, Owen. I tried to do things the old-school way. I got a couple degrees and with all my hard work I became a representative in the House. I could hardly put a dent in the system. Those fuckers filibustered me until they were blue in the face. I've been Washington's bitch, as have oh so many before me that have failed at fixing the system. What I realized, though, is you can't fix something that no one is admitting is broken. Those politicians who just want to keep themselves rich, hold those broken pieces together to make it seem like everything is fine, just long enough to make it to election time. Do you really want to waste your youth climbing the corporate ladder?"

"No," I mumbled. Honesty had slipped out.

"Exactly. We have a chance to create something monumental here, something that could change the course of American History. In the wake of one of the worst terrorist attacks in our nation's history, and in the wake of the worst stock market crash since the twenties, we will emerge. I'm getting old, Owen. I've already passed my prime. You've just barely taken a peek at yours. *That* is something special. Together we can go down in history as the founders of the party that changed the face of American Politics. Articles will be written about us in textbooks one day. That could be ours, all while simultaneously leveling the playing field…giving the power back to the people…back to the voters—the way it *should* be."

"Your idea…it makes sense," I admitted.

"See! Now you're coming around!" he hollered, roughhousing me.

"All right, all right—relax," I laughed.

"One day Owen, I'll be gone," he began, his tone serious. "The real question for you is, once you've left this world…how do you want to be *remembered?*"

Days Inn South – Raleigh, NC
08:47 10-14-2016

I awoke in tears. When I slipped away from the dream, the crying had begun. Hearing Cole's voice, even in a dream, was enough to make me hysterical.

He's *gone.*

Hearing those words in my head made me blubber.

I was still naked. The towel hung loosely at my waist, and I had somehow managed to make my way onto the bed in the middle of the night. I shivered; cold air sneaked in through the cracks in the door. The weather stripping was gone. Angrily, I wiped the tears from my eyes and sat up. In the mirror on the dresser, I stared back at my new appearance. Bleach-blond Owen Marina. I hoped this would help conceal my identity. The chase I endured yesterday was exhausting. If I could, I'd stop running from them. But what else could I do?

I couldn't run forever, though. I needed a plan. I needed *answers.*

My dream felt so real, so vivid. Our conversation that day was when I finally agreed to go along with his plan. It took him weeks to convince me. The last words he said before I woke up still echoed in my mind.

"One day Owen, I'll be gone. The real question for you is, once you've left this world…how do you want to be remembered?"

His voice caused me to cry again. I never imagined he would be gone so soon.

That question—how did I want to be remembered? It was what sold me, that day. It made me realize that my effort could go towards a cause that was bigger than myself…something that could potentially change the course of history. In the months following the Confinement, after our party's inception, he was right. It *did* spread like wildfire. From the soot-covered ground, we emerged.

Now, though, the words which Cole said the most often during our time in the Confinement plagued me. That we being assigned bunks side-by-side was *fate.* I sat here, on this creaky old bed, all alone, naked and depressed. How could *this* have been our fate? It didn't add up. Everything we had worked for was in the shitter. I was boxed in and had nowhere to go, nowhere to hide. I just hoped that fate had something else up its sleeve. Something that would save me from this situation—a miracle.

5th Ave Coffee Café – Garner, NC
09:21 10-14-2016

"Have a good one," I said as I tipped the taxi driver. He pulled off and I turned around to face the coffee shop. It was in a long strip mall. I left my bike in the bushes back at the hotel, it wasn't worth the risk being seen on it. I would ride it during the night.

From the outside, this coffee shop appeared typical to the South. It was in a strip mall, with a catchy name to stand out. The weather was overcast, and as I walked in the warmth relieved me from the cold.

Ahh, that smell. Coffee overwhelmed my senses. It was my life-blood.

As the door closed behind me, I walked into line. Behind my sunglasses I was glancing around at everyone, and not a single person seemed to have noticed my entrance. Or, at least, they didn't know who I *really* was.

More people came into the shop and stood behind me. The baristas were swamped, and the line was kind of misshapen and awkward. The woman in front of me stepped forward. When I followed, I caught the sweet smell of coconut and a light perfume.

A guy walked from behind and cut in front of the woman ahead of me. He patted the guy's back and they began conversing. The woman took a step back to give him room, as did I.

I blinked. Immediately I flashed back to snow swirling around, and I saw the man cut in front of the pregnant mother and child during the Confinement. I tried to forget his face, but anger percolated throughout my body.

Should I say something?

If I drew attention to myself, I could possibly be recognized. Was the principle more important than my safety?

"Always do what is right, Owen…even if it's not easy." My mother's voice echoed. Emotion tugged at my soul as I heard it.

I reached over the woman's head and tapped the man who cut in line on the shoulder.

"Hey man, you passed all of us in the line," I said.

He turned back with an irritated demeanor.

"I just hopped in line with my friend," he explained.

"Well, that isn't right, passing all of us."

He shrugged his shoulders nonchalantly.

"My bad, man," he said apologetically but didn't move to the back of the line.

I strained to ignore my gut. It was pushing me to say more. I *knew* I couldn't, though. It was far too risky. The brunette who was between us had slid sideways when I told the man he had passed us. She hadn't acknowledged that anything had occurred.

After a few minutes, I reached the counter.

"What can I get you today?" the chipper woman asked.

"Coffee with milk, please."

"Steamed or cold?"

"Cold, two-percent is all right."

"Sure thing! Is that all for you?"

"Yes, ma'am."

"It'll be $2.39," she said.

I studied her expression as she assisted me. I was looking for indications of whether or not she knew who I was. On the outside, I tried to appear calm. Internally, I was petrified. For the past year, there hadn't been a public place I could go without being recognized. I hoped my disguise was enough. I wore sunglasses and the hoodie Laura bought me last night. My goal was to keep my face as concealed as possible.

"Here you go," the barista said and gave me my coffee.

I didn't smile and kept a straight face.

"Thanks," I muttered.

I kept my head low as I walked to the corner of the room. I sat at a two-top table against the window. Part of me wanted to face away from everyone, but something inside told me it would be smarter to keep an eye on the other customers. Many of them were typing away on their MacBooks with their earbuds in. None of which were paying attention to me, and that was *exactly* what I wanted.

I sipped my coffee and let my eyes roam around the room. The anonymity of the sunglasses was comforting. I could just stare at people and they had no idea I was looking.

I locked eyes with a woman. She immediately looked down at her phone.

It was the brunette that was standing in front of me in line. I could tell from her walnut-colored locks. Now that I could see her face, I studied her closer. She had big, almond-shaped eyes. Her skin was smooth and unblemished. Judging by her tan, she was Italian, or Hispanic. She glanced up at me again.

Then she looked down at her phone and up at me again.

Did she recognize me?

Shit. The angle she held her phone at seemed like she was looking at a picture or something. I drank more of my coffee and tilted my head away from her.

Her eyes were on me. I could feel it.

I looked over at her, and when I did, she glanced back down at her phone quickly. This time, I turned away from her direction and used my hand to prop up my head. This woman knew who I was, and I wasn't about to let her scrutinize my appearance any further. I fucked up. I should have sat facing away from the crowd. My plan backfired.

The chair in front of me slid back. The woman sat down and scooted it in. Startled, I just stared at her. She pulled together her pea coat and stared back at me with pursed lips, her facial muscles taut. She had high cheekbones. I found her very attractive.

"Can I help you?" I asked, standoffish.

"Actually," she began, "I was hoping you can."

"Uh…there's nothing I can help you with. I asked you because you just nonchalantly sat with me, and you're a total stranger."

She smiled and revealed perfect white teeth.

"I am a total stranger, you're right…but *you* aren't."

She turned her iPhone around and I saw a picture of me from a news article a few weeks ago. My stomach felt like it fell out of my ass.

"I think I'm gonna head out," I announced and stood up.

She grabbed my wrist, clutching it tight. I stared at her startled.

"*Wait*," she demanded.

My jaw clenched. Our eyes were locked in a stare. I slowly sat back down, silent, and she released her grasp on my wrist. She brushed her hair behind her shoulder, and in her caramel eyes I saw something I had seen before—*determination*. There was a fire burning behind them…a fire lit with passion. It was so strong I could feel it across the table. It reminded me of how Cole's eyes would look when he talked to me about our party, in the beginning.

"What?" I muttered under my breath.

"I am a journalist for the Raleigh News and Observer. I was wondering if you wouldn't mind answering a few questions regarding the recent accusations of your involvement in the attack on the final debate."

"Are you out of your mind?" I sneered.

"No, I'm not actually—"

"You must be. Look, miss, no offense to your profession," I leaned in, whispering, "but the last thing I want to do is have another reporter sensationalize me in the news all for a big bonus. I've been through it a hundred times. You say one thing, and they always tweak it to fit their story."

She shook her head with disdain.

"You know, as condescending your view is of us, I'm surprised you've become as popular as you are."

"I guess to the media I'm just another pretty face."

"Seems like it," she scoffed. "But thank you, for generalizing me, and lumping me in with reporters I've never even met. Despite what you may think, we aren't all the same."

"Why should I believe you're any different?"

"Firstly, I'm not a *reporter*. I'm a journalist. Secondly, I agree that much of the news you see on TV, the internet, or newspaper, is skewed by the opinion of the person who wrote it. Or worse, their boss, or someone else's opinion. I prefer to conduct myself in a more 'old fashion' manner. Journalism is dead. I hope to revive it."

There it was again—the fire behind her eyes, the passion. It was *so* attractive.

You can't stay here. She knows who you are. You must leave.

"What am I even doing?" I mumbled. "I need to leave. I can't stay here."

"Please," she pleaded, her eyes desperate. "This is totally off the record."

As much as I knew I needed to leave…something told me to *stay*.

"What do you mean?"

"Off the record," she repeated. "I'm not going to use this for an article. It's not for work."

"Then what is the point of even asking me?"

"Because I want to know the *truth*."

I stared into her eyes, as she did mine. In that moment, I felt a spark—chemistry.

"So, logically speaking, if you want to know the truth, then that means you believe what was said about me was the contrary."

"Correct," she said and revealed a small smile. "I think it's the biggest heap of garbage that's been on the air in over a decade. From a journalistic standpoint, it's very two-dimensional. With their story, they string people along with simple connections. There are no facts. Just some video footage of you standing up and your coincidental background that aligns with their story."

I agreed with a nod.

"They have reduced me to this," I whispered. "On the run, and changing my appearance with nowhere to go. I'm fucked. Royally fucked."

"For now…" She said with a smirk. "They are winning the battle, but perhaps you can win the war."

Her statement caught my interest.

"How?"

"Let's just say I have a connection in my industry that no one else has."

"Which is?"

"My godfather. Ian Westlake—"

"Like I'm supposed to know who that is," I interjected.

"If you'd let me finish…" She scolded. "He is the Editor in Chief of The New York Times. He has been in that position for over a decade and with the company for even longer."

"Are you hinting at…?"

"Yes. Maybe, just maybe, with the right evidence we could undo what they have done."

She said *we*. She was no longer thinking singular. *We*. I shook my head. Her hopes were too high, and if she knew what I had gone through in the past two days she wouldn't have been telling me this in the excited tone that she was.

"What?" she asked in reaction to my expression.

I opened my mouth to answer, and I realized I didn't know her name.

"What is your name?"

"Rachel."

"Rachel, sorry to bring you down a notch, but *we* won't be able to accomplish shit until we figure out who *they* are. That, and we have to figure out why. Why me?"

"I'm no idiot," she said with a deadpan tone. "Ian has information bombarding him from all directions twenty-four seven. In the meantime, *you* aren't going to accomplish shit either if you are behind bars. Once they've got you, it's game over."

I swallowed hard. She noticed my discomfort.

"I—I'm sorry for being so brash."

"No, it's all right. It's the truth."

She pressed her lips together. "Anyway. How have you gotten this far without being caught?"

"I had help," I answered.

"They must be good at what they do."

"He is."

"Why isn't he still with you?"

"Because one of us is wanted and the other is not. He can't help me if he is in the spotlight too."

She nodded. "Are you going to meet with him again?"

"I don't know. I can't talk to him unless I am at a computer."

"Interesting. So, if you don't mind me asking, what's your plan?"

"I don't have one."

Her eyes lit up. Then, it hit me. Rachel had no intentions of just asking me a few questions. She didn't seem to be in any hurry to leave. Behind her dark eyes, the wheels were turning. *She* had the plan. She had it from the moment she sat down.

"Spit it out," I said.

"What?" she asked with her face contorted.

"You have a plan. What is it?"

"Uh…I—I mean."

"Rachel, I don't have time for small talk. Give it to me."

She seemed taken aback by my assertiveness. She sat up and straightened her posture. Then, her demeanor turned rigid, and her stare intense.

"You won't make it another day riding that bike—"

"Watch me," I interjected.

"I hope I don't have to. You asked me what was my plan, so *please* don't interrupt me again."

I barely nodded out of embarrassment.

"Every cop from D.C. to Miami is looking for that bike. You can't use it as your escape forever. It can only go so fast. They have more firepower than you. It's simple."

I stayed silent.

"Like you said a minute ago about your friend. You are in the spotlight, and he is not. I am also not in the spotlight. We have no ties on social media. We've never met before. With me, you're safe."

Safe. The word beckoned me as I heard it.

"The problem is though, with me you're *not* safe."

"Oh please, stop with the comic-book dialogue. Let me finish."

"Fine," I muttered.

"Look, you need to buy yourself more time. If you're with me, you have that kind of time. No one is going to be looking for me. If we can figure out who framed you and have some legitimate proof to back it up, Ian would have a headliner. He would have a story. There is a little over three weeks until the election. Don't you want to save what is left of your party?"

What is left of your party.

Her words stung terribly.

"Oh my God," she muttered. "I'm so sorry…I didn't mean it like that. My condolences."

"I am sorry too. I can't believe he is gone. I *am* the only one left now."

Those words tore away at me inside.

"Even more of a reason to expose the truth. In honor of him."

Who was this woman? She had just met me and I liked her more by the second.

"I like that," I said.

"As do I. So, what do you say?"

I paused. I had an extremely sexy journalist asking to give me a ride. This had to be the record quickest time I'd ever managed leaving somewhere with a woman. If I was still in college, I would have just said yes. It would have been a no-brainer. I knew how people were, though. My experiences dealing with reporters and journalists alike had shown me to trust no one.

"Why would you put yourself at risk for me? I am no one to you."

"Actually," she began, "before two days ago, you were *someone* to a lot of people. People looked up to you. You were revered for your impact on this country. My colleagues at work would always flip out when you were in a new interview. People wanted to hear what you had to say."

"How sweet of you, saying that," I teased.

"Don't flatter yourself," she said, pursing her lips.

"I don't have to, you already did."

She laughed. *I made her laugh.*

"I'm glad to see that throughout your dilemma you have yet to lose your humor," she mocked.

"Thank you," I fed into her sarcasm.

"I would put myself at risk for you in the name of journalism. For the sake of the real story."

"Damn, you're that die-hard of a journalist?"

She nodded. "The truth means everything to me. It is what sets apart the greatest journalists from the rest. You affect history, and we document it—inextricably linked."

"That's deep."

"I'd like to think so," she smiled.

"What happen Owen, is those people, make shallow story in shallow water. You and I, we deep. We know better."

Laura's words from last night echoed in my mind.

Rachel was deep *too.*

"What about your work? Won't they wonder where you are?" I asked.

"My job requires me to travel anyway. I can do my work from home, or anywhere. Regardless, this story is unlike anything I will get the chance to tackle in my career. It's worth the risk."

"It better be," I said, "because if it isn't, we will both be fucked."

"For now though, we are still fine. Let's not think too far ahead of ourselves."

I nodded. She was very intelligent, and so well-rounded.

"If only you knew what I went through in the past two days. You might be a little less optimistic."

"I've seen it on the news. Regardless, things like this don't happen by chance."

"Like what?" I asked.

"When I was in line, Ian and I were texting about you. You had successfully disappeared for the night, and we wondered where you ended up. At least, in my office, all the buzz was about that you were in the Raleigh area."

"I would assume. The CIA *is* looking for me."

"Well, yes. Anyway, I don't know. Since the news came out of your involvement, my mind has been awash with thoughts. I've lost sleep thinking about this."

"So have I," I added.

"Naturally so," she said. "Either way, I've just been thinking about how bogus this lie is. How they aren't trying to sway the opinions of the citizens who think for themselves. They are trying to sway those who let others think for them. It's so blatantly obvious that someone with power is injecting this story into the media. They are being forced to air this. There's no other logical explanation."

"If only that knowledge was enough to help me…" I mumbled.

"What's the use of knowledge if you do nothing with it? If Einstein wouldn't have written his equations of general and special relativity, he wouldn't have redefined the way we think of time and space. His knowledge would have been wasted."

"I agree."

"That's where I come in," she said with a smile. "If we can get the right information to Ian, we can potentially unravel their lie. Like I said, I've been brainstorming every waking moment about this. That if I just had the *chance* to get my hands on the real story, I might be able to fix it."

"You're a journalist, not a miracle worker," I countered.

She wasn't amused.

"I can't say that I am, but I am damn good at what I do."

"I believe you are…but do you really expect me to put all my trust in you? Expect me to go out on a limb with a stranger and hope for the best?"

She glowered at me.

"Right now, you're hanging from that limb by a noose, struggling to breathe," she hissed. "And I'm the only one around that has a knife to cut the rope."

Her analogy left me pondering.

"Like you said, you *don't* have a plan. I do. So what's it gonna be?"

I sat there confounded. Rachel had an energy about her. It was almost magnetic. It was something I didn't mind being around. She was definitely book-smart, and well-versed. She had the guts to sit down and approach me with this idea…but did I *really* want to let this gorgeous girl get involved? Let her risk her life for *me?*

"Owen," she said. Her voice pulled me from my trance.

My forehead creased in anger.

"Are you crazy? Lower your voice."

Her eyes became wide. She must have gotten comfortable and forgot.

"I'm sorry," she whispered. "Don't you feel it too, though? It can't just be me."

"What do you mean?"

"*This*—us meeting each other. What are the chances that *you*, of all people came into this coffee shop and stood in line behind me? If I would have looked over my shoulder while I was texting Ian, I probably would have passed out. The irony is just beyond me. I dreamt of a story like this since I was a little girl, and it sat right across from me. Don't you think that it's just too perfect to be coincidence…that it has to be *fate*?"

Her words pulled me in like gravity. Hearing her say *fate* caused my heart to beat faster. I could feel excitement coursing through my veins, and I didn't want it to stop. Everything had suddenly clicked in my mind. From the beginning of the conversation, the fire I saw behind her eyes, the passion, the confidence. She *had* the plan, and it was worth taking. The last time I had heard those words uttered they were from Cole's mouth during the Confinement. Looking back on it, I realized that when things were too ironic to be coincidence, *happened*, you couldn't ignore them. It just went against the universe, the ebb and flow of things. In that moment, Rachel sold me on her idea.

"I guess we will find out, won't we?" I said playfully.

She grinned. "All right, let's go then."

"I bought us some more coffee for the road," Rachel announced as she handed me my cup and sat in the driver's seat beside me.

"I'm liking you more by the minute," I replied with a smirk.

She revealed an unenthused smile. "Stop."

"What? Can a man not joke?"

She shook her head and rolled her eyes.

"Men. You're all the same," she sighed.

"And you don't think men feel the same way about women?"

"They may, but they're wrong," she chuckled.

"So are you."

"Owen, I highly doubt that you'll change my mind. Chivalry is dead."

"Whoa, kind of grim there, don't you think?"

"I'm just being honest."

"I mean come on, look at you."

"Is that your way of telling me I'm attractive?" she asked, her eyebrows quirked.

"Well…you definitely aren't ugly," I teased.

"Wow, way to kill a compliment," she scoffed.

"I'm sure you get plenty of them."

"There you go again, back and forth. How old are you?"

"Five. I turned five today," I answered, mispronouncing my words and imitating a child's voice.

She tried to suppress a smile.

"That would make a lot more sense."

"And how old are you? I wasn't aware you have to exchange your sense of humor when you get a degree in journalism."

"Oh please, bite me. I prefer sarcasm. I'm too much of a cynic to survive in this world without it."

"You don't look like a cynic," I added.

"You don't look like a politician."

"Now why is that, because I'm not old, fat, or bald?"

She chuckled. "You tell me, pretty boy."

"Aha, I see what you did there."

I heard the grumble from the inline-six engine accelerating as we merged onto I-40 East. Rachel leaned forward and hit two switches, and moments later I felt my bum heating up. Her car was a black, convertible BMW 325ci.

"You have a nice cage," I blurted.

"Excuse me?

"You have a nice cage," I said, repeating myself.

"That isn't some sort of innuendo, is it?"

"No, no," I laughed. "Your *cage.*" I held my hands out and waved them around the cabin.

"My car?" she asked bewildered.

"Yes, that is what us riders call them. On a bike, you're out in the open. A car is a cage. There's just not as much freedom involved."

"You're a lot freer in my cage than you were on your bike," she pointed out with a smirk.

"Ouch. Touché."

"So is this how you are with all women? You hit them with a barrage of random comments and just roll with it?"

"Sometimes. Although, I don't see any evidence you have a boyfriend, and judging by your snide remarks you wouldn't keep one."

She glanced at me glowering. "Ooh, you are *so* lucky this story matters to me, because I would have left you on the side of the road for that one."

"I'm sure that's the only reason…" I said, flirting.

"You know, we aren't in high school anymore. You don't have to pick on women you like just to get a rise out of them, that doesn't work with a *real* woman."

"What makes you think that I am?" I answered with a wink.

"Ugh," she huffed. "Look, we have a long ride ahead of us. So could you please stop acting like a teenage boy and grow up a little?"

"All righty then," I said, and looked at her with wide eyes, like her comment was uncalled for. "So, where are we going?"

"Orlando," she said, without looking at me.

"What? Why all the way to Florida?"

"I have a friend who lives there. I think she might be able to help us. Well, to help you, mainly."

"She doesn't know you're coming, does she?"

"I've only asked her if she was home. We'll explain everything to her once we get there. And don't worry, I haven't told her or Ian I am with you. I'm not that stupid."

"Good to know," I said.

We became silent. The ride was smooth, and I couldn't hear a single thing going on outside of the car; it was a quiet cabin. I saw signs that said I-95 was approaching. Just thinking about the chase yesterday was enough to make me nervous about getting back on it. Every once in a while I kept glancing at Rachel. Her thick, brown hair fell past her shoulders, and her skin had a sun-kissed glow even though it was late autumn. I didn't know why I was being such a dick. It had been over five years since I wooed a woman into liking me for more than just an evening. Back when I met Megan, our teasing each other built up a thick sexual tension, and the majority of our time spent together early on was just that—*sex*. We were interns at a lab together. We'd fuck in storage closets, empty rooms—anywhere we could escape for just a little while. As time passed, the high that accompanies a new relationship fizzled out, but we had fallen in love. Part of me was still torn that she left, all because of my new title. I didn't have as much time, and she wasn't going to give me hers for the little bit that I *was* around. Perhaps that was why Rachel was indifferent towards me, because I was trying to attempt a puzzle with old pieces. Pieces that used to fit for me, but now they didn't. I just didn't know any other way.

"So, are you a daddy's girl driving around this nice Beamer?"

Her eyes turned cold and her lips were pressed with anger.

"Are you *seriously* that much of a douchebag?" she sneered. "I mean, I'm really starting to rethink approaching you with this idea in the first place. How in the hell are you this charming, intelligent person on TV, but yet in real life you act like a burnt-out frat boy?"

Damn. That stung.

She noticed my silence, but that didn't quell her temper.

"And since you are just *so good* at icebreakers," she began, her voice trembling with frustration. "To answer your question, I'm not a daddy's girl. My dad is dead."

My gut wrenched from her words. Recalling my question, I realized why she got so upset. She kept her eyes straight on the road, and I saw her brush her hand across one of her cheeks. I made her cry.

"I'm sorry Rachel..." I apologized.

She let out a long, drawn-out exhale.

"Maybe the next time you start a conversation with a girl you don't know, you won't be as brazen," she chastised.

I didn't know what to do or say.

"Can you tell I've only had one girlfriend since I was twenty-one?"

"I'm surprised that you've had any."

Rachel was pissed. I had shot myself in the foot, and she didn't care that I was limping.

"I'll take that. Look, I'm sorry about being such a dick. I'm just going to put aside my ego and tell you the truth. I am intimidated by you."

"You're kidding me, right?"

"No, I'm not," I answered. "I mean, come on, you're as sharp as a knife, and you're a beautiful woman to say the least."

Her expression softened as I said that.

"That's hard to believe. I was probably the first girl who didn't approach you like some fan-girl groupie."

I nodded. "Now that is the truth."

She chuckled, exhaling sharply through her nose.

"Owen Marina is intimidated by me. I would have never thought."

"Why is that so hard to believe?" I asked and laughed with her.

"Well, you're kind of the pot calling the kettle black. Do you honestly think I wasn't intimidated to sit at your table unannounced? I felt like I was going to throw up."

"No way," I countered, playfully dragging out the words.

"You aren't exactly the ugly duckling of your family, either."

"I'm an only child."

"You must have some good genes," she said with a smile.

"Is that your way of telling me I'm attractive?" I mocked her from earlier.

"Oh, you're smooth. Don't mimic me."

We were laughing. She was loosening up.

"Hey, I'm sharp too…or at least, I'm good at faking it, like most politicians."

"Probably the latter," she teased.

"So," I said, and shuffled in my seat to face her. "What's your story?"

"I was born in Brooklyn and I lived there until I was seven. That was when my father passed away. My mother hated the cold, so she packed up everything and moved to Miami."

The pain returned to her eyes. The same pain I saw when I joked about her dad.

"Damn, that's so young…" I consoled. "Why Miami?"

"Most of our family was already there. Both of my parents are from Puerto Rico, if you couldn't already tell."

"Nah, I thought you were white."

She giggled. "You're quite the comedian. I like this side of you better."

"I would hope so. I'm trying not to be nervous in front of such a pretty woman."

"Stop Owen, you're making me blush," she said with sarcasm.

"So, if you don't mind me asking…what happened to your dad?"

The normal energy she gave off disappeared. The happiness was wiped from her face.

"He was one of the people murdered in the Račak Massacre in Yugoslavia, during the Kosovo War. He and forty-four other villagers were led up a hill and executed."

"Rachel…that is horrible, my God. I'm so sorry."

"It's okay," she murmured. "It has been a long time. It's much easier now."

"Was he in the Army or something? Why was he over there?"

"He was one of the lead reporters for CBS news in the late nineties. He was the best at what he did…at least that's what Ian tells me. When I was born, he left his position as a journalist and took the job at CBS. It was more money and he wanted to get out of Brooklyn and have a nice place in Manhattan, closer to work. Sometimes, I wonder if he would have stayed at the New York Times maybe he would still be alive."

"So he and Ian worked together. I understand now."

"Yes, for years. They were both journalists, and after my father died, Ian stayed with the company and moved up into management. My mom said they were inseparable, and when I was born, he made Ian and his wife my godparents."

"That's your connection to the industry. You're the goddaughter of the Editor in Chief."

"Exactly," she replied and glanced at me with a smile. "He was like a father to me when my dad passed. Came to all my birthdays, school plays, and my graduations. He would fly down to Miami just for an evening if it need be."

"He sounds like a good man."

"He is a great man. I think the reason why he did so much though, and now I realize it that I'm older, was he knew how much I meant to my father. He knew my dad inspired me to reach high in life and do great things. With him being gone, Ian tried to fill the shoes the best he could."

"Did your mother ever remarry?"

"She did, around the time I was in middle school. I was never angry because I saw how lonely she was, and I couldn't help her fix that. My step-dad was all right, but I always looked forward to Ian's sudden visits more than anything he ever did for me."

Rachel had been through a lot. I lost my mother. She lost her father. I understood her pain.

"It sounds like you two have a strong bond."

"Definitely," she said.

"You said you were seven. How much do you remember of him?"

She smiled before she spoke.

"I remember a lot, surprisingly. The clearest memories were towards the end when I was getting a little older, and he had taken the reporter job. He would be gone for a week or two, covering something in another country. I used to get so excited when the news came on. I would always do my homework just to watch it in time. There was just something so fascinating about seeing my dad through the TV. At that age I would greet him when he came on, and sometimes I would try and touch him on the screen."

I laughed at her.

"What? You remember what it was like being a kid. You do weird stuff!"

"Yes, yes. I remember."

She opened her mouth as if she was about to speak, exhaled, and let out a small chuckle. She was shaking her head—like she had dismissed a thought.

"What?" I asked her as I noticed.

"No, it's nothing really."

"Oh, come on. You stopped yourself. Just tell me."

"Okay, okay," she gave in. "I just, I've never told this to anyone besides my mom. I mean, it had relevance with my journalist friends, but this was personal and very sentimental to me. The crazy thing is, it relates to your situation so well. Maybe that's why my mind decided to bring it back out again."

"Damn, I'm excited to hear this now."

"This memory is what made me want to be a journalist. If I get emotional, forgive me. It was also the last time I saw my dad."

"In Yugoslavia, things were getting pretty bad in 1998. He was gone most of the fall but then came home a week before Christmas. I was so excited. I was actually still six when he came home. I turned seven a week before he passed away. I look back, and that is the Christmas I cherish the most. The night before he flew back with the rest of the crew, he brought me onto the balcony that overlooked the city. He told me, 'Rachel, I'm going to show you something that you can't ever forget.'"

I heard her sniffle and she wiped her eye with her fingers. She took a deep breath and composed herself. There it was again, that *fire* behind her eyes. The passion.

"He got one of my toys and hid it underneath a section of the newspaper. He asked me, 'Rachel, you like your toy, right?' Of course at six my answer was yes. Then he said, 'The truth is you like your toy. You know that for sure, right?' I said yes again. He asked, 'What if I were to show a stranger, would they believe you like your toy? Would they believe it's a toy underneath the paper?' I still hear my little voice answer him back, 'but I could tell them I did, Daddy. I could tell them it was underneath it.'"

I saw her start to get emotional again.

"That's when he leaned down, looked me in the eyes, and said, 'But they wouldn't believe you. They wouldn't know for *sure*. They wouldn't believe the truth that *you know*. That's what I do sweetie, I write the truth so people will know. When you write the *real* truth, that is a very special thing. Watch.'"

Her lip trembled and she struggled to finish the rest.

"He got a lighter," she said, "and caught the newspaper on fire. After it had burned to ashes, he asked me, 'What do you see?' I answered, 'My toy.' I'll never forget that smile as long as I live. He said to me, 'You see the truth, Rachel, and if a stranger looks at it, they can see the truth too. Justice is like fire; if you cover it with a veil, it *still* burns.'"

She glanced over at me, her eyes glistening. I was speechless.

CIA Headquarters – Langley, VA
10:34 10-14-2016

"Where the *fuck* is he?" I shouted. My breath was shallow. I walked around the room and waved my hands at the screens behind me. "We have technology that's decades ahead of what's available to the public, and we *still* can't find him? Have any of the street cams found a match with facial recognition?"

"No ma'am," someone muttered.

"That is bullshit!" I screamed, and knocked over a mug and some papers. The ceramic shattered loudly. "You heard what your director said earlier. We have six hours until we reach the twenty-four-hour mark. In six hours our chances of finding him go down by fifty percent. Everybody better get their shit together! I want something in the next six hours!"

I had to scare them. If they were scared of me, they would listen. The consequences of *not* listening far outweighed taking orders. The colors on the screens behind us flickered and began to change. A new feed was being displayed.

"Ma'am, Raleigh PD just found Owen's bike in some trees behind the Days Inn South. They checked the guest names from last night and he was never registered."

My blood boiled, but behind the anger an idea came to me. I turned to the screens and saw the footage playing of the cops around the bike.

"It looks like Owen found a ride," I announced. "Effective immediately, I want as many roadblocks as we can off the I-95 exits. Owen Marina has to be found before he gets too far, before he disappears like Viktor Ivankov. Make it happen, now!"

I-95 South – Brunswick, GA
14:49 10-14-2016

We were half an hour from the Florida state line, and the drive had been filled with conversation. Rachel and I kept exchanging stories and getting to know each other. It had been so long since I did this with a woman, and it was refreshing. I found out that Rachel went to college at UNC Chapel Hill for journalism, and her mother lived on the ocean in Melbourne Beach. Her father's name was Emilio Flores, and he left them a small fortune when he passed away. Rachel was thankful, but that wasn't important to her. She would have traded it all to be with him again. I was beginning to see that materialism wasn't significant to her. Despite the foreign car and the clothes, she hadn't spoken of any of it.

With her, it was like I had forgotten that I was in trouble to begin with. She made it all melt away.

"Have you been to Florida before?" she asked.

"Only to Disney World and Universal."

"Typical answer from someone not from Florida," she laughed.

"Oh, come on, Florida is like the Devil's armpit. The humidity is miserable."

"Yes, it is horrible, but Central Florida is the worst. The coast is breezy, it keeps you cool. So I understand why you think *all* of Florida is like that, but it's not."

"Well, that's what it's like where we are going."

"Not now," she smiled. "It's fall. It's starting to cool off."

"I thought you were a journalist, not a meteorologist."

"I wear a lot of hats in life."

I chuckled at her idiom.

"I assume you do too," she said. "Chemist turned politician?"

"Don't forget terrorist," I replied, keeping a straight face.

"That's the one we are trying to get rid of."

"We could at least donate it," I joked. "Give it to the real criminals."

"We have to figure out who they are first."

I nodded in agreement.

A chime sounded.

"The gas light just came on," she said. "After all of this talking I wasn't paying attention."

She got off exit 36 in Brunswick. The moment the ramp declined I saw something that made me cringe—cop lights.

"Oh my God. The cops. It's a roadblock, Owen. What do I do?"

I was already pulling at my hoodie and putting my shades back on. My heart was pounding.

"Rachel, stay calm, please. They aren't looking for you, remember? Just act normal and give them your license."

There were only two cars ahead of us.

"Okay, okay—but what do I do if they question you? I need to know what to do. Fuck! There's only one car ahead of us."

I could feel my gut tremble. "If they ask me for my ID, floor it."

"Are you serious?"

"Yes. Floor it," I said, and put my hood as far up as it could go.

I tried to control my breathing as I heard the power window slide down.

"License and registration, please," the cop instructed.

Rachel grabbed the registration from the dash and looked at her feet for her purse.

"Honey, can you give me my purse?" she asked in a loving tone and stared at me with wide eyes.

I didn't answer. I scrambled to grab it and hand it to her.

She quickly slid out her license and gave it to him. In my peripheral I could see him hand the license back to her. There were two cop cars on each side. My palms were sweaty.

I saw the cop lean in toward the window.

"Sir, if I could see your ID also?" his gravelly voice asked.

My heart sank. I barely turned to him.

"Officer, my husband was released from the hospital yesterday. He had a tumor removed from his kidney. I'm taking him to see my family in Jacksonville. You don't really have to see his, do you? That can't be standard."

Good. She lied.

Her voice was feminine yet firm. I saw her adjust her hair, and I couldn't see clearly, but I thought she was flaunting her bust to the officer.

"Ma'am, your husband is going to have to give me his ID. This *isn't* a standard roadblock."

She didn't respond. She just stayed quiet. My heart was in my throat.

"Ma'am, is there a problem?"

My head slammed against the headrest. The smell of burnt rubber filled my nose. The shrill sound of tires screeching along with bullets being fired were a deafening combination. She drifted left into traffic and accelerated as fast as she could.

She *did* floor it. She listened.

Jerkily, she darted around other cars. I saw cops far behind us in the rearview. We had a head start.

"Owen! What the fuck do I do?" she shouted.

"Drive! Just drive!"

I had no idea what to do. The back windshield was cracked from a bullet. The low-gas chime sounded again. Fuck. We had to get *somewhere.* Horns were being honked all around us. People swerved out of our way. The signs said Highway 25. The road was becoming smaller and we were coming into town. Rachel blew through red lights and laid on the horn as she approached them. If we got hit it would all be over.

"We are gonna run out of gas! Where do I go? Tell me where to go!"

"Calm down! Go as fast as you can like you are! We wait till the road ends."

I heard the back windshield shatter. Rachel let out a piercing scream.

"Faster!" I yelled.

"I'm going as fast as I can!"

I saw a bypass road on the right. Highway 341.

"Take that right!"

She turned and the rear end fishtailed before it straightened back up. I didn't see the cops. I prayed their route wouldn't intersect ours.

"You got this Rachel! Go! Go! Go!"

"I'm going, I'm going!" she yelled as the engine growled in the background. I saw a turn approaching and before I could say anything she braked, then gunned it as she made the corner. Water was to my right. The bay. We were close to the ocean. I saw a bridge in the distance.

"Owen! Owen, the road ends!"

I turned to see a T in the road a quarter-mile away. We had to make a left or a right.

"Lay on your horn and turn right!"

The traffic that passed was minimal. *Please, let us not get hit. Please.*

She slammed the brake, whipped the wheel, and floored it as she turned. We drifted and cars behind us honked. I glanced in the rearview. The cops were a half mile behind us.

"Floor it!" I shouted.

"I am!"

We accelerated to over 110 miles per hour. The other cars looked blurry. What I did notice though, was our surroundings were *flat.* Barren marshlands in every direction, with no place to hide. The bridge was coming up, and when I checked the mirror again I saw we had gained more distance.

The low-gas chime sounded a third time.

I tried to press the button near the cabin lights to open the convertible. Nothing happened.

"What are you doing? We are going too fast, it won't open!"

"It has to open. We are going to run out of gas any moment."

"I have to slow down to 30 miles per hour!"

"Do it! Do it now, and quick, before they catch up!"

She braked until it was below thirty. I held the button down and it began opening.

"Owen....Owen! Hurry! They're coming!"

"Just a few more seconds!"

"We don't *have* a few more seconds!"

I used my strength to push against the electric motor that opened the convertible.

"Gun it!" I screamed.

The tires screeched and we were now on the bridge. It was a long, smooth incline. I realized how high above water we were. A fall from the apex of the bridge would kill us. It looked to be close to two-hundred feet.

"Rachel, when we reach the lowest part of the bridge, I want you to slam into the guardrail as hard as you can."

"What? We can't! Not my car!" she yelled hysterically.

"We don't have a choice! Say goodbye to your phone, say goodbye to your car! We have to get off this bridge!"

"We could die!"

"If we don't, we are already *dead!*"

We were descending the bridge.

"The guardrail is weak, do it now, and keep your feet straight down towards the water!"

We readied ourselves on the edge of our seats and she glanced over to make sure our right lane was clear. My backpack was on both shoulders securely.

"Now!" I screamed at the top of my lungs.

She whipped right and we hit the guardrail. Metal crushing metal hurt my ears. We were catapulted off the bridge. I put my hands up and feet together, trying to do a pencil dive. Rachel copied me, and the murky water raced up to meet us. I sliced through it. The pressure of the water slamming against my ears as I displaced it was excruciating. The temperature was unbearably chilly. My backpack was filled with air, and I could feel myself floating up towards the surface.

There were no sounds. For a blissful moment, I let go of the worries that lay above me. No sirens, no horns, no bullets…just *silence*. My throat flexed from wanting to breathe. I broke the surface and gasped to catch my breath. I immediately whipped around to find Rachel. I didn't see her.

"Rachel!" I shouted in panic.

I used my hands to turn around in circles and didn't see her. Fear entered my being.

I heard her gasp for air behind me and I turned around to see her a few feet away.

"Rachel!" I yelled, and swam to her.

"O—Owen—it's so cold," she said, shivering violently.

"I know. I know it is," I panted.

I glanced at both sides of the bay, and we were moving fast. *Very* fast. We had already slid underneath the bridge. Once every few seconds, a bullet would miss us and hit the water. The tide was going out. We were being taken out to sea. I leaned back to see the bridge. Some of the cops were backing out to try and find a different route to us.

Rachel and I faced each other. Our bodies were inches apart, and we bobbed up and down in the tidal current that pulled us out to sea. She kept pushing her wet hair out of her face and breathed erratically. She was shaken up.

"How are we going to get out of this?" she asked, and choked as she let out a cry. "We are fucked. It's over. We're going to get caught."

I held her by her shoulders, unsure of what to say. Then I saw something promising. It was a boat.

"Rachel, I'm going to need you to do me a favor."

CIA Headquarters – Langley, VA
15:03 10-14-2016

"We've found him," a voice behind me announced.

"Where? Pull up what we've got," I said.

My voice sounded crazed. I was frustrated and on edge.

"He went through one of our roadblocks off of 95 and was in the passenger seat with a female driver in a black BMW."

"Where are they now?"

"They just crashed the car into the Sidney Lanier Bridge in Brunswick, Georgia."

"Come on, I told you to pull up *anything!* Do we have any cameras?" I yelled.

The screens displayed a video-feed. It was a security camera on the bridge. There was the BMW, barely recognizable and mangled. Smoke rose up from the engine and there were dozens of cop cars behind it.

"What do you have on the girl?" I asked.

The keyboard clicks from the agent were followed by the sound of the data populating the screens.

"The car is registered to Rachel Flores. She is twenty-three years old, born in Brooklyn, New York, and now lives in Garner, North Carolina. She is a journalist for the Raleigh News and Observer."

"A journalist," I murmured. "Tell me more."

"Puerto Rican descent, moved to Miami from New York when she was seven. Her father was Emilio Flores."

"Why does that name sound familiar to me?"

"He was one of the lead reporters in the field for CBS News in the late nineties. He was killed by rebels in Yugoslavia during the Kosovo War."

I remembered him.

"Why Florida? What is there for them?"

There was a pause. I pressed my lips together, impatient for an answer.

"Ma'am, from as far as we can tell, it is her mother. She lives in a house in Melbourne Beach."

"Get some undercover officers in the surrounding area, stat. We don't want her to know she is being watched, though. Get on the line with the Coast Guard, we need them mobilized immediately to apprehend Owen and Rachel. They can't get too far in the ocean."

"I'm on it," the man said.

A journalist...I stared at Rachel's brown eyes on her driver's license displayed on the massive screen in front of me. Her smile was beaming and symmetrical. The bitch looked so damn happy I figured she thought she was in a photo-shoot and not the DMV.

They were up to something, and whatever it was—I would *stop* it. She was in for a wake-up call. She had put her allegiance in the wrong place. When I took Owen down, she was going down with him.

Saint Simons Sound – Brunswick, GA 15:06 10-14-2016

"Help, help!" Rachel screamed, waving her hands around wildly to the boat that approached us. She purposely let herself sink in the water and coughed when it went into her mouth. "Help me, help, please! I can't swim!"

She was a great actress. I was impressed. I also bobbed up and down behind her, but I didn't struggle. I wanted *her* to be the center of attention for a reason.

I could hear the boat motor begin to idle. *Yes.*

It was a standard fishing boat, good for deep sea fishing, about twenty or so feet long. I scanned it as it stopped beside us. The guy driving it was alone. He had a scraggly brown beard and a Georgia Bulldogs cap atop his head.

"Here, grab onto this!" he called out as he left the wheel and dropped the ladder on the backside of the boat. The boat lurched up and down with the receding tide. Rachel went toward it first.

"Be careful! Watch out for the propeller!" he yelled over the sputtering gurgle of the motor.

She flinched as he said that and latched onto the ladder. She slipped and lost her footing. The man grasped her by her forearms and pulled her into the boat. I heard her make a choking noise, like if she had swallowed water. She continued choking and coughing violently.

Perfect.

The man scrambled over to her for a moment and I heard him slapping her back, hard. It was just the amount of time I needed to remove my backpack and take the pistol out from it. I slid it behind the breast pocket of my jacket and put my backpack back on.

"Come on, son. Tide's goin' out fast!"

I made it to the ladder and up the steps. He pulled me up by my arms until I was standing on the deck along with him. My eyes met

Rachel's. She gave me a quick nod. *She knew what to do.*

"Ow!" she yelped. "I hit my nose when I slipped on the steps. I think it's bleeding. Can you take a look at it?" her voice was muffled as she cupped her nose.

The man returned to her side. I pulled out the gun and held it behind his head. When she revealed her undamaged nose, he turned to me.

"Whoa, partner!" he cowered back. "I don't want no trouble with ya'll."

"We don't either," I responded calmly.

"Well is this how you treat someone who just pulled you out of the cold water? What kinda shit is that?"

Anger riddled his words. His southern accent was thick.

"We are thankful. We just need your help."

"No shit ya'll need help! If you two were the ones who wrecked on the bridge you both need to be in a hospital!"

His body-language was becoming more volatile. I was worried he might try to attack us.

"I promise we are both fine. We don't have time for this shit! I need you to get the hell out of this bay and go south, now!"

He seemed hesitant. "Ya'll know the Coast Guard is just over yonder. They'll get ya before long anyhow."

"I don't think you *understand* me!" I shouted through gritted teeth and pressed the gun against his chest. "I'm going to need you to take us south, *now*."

He turned around and grabbed the wheel, and pushed the throttle up. The double motors roared to life and expelled a massive stream of water. I held onto a rail, and the bow of the boat rose up with the sudden propulsion. Rachel crawled on her knees and wedged herself in the narrow walkway that connected the deck to the bow. She grasped the railing along the edge and shuddered from the cold air that rushed around our wet bodies.

With every rise and fall of the hull, I received a splash of saltwater-mist. I struggled to keep my footing while also pointing the gun at the man's head. He continued to speed up, and once we were out of the cut, the rolling waves of the ocean were even more jarring. He turned the boat to the right, and we began heading south.

To my right was an island. Judging by the signs I saw on the interstate, it was Jekyll Island. It moved slowly. We were but a tiny blip in the vast Atlantic Ocean. Rachel was silent. She just wrapped her arms around herself and looked out at the water. I had so many thoughts running through my head…all of which were jumbled and uncertain. The man had mentioned the Coast Guard. If they *were* close by, they wouldn't take long to get to us.

I saw another opening, to an inlet, and then another island. This island appeared lusher and overrun with dense forest. The farther we made it alongside its coast, the longer it appeared to be.

"What is that island?" I asked over the groan of the engines and pointed with my gun.

"Cumberland Island National Seashore."

"Is it deserted?"

"Pretty much," he said. "More animals than people."

"How long is it?"

"Fifteen miles I reckon."

"Hurry," I demanded, pointing the gun closer to him.

"Look, I'm getting low on gas. I can take you to the St. Mary's cut and I have to turn back around."

"Fine."

Close to half an hour passed. I glanced up at the sky often, paranoid of a helicopter spotting us. I knew we were running against the clock. It was only a matter of time before the Coast Guard received the orders to come searching for us. Suddenly, the island began to end and another inlet appeared. Before I could say anything, the man whipped the boat in that direction. The sky was a dreary gray, and I couldn't tell whether it was beginning to rain or if it was just ocean spray.

In the inlet, the man positioned the boat halfway between Cumberland Island and the mainland. Both directions looked swampy. The engine slowed, and the boat rocked back and forth as it came to a stop. He turned around and stared straight at me—his face was inches away from the barrel.

"Well, here's where the road ends," he announced.

Rachel stood up and she glanced between me and him nervously.

"Thank you," I said. I slid the backpack off and slung it toward Rachel. "Rachel, if you could take out a bundle and give it to this man, please."

She quickly unzipped it and pulled out a bundle of ten-thousand dollars.

"That is for you," I pointed at it with my gun.

He just stared at me and didn't respond.

"You go first, Rachel."

There was no contest from her, just the metallic cling of the ladder against the hull, followed by a splash.

"Don't do anything stupid," I said, and slowly lowered my gun into my backpack.

"I don't have to," he laughed. "I'm already watching ya'll do that."

I didn't respond. I just zipped my backpack closed.

"Thank you," I called back to him and jumped into the icy water. The shock took my breath away. Rachel was treading water a few feet ahead of me.

"Thanks for the cash. Watch out for them gators!"

We were splashed by the wake from the boat as he pulled away.

"Alligators!?" Rachel shouted.

The fear of encountering one of those massive creatures was nothing short of terrifying. I could see the shore. It was maybe a half to a quarter mile away. We had to get to land—fast.

"Just swim. Let's get out of here."

I put my face just below the water and swam as if I were a swimmer doing laps. I would take a breath every few seconds and see how far away the shore was, and how far Rachel was from me. My backpack dragged me down significantly. Every time I took a breath and looked around, it felt like I hadn't even moved a foot or two.

The tide was *still* coming out.

I tapped Rachel's arm as we were swimming and she picked her head up.

"What?"

"The tide is still going out. We need to swim as fast as we can to get to shore. Give it all you got."

She nodded, panting heavily. I put my head down and swam so fast my arms and legs began to burn. Every breath I took, I made sure Rachel was still beside me. Minutes went by. With every glance, we grew closer to the swampy shoreline.

Suddenly, my feet scraped against something sandy as I swam. Then my arms. I pushed upwards with my hands to see we had reached it. I tried to stand on the gunky, swampy ground. It was difficult, but not impossible. I pulled Rachel onto the porous ground and she just lay there, completely out of breath. I sat down with her until she regained herself.

"That…that…was the most cardio I've done in a year," she gasped.

I laughed, and she began to laugh with me.

"I feel your pain," I said. "Let me know when you're ready."

She pushed herself up onto the ground and looked at me with a smile that began to fade. She was looking over my shoulder. I turned around in curiosity.

Endless swamps. That's all that laid ahead.

"Let's go," I said.

She didn't respond, she just followed me. If we took a wrong step our feet would sink into the sludge-like ground beneath. It felt so slimy, and it made the most grotesque squishing noises when we tried to pull our feet out. I had no idea where we were going. The sun was somewhere above the gray blanket of clouds. The rain wasn't helping any. It caused us to slip around on the sections of mud we *didn't* sink into.

I heard a raspy growl and the snapping of teeth.

"Ahh! Run! Shit!" Rachel shrieked. She was in front of me in an instant.

I looked behind me and saw an alligator ten feet away, just sitting there with its scissor-like jaws open. My heart jumped in my chest. It wasn't chasing us, but seeing it a few feet away was *too* close for comfort. I struggled to keep my footing on the muddy terrain. Rachel was now twenty or more feet away.

"It's not chasing us! Slow down!" I yelled.

"I don't care! If there's one, there's more. We need to get out of—"

She lost her balance and yelped. Her face smacked against the mud. For a moment, she didn't even move. She positioned herself into a pushup, and I could actually hear a suction noise when her face peeled away from the mud. When I reached her side I couldn't help but laugh. Her face was covered with a layer of mud so thick her features were indiscernible.

She used her hand to wipe off the big slab that covered her eyes and nose, then she did the same with her forehead and mouth. I knelt down and gently used my thumb to brush off the remainder, and then she looked into my eyes. I felt something, something I hadn't felt in years looking into the eyes of a woman. It wasn't just lust, or chemistry. It was something *more.*

"Excuse me while I blow the mud out of my nose," she said with her voice stuffy.

"Be my guest," I laughed.

She turned her face away and rid her nose of the dirt. When she turned back around I was standing, and I offered her my hand.

"Thanks,"

I nodded.

My body felt fatigued. Although, the constant adrenaline was keeping me going, numbing me enough to survive. Once we were safe…*if* we were ever safe…I would crash. I knew to my right was the north, and to my left was the south. We had to keep our original destination in mind. Orlando—but how would we get there? Willpower was one thing, but having all the odds stacked against us made it nearly impossible to do anything.

We crossed rivers. We waded through swampy fields of cutgrass so tall it sliced our hands and arms. The light behind the clouds was beginning to fade. Dusk was approaching. In the distance, I saw acres of trees. As we approached, I could tell they were oaks. Spanish moss draped the thick branches. It was the same type of flora you might find at an abandoned plantation in the South. The ground beneath my feet was becoming firmer. We had slowly retreated from the coastline.

"There," I said, pointing ahead. "We will rest there."

Rachel nodded. "About time."

We reached the edge of the woods and cautiously entered them. I hadn't seen any houses. The last thing we needed was for someone to blow us to smithereens for trespassing.

"Here," Rachel announced and changed direction. She led me to a massive tree. The trunk had a natural curve at its base. We plopped down and scooted backward to where our backs leaned against the trunk.

It was so relieving. I exhaled, and tried to expel some of my stress along with it. There were times since we had left the boat that I thought I had heard a helicopter. It could have been my imagination, but regardless, *they* were out there, somewhere…trying to find *me*. Despite that fact, I felt safe. I was still free.

"I could not move an inch for the next week and be completely fine," Rachel said with a sigh.

I turned to her. She looked exhausted. Dried mud caked her hair and the edges of her face.

"Same. Unfortunately, we can't stay."

"Why not? This spot is perfect."

"No, it's not. We are too close to our wreck."

"I feel like we've done a triathlon."

"I do too. I'm impressed, actually."

She cocked her head and gave me a smirk.

"Why, because I kept up with you?"

"Well, not only that, but just your willingness to do it in the first place."

"This story is important to me," she answered matter-of-factly.

"It seems so. Most women I know wouldn't crash their fancy foreign cars into a bridge."

"I'm not most women."

Her brown eyes oozed affection. Physically, it was subtle. She kept it hidden, but I could still feel it. I knew it was there.

"I can tell."

"So, if we can't stay here, can we at least take a nap? I can barely move my arms and legs. That swim was unreal."

"Mine are dead too," I agreed. "Yes, let's rest until nightfall. Then we can keep moving."

"All right."

A few seconds of silence passed. Then, her head leaned up against my shoulder, and she snuggled against my body. Just feeling her hair tickle the skin on my arm gave me chills. Who was this girl? Rachel Flores jumped into my life less than ten hours ago, yet it felt like I had known her for longer. By whatever slim chance I had of meeting her, I was glad she was here, by my side. I wasn't *alone.*

"Owen, wake up. Wake up."

Rachel's voice pulled me from my sleep.

"Mhmm…" I mumbled incoherently.

"Wake up. It's been two hours. Let's go."

Two hours.

I opened my eyes and rubbed them. Rachel was staring, just waiting for me to come to my senses.

"You awake now? Come on, get up."

She grabbed my hand and helped drag me upright.

"All right, all right. I'm up."

"So, where to, Mr. Criminal Mastermind?"

I pointed to the left.

"South."

We meandered our way to the exit of the woods and trudged through unkempt grass. I was still lethargic. Our nap had passed in an instant. It was one of those black, dreamless sleeps. Rachel and I didn't talk, we just forged our path farther south. Minutes felt like hours. The land was flat and vast. It looked the same in all directions. There were palm trees that lined every wooded area. I wasn't the best at geography…but as far as we had gone since the boat, we had to have been in Florida.

"We still could have been sleeping, you know."

I didn't even turn to look at her. I was so exhausted.

"I know. It isn't safe to stay put."

"I disagree. Look how out in the open we are. If anyone was looking, they'd find us."

"We will be fine. Don't worry."

"I'm not worrying," she said. "I'm a realist."

"Are you suggesting I'm not?"

"No, we are both tired. I'm just saying we could have *really* rested. I shouldn't have woken you up."

"Well, that opportunity has passed. Look, all I'm saying is the CIA and FBI are going to be all over the area where we crashed. The farther we are away from them, the better."

"True."

More time passed. The land became even vaster with little to no trees around. Just flatlands surrounded us. I had seen a house tucked behind some woods a few minutes back. Hopefully, if anyone was home, they weren't keeping a close eye on their property.

"Do you hear that?" Rachel asked. She grabbed my arm.

My senses heightened as I stood still to listen. It didn't sound too far off, whatever it was. The ground beneath me was vibrating slightly. The sound was rhythmic. It churned and pulsed, yet was mechanical and deep.

"It sounds like a train," I said.

"I wonder how far away it is."

"Come on, let's go. Run!"

I began to run in the direction of the sound.

"What? Wait up!" Rachel called from behind me.

"Hurry!"

She made it to my side and we both ran across the flatlands. I was breathing heavy, but the sound was growing louder. We were close.

"Why are you running?" she asked, her voice bouncy and struggling to speak. "If it's a passenger train it's pointless."

"It sounds too slow to be a passenger train."

We kept running, and then I saw it. It was a black freight train…and it was going *south.* I sped up, and as I neared the track, I looked to the right and saw the last railcar come into view.

"Rachel! Sprint!"

I pumped my arms and used every last bit of energy I had to keep up with the train. It was sliding past me, railcar after railcar. Suddenly, the caboose passed my side. The thought of losing the train pumped adrenaline through my veins, and with one final surge of energy I launched myself into the air. I grasped onto the metal rungs of a ladder and turned around to see Rachel just feet behind me.

"Come on!"

She strained and pushed herself harder, trying her best to speed up.

"I can't!"

I held the rung with one hand and made sure my feet were on the ladder firmly. I extended my left hand as far as I possibly could. My arms were stretched out to the full length of my wingspan.

"Rachel, you can do this! Give it all you got and grab my hand!"

Her face was beet-red and she pumped her arms up and down in a final sprint. She neared my hand, and I knew it was now or never.

"Jump!"

She leaped into the air and wrapped her hands around my forearm. I clutched her and swung her up into a half-hug. She panted in exhaustion. Her breath was hot against my neck. I glanced down at our feet, and they were squished together on the thin, metal rung. I hoped it would hold our weight.

"Grab the ladder!" I yelled over the raucous sound of the train.

She used one hand to latch on first, then released her grasp from my neck with the other. Once she was secure, I began to study my surroundings. To my right, there was an iron door.

I clasped the door handle with my four fingers. Once I gripped it with my other hand, I planted my feet on the body of the train and used my strength to tug at the door. It was unbelievably heavy. I continued to pull, and suddenly it swung open. It threw me backward and my legs swung like noodles as I held onto the door handle with all my strength.

My struggle was far from over. Now wide open, I had to find a way inside without closing the door.

I rocked back and forth and pushed the door closer to the closed position. I swung my left leg around the underside of the door and straddled it like a monkey would a tree limb. I rocked harder, to the point where my head was slamming against the iron frame. All I needed was for—

My butt cheek caught the surface of the floor, and that was it—solid ground. I used my left hand to keep my balance, dropped my right leg beneath the door, and pulled it inside. I had made it.

I quickly stood up and opened the door, peering up to my right to see Rachel still clung to the ladder. Her hair whipped wildly around her face.

"Rachel!" I called to her.

She turned and looked at me.

"Do what I did! Climb down and jump!"

She nodded. I caught fear in her expression.

When her feet hit the last rung, she looked down at the track moving fast below us. She was hesitant.

"You got this! You've made it this far!"

"Jump!"

"Ahh!" she screamed and stretched her arms skyward. I lunged for her and grabbed her wrist. My abs quivered from trying to keep balance. It took all my strength not to fall forward with her weight.

"Don't let go! Please!" she cried.

I felt vibration through her arms. The tips of her shoes were dragging across the tracks. My eyes widened at the thought of what kind of pain she might have been in.

"It hurts," she winced. "Pull me up, please!"

"When I pulled her up, I would slip closer to the edge. She was literally *in my hands*. Our weight was linked and I couldn't adjust my position.

"I need you to push! Push with one foot! I will pull you in!"

"They are numb…" She cried. "The pain…"

"I need you to *push,* Rachel! Now!"

I felt the motion of her moving up a few feet. I used the momentum and threw myself backward into the caboose, slinging her in by the wrist. I collapsed onto my calves, and my body folded onto itself like a lawn chair. Rachel lay on top of me, crying and panting.

"Thank you," she sighed. "Thank you…"

She was on top of me. We were chest to chest. Our breath was in sync, and although I was in pain from halving my feet wedged underneath my body—it felt nice. I didn't want her to move.

"We made it," I said. My voice was shaky. I was still catching my breath.

"Your heart," she blurted, with her head atop my chest.

"What about it?"

"It hasn't slowed down a bit. It's still beating just as fast."

It sped up even more as she said that.

"It's going faster," she added.

I smirked and tried not to laugh.

"What is your diagnosis, Dr. Flores?"

She chuckled. "I think you have a case of the butterflies."

I craned my neck up and looked at her.

"You really do wear a lot of hats in life."

She shook her head at me.

"When was the last time you had a woman on top of you?"

"Two weeks ago."

"You dog!" she scolded.

"She wasn't nearly as beautiful as you, though."

I felt affection as her eyes met mine. I had hit a soft spot.

"I have to admit," she began. "You are mighty charming if I do say so myself."

"Oh really? I thought I was a douchebag that needed to grow up."

"I don't know who that Owen was. It definitely wasn't the same guy I'm with now."

"I'll give you that…"

"You're actually not half bad to be around," she teased. "You act no different than you do in all your interviews."

"I strived to be an honest politician. I had nothing to hide."

"What an oxymoron," she laughed. "Honest politician."

"No joke."

"It showed, though, those times I saw you on TV. Everyone knew you were genuine. It is something this country has lacked for a long time."

"Thank you," I said. "Funny how the media can turn on me so quickly. One day I'm a hero, and the next day I'm a villain."

"Now *that's* what I am here for."

"To expose the truth," I repeated her words from earlier today.

"Of course. A truth will erase any well-executed lie. Especially if the evidence is tangible, and from a credible source, that will make a story irrefutable. That is what I aim to do."

I admired her intellect. It was so mesmerizing.

"Rachel, that plan sounds just as good as it did this morning…but, my legs are numb. Do you mind?"

She slid off of me and I strained to slide my legs out from underneath of me. They were deadweight. Once separated, everything was different. I could feel other sensations besides the warmth of our bodies together. The air was temperate and humid, but there was a slight chill in the caboose. She sat a few feet away and stared at me silently.

"So, two weeks huh?"

My heart jumped at her words. *Yes!*

"Yup," I answered smugly.

"You know, I don't blame those women at all. Your personality reflects your looks. They are both great."

She is really coming on to me right now…

"I can say the same thing about you."

The sexual tension only heightened.

"Oh really?" she chuckled and tossed her hair behind her shoulder.

"*Really*," I replied, emphasizing the word. She moved closer to me. I knew she wanted me to make the first move.

"It is chilly in here…why don't we keep ourselves warm?"

I propped myself up with my elbow and stared into her eyes, just inches away from her face. It was almost pitch black, with the exception of some moonlight that slipped through the hatch in the roof. She didn't answer me, and I went in for the kiss. Our lips touched, and I started off delicate. Her lips were amazing, they were soft and plump. She would pull back for a second, teasing me, and I gently sucked on her bottom lip. She rolled over on top of me and her long hair dangled around my face.

We continued with more passion than before. I ran my fingers through her hair, massaging her scalp. Our kissing was deep and in sync. She sucked my bottom lip so hard I could feel it enlarge. She tossed her hair back and moved to my neck, kissing my face and chin as she went down. I could feel the tingling sensation of the skin being filled with blood just below the surface.

I moaned in pleasure. Hickeys were my favorite, and I was hard as a rock. She noticed, and tickled my stomach and slid her hand down to my crotch. She rubbed me through my pants, and I took my free hand and slid my two middle fingers down her pants like you would hold a bowling ball.

She let out a moan. We played with each other for a few minutes, and we continued making out with more intensity as time passed. I removed my hand from her pants and began to reach for my waistline. I felt a firm hand on top of mine. She pulled away from our kiss.

"What do you think you're doing?" she asked in a sexy whisper.

"Getting naked."

"There's no need," she replied.

"What? Why not?" I questioned. Confused, I began to pull at her clothes to assist her in undressing.

"Do you really think I fuck on a first date?"

"Wha—? I mean—"

"Shh," she said, kissing me more and then pulled back.

"What kind of girl do you think I am? Do I come off as easy?"

"No. Sex is a stress reliever, and after the kind of day we've had, anything would help."

"Sorry to disappoint you, but we met less than twelve hours ago. I'm not going to give it up that quickly."

She dry-humped me through my pants. I could barely contain myself.

"Oh, come on," I pleaded and kissed her all over her face.

"Shh. Don't ruin the moment, Owen. We can still have our fun."

As she said that, she gave me a final kiss and slid down to my waist. She pulled down my pants and freed me from the constricting fabric.

Yes. Oh God, yes.

I moaned as she began to blow me, and God was it wonderful. I placed a firm, yet gentle hand behind her head. The erotic sounds filled the caboose, and we both took turns pleasing each other for what felt like hours. Our sweaty bodies were perfect together. Her voluptuous curves, and my muscles. Although it wasn't sex, it was the strongest connection I have had intimately since I was with Megan. What intrigued me though, was I spent five years with Megan, and this was so much more *raw*.

Rachel's head laid upon my bare torso. Her hair was matted and damp. Sweat beaded off my head and dripped down my neck. I was so relaxed. My back was up against the rough iron wall of the caboose. Her breath hit my chest. The warm exhalation a reminder she was still with me. I ran my fingers through her long, thick hair. Her Puerto Rican ethnicity was apparent in its texture. As I combed it, my fingers would sink inches in—it was voluminous and soft. I cherished this simple moment. I wanted to forget about my dilemma. I wanted to let it go. Part of me wanted to ride this train until the tracks ended. We didn't need to have a destination. As long as she was with me, everything would be fine. It was refreshing to forget, to let go. That kind of blindness was dangerous…but in the short-term, it was blissful. It was necessary for my peace of mind.

Gently, Rachel kissed my chest and neck, and the underside of my chin.

"You're so beautiful…" She whispered.

My heart swelled in euphoria.

"So are you," I said.

She caressed my abs with her pointer finger, tenderly drawing patterns; it was soothing. With Rachel, I felt whole. Ever since that dark day, when Megan gave me my ultimatum, and I chose my party over her—the loneliness had been unrelenting. It only made the void within me grow larger. The emptiness I couldn't seem to fill. It was the emptiness I'd taken with me every day since my mother died. It was so sudden. There were no goodbyes, no last words—just death. Now, for the first time in almost a decade, Rachel made that emptiness *smaller.*

The day replayed in my mind like a film reel. Rachel sitting down in front of me during my morning coffee, the five-hour car ride getting to know each other, and then the roadblock and the pursuit that followed. She destroyed her car just to keep us safe. She stuck with me through a journey most athletes would have found challenging. We were dirty, we were exhausted, but yet, she was *still* here. She was the perfect partner in crime.

"Nice. Remind me of movie I once saw, Bonnie & Clyde. But where is Bonnie?"

Laura's words from last night resurfaced in my mind. Her heavy accent sounded just as clear as it was in real life. The memory sparked an idea.

"Rachel…" I murmured.

"Yes?" she asked, still playing with the skin on my stomach.

"Will you be my Bonnie?"

She craned her neck upwards and stared into my eyes.

"Bonnie?" she repeated the name.

"Yeah, like Bonnie and Clyde. The outlaws."

"I know who they are."

"Well then?"

She gently held my cheek with her hand and kept gazing into my eyes. In the darkness, I thought I caught a small smile emerging.

"Will you be my Clyde?"

Sofra Bakery & Café – Cambridge, MA
07:57 10-15-2016

"What is your next move?" Emily asked.

I took another sip of coffee before I answered.

"I need another sample."

"Stefan, you're joking, right? The evidence is undeniable. It's plain as day."

"I know it is, but it's not enough."

"In what universe?" she sneered. "The only thing we need is someone in that field to peer-review your research. We go to MIT for God's sake, there are PhDs in and out of the lab all day. All of whom we are friends with."

"It doesn't matter. I need a second sample."

She stared at me dumbfounded. Her mouth was agape.

"You've got to be out of your mind. You even said it yourself. We don't want anyone else to find out what we are doing. That kid almost barged in and ruined everything."

"I know what I said—"

"Then *stick* to what you said," she interjected. "You and I both know if the wrong people were to find out the kind of experiments we are conducting, we could both wind up in a federal prison. Any institution caught with samples from the Danger Zone could be cut off from funding. Graduate school is hard enough to afford in this economy. It's not worth the risk."

"Why *is* that, though?" I said, tapping the wooden table. "We are in grad school at the most prestigious research university in the world, and just because we aren't the damn EPA we can't touch anything from the Danger Zone. It's fucking ridiculous…"

"You're telling me something I already know."

She stared at me with a serious expression. Her lips were pursed. She lightly smoothed a few misarranged hairs from her bangs behind her ear. Her hair was short and jet black. The one time I had asked her why she kept it short, her response wasn't surprising. *'It's convenient and manageable.'* That was the scientist in her speaking.

"I'm sorry, I shouldn't be so redundant."

"No, you shouldn't," she added.

I shook my head from her comment.

"Look," she began, "I'm not trying to say I won't take this risk with you again, because you know I will. I'm just saying to listen to your own advice. *You* said it was too risky to let Professor find out. We need to be practical…and having our PhD gives us a significant advantage to land a job. There isn't any steady increase of jobs like before the Confinement. Our economy is shot. Please keep that in mind and base your decision off of logic only."

She had a point.

"Well, logically speaking, I need another sample before I can approach my dad."

"Why?"

"Have you ever met him? He's the busiest person I know. I have to make an appointment to see my own father."

"Are you serious?"

"Yes. If I give him this research without more research to back it up he will send me packing. I'm almost a doctor and I still have a hard time impressing him."

"You've been published in scientific journals. You're one of the best."

"I know. His work blinds him. He's just so busy."

The truth I had just reminded myself of was always difficult to swallow…living in my father's shadow. I knew though, with *this*—it would get his attention. I had to have more than enough evidence.

"I'm sorry…" Emily mumbled.

"It's fine."

"Well, anyway, I was curious. Who was that phone call to? When I was cleaning up and preserving the samples. You asked for Ms. Walling."

"Oh, it was my ex."

She chuckled. "Since when do you date?"

"I could ask you the same thing," I teased her.

She rolled her eyes.

"I barely have time to do homework, let alone have time for a man in my life."

"I didn't tell you? She was vacationing in Boston. We met, fooled around a little, and hit it off. I visited her a few times in D.C. and vice-versa. It was long distance. I was the one who ended it, but she still likes me. That's why I knew she would be willing to talk if I called."

"And what did she have to say? Or more importantly, what did you ask her?"

"She said exactly what I expected. She lied. Just as she always has since I shared my theory with her."

"That it's not Strontium."

I nodded.

"She probably doesn't want to risk her job."

"That's what I'm thinking. I told her what we found, and I told her to tell me the truth."

"What exactly is her position again?"

"She works in the office. She deals with paperwork."

Emily's eyebrows quirked.

"Now why would some paper-pusher know the truth about Black Monday?"

"She is the manager. She has access to the archives in the EPA."

"And how do you know this?"

"She let it slip," I answered. "That's why I am so convinced she has seen some evidence herself. She told me she had access to the archives right after I told her my theory. To me, it seemed like she had something she wanted to tell me, but couldn't."

"So how exactly did she word this lie? I mean, you did blatantly tell her you had evidence."

I glanced down at the table, frustrated. I chewed on my bottom lip.

"She said the evidence I was looking for doesn't exist, and hung up."

Emily's eyes grew wide, and she opened her mouth, but nothing came out.

"You know," she said. "You better hope that your ex doesn't rat us out in fear of losing her job."

"No," I dragged out the word. "She wouldn't do that."

"How long did you date?"

"A little over six months."

"That is thin ice you're walking on, Stefan. *You* were the one that broke up with her, and the first phone call you make to her is to ask about something confidential? Women remember everything…and some are very spiteful."

My stomach turned from her comment.

"Are you speaking from experience?" I joked out of nervousness. Her words made me unsettled.

"No, I'm speaking from observation," she countered.

I swallowed.

"Regardless, I'm going to stick to my plan. I'll drive to the Danger Zone today and see if I can find another sample. Let's plan on being in the lab at 5 a.m. tomorrow."

She pursed her lips and tilted her head in uncertainty.

"I hope that ex of yours is trustworthy. Because you and I both know after what we discovered in our experiment, that they *are* trying to hide something. Something the American public isn't privy of knowing."

Hwy 50 West – Titusville, FL
08:34 10-15-2016

The long, prickly grass made the skin on my arms itch and I scratched it to relieve the urge. I lay as flat as I could against the ground to remain hidden. I kept my head propped up just enough to see Rachel and the highway that was just a few feet ahead of me. Hidden in a small ditch, I watched patiently. Rachel had an idea a while ago. She jokingly said, '*Bonnie would be proud.*'

She was playing the role excellently.

Last night we rode the train for around four hours. Rachel relied upon her own judgment to determine how far we had traveled. We got a little scraped up from jumping off the train, but after wandering around for a while in the early morning, we realized we were in the outskirts of Titusville. She was familiar with where we had to go, and we continued south through field after field, until we ran into a two-lane highway that bisected the fields. It ran west, and we walked parallel alongside it, far enough away to remain out of sight from the passing cars. Now, being so close, I noticed there weren't too many—maybe one every minute or two.

There was a creek we had stumbled upon. Rachel rinsed the mud out of her hair and cleaned her legs and face. It was an essential step in her plan.

It was time to execute it.

She had her hair in a loose ponytail. I was holding her business pants in my left hand, and I had let her borrow the sweatpants I was wearing. The cuffs were rolled up to her knees and her shirt was the white undershirt she had worn yesterday. Although she seemed like she might have just wandered out of a trailer park, her body was still amazing. Some foolish guy would roll up, gawking at her, and fall into our trap. That was *exactly* what we wanted.

Rachel was the perfect candidate for a hitchhiker. Her tan legs were long and caught the light of the rising sun. They glowed a rich, orange-brown. Her undershirt showed off her bust, and I knew it wouldn't be long until someone stopped. She had thought of the idea, but *I* came up with the signal.

We wanted someone riding alone. Judging by her outfit, it would be a man. She stood there with her thumb out at shoulder level. When a vehicle approached, once she could see the driver was alone, she would raise her thumb up to eye-level. That was the signal. She knew that if a car *did* stop with children in it, she was to make up a false destination and tell the driver she was going somewhere else.

Two cars passed without stopping. I waited anxiously.

An SUV slowed down, and they rolled down their passenger window. Even from my vantage point, I could tell there were more people in the car. I watched as she shook her head and pointed in different directions. She was lying. The SUV drove off.

She looked in my direction, her thumb still in the air, shaking her head side to side. I nodded and gave her a thumbs up to encourage her.

A minute passed. To my right, I saw what looked to be an old, beat-up Nissan. My pulse quickened as it approached her. I noticed that *both* windows were rolled down.

Even better.

She raised her thumb to eye level. I knew that this was the one. I saw her lean in and seductively twirl a lock of her hair as she spoke to him. She nodded, and I saw her reach for the door. It was time.

I stood up and hurriedly made my way across the highway. Glancing left and right, there were no cars coming from either direction. The mild Florida air swept around my man parts. I was only wearing boxers. Rachel had my sweatpants.

I pulled out my gun and just as Rachel sat down in the passenger seat I reached the car. I held the gun at the man's temple.

He froze up, and I saw his Adam's apple bob. His eyes glanced left at the barrel.

"Get out," I demanded.

"No," he stammered.

"*Get out!*" I shouted.

He slowly lifted his hands off the steering wheel and popped open the driver door. He paused before he stood up. He was a chalk-white man, with freckles that covered his face, and he had orange hair. He winced like he was about to cry.

"I just bought this car a week ago," he hiccupped. "I've been saving up for it forever."

I glanced at the exterior of the car. It was a faded, dark-purple. There was rust along the side molding. Something inside me felt sympathetic for this man…but we *had* to get to Orlando.

"I need you to trust me," I said. "Get out!" I yelled once more.

He scowled and stood up. I held the gun against his head and threw my backpack into the open window. It landed in the driver's seat.

"Rachel. Please give this man a bundle."

She nodded, and I heard the sound of a zipper. The man's eyebrows quirked from my words. He was lost.

"Here," she said.

I leaned over and grabbed the bundle with my free hand.

"Take it," I said, pushing it into his gut.

"What? Are you serious? I thought you were taking my car."

"We are, but that doesn't mean you can't get yourself another one."

An awkward smile emerged on his face.

"How much did you pay for this thing?"

"Three thousand," he answered.

"Well, there is ten. Call yourself a cab, and go buy a better car outright."

"Uh, okay," he mumbled as he groped the large stack of hundreds in his hands.

I sat in the driver's seat, and when I glanced to see what belongings he had in the back, I discovered a nylon, string-strap backpack. I threw it to him.

"Put that money in there. Don't want anyone to take it from you."

The man nodded.

"Oh, and, if you could—don't call the cops."

"Okay," he said.

With my request, we drove off.

I glanced over at Rachel beside me. Her messy hair was flowing around the cabin from the windows being open.

"Good job, Clyde," she said with a wink.

"Not too bad yourself, Bonnie."

She leaned in over the console, and as I turned to look at her she gave me a kiss. It was electrifying.

"Sorry, I'll let you drive," she teased playfully.

I shrugged my shoulders with a flirty grin.

"You can kiss me whenever you want."

"Oh really?"

She kissed me again.

"All right, all right," I laughed. "Let me drive."

"You just can't make up your mind, can you?"

I could see the road for miles. It was flat in all directions. Occasionally, we would pass fields of oranges or a house. When I would see a cop, my whole body would clench up. Every single one just drove past.

"How long to Orlando?" I asked.

"From here, maybe half an hour."

"Do you know where we are going?"

"Kind of," she muttered.

"Kind of? You can't be serious."

"Don't worry, I'll get us there. It's just been a while since I've visited."

"How long?"

"Almost two years."

"Two years?!" I threw my hands up. "She could have moved for crying out loud!"

"Relax, I remember where she lives. These apartments off of Conway Gardens Road."

"I hope your memory is as good as your oral."

She slapped me hard on my bicep.

"Ouch! God, I'm just playing."

"Men…" She muttered.

Conway – Orlando, FL
09:21 10-15-2016

We pulled into an apartment complex. The parking lot was half-full, and I saw a dark-skinned guy leaning into the window of someone else's car. On the drive in it appeared like the rest of Florida—flat, palm trees, and clay-tiled shingles on many of the roofs. I had never been here before, but these were definitely the outskirts. Downtown was farther west.

Rachel turned the car off and just sat there for a moment. She pulled her hair out from the bun and began sliding off the sweatpants I gave her.

"Here are your pants back," she said.

I handed her business slacks back to her.

The building in front of us was beige-colored and three stories. I counted, there were twenty units, and as I looked to my left and my right, there were at least ten buildings.

"Do you remember her apartment number?" I asked.

She glanced at me with uncertainty in her eyes.

"I remember it was on the bottom, and a corner unit. I sent her a Christmas card last year. I think it's apartment 1A."

"I hope you're right. I wouldn't want us knocking on the wrong door in this kind of area."

She gave me a bizarre look as we stepped out of the car and began laughing.

"This kind of area?" she mocked. "Orlando is nothing compared to Miami."

"I grew up in a small town. D.C. is the biggest city I've lived in."

"Aren't there bad areas up there?"

"Yeah, I avoid them."

"Some of us aren't so lucky," she pointed out with pursed lips.

I shrugged, and we approached the corner of the building. Once inside the breezeway, I saw these apartments were labeled 1A, 1B, 1C, and 1D.

"This is the one," Rachel said, pointing to her left.

I grew nervous as we approached the door. Almost *two years* since she had visited? We could have been knocking on a cop's door for all we knew.

Rachel rang the doorbell. I waited anxiously.

Nothing.

Rachel glanced over at me, shrugging her shoulders.

She rang it a second time. I counted the seconds. I was beginning to doubt anyone was home to begin with. Rachel's face revealed a slight frustration.

This time, she knocked on the door. She gave it three solid raps.

"*Briana,*" Rachel said, her accent switching over to Spanish. "*Es Raquel—abre la puerta, por favor.*"

She continued to knock persistently.

"It's probably the wrong person," I said.

Rachel opened her mouth to respond, and the door swung open. A woman around Rachel's height with dark, mocha skin stood in the threshold with a stunned expression.

"*Raquel, ay Dios mio!*" Briana shouted.

They embraced in a long hug and jabbered in Spanish to each other. Their voices fluctuated with momentary laughter. Briana pointed at Rachel's dirty clothes. Rachel said something, and then Briana's eyes darted to me. She gave me a look that a foreigner might give a loud, obnoxious tourist who didn't belong. It wasn't pleasant. Rachel grabbed her attention and muttered something else. Briana's face turned worrisome.

"Come in," she motioned to us.

We walked inside. The dining room was to the left, and the den was of good size. I scanned the walls in awe of all the decorations. There were pictures of what I assumed to be family and friends. I saw Rachel in one of the photos, but she was much younger. There was a small Puerto Rican flag on the wall in the kitchen. The apartment had the faint scent of Hispanic food; it made my stomach growl. We hadn't eaten in over a day. Rachel sat on one of the barstools that lined the eat-in kitchen counters. I remained standing.

"Rachel. Girl, what's going on? Be real with me, I've seen the news and I almost didn't believe it was you."

"Well," she began. "Owen here was framed. He wasn't behind the terrorist attack at Georgetown."

"How do you know for sure?" Briana countered.

"He's—I mean, it just doesn't make sense."

Briana pursed her lips in a duck-face.

"It sure makes a whole lotta' sense on TV."

"You can't believe everything you see on the news—"

"And you can't believe every pretty boy that has a good story," she interjected.

Rachel's mouth was agape. She glanced between Briana and me. I became flustered listening to them go back and forth. Briana acted like I wasn't even in the room. She had her hair slicked back into a ponytail, and out of it sprung golden-blonde ringlet curls. They bounced around as she talked.

"He doesn't have a story," Rachel said. "The media is telling it for him."

"Then what did he tell you?" she pressed.

"Brianna, I am completely innocent. I devoted the last two years to my party and to this election. They are trying to take that away from me, whoever they are."

She raised an eyebrow.

"Listen to him talk like the *gringo* he is," she snorted. "My name is Bri-*ana*, not Bri-*anna*."

"Bri-on-a," I repeated, enunciating the syllables. "I know to you I'm just a white guy, but I am innocent. I wouldn't lie to Rachel. Anyway, she approached me."

"Really?" Briana asked, turning to her.

"Yes," Rachel answered. "I saw him in a coffee shop where I live."

Briana seemed hesitant. She studied me up and down and kept glancing between Rachel and me.

"No one followed you guys here, right?"

"Not that we know of," I answered.

"You better be right. Rachel, you know I love you, *amiga*, but if the feds come I can't get caught hiding you. You know my history."

"That is *exactly* why we are here."

Briana's eyes grew wide. Rachel's pressed lips and stony glare screamed tension. Something sensitive was just brought up.

"No, no," Briana nodded her head and walked towards the door. "I need you to leave. I can't believe you just said that."

"Are you seriously going to kick us out just like that? So easily?"

"Don't even fucking go there, Rachel! You spend three years in prison and tell me how easy it is to kick you out. It's the easiest decision I've made in years! Get out!" she repeated, fuming.

"No," Rachel huffed. "I'm not going anywhere."

Briana's face turned red.

"Don't try me! Every pig in the country wants you two. I could have you out of here in a second."

"*No eres una rata!*" Rachel shouted in Spanish, her expression stunned.

"*Ay, por favor, Raquel!* Don't call me that!"

"Is that what you're gonna be? A fucking rat?"

Briana's eye twitched and her lower lip trembled.

"We have been through thick and thin, *hermana*. Don't make me do something I *don't* want to do. Get out!"

Rachel crossed her arms and shook her head. She wasn't budging.

"Please, can you just listen? Just for a few minutes? We are dirty, tired, and hungry. We can't show our faces anywhere. Just let us be safe for a few hours. *Please*."

Rachel's comment seemed to placate Briana's temper. I stood, glancing between these two Latina women yelling in Spanish to each other. I wasn't going to *dare* butt in.

"Fine, I'm listening," she conceded.

Rachel exhaled and composed herself before speaking.

"We need your help getting Owen out of the country."

"What?" I asked, yelling.

"Look, Owen, we need to figure out the truth, I get that…but you can only run for so long. You have to get out of this situation, and I don't mean in handcuffs."

"I—I need to help you, though," I stammered.

"What good does the truth do if you're behind bars before the world knows? Then you will have to spend years in a jail cell until you go to trial, and God only knows what kind of false evidence the government might have."

Her plan was well thought out. It was the truth. Frightening, but still the truth.

"But this is my home…"

"I know," she said sympathetically. "Your freedom is more important than staying here, don't you agree?"

"Yes…but, where would I go?"

"We can figure that out later. Obviously, it needs to be a country that doesn't extradite to the United States. China, United Arab Emirates, Russia."

"What great choices…" I mumbled.

"Owen, you're like the new Edward Snowden. Except, you didn't expose anything. Well at least, not yet you haven't."

"I'm sorry to interrupt your grand plan," Briana began. "But, I have a feeling I know where Rachel is going with this. I refuse. You can stay here, but I'm not doing it again. It's not worth the risk."

"What is she talking about?" I questioned Rachel.

"Briana used to make fakes. Fake IDs, fake documents, whatever you wanted—she could do it. It made her a lot of extra money…but when one of her IDs was connected to the biggest insurance fraud this area has ever seen, she had to do time for it. Three years and probation for no previous record."

"And that's *exactly* why I can't help you," Briana added. "I am still on probation. I can't even leave the state without permission."

"You don't have to leave the state," Rachel pressed.

"*Ay Dios mio, Raquel! Te dijé no!*"

Rachel was shaking her head. Briana's resistance to persuasion was making her irritated.

"Do you remember the Confinement?"

Briana's forehead scrunched up.

"Of course. What kind of question is that?" she retorted.

"Did you like it?"

"Seriously, Rachel? What the fuck."

"So you *didn't* like it, then."

"Stop playing dumb."

"I'm not," Rachel replied firmly. "But you are going to have to take a step back and think about Owen's situation from a broader perspective."

"Broader as in…?"

"Who are you going to vote for in November?"

"I—um. What does that have to do with anything?"

"Answer the question," Rachel said.

"Convergence Party…" She mumbled.

"What about after the bombs?"

Briana blinked and glanced at me sheepishly, then turned her eyes to the carpet. For the first time since we had entered, she seemed nervous to speak because I was in the room.

"It made me question who I was going to vote for…"

"See!" Rachel exclaimed. "That is the first glimpse of the big picture. Why else would these bombs happen less than a month from the election? It just doesn't make sense. Why would Owen ruin everything he has worked for in his party? Someone with power is trying to slant the election in their favor."

Briana just stared at Rachel and didn't respond.

"You know," I spoke up. "That night, at the debate, the Russian guy who was sitting a row in front of me was wearing my colors. I had never seen him involved with our party before. It wasn't even that big of an amphitheater. It was strictly invitation only. It was as if Alexei Malchikov appeared out of thin air…like he was *placed* there."

"He was wearing your colors." Briana repeated.

"Yes, purple vest and tie."

She bit her bottom lip.

"The whole thing seems fishy to me, now that you told me that."

"So, will you help us?" Rachel asked.

Us. There it was, that word. Rachel thought of me and her as *us*. Hearing it, though, made my soul swell up in love. After last night's escapade, just the way she looked at me was different. She was enjoying being my partner in crime, and so was I.

"What's in it for me?" she retorted.

"Are you serious? After everything we've been through…"

"Don't even go there! Yeah, we are from the same *barrio en Miami*, but we are different now! Look at you, with your perfect life and your fancy college degree. You weren't even around to see the shit I went through in the past five years. So *fuck* you for judging me for not wanting to risk my freedom for a stranger!"

I quite literally watched the blood rush to Rachel's face.

"*Briana*, you don't seem to understand," she said, rapping the counter with her knuckles. "If the people who framed Owen win, then *all* of our freedom will be at risk."

"And if we *lose*, then not only will you and Owen be in jail, but so will I!"

"Well if you want to live your life afraid of *ifs*, then let me make something really clear for you. *If* the people who framed Owen get away with this monstrous lie, then we might all be imprisoned! Who knows? Maybe we were *never* supposed to be released from the Confinement!"

I glanced at Rachel in shock.

"What if they never let us go?"

The question I had posed to Cole that day during the Confinement reentered my thoughts. He had told me, *"You can't think like that, Owen. You can't."* The purpose of his statement was to keep me hopeful. So that one day, when we were released, we could create our party. We *were* released, but Rachel's statement brought forth a terrifying possibility. What if we were never *meant* to be released?

"But we *were*, though," Briana sneered. "Why would you even think there would be another Confinement? There hasn't been a riot in almost two years. There's no reason for that to happen."

"The reason is standing right beside you!" Rachel shouted and pointed at me. "Just three days ago he was America's sweetheart and now he is a wanted terrorist. Now, he looks bad. His party looks bad, and the polls *will* look bad. All in time for the election! Something is going on that is far bigger than what we can see. As a journalist, I am obligated to expose the *true* story since I have the chance to! And now, I'm standing in front of someone I *thought* was my best friend and she is asking me what's in it for her!"

Briana's jaw dropped, and I saw tears form in the corners of her eyes.

"How *dare* you, Rachel. How dare you come into my house out of nowhere and just throw all this shit on me, asking me to take a huge risk on the *slim* chance that we will be able to expose anything! Let alone get Owen out of the country. Fuck you for even asking me to take a risk like that! You wouldn't want to know what would happen to a Barbie doll like you in a women's prison. I don't want to go back! Not a damn thing could make me take that risk again!"

"1.4 million dollars," I interrupted.

Rachel and Briana whipped around, staring at me.

"*What* did you just say?" Briana asked, her face streaked with tears.

"1.4 *million* dollars," I repeated.

"But Owen," Rachel gasped, her expression confused. "We've been handing out bundles of cash left and right. You can't possibly have that kind of money."

"I don't, but Grey does."

"Who?" she asked.

"Remember when you asked me if I had help, and I told you he was good at what he did. Grey Maxwell—my best friend from high school. He is an IT genius, and he helped me rob the bank. He also wired and stole one-hundred thousand dollars from fourteen separate squatter accounts. All of which came from the grand larceny committed by the VP of the bank where Grey works. The grand total of the money siphoned from the illegal activity being 1.4 million dollars. Grey is in on this, and perhaps, *Briana*…if you help us, the compensation might be well worth the risk."

She stared at me, completely dumbfounded. In the corner of my eye, I thought I saw Rachel begin to smile. Briana bit her lower lip and looked down at the ground. I heard her exhale sharply out of her nose.

"How much?" she asked.

"Twenty-five percent. That would be three-hundred and fifty thousand dollars."

Briana stared at me silently. Behind her eyes, the gears were turning. She was *considering* it.

"What exactly do I have to do?"

"Get Owen out of the country. A fake passport is what he needs from you," Rachel said.

"And what if I fail?"

"Well, then we are all fucked," Rachel answered.

She glanced between Rachel and me. The nervousness in her expression was palpable, but my offer was more than tempting to her. This wasn't the greatest neighborhood, and for an ex-con who wanted to better her life, 350K could get her a lot.

"Okay. I'll do it. I'll help," she conceded.

"Yay!" Rachel hooted. "*Gracias, amiga, muchisimas gracias!*"

I waited until the girls calmed down to say anything.

"Briana, thank you. I really appreciate it."

"You can thank me later," she laughed. "When you're out of the country."

Out of the country…

The words stung. Rachel's plan was necessary. She was right, I couldn't stay in the States much longer. Eventually the FBI and CIA would have us cornered. Once arrested, my voice would be silenced, and so would Rachel's. Our hopes of uncovering the truth would be but a failed attempt. *That* was something I couldn't stomach thinking about.

"So, what now?" Rachel asked.

Briana shrugged. "You guys said you were hungry. Want some breakfast?"

Rachel and I both nodded quickly in response.

"Great. I still have some *arroz con leche* from this morning."

"*Mi favorita*," Rachel added.

Before Briana could walk to the kitchen I stopped her.

"Briana."

"Yes?" she turned back to me.

"Do you have a laptop? Or a desktop?"

She seemed confused by my request.

"Yes, I have a laptop. Why?"

"I need to contact Grey."

I could still taste the sweet, milky flavor from the *arroz con leche* in my mouth. The meal was simple and filling. It was great, considering we hadn't eaten in so long. The girls were sitting on the barstools that lined the kitchen counter, catching up with each other. I had shut down the computer, and when I restarted it, I immediately pressed F2. When the USB option did not show up, I quickly pressed F12.

Whew, it appeared. Grey's flash drive he gave me was blinking red every second, already ready to go in the USB port. When I chose his drive to load the OS from, the startup screen was plain and simple.

There was one icon on the desktop. Bitmessage.

I made sure I was connected to the Wi-Fi and clicked it. It loaded a login screen, and I fumbled to get my wallet out of my pocket. From inside one of the slits, I pulled out the piece of paper he had given me the morning I robbed the bank.

I typed in the username, **anonymoususer159753258.**

The password was a lengthy thirty characters. I nervously pressed the button to log in. It took a moment to load, but when it did, I was looking at an extremely rudimentary email inbox. No fancy colors or designs, just two tabs to click on. **Inbox** and **Sent**. There was no trash. I assumed that with Bitmessage, if you were to delete a message, it was gone permanently.

I noticed there was the number one next to my inbox. I had a message. The received date was two days prior when I was last at Grey's.

From: intheshadows842679513

Body: *Respond to this message to reach me.*

I smiled. Typical Grey—vague, cautious, but yet the message was enough.

I hit reply and began to type.

Hollygreen Apartments – Virginia Beach, VA
10:02 10-15-2016

My phone beeped. I pulled it out of my pocket, and my eyes lit up from what I saw. It was a notification from Bitmessage. Owen finally messaged me.

That fucker is still safe. What a lucky dog.

I glanced over at my friend. He was still asleep on the futon. Daylight spilled through the cracks in the blinds. He had one too many shots at the bar last night, and it would be hours before he woke up.

I stood up, went to the desktop in the corner of the living room, and logged into Bitmessage.

There it was. A message in my inbox from ***anonymoususer***.

I laughed at the simplicity of the name. I opened the message and began reading.

Come to 2700 Conway Gardens Road Apt 1A. Orlando, FL 32806.

We have a plan.

Damn. I was proud Owen didn't use my name or wasn't outspoken with any other details. He wrote, *we have a plan.* Who was *we?* I recalled the newscast from yesterday. Perhaps it was the hot brunette he hitched a ride with. I was still surprised they survived the crash on the bridge. I stood up, walked to the kitchen, and grabbed a pen that was sitting on the counter. I began to write a note to my friend who was sleeping on the couch, expressing my thanks to him for letting me crash here for the past couple nights.

He had no idea that I was involved in the bank robbery. I just showed up, bought a few rounds of drinks every night, and treated him to dinner. It was money well-spent for a safe place I could pass the time in. Logically speaking, I knew the chances of Owen ever contacting me were slim—almost nil. The government's arsenal of technology was nothing to sneeze at. Advanced facial recognition, phone taps, access to security cameras—the list was endless. By some miracle, he had yet to be captured. I hoped this plan was a solid one.

I unplugged my charger from the living room wall and grabbed my belongings. I walked back to the desktop and typed a quick message before removing my jump drive.

Body:

Leaving now.

Briana's Apartment – Orlando, FL
23:17 10-15-2016

The bloodcurdling scream of a younger Jamie Lee Curtis filled the living room. We were watching the original *Halloween* on Briana's Netflix. Rachel shifted her feet and they dug into my hamstring. I flinched in reaction.

"My bad," she said and pulled her feet back a little.

"You're good," I replied, smiling and gave her a wink.

She rolled her eyes, but still revealed a half-smile.

Rachel and I were sitting at opposite ends of Briana's couch. Each of us with our backs against the armrests and our legs interlaced. We had two separate blankets, but after hours of lying here they had merged into one messy bundle. Briana had made us lunch. It included rice, tortillas, and heavily-seasoned flank steak…and although I couldn't pronounce it, it was still delicious. She brought us Chinese take-out for dinner, and was still noshing on the remainder of hers, sitting in a large, puffy recliner.

Eating only temporarily suppressed the anxiety I felt from waiting. Grey's response was in and out of my mind every few minutes. *'Leaving now'*, he said. I glanced at the clock on the wall. It was almost midnight. I vaguely remembered the last time I spoke with Grey. He had mentioned something about a friend in Virginia Beach. If that *was* where he went, it would be a little over an eleven and a half hour drive. I used Google Maps to plot his route. He should have been here by now. Maybe there was traffic, or he stopped and ate dinner. The possibilities in my mind couldn't be silenced. They worried me because with Rachel's plan, Grey was an indispensable player. We *needed* him.

Another yelp from Jamie Lee Curtis on the screen. She had tripped and was shimmying backward down a wood-floor hallway. Michael Myers lumbered towards her slowly, step by step.

"Please! Please!" she begged and trembled as she cried. "Leave me alone!"

She stood up and pounded on the windows. "Somebody help! Help me!"

Michael moved closer with every step.

Suddenly, my mind drew a parallel from the movie. Would *that* be what it was like if I had nowhere to go? If I was cornered, would I beg them to leave me alone? Would I sob in defeat?

I got chills just thinking about it. I prayed that moment would never come.

The doorbell rang.

My heart sped up drastically and my stomach quivered. Rachel and Briana stared at me with wide eyes.

"Is it him?" Rachel whispered.

I shrugged, clueless. It *had* to be him. We were watching a scary movie...but in our situation, it wouldn't be Michael Myers at the door—it would be the FBI.

And the FBI *doesn't* ring the doorbell.

"It's your house. Answer it," I said to Briana.

She cautiously stood up and set her take-out box on the cocktail table. She tip-toed to the door and glanced through the peephole. The doorbell rang a second time.

"What does he look like?" she asked just above a whisper.

"Black hair, and a big, scraggly beard."

"I think it's him."

"Open it then."

I heard the door creak open and then shut. I couldn't see anyone yet. They were still in the foyer.

"Uh…hello, um. Well, this is awkward. My name is Grey."

I felt the biggest wave of relief I've had in days.

"Briana," she introduced herself.

Grey came around the corner into the living room, looking just as he had when I saw him last. Except now he appeared well-rested. He grinned as he saw me on the couch.

"I never thought I would see you again," he motioned for a hug as I stood up.

I patted him on his back roughly.

"I understand why," I laughed.

"No shit," he slapped my shoulder, roughhousing me. "You two have some incredible luck."

"I guess that's what you can call it," Rachel answered with a small smile.

"Owen, how rude of you not to introduce me," he winked at me.

"Rachel Flores, this is Grey Maxwell."

He leaned over the cocktail table, and she delicately placed her hand in his.

"I've heard a lot about you, Grey," she announced. Her expression was somewhat flirty.

"Oh really?" he turned to me. "What kind of things have you been telling this beautiful lady? Let me guess. That I'm dashingly handsome, intelligent, and can grow a *real* beard."

"Something like that," I played along.

"Actually," Rachel began, "he informed me that you assisted him in the bank robbery…and you stole 1.4 million dollars from the VP, who is apparently a thief."

"Indeed he is," Grey nodded.

"That's quite a feat," she complimented. "Owen says you are an IT genius."

He shrugged, cockily.

"Something like that," he winked at me.

Briana stood beside Grey, glancing around at all of us. She pressed her lips together. She seemed annoyed she had been overlooked.

"So," Grey split the silence. "What is this plan?"

"On that note," Rachel raised her hand. "Grey, this is Briana

Pittman. My childhood friend. She is the first piece of the plan."

They shook hands and introduced themselves.

"Enlighten me," he said, and sat down on the ottoman.

I didn't say anything. It *was* Rachel's idea.

"Grey. We need to get Owen out of the country."

Grey's face was deadpan. He didn't even blink, just let out a loud laugh.

"You've got to be joking."

Rachel opened her mouth and tried to form words.

"No, I'm not," she replied flatly.

Grey's eyes darted to each of us. His expression indicated that he thought we were all crazy.

"Okay, so let me get this straight. You want to get Owen, the most wanted fugitive in the United States, on a *plane* leaving the country?"

Rachel pursed her lips. Her face flushed. She wasn't enjoying Grey's mockery of her plan.

"*Yes*," she forced the word out.

"Well, first off, let me make something apparent to you. Bringing Owen into *any* international airport is a deathtrap. I don't even know where to begin. There are hundreds of cameras, not to mention getting through security. If the CIA were watching, they would have ample opportunity for facial recognition. It would be a shit-storm in minutes—complete chaos."

Rachel shook her head, glancing at the ground, and let out a chuckle so small it was exhaled sharply through her nose.

"*That* is why Briana is the first piece of the plan."

Grey's brow quirked and he turned to Briana.

"What? Don't look at me like that," she sneered in response to his surprised demeanor. Her dyed, golden-blonde ringlet curls bounced around from her ponytail as she shook her head in disdain.

"I just—I," Grey stammered.

"What?" Briana cut him off. "Just because I'm not some white boy nerd who went to college, you're surprised I have something to offer? Let me make something clear to you, *gringo*. I learned my skills in the streets of Miami, and my teachers were harder on me than any one of yours could have been."

"I'm sorry, I just didn't expect—"

"Is it because I'm black?" she raised her voice and cocked her head towards Grey.

"*Ay, Briana, por favor!*" Rachel interjected. "Stop with that shit. Your dad's black. You are mixed."

Briana huffed as if she was going to say more. She bit her bottom lip and stopped herself.

"Look," I began. "We are all here for a reason, to make this thing work. Let's not get ahead of ourselves."

The tension in the air lessened. Rachel was quick to pick up where I left off.

"Grey, Briana was the best at what she did. She made fake documents…*a lot* of them. One of those documents was connected to a massive insurance fraud here in Orlando. She served three years."

"If she was the best then how did she get caught?" Grey mumbled.

My eyes grew wide.

"You know what? Fuck you!" Briana shouted. "Fuck this shit!"

She stood up and Rachel grabbed her wrist. "Please, don't leave."

Briana's lower lip trembled. Her anger exuded from her.

"Grey, that was a little uncalled for," Rachel said.

"A little?!" Briana snorted.

"Come on, dude," I added. "That was fucked up."

His expression remained nonchalant. Briana was still standing from when she tried to leave the room, and she turned to face Grey sitting on the ottoman.

"Unfortunately for me, Grey, my line of work dealt with things that were *real*. Paper, IDs, legal documents—all real evidence a court could use against me. Let's say, when a middle-aged man was facing fifteen years in prison for a huge insurance fraud, he decided to rat out the person who made him the documents for a lesser sentence. And that's how I got caught. I couldn't just hide behind a computer like you, and when this is all said and done, and I *do* make Owen a passport that gets through unnoticed, three hundred and fifty thousand of those dollars are mine. Or, if your abilities fall short of what is needed to help him leave, and we all get caught, then I'll see your ass in prison. Because even the *best* get caught. I wouldn't be so damn cocky if I were you. I did three years—try a lifetime."

Briana stopped pacing and sat back down on the edge of her recliner. Grey finally didn't look so smug anymore. Her words had sunk in.

"So, Briana…" He began humbly. "How are you going to get a valid passport?"

"The Darkweb," she answered. "Do you know what that is?"

Grey's eyes grew wide. "I do, but they don't."

Briana glanced over at Rachel and me.

"Have you gotten one off of there before?

"No. I've actually never made a fake passport before."

All three of us turned to her, surprised.

"What? I know what it takes to make one. The hard part is getting it."

I could tell that Grey was intrigued. He might have doubted Briana upon meeting her, but when she mentioned the Darkweb, his eyes lit up in interest.

"How do you plan on doing that? The websites on the Darkweb are on the internet, it's just essentially they are invisible—hidden in plain sight. You have to know exactly what you are looking for."

"I know," Briana rolled her eyes, but smiled instead of getting upset with him. "I still have connections…people I used to do work with that might be able to get us what we need."

"How certain are you they would still do business with you? I mean, after your charges and all. Maybe they wouldn't trust you."

She shook her head. "They will. I used to pay good money for the things I needed. They know I take my work seriously."

"I can tell you do," Grey complimented.

Briana laughed. "Thank you. So, I was thinking. By the looks of Owen's hair, I should try to find him a European passport. He needs something that gives him access to the rest of the world. I was thinking, Sweden."

"He sure looks like a Swede," Grey went along and laughed with her.

"I know I do," I said. "Having these blonde eyebrows is killing me. They are practically invisible."

"You look like a grown up Macaulay Culkin," Rachel giggled.

I shrugged and nodded in agreement. We all laughed together.

"So, I was just curious, what airport would he leave from?" Grey asked as the laughter subsided.

Rachel and Briana looked at each other.

"Well…" Briana began. "It would have to be Miami International."

"Why?" Rachel questioned, her eyebrows quirked. "Orlando is international too, and that way we could stay local. After what we went through yesterday, we don't want you guys to have to go through something like that."

"No shit," I added.

Briana's expression was as if she had just eaten something sour...like she had bad news to deliver.

"That's the thing, I don't have any of my old stuff I used to make fakes with. When the cops searched my house before I was arrested, they kept it all as evidence. Since I'm on probation, I would never risk having something related to my old life in this apartment. My friends in Miami, they are still involved in some shady stuff. Whatever they don't have, I will have to purchase. I'll start from scratch.

"After seeing the news yesterday," Grey looked at Rachel. "I'm assuming we are taking Briana's car?"

"Yeah, I'd say so." Rachel smirked, unamused.

"I will call my work now and tell them I've come down with the flu. I will use my sick hours," Briana said.

"Well then," Grey smiled behind his scraggly beard. "Tomorrow, we go to Miami."

CIA Headquarters – Langley, VA
00:02 10-16-2016

I could see light from the dozens of screens along the wall through my eyelids. It annoyed me. My nerves felt frayed. They were shot. My elbows were propped on the cold metal desk, and I cupped my forehead with my hands.

I wouldn't open them. I couldn't watch that same goddamn video another time.

The convertible BMW slamming into the guardrail and Owen and Rachel flying out into the inlet. I'd seen it thousands of times today. It was making me fucking nauseous.

If only they would have crashed in the middle of the bridge, they would have died from the impact in the water. Owen would be dead, like he was *supposed* to have been at the debate. He was never supposed to live. His survival had been haunting me, nagging me. It felt like an ice pick digging into my brain. My migraine had yet to cease…but how would I sleep? How could I rest, knowing *he* was still out there?

It was nine hours past the twenty-four-hour mark. Now, there was a fifty-fifty chance that he would end up like that elusive vermin—Viktor Ivankov.

His name gave me chills…it always had.

Although Viktor had successfully disappeared off of our radar, we knew he was still around. He lurked in the shadows, trapped from living freely because of his infamy. I wasn't worried about Viktor. We had won that battle a long time ago. I was worried sick over Owen.

Owen had a following. Everybody loved him. That was until we framed him to destroy his reputation. With the election so close, it was our only hope to finish something that began years ago. Something that was imperative to keep ourselves in power. The polls were slipping. The Convergence Party had a lower percentage of support every day. The media was fulfilling its duty masterfully. Although, the longer he and Rachel were missing, the greater likelihood there would be of them lashing out in retaliation. Would they be hostile? Or, would they be passive-aggressive, like when Viktor left the note in the cabin. It didn't do any *real* damage, but it only added to the complete distrust the country had for their government, and that was the *antithesis* of what we wanted. We wanted them to believe everything we told them. Luckily for us, we had the news. Paid lies were the best kind. They ensured compliance.

I burped. The acidy bile burned the back of my throat. The taste entered my mouth—it was disgusting. A migraine, heartburn…what else could go wrong? Fuck this menial bullshit I had to deal with.

"Somebody get me some Tums!" I groaned.

A moment later the roll of antacids was in front of me. I blinked, gradually opening my eyes. They were so sensitive to the light on the screens my vision was blurry.

"Can we turn off these screens for God's sake?"

They shut off. Thankfully, the room was dim. Just the soft glow from computer screens. It hardly helped ease my stress, though. I shouldn't have fucking been here. This was supposed to end the night of the debate. It was supposed to set our plan back in action. Now, the perfect execution had failed, and I was put in charge to fix it quickly.

"Ma'am, I think you'll want to hear this," a man said from behind me.

I craned my pounding head around.

"Is it him? Did you find Owen?"

"No, I'm sorry to say we haven't…but this is equally important."

His idiocy made me cringe.

"Although I highly doubt that, go ahead. Give it to me."

"We just received a tip from someone who works for the EPA. They said they have knowledge of two grad students at MIT who have been conducting experiments with live animals from the Danger Zone.

She said they both *know*."

I tilted my head and my lower eyelid began to twitch.

"Did you just say, *live* animals?"

"I did, ma'am," he nodded nervously.

My jaw dropped, and I could feel myself begin to breathe heavy. *Another* loose end we would have to tie. I was livid.

"How the hell is this happening!? I thought they were all *dead!* Goddamn it!" I balled up my fists and pounded on the metal desk.

I could barely see their faces with the migraine affecting my vision. I could tell they were scared of my anger.

"Do y—you want me to call Boston PD?" the man stuttered as he asked.

"Oh no," my voice trembled. "I want our guys up there."

"But ma'am, it might take hours."

"I don't care!" I shouted. "Police officers won't do the trick, we need the FBI to shake them up a bit! Scare the shit out of them."

I panted. My breath was uneven, my heart in my throat.

"I'm on it," he said.

"Shut it down! Shut the whole damn thing *down!*"

MIT – Cambridge, MA
05:23 10-16-2016

"How we lookin', Em?" I asked, delicately positioning the sample on the slide.

"*Emily*," she corrected. I thought I saw her smile in the corner of my eye. "You aren't my grandmother. The hallway is clear. No traffic—for now."

"Good."

The sound of her footsteps grew louder until we were shoulder to shoulder.

"So, it looks like you lucked out again in Manhattan?"

"We will find out here in a moment. I walked circles for hours."

"Searching for your beloved cat-lady?" she teased.

"Indeed," I chuckled.

"What did you give her this time? Your father's trust fund?"

"Not quite. She was a little more resistant. I gave her two-hundred."

"She probably would have demanded more if she knew you were killing her cats."

"Probably," I smirked.

She walked back over to the lab door to peer out of the glass, then returned. I began to prepare the microscope to fire the electron beam.

"So, *Emily*. Why can't I call you Em?"

Her brow furrowed. She tucked her hair behind one of her ears. Its jet-black color was always such a drastic contrast against her white lab coat.

"Well, I—that's what I was called as a child. I am about to become a doctor in a field primarily dominated by men, and I want to be taken seriously. So I guess when I hear Em it reminds me of a time when I was forced to play with Barbie dolls when I would have rather been reading."

"Makes sense," I shrugged. "Don't let yourself feel so slighted. Your intellect is unmatched, and you will be a superb Nuclear Engineer. Why do you think you're here right now?"

Her lips tugged into a smile and she shook her head, letting out the tiniest exhale of a laugh.

"Actually, I was under the impression you enjoy my company."

I snorted. "Now as a scientist, what evidence do you have to support your hypothesis?"

She pursed her lips and restrained a smile.

"I'm a woman," she began. "And, although you compliment my intellect as an engineer, our intuition is also unrivaled. It tells me you'd *much* rather it be me with you in the lab, than one of our colleagues. Remember? Our field is made up of almost eighty percent men. I'm a rare bird."

I fired the beam. The electrical buzz was momentary.

"Bravo," I exaggerated. "So, what does your intuition envision for the results of this second specimen?"

"If it really was in the Danger Zone like the first…then logically speaking, the damage wouldn't be the kind seen with Strontium. It would be distributed in tissue rather than bone."

My stomach knotted as the image on the screen was ready. Emily jumped to my side.

"Take a look for yourself…" I mumbled.

Her warm breath hit my neck as she gasped.

"It's the same—stuck in a pre-cancerous mitosis."

A comforting warmth settled in my chest. I was finally ready to approach my dad. With two sets of the same, irrevocable evidence, he would have to use my research as fact. *Someone* besides Emily and me had to know the truth. Since the discovery, I had lain awake late at night…tossing and turning…pondering at the *why*. Why did they lie? What motive did they have? We were told the radioactive material was Strontium almost two years ago. Now, with the bombings at Georgetown just a month before the election and the false information they had given the public regarding Black Monday, it only added to my suspicions. Behind the marble-clad walls of our Capitol, corruption was rearing its ugly head in the form of a lie. A lie that I now knew. That knowledge gave me a *feeling* in my gut. It was strong, and kept my stomach in knots at all hours of the day. It told me that it was *dire* to get the truth out. No exceptions.

"Stefan!" A hard whack to my shoulder jarred me from my thoughts.

Emily stood facing me with large, cylindrical Pyrex vials and a jug of formaldehyde. Judging by the sloshing in the jug, she had hit me with that.

"Can you move, please?" she huffed, wide-eyed and chuckling at my phasing out.

I stood up and let her preserve our specimen.

While she did that, I walked over to the glass and peered out into the hallway. Nothing. Just the clean white tile and chrome railings I had seen for years. The life of a scientist.

"So," Emily called from behind. "Have you heard from 'Ms. Walling' since we spoke last?"

"No." I turned back to her. "I texted her to see if she was all right."

"And?" her eyebrows quirked at my sudden pause.

"Nothing. No answer."

I saw fear sweep over Emily's expression. She was worried, and I knew that from her lengthy explanation at the café of why I couldn't trust my ex to keep her mouth shut. The most frightening thing was, I thought she might have been right.

"You better pray she doesn't talk."

"I never thought of you as the religious type."

She pursed her lips and nervously arranged the vials on the counter. "You thought right, but that still doesn't mean I don't pray."

I snorted. "Did you, just? Am I the only one that heard you contradict yourself? You're not religious, but you still pray. To whom, Albert Einstein in the sky?"

She laughed and nodded her head in dismissal of my trivial statement.

"Well, in light of all the science I've learned in my life. Some facts are just hard to fathom. Don't you think?"

My face scrunched up from her words.

"Examples?"

"My favorite, one I'm certain you know. Atoms. They never touch." I nodded, rolling my eyes in response. I knew that from the eighth grade. "Don't give me that look," she scolded.

"Sorry."

"Anyway, they never touch. Their electrons, although incredibly close, never touch. There is always space between the atoms. Also, the volume of an atom according to physics is 99.99 percent to the umpteenth-power repeating—empty space. The physical matter that makes up the visible world is but an infinitely small fraction of the whole. We are all quite literally empty space. We are the universe observing itself."

What a parallel. I was impressed.

"So, perhaps my thoughts emit a frequency…a cosmic resonance, per se. Perhaps the rest of the known universe can pick up that frequency, and it returns another back to me. It could be measurable, one day. Who knows?"

"Is your PhD in Metaphysics?

"Funny." Her face was deadpan.

Beep. The electronic lock clicked open. I whipped around to see Professor Trantham in his pajamas with four stony-faced men in black suits behind him. I met eyes with Emily. Her hands were shaking as she held the vials. The sound of their dress shoes hitting the tile floor grew closer.

"Professor Trantham!" Emily gasped shakily. "What are you doing here so early?"

He didn't respond, just lingered by the entrance. The four men approached our station. That's when I knew it—we were screwed. My ex had squealed.

"This laboratory is off limits to all students and professors alike. The CIA has full control over these premises' by executive order. Effective immediately." The tallest of the men announced those words emotionlessly. The other three went for the vials in Emily's hands and the specimen that laid on the station. She drew back, holding on to the vials.

"This is ours!" she struggled to keep a grasp, and they forcefully pulled them away. She staggered backward from their strength. My heart was pounding in my chest.

"Ms. Stevens, it is in your best interest to cooperate with us."

"Is it?" she spat, and her nostrils flared.

"I wouldn't recommend attempting to find out the contrary."

Did he just threaten her?

Emily's mouth hung open in fear. The tallest one, who I assumed was the leader, mumbled something into his watch, and then turned back to us. His jawline was strong. His face was square, and he sported a buzz-cut. The others cleared our workstation before I could even take a second glance at what they were doing.

"Everything in this lab is property of the federal government. If you do not comply with our requests, we will charge you with tampering of evidence from the Danger Zone. Which infringes H.R. 1649—a crime punishable of up to twenty-five years in prison or loss of citizenship and becoming a known traitor of the United States."

My breathing was shallow. A cold line of sweat formed along my hairline. I glanced back at Professor Trantham. His head was hung towards the floor.

"This is ridiculous. We have rights!"

A minuscule smile emerged on the man's face. He was amused. He knew he had the power to do whatever the hell he wanted.

"Sorry to be the first to inform you, but in matters of National Security, you have no rights."

My stomach clenched up. Pure, undiluted terror swept over my body. My blood felt hot and a vein pulsed in my forehead.

"National Security my ass," I coughed.

The man didn't react. His lips pressed together, and he held his composure.

"Are we almost clear?" he asked.

"Clear." One of the other agents behind me answered.

"Good. Destroy all of it."

Emily shook her head in desperation. "No, no! You can't!"

Excellent. She remembered our emergency plan.

I felt the cold metal handcuffs clamp around one of my wrists. My instincts caused me to jerk my arm, and my head was slammed against the workstation.

"Don't resist," a voice behind me said.

The clicking noise of another pair of handcuffs sliding shut caught my ear. Emily was now in the same position as me. From across the opposite side of the table, our eyes locked. She gritted her teeth and her forehead creased from strain. Her prediction came true. She had warned me for days, but I didn't listen.

"Did you do what I asked you?" I whispered across the table.

Emily's lips tugged into a smile, and with her cheek pressed into the metal workstation, she nodded *yes.*

We were jerked upright violently and pushed towards the lab door. The tallest one stepped in front of me, blocking my path. The agent held my wrists and waited. Emily was led out ahead of me.

"What did you just say to her?" His eyes turned to slits.

"Nothing," I muttered. He wasn't the least bit pleased.

"I *heard* something. She nodded back at you."

I exhaled heavily and puffed up my chest. I wouldn't budge for this prick.

"Fine. Take him away."

"You can't arrest us," I said as we began to walk away.

"We aren't—yet. You and the girl are being detained for questioning."

FBI Field Office – Boston, MA
06:11 10-16-2016

The ride across town was silent. The kind of silent that was unsettling, which caused my thoughts to race endlessly. It was a conscious effort to hear something other than the soft hum of tires on pavement. I was shoved into the back of a black Yukon Denali. Emily must have been in a separate vehicle. After the leader noticed me whisper something to her, there wasn't a chance in Hell we would be taken together.

There was a faint red glow emanating from the controls on the dash. The stick shift was a faux-mahogany, and the doors had a trim in the same material. An advanced navigation system was jutting out from the dash. I spotted the police lights hidden in the corners of the windshield. This SUV was loaded.

I was glad our tax dollars were being spent so prudently…not. No, instead, our Post-Confinement tax dollars were going to the extortion of innocent citizens like myself. All for conducting research that violated the heinous law the government enacted to keep the lie hidden from the public. They were scared. Scared that our research might abate the trust people had in the EPA's findings. I exhaled slowly and glanced between the two men in the front seats. They weren't talking, just fulfilling their orders. I wondered how much their salaries were. Perhaps they were paid enough to keep quiet about the corruption taking place.

My face flushed with heat. My breath shuddered from just thinking about what had just occurred in the lab. I owed over two-hundred thousand dollars in student loans to two of the most renowned universities in the US, and now I was being punished. I was being told by the feds that I could not conduct research. Research that was not harming anyone, nor a threat to National Security. To Hell with them. They fucked with the *wrong* scientist.

I stared at my reflection in the two-way mirror across the room. I knew they were watching. The agents had led me in here a few minutes ago and left without saying a word. I sat at the end of a long, rectangular table. There was a box of doughnuts and a pot of coffee sitting in the middle with a few Styrofoam cups nearby. It was as if they were trying to say, *'Hey, open up to us. Oh, and here's a donut. Maybe that will make you feel a little more at home.'* I snorted, shaking my head at the thought. They had released me from the cuffs. I guess they saw a thin white guy in a lab coat and figured I wasn't a real threat. If only they knew.

The door swung open. It was the same tall agent who did all the talking back at the lab. The leader. Why wasn't I shocked? I was certain he wanted to get to the bottom of what I whispered to Emily. He pulled out the plastic seat and sat down. His face was vacant, and his eyes were sullen. He poured himself a cup of coffee, all while acting like I wasn't there. I didn't care how long he took. He wouldn't make much headway with me regardless.

Finally, he glanced up and met my eyes. There was a manila folder he had brought in, and from it he removed papers and began sorting through them.

"So, Stefan, is it?"

Why did he ask such a dumb question? He knew exactly who I was.

"Yes."

He didn't answer right away, just kept his impassive expression. "Salutatorian of your high school class back in New York, graduated Magna Cum Laude with your bachelor's from Columbia University, got your master's at MIT, and continued to pursue your PhD there in Nuclear Engineering. You are quite the overachiever, wouldn't you say?"

I didn't even bother answering. It wasn't worth my breath.

"Now let me ask you a question," he began, setting down his papers. "What is an up and coming Nuclear Engineer doing wasting his time testing animal tissues? Why bother?"

I bit the inside of my bottom lip, trying to hold back going off on him. It infuriated me how he was playing dumb.

"It's a side-interest," I muttered.

His forehead scrunched up. "You got your specimen in Manhattan, judging by your research. I mean, last time I checked, Boston to New York is nearly a four-hour drive. Hardly a side-interest, I'd say."

I glowered at him. I wanted him to know I didn't like him, and everything he stood for. I knew though, the longer I stayed quiet, the more intense the questioning would become.

"Emily Stevens. What is her involvement?" My Adam's apple bobbed up and down as he said her name. I didn't want her to be the least bit responsible for this.

"None. She just assisted me with the handling of the specimens."

"I find that kind of hard to believe."

"I find *a lot* of things hard to believe," I spat back.

The man snorted and let out a hiss-like laugh. "Is that what compels you? Driven by the notion that the EPA lied about what type of radioactive isotopes were found on Black Monday. I wonder who would believe you, when that story has been forgotten of long ago."

"I have proof."

He revealed a smile so sinister it was disturbing. His eyebrows quirked.

"Proof? What proof? Your proof is gone—toast."

"Is it now?" I countered and revealed a smug smirk. That caused the man's eyes to grow wide. I could see the fear on his face from having realized what I was insinuating.

"You thought you could fool us, Stefan, but you can't. We see and hear everything. We also found your first samples from the specimen you brought back from the Danger Zone a few days ago. All of it is destroyed. There's nothing left."

I did my best to fake a distraught reaction. I displayed a somber look in my eyes as I stared back at the man. I needed him to think he had won, that the first specimen we took samples from was confiscated and in his control. That was what we wanted. For them to believe we were at their mercy, but actually, it was the *other* way around.

"My research…it's gone…" I mumbled. He relished my words. A smile tugged at his lips. "Yes, it's all gone. Which is why I am curious as to what you said to Ms. Stevens. She smiled and nodded yes. What did she say yes to?"

My instincts told me not to say a word, but I couldn't resist.

"Wouldn't you like to know?"

He laughed, shaking his head at my comment. "I told your friend, and I'll tell you the same thing. I don't recommend trying to find out what happens when you don't cooperate with us."

I didn't respond. I kept my lips pressed together and stayed silent. He caught on to my resistance but didn't let his expression display any reaction. He organized the papers, shuffling them against the table, and then put them back in the manila folder.

"Since you won't speak. We are done here," he announced.

My brow furrowed. "Really?" my voice sounded surprised. I didn't expect him to let me go so easily. "Legally, I could arrest you and the girl for the research you conducted—"

"Then what is stopping you?" As the words slipped out I immediately wished I hadn't been so brazen, but as a scientist, I had to know. They had all the power in the world to keep us here indefinitely, so why didn't they? The agent gave me a bizarre look as if I were insane.

"There are reasons…" He began, almost hesitantly. "Based on your file. We would have to set a bond above the tens of millions to keep you imprisoned. We aren't trying to draw any attention to ourselves..."

'We aren't trying to draw any attention to ourselves...'

My stomach clenched as the words repeated in my mind over and over. They *did* know everything about me. They were afraid the media might catch wind of our arrest. *Drawing attention.* They knew who my father was. They knew what he was capable of, and they didn't want to risk a person of such a high title finding out their son was imprisoned. I fought the urge to smile, and luckily it worked. I kept my expression blank.

"Am I free to go?" I asked.

"Yes, for now. One of the agents will escort you out, but I must inform you of what is about to change for you and the girl." His know-it-all tone gave me goosebumps. "Excuse me?"

"If you come within one mile of your campus, we will be on you like a fly on shit. If you talk, we will be listening. If you even happen to look crooked, we will come down on you so hard that you will forget what the hell you were going to school for. If you have a feeling that you are being watched, you probably *are.* I am giving you fair warning. Is talking worth losing your citizenship over?"

His question angered me down to my core.

"I want to speak to my lawyer." I stood up.

"Not so fast," he pointed to my seat. I slowly slid back down into it. The plastic was warm from where I had sat. "The stipulations of your release are simple. You cannot go within a mile of campus. You cannot talk to *anyone*—including your lawyer. If you would like to break either of those conditions, we will arrest you indefinitely, and then you can talk to your lawyer. In matters of National Security, a lawyer would be of little help to you."

"Not the best lawyer," I countered.

"All the money in the world couldn't help you once you are in our crosshair." The volume of his voice raised. He didn't like that I was testing his authority. The rebel in me continued to rage and think of ways to exacerbate the situation. The agent's words though, echoed. They were frightening. *'Once you are in our crosshair...'*

"You said I was free to go, and I am leaving." I stood up and strode to the metal door without hesitation. I heard the scraping of the agent's chair against the floor. I pulled the handle hard and the door only opened a few inches before being slammed closed by the fist of the agent. We were eye to eye. I could feel his breath hit my face. There was malevolence in his dark eyes. His whole presence was unnerving.

"Let me make something *very* clear to you, Stefan. The CIA are the wrong people to fuck around with. We were sent here to neutralize a situation, nothing more, nothing less."

"You were sent here to erase the truth, *nothing* more, *nothing* less," I mocked his wording. The muscle in his jaw twitched, and the planes of his face tightened. I pulled the door and he slammed it closed once again.

"Listen here you little shit," he frothed, accidently drooling as he spoke. "You better fucking watch yourself if you want any sort of a future with a good career. We could take away everything you have worked for in the blink of an eye."

I could feel my eye twitching, and my lip began to tremble.

"Good luck," I said.

He released the door and hoisted me up against the wall by the collar of my button down. His constricting grip on my neck caused me to gasp for air. Blood rushed to my face.

"I don't think you understand the kind of power we have."

I gasped, writhing around under his grip. The pressure in my eyes was building quickly. My heart pounded from the starvation of oxygen. His eyes were snake-like, and there wasn't a bit of goodness in this man's body. He was an extension of a greater evil.

"If you fuck up once, and I *mean* once. We could have you put away for the rest of your life. No lawyer and no amount of Daddy's money would set you free. You *are* a scientist…" He mumbled, and I struggled to push away his hand with my own. "Who is to say you and Emily didn't help Owen Marina secure the explosives to create his pipe bomb?"

My eyes bulged and I opened my mouth wide, trying to breathe. The room was becoming fuzzy. The clean white tile and walls began to fade away. He released his grasp from my neck and I inhaled violently, coughing from the lack of air for so long. My neck felt bruised.

"Yeah," he huffed, wiping his hands off as if I were dirty. "Don't underestimate what we are capable of." He pulled the door open and pushed me through it. The two agents who assisted my interrogator earlier in the lab were waiting outside. They still donned their perfectly pressed, black suits, and they waited with their hands resting in front of their waists.

"Take him home—now," the man demanded.

One of the agents grabbed my wrists and held them behind my

back. The other agent walked in front of me. We began down the long hallway illuminated by overly-bright fluorescent lights. My breathing shuddered from the outrage that flooded my body. He threatened to *frame* me. To involve me in a crime that was completely unrelated. His words made me wonder. If they could make Emily and me accomplices to a crime we didn't commit, who is to say they didn't do that to Owen? He was the country's hero and look at him now…on the run from the same people who barged into the lab. All it took was the final debate to send the polls spiraling down day by day.

The final debate. I almost gasped from the thought that entered my mind. They were trying to put an end to the Convergence Party. A month before the election they were trying to dismantle everything. The co-founder died, Owen was now a terrorist. *My God.* How could I have not pieced it together sooner? They were trying to snuff out every last bit of their influence. They tarnished their solid reputation and their loyal following, me being one of them, was dwindling before the country's eyes. The media covering Owen was entirely one-sided. My heart was practically in my throat. It all made sense. The terrorist attack was all a sham in order to slant the election in *their* favor. But *who* could be behind such a contemptible lie?

"Walk a little faster there, buddy," the agent behind me said and gave me a shove forward. A vein pulsed in my forehead and I could feel myself begin to sweat. They *thought* they destroyed all the evidence, but they couldn't have been further from being right. Emily and I had prepared for this, just in case of an emergency. We couldn't have let over a year's worth of effort slip out of our grasp that easily. I would not let our endeavor be in vain. They could intimidate me, rough me around a little bit, and kick me out of school, but they could *not* take away the truth that I knew. They couldn't erase it…and that fact was what scared them shitless. They knew our research was another hole in their porous plan. It was a potential voice that could unravel their lie.

The footfalls were all I heard besides my thoughts. The ding of an elevator sounded, and we stepped inside. I began to smile. I was no longer fearful or frightened. I could still feel the sensation of the man's hand clasped around my throat, crushing in around my windpipe. I didn't have to worry about fighting them back *now*, for today they won. They stripped me bare and expected me to remain petrified. They wanted to keep me in submission. I didn't feel any of that. I felt *empowered.* I had to be patient, I had to wait long enough to let their gaze wander off from me. In order to slip away and *finish* what Emily and I started.

It was time to go see my father.

Palmetto Expressway – Hialeah, FL
13:13 10-16-2016

The ride was long, and the road flat. It had been nearly three and a half hours. Rachel and I wore hooded jackets to help conceal us in the back seat. She was snuggled up against my shoulder and had slept the majority of the journey. Briana and Grey talked intermittently over the soft music playing from the radio. I wasn't paying much attention to their conversation, but from what I could hear, it seemed like they were discussing their abilities and comparing skills. Cool air blew from the AC, and it kept me comfortable, but through the window, the strength of the Florida sun made itself apparent. It heated up my arm to the point of being uncomfortable. I tried to readjust my position without waking Rachel.

We had taken the turnpike all the way down from Orlando. Briana had a SunPass—a device that stuck to the inside of her windshield, allowing her to drive through the tolls without having to stop. It was a huge advantage when she was carrying dangerous cargo. Before the turnpike ended and put us onto the Palmetto Expressway, I got to see the Miami Skyline from afar. It was just like I had seen in movies. The buildings lined the bay, and some of the glass panes glinted from the sun reflecting off of the water. *CSI: Miami, 2 Fast 2 Furious, Dexter*…all films and shows I had seen Miami in growing up, yet it was different. The lighting was natural, and not the saturated orange tint that was used when filming this area. You couldn't escape the palm trees, they were everywhere. As we got off the expressway, I noticed this area looked much different compared to the sleek and contemporary skyline of downtown. It was almost jungle-like. The houses were so close together they were almost side by side. I saw people of all ages walking, riding their bikes, everyone was out and about. It was a melting pot. I saw the entire spectrum of possible skin tones just from passing a few blocks. Some of the area seemed run-down, with a few broken down cars on cinderblocks in the yards.

"*Bienvenidos à Hialeah,*" Briana said.

"Hialeah," I repeated.

Rachel began to stir. She inhaled deeply and stretched her arms out.

"We're already here?" she asked while yawning.

"Yep. I was about to have Owen wake you up."

Rachel rubbed her eyes and peered out of both windows. "Wow, we are near the street Briana and me grew up on. That was quick."

"Yeah for you, Sleeping Beauty," I said, poking her in her side. "I was awake the whole time."

"I could sleep for a week after what we went through in the past two days."

"I can see that."

"Rachel," Briana called to her, "What street is Vinny's garage off of? 37th of 44th? It's been too damn long."

"You should be ashamed," Rachel answered. "You're forgetting your roots, *amiga.*"

"Oh please, it's been over a decade. Which is it?"

"This one! To the left!" The car whipped around and Briana's tires screeched. I used my forearm to keep myself from being thrown against the window. We were all shaken up from her sudden turn. "37th," Rachel said and let out a giggle.

I could see Briana's sarcastic glare in the rearview mirror.

"A little too late, don't you think?"

Rachel shrugged. Towards the end of the street, I saw what looked to be a concrete building. Apparently, Rachel had two cousins who owned a garage here in Hialeah. She told me before we left Briana's this morning that their names were Vicenzo and Luciano, but to call them Vinny and Luke. I would come to find out they were *very* opinionated.

We pulled up in the small parking lot. As I stepped out, I noticed some of the asphalt was crumbling and deteriorated. My guess was that this building had been here long before Rachel's cousins purchased it. There were three garage bays, all of which were open. I passed a souped-up Mitsubishi Lancer Evolution, and a few feet from it was an equally nice Toyota Supra. I took a second glance when I saw it. *That* was a desired car amongst racers and car enthusiasts. Rachel took the lead ahead of us and strode into the garage like she lived there. I couldn't help but glance down at her ass. She had borrowed some shorts from Briana. Our clothes were dirty, and Florida was shorts weather all year round. I wasn't complaining.

"Is that who I think it is?!" a gruff voice asked from inside the garage. It was accompanied by another with the same Hispanic accent. "No fucking way!"

"It's me, *primos!*" she shouted in a singsong tone. Two men barreled into her. The first embraced her in a bear hug. He picked her up and swung her around in a circle. She laughed and I heard him mutter something in Spanish with a huge grin on his face. Rachel rubbed his shiny bald head. "What happened to your hair, Luke?" He laughed, putting her down and rubbed it himself. "It started to go a while back, I had to shave it off. I look like Pitbull, right?" She shook her head and chuckled. "You wish!"

By now Grey, Briana, and I had settled in behind Rachel. Vinny greeted her next, and when he pulled her tight in a hug, I noticed how massive his arms were. The ridges in his biceps and triceps were stone-like. He had a tattoo sleeve on each arm, tribal designs in various patterns. The black ink ended at his wrists. He also had a shaved head. I assumed balding began early for the men in Rachel's family. When Vinny released Rachel, he straightened his posture and his towering frame became apparent. I couldn't help but stare. He must have been well over six foot, and his t-shirt looked a little too tight for a man of his size. Perhaps he was trying to flaunt his muscles. Besides his Hispanic features, he almost looked like Dwayne "The Rock" Johnson. Luke was around my height, maybe five-eleven or six foot, but not nearly as built as Vinny. He had muscles, but he also was a little huskier.

By the looks of them, I wouldn't want to be around when they saw red.

The garage smelled of rubber and motor oil. Rachel hadn't introduced us yet, so I took this time to survey my surroundings. There was a car in the far bay with the hood open and movement visible from the mechanic's well underneath. Judging by the fact Vinny and Luke hadn't a trace of dirt or grease on them, I assumed they were the owners.

Luke's demeanor turned serious and he glanced at all of us.

"Rachel, what the hell is going on? We saw you on the news. You are wanted big time, *chica...*" His baritone voice softened. He seemed concerned about her well-being, which made me happy. I then realized that now *I* also cared about Rachel, and it kind of alarmed me. I'd only known her for three days. Maybe it was fear that caused me to question the sensation as it swept over me. Megan made me bitter when she left. I was afraid to care, to invest so much into another human being again. There was something gravitating about her presence. It wasn't just her looks, it was the energy she gave off. It made me want to be around her.

Regardless, a little voice inside told me that my road would be a short one. Albeit we were intelligent people, I had my doubts. Images of a future with Rachel swam around my head. A future where we wouldn't have to hide, wouldn't have to run, and could be free again. It all sounded a little too sublime, too good to be true. At this point, I was living day by day, uncertain of what was to come. I couldn't get too attached to Rachel. It would cause her more pain than I'd like to imagine. For that little voice was incessant, and seldom had it quieted since discovering I was a wanted terrorist. It said my road would be a *short* one…and that very thought terrified me to my core.

"Owen! What are you waiting for? We have some things to discuss."

Rachel's voice jolted me from my daze. As I became coherent, I saw Grey and Briana trailing her and her cousins. I scurried behind them and we walked up concrete steps into a loft. It was spacious and had a pool table with burgundy fabric. The room had a faint smell of cigar smoke that lingered in the air, and even with the dim lighting, I couldn't keep my eyes from the walls. There were all kinds of pictures of their family, posters of the Miami Heat, cars, and I saw one of the Wu-Tang Clan. In just a few glimpses, I saw most of what made up their interests.

"I like what you've done with the place," Briana said.

"A lot different from when you were a little girl, huh?" Luke smiled and let out a throaty laugh. I caught the glimmer of a gold molar in his mouth. There was a long, saggy, beige couch against the wall, accompanied by another perpendicular in the corner. Her cousins both sat on the smaller sofa and let us four sit on the longer one. Rachel daintily crossed a bronze leg over the other and rested her hands, intertwining them around her knee. None on our couch said a word, but Vinny kept glancing over me as if I were an intruder of some sorts. His forehead was scrunched up, and he didn't look very pleased.

"So, *prima*, tell me why the fuck are you risking your life for this *gringo?*" Vinny waved a hand in my direction. My anger caused me to flinch, and I almost jumped off of the couch, but Vinny's rocky build made me think twice. Still, I was no coward. "What the fuck? Nice to meet you too, asshole."

He jumped up and lunged at me with fiery eyes, and Rachel was between us before either of us could lay a hand on each other. "*Ay, ay, ay!* Calm down. No fighting!" Rachel shouted, pushing us farther apart.

"Fucking *gringo*…" He muttered some hateful Spanish, I assumed. Luke also stood up with him, but was now easing back down onto the couch. He eyed me just as Vinny had—distrusting and loathing.

"What does that word even mean?" I whispered to Briana.

"White boy…"

Rachel, still standing, huffed and began to wave her arms around heatedly.

"Now are you two ready to stop acting like thugs and listen to what I have to say? Owen—"

"Before you continue," Grey interrupted. He seemed uncomfortable in this environment. "Take your batteries out of your phones. Now."

Vinny and Luke looked at him as if he was insane. "Why?"

"Because *they* could be listening." He pointed to Vinny's phone which was now out of his pocket. "Take out the batteries." They both glanced at Rachel to silently confirm Grey's demand. Rachel crossed her arms and nodded. They reluctantly popped out the batteries and set them on the cocktail table between the couches.

"Owen is in deep shit, and it runs a lot deeper than you think."

"He's not my blood," Vinny shrugged in my direction, making a sour face as if he could smell my *gringo* self from where he was sitting.

Rachel snorted. "He's not your blood, but when whatever it is they are planning goes into action, you will both wish you would have treated him like he was."

"What are you talking about?" Luke questioned.

"Owen was framed for the bombings at Georgetown. We think someone, or a group of people wanted Owen's party to lose the election."

"Why?" Vinny still glowered at me like I really *was* a killer.

"As a journalist, I am inclined to believe someone wants to keep themselves in power. With all of this happening weeks before the election, who knows what else they could be hiding?"

"Is that what all of this is about?" Vinny scoffed and stood up, pacing around. "You just trying to get a story for a big bonus at work?"

"It's not *just* a story, Vinny! Something tells me this all goes back to the Confinement."

Vinny and Luke froze. Their demeanor turned grave.

"What? What do you mean? This all goes back to the Confinement…"

The change in Luke's tone was palpable. It was the first time since meeting them that they didn't appear so callous. It was hard to tell, but it almost looked like *fear.*

"I've thought…that maybe we weren't meant to be released from the Confinement."

Rachel's words pierced like daggers, and the reactions from Vinny and Luke were evidence.

"There's no fucking way that's true. I can't believe it. After everything we saw happen, there's no way…" Luke stumbled over his words and he rubbed his forehead with his palms. Was he beginning to sweat? Rachel sat down next to Grey at the end of the couch, closest to Vinny and Luke.

"Was the Miami Camp bad? What did you see?" her voice was soft and empathetic. Vinny's eyes jumped up to meet Rachel's. "It was a nightmare. Six million people, from all walks of life, different languages and cultures, stuck. Hundreds died every day because they would fight, and the guards would kill them. Imagine, all the gangs behind one fence, all the drug dealers *forced* to be together. I could only imagine how bad it would have been if it was in the dead of summer, the winter kept the temperature mild. Regardless, they didn't have enough supplies to feed everyone—"

"Are you serious?" Rachel interrupted. "Yes, I'm serious, *prima.* Kids died right in front of my own eyes from starvation. It was horrible. I have nightmares sometimes." There was pain behind Vinny's voice. Luke didn't add anything to Vinny's statement, he just stared at the concrete floor. I glanced at the scar on my left forearm. I had nightmares too, just like Vinny. The faded dot on my arm from the cigarette was a physical scar…but the Confinement's damage ran much deeper. It scarred us mentally more than anything.

"I wish you had pictures." Rachel's voice was distant.

"I don't have any pictures," Vinny answered, "but you do have our word. We are witnesses."

Rachel nodded. She seemed to be daydreaming.

"So, tell us about this plan," Luke said. Rachel pulled herself out of her daze. "Well, Owen and I have made it all the way here from North Carolina, and we can't keep running. We are running out of time. We have to get Owen out of the country—"

Vinny started laughing. "You gotta be kidding me." His chuckles were guttural and raspy. Rachel wasn't amused, and she began to open her mouth to speak.

"No, it's possible. I can do it," Grey interjected. We all turned to him. "I've actually been thinking of how we would go about doing it."

"No offense," Vinny spoke over his subsiding laughs. "You think you're going to be able to get Owen Marina, through security, and on a plane in the second largest international airport?"

"Yes." Grey nodded confidently.

"*Gringos*, man…" Vinny patted Luke on the back. "They are *loco*." Luke didn't laugh, but a smile emerged. "I was laughing, too," Briana added. "Until Grey and I talked. He's the real deal, he's not crazy. His computer skills are unbelievable." They glanced at Grey again. I couldn't tell if he was smiling behind his scraggly black beard.

"I'm interested in hearing about this later, Grey," Luke said, "but what about you, Rachel? Maybe you forgot, but you are just as wanted as he is. Why don't you go with him? And where is he going?"

Luke's words struck a chord inside of me. The thought resonated in my mind. *'Why don't you go with him?'* The idea was alluring, Rachel coming with me. Part of me was excited to hear her answer. The slightest possibility of Rachel still being in my life gave me butterflies. I knew, though. I knew she couldn't. The story meant more to her than remaining by my side.

"I—um. I can't," the words tore away at me, even though I already knew them before she spoke. "I have to get the truth out to people before it's too late. Before the election."

"And how are you going to do that?" Luke countered.

"Uncle Ian."

"Damn, that's right. I forgot all about him. I'm still lost, though. What proof do you have besides Owen? I know you, Rachel, and if you had a story you wouldn't be here right now asking us to get involved in this crazy mess."

Rachel huffed and her lower lip began to tremble. Luke asked a valid question, one which frightened me. I knew she wanted this story more than anything, but how would she get it? My words and experiences were just one voice in a sea of lies. Who would believe her story?

"You know what?" her voice was heated. "We can't think about the end yet. Right now, we have to keep everybody safe. That means we have to get Owen on a non-stop flight to Moscow, where the United States Government will have no chance of extraditing him for the crime he didn't commit."

"And?" Vinny split the silence. Rachel shook her head, and I thought I saw tears forming in the corners of her eyes. Vinny and Luke were making Rachel face something that she couldn't face. The fact that her plan had gaps. It had loose ends that didn't work. She had no *real* story.

"There is no *and!"* she shouted. "Give me a break! Let's just focus on what we have to do here and now. I will worry about the story after Owen is safe again. Like I told him when we first met, Ian has information bombarding him twenty-four seven. What if someone else knows something that we don't? Maybe there are more pieces to the puzzle than what we have to offer."

"You know what, fuck this…" Vinny stood up and looked at all of us, but mainly at Rachel. "We haven't seen you in years, *prima*, and you think you're just going to walk on into the shop like you are still the old Rachel we used to know? You got all your fancy degrees and forgot about your old life back in the *barrio* with us. You didn't even call us after the Confinement! So *fuck* you, and *fuck* your friends! You are risking everything we have worked for by just being here! Who knows? The fucking FBI could barge in at any minute, all thanks to you being so damn inconsiderate and just like always making everything about you!"

Vinny was fuming. Part of me was about to defend her, but something kept me seated. This was a family matter, and I wasn't family.

"Calm down, man." Luke stood up and tried to get him to sit down. He shrugged off Luke's grasp and kept pacing around. "No, hell no! It just blows my mind she expects us to risk our freedom, our garage, our whole lives for nothing!" I heard Rachel crying. Grey rubbed her back gently, and Briana sat beside me glancing at Vinny and Luke.

"Three…three hundred…" Rachel hiccupped in tears. "And fifty…fifty thousand dollars."

Vinny and Luke froze. The air was tense and Vinny's angry expression didn't lessen.

"What did you say?" Vinny asked.

"She said, three-hundred and fifty-thousand dollars," Briana announced matter-of-factly.

"We…we will give it to you…for helping us."

Vinny glanced around at all of us as if we were hiding some secret or lying. "Rachel, stop crying," he said. "What are you talking about, *prima*? How in the hell would you get that kind of money?"

"I stole it," Grey answered nonchalantly.

"Stole it?" Luke asked, bewildered and wide-eyed. "Well," Vinny began, "don't you think the person you stole it from will want it back?" Grey shook his head no as if it was nothing. "I stole 1.4 million dollars from someone else who stole it. It was my job to stop grand larceny from occurring at my bank, and I failed. So, I stole the money that was stolen in order to help Owen."

Vinny and Luke digested Grey's words. They didn't respond, just glanced around at the ground in front of them.

"If you help us," Rachel composed herself enough to speak, "we will give you three hundred and fifty thousand dollars. We will give the same to Briana."

"Seriously?" Luke questioned with disbelief.

"Yes. Owen needs to get out of this country alive. We plan to do that with Briana and Grey's help." Vinny's forehead scrunched up as Rachel finished her statement. "Then what do you want from me and Luke?"

I was curious to hear this answer myself. Rachel had yet to tell any of us why we came to see her cousins in the first place. Obviously, it was partly because of protection. This loft on top of the garage allowed us to hide in plain sight.

"We want your muscle. We need a backup plan, and that's the role you will serve."

"You'd give us 350K just to be a *backup* plan?"

"Of course. It is the least we can do for agreeing to be a part of this. Your involvement is a major risk to take, especially if we fail."

"We won't fail," Grey spoke up.

"And if we do?" Luke asked, nervously.

"Then we are all fucked," Briana replied. "At least, that's what they told me when I asked them the same question." She chuckled.

"So, it's that simple," Luke retorted. "If we fail, we are fucked."

"Indeed," Grey said. "We aren't going to fail, though."

"And how can you be so damn sure?" Vinny pressed with a skeptical glare.

"Because. Briana and I have discussed the plan of action, and if we follow it—it will actually work, quite well if I might add." Briana suppressed a smug smile that tugged at her lips.

"What's your role in all of this?" Luke nodded to Briana. She glanced around at all of us before answering. "Well, I have to get in touch with my old contact on the Darkweb. I used to work with Silk Road, but that was shut down by the feds. Given our time frame, I highly doubt a rush delivery from Sweden would work. I should be able to find someone who can give it to me in person. Then, getting Owen's photo on the passport once we get him an adequate disguise will be the hard part. It has to look real enough to fool the security agents."

"What about you, Grey?" Grey flinched from Luke's sudden question. I had yet to hear his plan either. "I would assume, that with as badly as they want to catch Owen, they are using facial recognition to find him. Once he is seen on the airport security cameras, we could believe with good reason that they will swarm the airport as soon as they can. I will have to create a diversion."

"What kind of diversion?" Luke continued barraging them with questions.

"That's what I still have to figure out," Grey answered. "I have the idea. It's just, I still have to work out the logistics of it."

I had stayed quiet this entire time. I was just listening to them discuss how they were going to get *me* out of the country. I tried to stay relaxed, but I felt unsettled in my gut. It hadn't even been five days, and I was the polar opposite of being free. I couldn't make any of my own decisions. Now, I went along with Rachel's plan because it was the only chance I had. The morning after Cole died, I knew I would need a miracle to get me out of this, and I met her. That *had* to have meant something. She said it was fate…

"So what about you, Rachel?" Vinny's deep voice pulled me from my thoughts. "Where do you fall in all of this? What is your role?"

"I don't have a role. I will say goodbye to Owen before he walks in. I can't risk getting caught because I must be able to communicate with Ian. The country has to find out what is really going on."

"And what is *really* going on?"

Vinny's tone caused Rachel's normal glow to fade away. The passion I first saw in her eyes when I met her wasn't as visible. She was reluctant to answer. She didn't want to have to face the truth.

"I don't know yet," she stammered. Vinny huffed and didn't let up. "And what makes you believe you ever will?"

This time, even his words hurt me.

"I have this feeling…" She mumbled. "That Ian might know more than we do. I have a feeling that it will all work out."

"Well, I hope your little *feeling* is right," he scoffed, "and it doesn't land all of us in prison for the rest of our lives."

Rachel swallowed and nodded in acknowledgment. She brushed her hair behind her shoulder and looked at the ground.

"Here's the deal," Vinny continued. "The moment we are done at the airport, whether you needed our help or not, that 350K will be ours. Are we clear about that?" He glanced at Grey.

"Crystal," he replied.

"Good. Now, it seems like we have some work to do." He stood up and Luke followed suit.

"I'll go get my laptop out of the car," Briana said. Grey began to open up his backpack. "I have to make whatever wireless you have here secure before we do anything. It won't take long," he added. I didn't have anything to do. Anyone connected to me would be in deep shit. I was helpless.

"Vinny," Rachel began. "I need you to go buy me a pre-paid phone. I have to call Ian."

Avalon North Point – Cambridge, MA
09:44 10-17-2016

The sun that slipped through the blinds warmed my face. The Weather Channel said it was a record-breaking cold temperature today. It was not like I would know. I'd been stuck in my apartment, being held hostage by the FBI.

I peered out the window, just as I had countless times in the past twenty-four hours. Like I expected, there it was—the black Yukon Denali sitting in the parking lot of a gas station just across the street. I knew they were listening, monitoring my every waking move.

It felt like the only time I was free was in my sleep. Although, I hadn't done much of that either. I got maybe an hour or two of *real* sleep. Every time I closed my eyes, I was plotting how I could get to Manhattan to see my dad. Everything was ready to go. I was just trapped and I didn't know what to do. I couldn't talk to anyone. It would be pointless. I did text Emily a simple *'how are you?'* To which she replied, *'I'm okay.'*

She wasn't stupid. She knew we couldn't talk.

CNN was on TV across the living room. Although Owen and the girl, Rachel, hadn't been seen since the 14th—three days—they were still giving it all of their airtime. The most important thing in the media at the moment was to find Owen Marina. Even more evidence to back up my newfound revelation. The bombs were a sham, Owen was framed, and *someone* was trying to slant the election in their favor.

I stood up and paced around my apartment. The transition from the carpet to the cold tile of the kitchen caused a chill to race up my spine. I wanted to brew a cup of coffee, but I knew that wouldn't be smart. My heart was racing as it is. Eating was another option, but I was also nauseous. This whole situation had my stomach in knots. I felt like I was running out of time.

My dad was only four hours away. Four hours and that godforsaken FBI agent outside my apartment complex were all that kept me from getting my father the truth. I could almost taste the satisfaction, knowing that I would have finally disassembled their lie told so long ago. But how? How could I get there without being followed?

I would have to wait. A thought plagued me, though. What if they never left? I had to find another way. Time was *not* on my side. It was only three weeks till the election and the polls were plummeting day by day. They were watching. They were listening. How would I?

That was it. I had an idea.

Garage Loft – Hialeah, FL
16:24 10-18-2016

I couldn't remember the last time I had seen Grey smoke a cigarette. The tobacco odor intermingled with the smell of coffee. He was drinking it non-stop, as was everyone else. Briana was out with Vinny. Apparently, they were going to meet the contact for the passport at some Cuban restaurant in Downtown Miami. Grey, on the other hand, had purchased my ticket to Moscow. The flight left the day after tomorrow, and I still wasn't all that convinced Grey and Briana could pull it off in time. When he printed off my ticket, I almost got sick. It had hit me like a train in the gut, harsh and swift—it was really happening. In forty-eight hours, I would be on a plane headed to Moscow. That was if we even made it that far.

A couple ashes fell onto Grey's beard.

"You better watch out, Grey. If you're not careful you'll catch your beard on fire."

He chuckled. "That's the least of my worries."

The deep grooves along Grey's forehead spoke louder than his words. He was very confident our plan would work, and that was why he was working so hard to make it perfect. He also bought a ticket, a one-way from Miami to Atlanta. A relatively cheap flight, and he told me that was for a reason. Apparently, with the help of some wacky Chinese module and his plane ticket, he could create this *'diversion'* he spoke of. Something about the fact the ticketing system used a common SQL database, helped him. The system scans the ticket, queries the database for the correct flight and passenger information, and prints out the correct boarding pass. When the ticket is scanned, it was basically a comparison of the data from the database to the encoded information on the ticket, or so Grey said.

Grey's idea was to encode a piece of information on the ticket with the Chinese module that would infiltrate the database and perform an execution, instead of just comparing the data off of the ticket to the data in the system. He called it an *'SQL injection'*. He said it would cause something in the mainframe to mess up. How he knew it would work was beyond me, but Grey was an incredibly talented individual. If he was working for the CIA, they probably would have already caught me by now. I was glad he was on my side.

Rachel was on the sofa taking a nap. Grey had convinced her to wait to call Ian. He insisted that we didn't use the pre-paid phone at all, because of the potential risk of Ian's landline being monitored. They could triangulate our location and then all of our effort would be wasted. He proposed we call through a computer and heavily encrypt the connection to ensure no one could trace it back to us. Not being able to call him, Rachel felt useless, and so she had gone to rest. Her long hair was put up into a bun, and her caramel skin looked so flawless, even after all the stress we had been under lately. Her chest gently moved up and down. I wondered what she was dreaming about, or if she was dreaming at all. Maybe it was a nightmare…

I saw a flash of the mother and daughter, holding hands in the snow in front of the Capitol. The mother whispering, *'Thank you'*.

I shook my head quickly to forget about my reoccurring nightmare. I tried to forget, but I had come to accept it would haunt me forever.

"What is all of this shit?" I asked, setting it back down on the pool table. Briana wasn't amused. "It isn't *shit*, Owen. It's your disguise. Believe it or not, your hair is already growing. The sandy-brown is coming through." I walked over to a nearby mirror to confirm her claim.

She was right. The bleach-blond was already beginning to fade, the culprit being how short my hair was. "And this?" I held up the plastic packaging. "You trying to give me a Hitler mustache?"

She rolled her eyes. "No, it's a fake goatee. A blond one. And you better damn appreciate it because it took half the day to find. By the way, your cash is getting low."

"How low?" I asked.

"Thirty-five thousand."

I laughed at Briana's statement. Our cash might have been getting low, but Grey had seven hundred thousand dollars at our expense, and that was including what we owed Briana, Vinny, and Luke. All he had to do was wire it into an account or a pre-paid card. I heard Grey chuckle as he processed Briana's words. He was hunched over his laptop, sitting at a desk in the corner of the room. There was a table-lamp he had tilted down, shining it on the papers and ticket beneath it. An ink pen between his fingers zipped around the paper and the scraping noise was constant. I sat up a little farther and could barely make out what he was drawing—it almost looked like a QR code.

"You said you have a printer, right?" Grey asked.

"For the last time, yes! It's downstairs at the reception desk, just like I told you." Vinny's tone escalated. Grey didn't react, just continued working and took a sip of his coffee. "I'm just making sure. It's important."

"Why?" Rachel asked from her seat on the couch. Grey spun around in the desk chair. "Well, I'm drawing a rough sketch based on some designs on how the code is formed. Once I get the execution code written in, I will have to design it on the computer and print it off. A drawing wouldn't work on a ticket."

"What kind of diversion are you trying to make?" she questioned further. Grey seemed nervous. He chewed on the bottom corner of his lip and tapped his pen against the arm of the chair. "I'd rather not say. I just don't want to jinx it, you know?" Rachel shrugged off her curiosity and turned to me. It was honestly the first time our eyes had met since she woke up. Staring into her warm brown eyes made me melt inside. As difficult as it was to acknowledge given my circumstances, it was still happening. I was falling for Rachel—*hard.*

"All right, it's time I get to work," Briana announced. Her ringlet curls bounced around like rubber bands that sprung out of her ponytail. I was amazed she never complained of headaches as tightly as her hair was slicked back. She threw me the plastic container with the goatee hair and adhesive. It landed on my crotch and I winced from the pain.

"Sorry," she said, nonchalantly. "Go take a shower."

"Excuse me?"

She pursed her lips. "Once the goatee is on, you won't want to shower because it might mess with the glue. I would say wait until tomorrow, but I need time to get your passport ready. So I have to take the picture as soon as possible." She pulled out a camera I hadn't seen before. "Where'd you get that?" I asked. "Wal-Mart. It was on sale."

I had the sudden sensation of Déjà vu. Briana's purchase of the camera reminded me of when Laura bought one for herself back in Raleigh. I wondered if she was doing well…

"Nice," I muttered.

I heard Grey's chair squeak and he stood between Rachel and me.

"Rachel," he began. "I've got the line secured. Are you ready to call Ian?"

620 8th Ave. – New York, NY
17:39 10-18-2016

I scratched the back of my head, troubled by the front page story of tomorrow's paper in front of me that I had to approve. Never in my life would I have imagined that I would be looking at the face of my goddaughter as the headline article for my paper.

Emilio was probably rolling over in his grave right now. I shook my head, distressed at what to do. It was killing me, having all of these baby-faced journalists fresh out of college, who didn't know shit about what *real* journalism was, putting this garbage on my desk. How could I allow us to publish another day of this tabloid nonsense? Just because that was what USA Today, The Washington Post, and every other major newspaper was spewing out as fact.

Emilio was a real journalist, and he was my greatest friend in life. Even after almost twenty years he was still on my mind. Although he was in Rachel's life for such a short amount of time, he instilled a lot of wisdom in her. Rachel was just as good as her father, perhaps even better. She just hadn't had her moment to shine. I wanted her to get a few years under her belt in a smaller paper before I brought her up here.

I set the papers down. Frustrated, I let out a long sigh. Something didn't feel right. I knew it had been a year since I had seen Rachel, but she wasn't the type to befriend a bad person, let alone a terrorist. I knew her. I watched the girl grow up for Christ's sake. I was dubious to say the least when Owen was first wanted for the bombings. As genuine as he seemed in all of his public appearances and interviews, I saw it as a rumor at most. Once Rachel became involved, that rumor seemed more like a blatant lie. Rachel had to be with him for a reason, because there was *no other* logical reason. Their combined talents must have done them well because they had been off of the fed's radar for four days now.

Police sirens echoed in the streets far below me. After living my entire life in New York, you would have thought I would have been used to them by now…but they always bothered me. This city never slept, and that was the truth. I glanced over at my faint reflection in the floor to ceiling glass that encircled my office. Damn, did time sure do its toll. My hair was almost entirely gray.

I signed my name on the black line at the bottom of the final draft, putting my seal of approval on tomorrow's cover story. My gut panged as I did so. It hurt to have to publish these hideous articles about Rachel, but I had nothing else. I had no other leads. Part of me wanted to use some of my sick days just so someone else would have to make my decisions.

I picked up my briefcase and stood up. I winced as my lower back trembled—the pain just became worse as the years passed. I rubbed it and headed toward the door.

Ring…Ring…

I had taken two steps before it rang. My jaw clenched up, and my exhale shuddered. It was the final straw to an already hectic day. Normally, I would have just ignored it…but with everything going on, it was necessary. I didn't get this far in life by dodging calls just because of my status.

I glanced at the red light on the phone and saw it was coming from my assistant's line. I pressed the speakerphone button.

"What is it, Sharon?"

"I have a call on hold. Line four." Her voice was shaky. I hadn't heard that kind of tenor from her since the bombs went off outside of

Wall Street.

"Then why didn't you transfer it to me?"

"Because. I was afraid you wouldn't pick up."

"All right, Sharon—stop the nonsense. I have to go."

"You'll want to take this call."

Something tugged at my gut—intuition. Maybe it was something greater? Like a God, if there was one. I had covered too many stories that kept me sleepless for me to believe in that anymore.

"Thank you. I'll grab it."

"Mhmm," the line clicked off.

The red light on line four blinked every other second. My breath was shallow. Why was I so damn nervous? I picked up the cold plastic phone and pressed the button.

"This is Ian," I said in the unfluctuating tone I had for years.

"Ian—it's me…"

My stomach sank in relief. Her soft voice was soothing even when talking to a bundle of nerves like myself. Suddenly, my relief turned into alarm. What if *someone* was listening to her? To me?

"Ra—," I stopped myself from saying her name. "Are you okay?

"I'm okay as I'm going to be in a situation like this."

Fear welled up throughout my body, for her safety and mine.

"Are you crazy? What if *they* are listening?"

"They might be."

"What?! Why do you sound so calm then?"

"My line is secure."

Thank God.

"Good. Why did you call?"

"I figured I owe you some sort of explanation," she chuckled. I couldn't help but smile.

"I was worried about you, you know."

"I could imagine."

"I've been wondering. Why were you with him in the first place?"

"You know," her voice was short.

"Do I?" I countered.

"I believe so."

She was right. I *did* know.

"Guilty as charged."

"Anyway," she began. "I called you for a reason. I have a very important question to ask you."

"Shoot."

"Have you been given any…confidential information?"

"Regarding?"

"This, Ian. All of this."

"This is the most confidential conversation I've had all year."

There was a long pause. I thought she had hung up.

"Hello? Are you there?"

"Yes."

"What did I do? You sound upset."

"I'm not gonna lie. I'm a little disheartened."

"Why, because I don't know any more than you do about all of this?"

"Yes. I'm sorry, it's…it's not your fault."

I wiped my hand up my forehead, stretching the skin and rubbing all of my hair back. I wished I had more to give her.

"Any way I can help you, I will. You know that. I promised your dad when you were born that I would."

"I know…" Her voice now a whisper. That somber tone in her words was hard to swallow. I knew I was only her godfather, but she was like the daughter I never had. I loved her.

"What is it exactly you are trying to do?"

"Piece together this lie before it's too late."

"You sound just like your father."

"Really?" she asked. "I wish I could say that I know."

I exhaled. The pain from losing her dad was a colossal weight she carried with her. I still felt that same weight on my shoulders every day. Such a great man Emilio was. Why did the good always go so young?

"You do. He was always trying to look at the bigger picture. That's what made his work so great."

"I know. I still read over the articles you gave me."

"Good. I'm sure you will follow in his footsteps."

"I hope to, Ian. I really do. There's just one problem."

"Which is?"

"That I am trying to solve the puzzle with only one of the pieces." I paused, reflecting over her statement…*only one of the pieces*. "Are you insinuating?"

"Yes, I am. I have a feeling…that there are more pieces out there. This lie is spread out so far, and its roots are so deep, that it must have affected far more than just you-know-who."

Owen...

"Go on," I said.

"He is the only piece I have. His story and his recollection of what happened at the final debate. That isn't enough, though."

"Enough for what?" I was trying to string together what she was getting at, but she was being vague in her explanations.

"What have been the cover stories lately? I haven't seen a newspaper in almost a week. I've only seen the TV."

Her question began to reveal the *real* picture to me.

"You and him. It's all anyone wants to see. They want you in handcuffs, or worse—"

"Don't say it," her breath was sharp. It caused a momentary static in my ear.

"You aren't thinking..." I murmured.

"Oh, I am. The thought has been embedded in my mind so deep since the day I met him, it is all I can think about. It is possible. That is why I called you. We have to give the people the truth. The *real* story. I know you value that. It's what you and my dad established your reputations on. If anything, Ian, do it for him. In my dad's honor."

My eyes began to glisten just from the conviction in her tone. To hear the daughter of my best friend, now twenty-three and grown up, speaking like this...gave me chills. I was proud.

"All right," I conceded, "Let's do it. In his honor."

I couldn't tell whether she was laughing or crying in reaction to me accepting her proposition.

"Good. I knew you would agree. Thank you so much. I'm glad you didn't believe the lie about him was true...and think bad about me. I'm sorry if I—"

"Don't be sorry. You're fine. I had my doubts about...*him*. The coverage is just too basic. Their story doesn't have much depth. Just a lot of bells and whistles, like I told you when we were texting, the last time we talked."

"That was the day I met him," she added. "I recognized him at a coffee shop and made my move."

"Wow! Bold move, I'd say."

"It worked," she chuckled.

"How will I get in touch with you?"

"You won't."

My forehead scrunched up from her statement. How could she

possibly have wanted me to invest my effort into this story when I couldn't even talk to the first and *only* piece of the puzzle?

"I will contact you. Find one of your tech guys and get some sort of secure line. One that I can be transferred to when I call."

"Sounds good. Well, in the meantime…what do you want me to do?"

"Find the other pieces to the puzzle."

The Garage – Hialeah, FL
23:54 10-18-2016

A warm breeze blew past. It delicately tickled my bare skin, and I was still having a hard time processing the fact that I was wearing shorts and a t-shirt. If I were back home I'd still be wearing my business slacks and pea coat. It was difficult to imagine the weather here was like this all year. What a luxury.

Briana and Grey were working tediously on the task at hand…to get me out of the country unscathed. I didn't think I had ever seen Grey this stressed in my entire life. I bet whatever his plan was, it would have been unimaginably difficult for the brightest minds to execute. Grey was brighter. I gingerly touched the faux goatee on my face. It was so weird to feel, and I wished I could have ripped it off, but I knew it was necessary.

Necessary. Necessary. Necessary. I had heard that word thrown around loosely for days now. It made me so sick to my stomach I could have puked. Briana, Grey, and Rachel all said it at one point. I knew it was true. They were right…but nonetheless, it was still nauseating.

My elbows were propped up on my knees. I was alone, sitting on the sidewalk outside of the garage. I let my head sink forward towards my lap and I used my hands to cup my forehead. My knees bowed out from the sudden weight.

Fuck necessary. I was fed up with that word. I just wanted my old life back. To be able to walk into my office and know I was making a difference in this country. If I could just hear Cole's throaty voice again or feel his heavy-handed slap on my shoulder one more time. How did my life fall apart so fast? Everything I worked so hard for had slipped through my fingers in a matter of days. It felt like I had known Rachel for over a month, but yet it had just been under a week.

My mind was awash in negativity. If only I had my bike. It would have helped so much at a time like this.

I took a deep breath, pulling the humid air into my lungs. I controlled my exhale and attempted to unwind. The phone call Rachel made to Ian had been lingering in my thoughts. Since it was through an encrypted connection on Grey's laptop, the conversation was heard by everyone. Ian said something. Something that made my soul ache. I glanced down at my watch—it was past midnight. The feeling that accompanied seeing a new day had begun only added to the melancholy that enveloped me.

Tomorrow, I would be on a non-stop flight to Moscow. *Tomorrow.*

The words were like lead in my mind. I clenched my jaw in frustration from the utter lack of control I had over my life. Ian's words hit me like a freight train in the gut. It resonated so sharply when I heard it that it was frightening…because, it was almost as if I *knew* that he was right.

Rachel had asked him what the cover stories were about recently. He said they were about us, and that *they* wanted us in handcuffs, or even worse—

Dead. Rachel cut him off before he could say it. Most likely because I was in the room. With good reason. Rachel was on the target now, but I was the bull's eye. They wanted me. I wondered. The majority of the critical injuries in the bombings were in my row, maybe I wasn't even meant to make it this far? It was a possibility. A possibility that was truer than I would have liked to acknowledge.

Russia was my only hope to stay alive.

"I was wondering where you ran off to," Rachel's velvety voice called from behind me.

I craned my head backward and saw her approaching the sidewalk. Her wavy brown hair swung around at her chest, and a smile tugged at her lips as she plopped down beside me.

"Did you need some fresh air?" she asked.

I nodded. For some reason, words didn't form. She placed a gentle hand on my forearm, with her face concerned. "Owen, what's wrong?"

"I don't want to talk about it," I managed to get out.

"What, was it what Ian said?"

I turned to her, looking her straight in the eyes.

"How did you know that?"

She snorted. "You've been down in the dumps since I got off the call. I'm not stupid."

"Is it really that obvious?"

"You haven't said a word, you haven't smiled, and you just recently disappeared."

"You're right…" I admitted.

She brushed her hair over her shoulder and scooted in closer to me. Her eyes darted across my face and a tiny breath of a laugh slid out.

"I felt it too, you know."

"What?"

"The fear."

Her words clicked in my mind. What Ian said.

"Don't worry, you'll be fine," I said, rubbing her knee. Her expression became tense. "Why did you just say me? *You* will be fine, too. We are going to get you out of this mess. I promise."

"Don't make a promise you can't keep, Rachel."

She snorted and opened her mouth to speak, but nothing came out.

"You know, you have made it this far. *We* have made it this far." Her grasp on my forearm tightened. "So don't start being a cynic now just because there is risk involved."

"My life is the ultimate risk," I interjected.

She slightly cringed from my statement, but it didn't deter her.

"I know, Owen. I do. I could die too, you never know. We could have died when we crashed into the bridge, and we didn't, okay? Briana and Grey are working their asses off up there. All to get you out of this predicament safely. So don't belittle their effort."

"Your conviction is so fucking sexy."

She slapped me and rolled her eyes. "You're terrible!"

"I know you don't mean it," I nudged her playfully and wrapped my arm around her.

"Don't be so sure," her eyebrows quirked.

"Oh! Okay, I see how it is," I laughed.

The delicate skin of her palm gave me chills as she caressed my forearm lovingly.

"I'm serious, though."

"About?" I asked.

"Owen. This plan will not work unless you truly believe it will. Grey's code could work perfectly, Briana's fake passport could get you through unnoticed…but if you don't believe it will, it won't work. You are the most important aspect of the plan. You realize that, right?"

I let her words sink in. Honestly, I was distracted by her perfect voice. Anything she said always came out smooth and silky.

"Not really," I admitted. "I've sat in the loft doing nothing while everyone else is working to get me on a plane to Russia. All I can do is sit and wait, and it's killing me, Rachel. I think the fact that I know I have no choice is what bothers me the most. I like to be able to make my own decisions."

I heard a prolonged sigh, and her breath hit my neck. Her lips were pressed, and her expression troubled. "I know you do. I understand because I am the same way. But, if you truly value that—value your *freedom*—then you know just as well as I do that if you want to keep making your own decisions, you must go. You can't stay here, at least for now."

"What if I never get to see you again?"

She reached around and grabbed my far shoulder, centering me so I faced her. I felt ashamed of my sudden pessimistic mood. I had been like this for hours and I couldn't even turn to her.

"Owen. Look at me, please."

I gave in to her request and met her gaze.

"Don't say that. We will. When all of this is over."

"How can you be so sure?"

"I can't. I don't know anything for certain, but just like I told Ian. I have a feeling that this will all work out. What I *do* know is, is that if you stay here, those chances are reduced to slim to none. Although you will be on the other side of the planet…at least I'll know you're safe."

Her tone was nurturing and warm. It was comforting to know she was beginning to care about me because I was the same with her.

"That means a lot to me. That you want me to be safe."

She rubbed my arm more as I spoke.

"I do. You didn't ask for this to happen. You didn't deserve this. You will go down in history as an American hero, mark my words."

"Hopefully while I'm still alive," I muttered.

"Stop," she demanded. "You will be fine."

I nodded in acknowledgement.

"So, today is your last full day in the United States. What do you want to do with it?"

"What do you mean? I can't do shit. We are trapped here. Our faces unfortunately prevent us from going anywhere or doing anything fun."

She bit her lower lip and her eyes darted across the pavement. Suddenly, she glanced at me. There it was—that spark behind her eyes, the passion.

"How much cash did Briana say we had left? Like thirty-five grand?"

"I think so, why?"

A mischievous smile tugged at her lips. "*We* are the only two that are wanted. Briana and Grey are fine. They can go wherever they want without a worry."

My brow furrowed and I shrugged. I had no idea where she was going with this.

"Let's spend your last night in style," she said. Her smirk blossomed into a grin.

"What do you mean?"

"Maybe Grey can get the cash onto a card and we can stay in a hotel. It beats spending your last night here in that loft. I'm already tired of the cigar smell, so I'm sure you are too. We can have fun. *You* need that more than anyone here."

I laughed. Not because what she said was funny, but because it was absolutely crazy…borderline insane. Sneaking Rachel and I into a hotel didn't seem like the smartest idea, but the realization that she was concerned with my happiness made me happier than I have been lately. I couldn't remember the last time I had *fun*. What we did in the caboose, I admit was fun, but that was sexual. It was different. I phased back into the present, and Rachel was staring at me with her lips pursed—waiting for a response.

"You are really serious, aren't you?"

"Very," she said. "The most expensive room in all of Miami. It's in the Hotel Setai. I remember reading an article about it. Top of the line."

I began to smile at the thought of it.

"Let's get the money on a card, call the hotel, and get the room for one night. We can go to the airport from there."

"What type of room?" I asked.

"The penthouse. We are going to live large your last night."

CIA Headquarters – Langley, VA
00:10 10-19-2016

I heard the sharp clacking of her heels first. The hallways here were wide, with no carpet. Everything was marble or concrete. I missed the sun. We were working twelve-hour shifts. Well, that was what we were *supposed* to work. In reality, sometimes we would be here for sixteen hours or longer. Most of us left work in the middle of the night and we would sleep all day. Only to return in the evening. The higher ups manned the daytime shifts. It must have been nice, getting to see the sun. They were much older, though. Maybe when they died off I could replace them. I felt old enough—pushing forty seemed old enough to me.

I would never, though. I couldn't continue working here. Not after I figured out what was *really* going on. They threw around the word treason, applying it to innocent people, when in actuality they were the traitors. They were figuratively shitting on the constitution and spitting on the founding fathers' graves. If only people knew. If *only*…

Now, every night when I came to work and pressed the button in the elevator to go down, ten floors below the ground, it was blatantly obvious. They *had* to keep such atrocities hidden beneath the surface. Above the surface were all the mindless sheeple who struggled to keep their heads above water in Post-Confinement America. It was madness. As a country, we were being forced into oblivion by the hands of the unknown. Doomed by corporate greed and an insatiable thirst for control, for power.

But I knew. I knew *everything*. But what could I possibly do? We took an oath before we got the job, and that was years ago for me. I also took *another* oath, back when I was a soldier defending this country. I was one of the first deployed to Iraq and Afghanistan in 2003. My oath caused a rage to build inside of me, one that I could not quell.

I, Lucas Bolden, do solemnly swear that I will support and defend the Constitution of the United States against all enemies, foreign and domestic; that I will bear true faith and allegiance to the same; and that I will obey the orders of the President of the United States and the orders of the officers appointed over me, according to regulations and the Uniform Code of Military Justice. So help me God."

All enemies—foreign *and* domestic.

The enemies I wanted to protect my country from were domestic. I had proof. I had paperwork, and it was destroying me, knowing that I was helpless. Unfortunately for my colleagues and I, these *were* the orders of the President. Diabolical ones at that.

I had wondered, where did this begin? Was it George Bush Senior? Reagan? Or as frightening as it seemed to me, perhaps it all began with the killing of JFK. Maybe the conspiracies *were* true, but I couldn't be certain. All I knew was this *had* to be stopped. Our freedom depended on it. No one dared to speak out and warn the others. They knew what was at stake.

We were given immunity, or so they told us. I didn't believe them, not a word of it. I happened to be off work when the Confinement was initiated, and somehow my house ended up on the list. My family and I were awoken in the middle of the night to flatbed military trucks outside, to escort us to the Arlington Confinement Camp—District 4.

We were there for almost two weeks before they realized their mistake. Given my employment with the CIA, I was supposed to be excluded. To be left alone, even though I lived within the twenty-mile radius. Once we were back home, it was like living in a ghost town. Everyone was gone, my neighbors, and even the schools were shut down. What were we supposed to do? Wait? My kids were afraid. They missed their friends, and they asked me questions like, *'Why did they take everyone, Daddy?'*

It devastated me not to have been able to give them an answer. I had a feeling after Black Monday something was going to happen. We collectively knew. I mean, I was in the intelligence department. Our floor was dedicated to finding things out that the higher ups needed to know. Matters of National Security, they called it.

Her footfalls were growing closer, and the heels made such an unnerving sound. The fact that *she* was the one wearing them was the problem. I was convinced that she was Satan in the female form.

I was working the night she lost her shit about the two kids at MIT who were conducting experiments on animals from the Danger Zone. We knew they had been exterminated, but we didn't know why. Seeing her reaction only heightened my curiosity to why that was so important. My wife always joked around that I must know everything. The truth was we didn't. Anything the higher ups wanted to keep secret, they did. They wanted us to do the job and do it blindly, without questions, without resistance.

We knew the truth about *this*, though. We had pieced it together. Owen Marina was framed for a crime he didn't commit. He was their sacrifice—a pawn piece in their grand plan. All so they could keep one of their parties in power. That was why they were so afraid of the Convergence Party winning. It didn't matter which of the two traditional parties won the election, both were terrorists. The only difference was that in this country, some ill-informed person might have imagined a terrorist wearing a turban. The ones that were the biggest threat actually wore suits and ties.

I was exhausted. Tired of keeping secrets bottled up that would undoubtedly change the face of America forever. How could I let that happen? I had to find a way. My phone was tapped, my wife's phone was tapped. My immediate family's phones were tapped. My home and work computers were monitored. My car had a GPS tracker in it. They had me just like they wanted me—subdued.

She entered the control room. Angrily, she tossed her sandy-brown hair to the side. She stood at the front of the room and glanced around at us with her cat-like eyes. I despised every cell in her body. It was incomprehensible to fathom what was going on in her maniacal mind. I wanted to throw up every time she spoke. More so, I would have rather put a bullet between her eyes.

"The meeting begins now," her cold voice began. "As of ten minutes ago, it has officially been five nights since Owen and Rachel's disappearance. Our methods have failed, and we must implement a higher level of strategic planning. We know they are in Florida. I want each one of you searching a different major city. Traffic cams, convenient store cams, you name it. Tap into it all. Your jobs and your families' welfares depend on it."

There she goes again. Threatening us.

"I want *anything* that is suspicious to be blown up on the big screen for me to see. Remember, this is an order from the Commander in Chief. Don't fuck around with your time."

I struggled not to scowl. I gritted my teeth and imagined myself wringing her neck in front of a crowd of thousands. The crowd would cheer in liberation once they figured out she was hell-bent on creating a totalitarian regime. I swallowed and felt sick again. She was just as guilty as Obama. She was an extension of him, and he was ensuring the continuity of a plan that began long ago.

Veronica Hall was going to be the end of this great country, and I planned on finding a way to be the mutiny.

Garage Loft – Hialeah, FL
13:43 10-19-2016

Vinny and Luke were in the garage tending to business. Judging by the constant sound of torque drills and hydraulic lifts, today was busier than what it had been. It might have had something to do with the fact that they were going to close shop early and remain closed tomorrow. We were going to the hotel in the next few hours. Briana had called and booked the presidential suite. It was the entire top floor, apparently.

Rachel and I were all alone. We were lying on the couch, and she lay on me with her back against my stomach, with her head upon my chest. She was watching some Lifetime movie that I wasn't paying much attention to. I was content just having her lie on me like this with our bodies so close and so warm. She had been playing with the palm of my hand with the tips of her nails, and it felt so amazing.

Simple pleasures. Spending time with Rachel was all I wanted to do. Every hour that passed, the one that followed seemed to slip by faster.

The closer that tomorrow grew, the tenser I felt, but I tried to keep it out of my mind.

I heard heavy pairs of footsteps coming up the loft.

"Ah, hell! Can you two get a room?" Vinny's deep, Hispanic accent was unmistakable. The footsteps that followed must have been Luke's.

"We will have one tonight," Rachel teased them. "We are just watching a movie."

"Yeah, okay. It's pretty warm in here for a blanket…"

"You're crazy, cous. I just like being cozy."

I glanced over and saw him rolling his eyes.

"Guess who is back?" Luke asked, and Rachel and I shuffled sideways so we could see the rest of the loft. Two more sets of footsteps sounded from inside the stairwell, and then a moment later I saw…Briana? Was that even *her?*

"Oh my God, Bri!" Rachel shouted in the shrillest tone possible. She sounded like she was back in high school, calling one of her friends across the dancefloor on prom night. She jumped up so quickly from the couch she almost nailed me in my nads. I had to admit, my jaw dropped from seeing Briana's transformation.

Her hair was no longer slicked back into the overly-tight ponytail she always wore it in. Her golden-blonde ringlets were bouncy and fell to her shoulders. Her makeup was done impeccably, and her skin appeared flawless, along with lipstick that went along with her mocha complexion. She wore a black dress, white pearls, and what looked to be some form of diamond-like stud earrings. Her white heels finished off the look of wealth she was portraying.

She held up her wrist and the silver from the watch gleamed in the fluorescent lights overhead.

"Michael Kors, baby!" she shouted and laughed as if she had just won the lottery.

Grey entered a few seconds after, and his face was humble—as it always was.

"Whoa, dude! Is that you?" I jumped up and roughhoused him a little bit, grabbing his shoulders and looking him up and down. "What kind of suit is this?!" It was perfectly tailored. He looked like I did the night of the debate. He could have passed as a polished politician without a problem.

"Giorgio Armani…" He mumbled, still reserved, but I couldn't stop grinning. "Bro! Where did the beard go? It's all gone!" I stroked the bottom of his chin to mess with him.

"I know, I know. It's gone."

I stepped back to get a better look at him.

"This is the real deal. Look at you, with a tie-clip and everything. Genuine stud!"

He was turning red. "Grey, you better watch out. Briana might come on to you as handsome as you look all dressed up."

I heard Briana huff. She made a duckface with quirked eyebrows and her hand on her hip. "He look good," she began in a dramatic tone, "but he *still* a white boy."

Grey rolled his eyes at all of us analyzing his looks.

"I'll take him if you don't," I went over and put my arm around him. "You're crazy," Grey said. Rachel began outright laughing.

Briana pursed her lips and shook her head with a drawn-out sigh.

"White people," she muttered and turned back to face Vinny and Luke.

I turned to face Grey. "So why did you get rid of the beard, man?"

"I had to for the picture Briana put on our licenses. We stopped by her friend's house. Plus, I need to look clean-cut for what I'm going to do tomorrow at the airport."

I nodded. "Which is?"

"I told you, man. I don't want to jinx it."

"I never remember you being superstitious."

"It's just not worth risking," he said.

"Did you say licenses a second ago? What do you mean?"

Briana must have heard me because she whipped back around and pulled out two New York State driver's licenses. "We aren't Briana and Grey anymore…" She handed them both to Rachel. "Say hello to Rose and Gregory Johansen!"

Luke almost spit out his beer.

"No fucking way," Vinny croaked. "You made yourself married? Because there isn't a chance in Hell you two are brother and sister."

We all laughed at his statement, a lot. Grey just stared at his feet.

"It's 2016," she said. "Interracial is all the rage nowadays."

We continued laughing hard.

Rachel shot her a sidelong glance. "Am I reading this right? The city is Westhampton."

"You read it right," Briana affirmed. "Greg here is the heir to a Swedish entrepreneur, and he came to America as a child, and now that his father passed, he has invested money out west in renewable energy. He is a multimillionaire, and *I* am his beloved wife he met at an outing in New York City." She walked over and tucked her arm beneath his. He couldn't help but crack a smile.

"Gregory," I chuckled. I couldn't get over Briana's creativity. When Rachel handed me their driver's licenses I was incredibly impressed. Her talent was nothing to scoff at. I was curious to see how my Swedish passport had turned out, but Briana wouldn't let me see it. She said the chemicals used underneath the laminate were photosensitive, and she didn't want to risk them spoiling before they had dried.

"What about the credit card?" I asked.

"Taken care of," Grey answered. "Loaded thirty-five thousand onto a prepaid Amex card. They won't take a second glance at it."

"Nice," I said.

"Oh," Briana began. "Here are your prepaid phones we got today." She threw the simple flip-phone in my lap and did the same to Rachel, Vinny, and Luke. "I already turned them on and put each other's numbers in there. That way there is no confusion. They all have minutes, except Owen's."

"What? Why?"

"Because you won't be able to call us from Russia, Bozo."

I nodded in understanding.

"I added all of our numbers to the contacts though, Owen. It's an international flight, I would think there are phones behind every seat."

"Good point."

"So," Rachel said. "When do we leave?"

The Setai – Miami Beach, FL
15:51 10-19-2016

We rode in a black Tahoe and had made it onto I-95 South. We were only a few exits shy of Downtown Miami. The skyline was growing larger as we neared it. Vinny and Luke were in the front seats, Briana and Grey in the row behind them, and Rachel and me in the back. We took the exit for Biscayne Boulevard and US-1. Traffic was thick. Rush hour was approaching. A taxi laid on his horn and didn't let up. The sound blared for fifteen seconds, and the car in front of him honked back and stuck his middle finger out the window. I glanced out of Rachel's window and saw a red Lamborghini beside us. I imagined my face looked like a child's would on his first vacation to a new city. Rachel noticed and let out a chuckle.

"Welcome to Miami," Rachel said.

"The city of heat," Vinny added from the driver's seat. "Makes our tempers hot, too. Can you tell?"

"Just a little," I answered sarcastically.

On US-1 South, the bay was beside us. Rachel told me it was Biscayne Bay. Palm trees lined the median in the road, and I couldn't go a minute without hearing a horn being honked. This was the definition of hectic. Ahead on our left I saw a massive bridge.

"It's the MacArthur Causeway. That's how we are going to get to Miami Beach."

"Miami Beach is on an island?" I asked.

"Yes, the whole thing is a barrier island. The home of the famous South Beach."

Within minutes, we were going over it and Biscayne Bay was below us. In the rearview I saw the skyline of Downtown Miami getting smaller. Ahead, the buildings weren't as tall, but the design was different. More whites and pastels—it had a tropical flare to it. The roads in Miami Beach were narrower, and I saw a sign for Collins Avenue. We turned onto it and I saw many boutique hotels, all in Art Deco architecture.

"Our hotel is a half-mile on the right," Luke said. "Rachel and Owen, are you ready? They will have valet, so make sure your disguises are okay."

The moment he said that Rachel began whipping her hair up into a tight bun and put a Miami Dolphins ball-cap on. She pulled out makeup, and I watched her draw on a fake mole where Marilyn Monroe had one. I used the black, blank screen of my flip-phone to see my reflection. My blond goatee was in place and my eyebrows and hair were bleach-blond. I was ready to go.

We pulled up in the registration and came to a stop. I could already see the bellman standing nearby, ready to approach us. I hadn't been out in public in days—I was nervous.

"You ready?" I whispered to Rachel.

"We got this."

Briana opened her door and Grey his. Rachel and I followed him out and were immediately enveloped in the muggy Florida warmth.

"Welcome to the Setai," the bellman greeted us in a Bahamian accent.

I nodded. I didn't say anything back. There were hundreds of cars in the road behind us, and dozens of people were walking in and out of the hotel. I was in awe of its design. The main building looked like it was straight out of the ancient Aztec. There was a large tower behind it. It had to be close to fifty floors. Vinny handed the valet attendant his keys and Briana strode towards the hotel entrance without hesitation, with Grey by her side. We lingered a good distance behind them. We had planned that because we weren't dressed at the same caliber as *Rose* and *Gregory* were. I almost laughed out loud thinking about their aliases and how they were married.

With a deep breath, I went through the revolving door and entered the lobby. The refreshingly cool air hit me, and my eyes were overwhelmed. I glanced around, not knowing what to look at first. There were palm trees in clusters of four that jutted out from the black granite marble floors. There were stained wooden beams that went all the way to the ceiling high above. Low to the ground contemporary sectionals formed squares for sitting areas. It was nothing short of luxurious.

Briana was already at the registration with Grey by her side. She wasn't waiting on us, she knew the drill. This was her expertise, and she was filling the role just as an actress would. She faked her documents, so she tried to fill the shoes accordingly. I saw a hallway with a sign for the elevators. Not knowing what to do while we waited, I walked over to them. The hallway was extremely long, and I realized we were walking into the tower with the majority of the guestrooms. I had sunglasses on, but as I stared at all the faces, I was just waiting for the moment when someone paused to take a second glance at me.

I wasn't just a criminal. I was a criminal who had been on every major news network, newspaper, and magazine. That fact made me feel so exposed. My breath started to shudder, and I tried to relax myself.

Rachel's brow creased when she reached me by the elevator and noticed my distressed state.

"Chill out, Clyde," she muttered with a smug smile tugging at her lips.

"Oh, do we have aliases now?" I chuckled.

"It just adds to the excitement, don't you think?"

I returned her mischievous glare. "You might be right, *Bonnie.*" I winked.

The elevator opened and a group of people walked out of it. There was an older couple beside us, and they were glancing over at us peculiarly when we didn't step in.

"You go ahead," the elderly lady offered with an open hand.

I couldn't even open my mouth. I tried, but nothing happened.

"We are waiting on the rest of our family. Thank you, though."

Rachel stopped the elevator door from closing and held it open with her arm.

"Thank you, ma'am," said the older man's crackled voice.

Once they were in and the elevator closed, she shook her head at me with pursed lips. "Are you really that afraid of someone noticing you?"

I glared at her in bewilderment. "Bonnie, really? Not so loud. Okay? You never know who might be listening."

"Look at you," she wrapped her arm around my waist. "You're trembling. You look nothing like your old self. Relax."

"I was still blond when you recognized me. If you could do it, so can anyone else."

She bit her lower lip and stayed quiet. My eyes began to wander. I scanned the high ceilings and the walls by the elevator—cameras.

There were *cameras* filming us. I immediately turned my head to the ground.

"What?" Rachel asked, alarmed from my sudden movement.

"Cameras," I said. "Don't look up."

She followed suit and kept her eyes towards the elevator doors. I heard a set of heels hitting the marble. Briana and Grey approached us, with Vinny and Luke trailing.

"Success," she said, and held up the black keycard.

We gathered into the elevator and Briana pressed the button for the 40th floor. The elevator didn't budge.

"It says put your key in to access the penthouse," Grey spoke up.

She slid in our room key and we pressed the button again. The elevator smoothly accelerated upwards and extremely quickly. A lot quicker than what I was used to back home in my apartment. When the doors opened, my jaw dropped.

It was gigantic. There were no other words that sufficed. The living room was easily the size of an office space, there was a full kitchen with stainless-steel appliances, and the countertops were the same black granite used on the floor of the lobby.

Gasps from Briana and Rachel filled the air. Luke and Vinny ran to the glass door that led to the terrace, but I wanted to see the rest of the suite. Rachel and I went through, room by room, and I was keeping count. There were four bedrooms total, each with their own bathroom. I knew when we had reached the master bedroom because the bathroom was the size of its own room. It had two Jacuzzi tubs, and the shower appeared to have holes coming from the ceiling.

"This is unbelievable," I mumbled. No matter which room you were in everything was floor-to-ceiling glass.

"You guys! Get your asses out here!" Vinny's scream echoed throughout the penthouse. We hurried through the many rooms, and Rachel pulled open the door first. I followed through.

The terrace was so gargantuan it was dizzying. I could have almost passed out. The view was breathtaking. In the distance was the Miami skyline. The sun was setting, and the MacArthur Causeway glowed in deep purple lights.

"Look!" Rachel shouted.

I turned to my left to see an infinity pool. It must have been over fifteen feet long. I walked around the terrace to get a feel for things and saw couches that lined the half-wall balcony. There were also sunbathing chairs in the middle between the couches and infinity pool. The Atlantic Ocean was on our left, and Downtown Miami was on our right.

"Briana, how much was this a night?"

"Thirty-two *thousand* dollars," she said. "It's the most expensive room in all of Miami. Four bedrooms, four bathrooms, and a private rooftop terrace. Ten-thousand square feet."

"It's fucking unreal," Luke said with a laugh as he sat on the couch in the corner.

She nodded, and her curls bounced around.

"Not bad for a sending off, right Owen?" she asked.

"Not bad, I'd say."

"It's time to start the party!" Vinny shouted. "I'm going to the liquor store!"

"Cheers to a safe flight tomorrow for Owen," Luke announced, raising his shot glass to meet our own.

"Cheers!" the glasses clung together as they hit.

The vodka burned my throat as it slid down, but it wasn't nearly as bad as my college days drinking cheap liquor. Vinny had bought Grey Goose and other top-shelf brands. We were partying like celebrities do, celebrating in style.

All for *me*…

Maybe a fourth shot would help numb the pain I felt. As the liquor burned my stomach, I figured I should slow down. The thought that I would be leaving my home country indefinitely tomorrow made me sick to my stomach. What were we even *celebrating?* The fact I would no longer have to run from anyone? No longer hide?

I wiped the back of my hand across my lips to dry them from the little bit of liquor that still wet the corner of my mouth. Vinny and Luke had taken out their iPods to use on the Bose surround-sound system that was installed throughout the penthouse. They were playing some rap music, and I didn't mind. Briana had gone with them on their liquor run and she bought bathing suits for Rachel and her. After our toast, she ran to the bathroom to change. She had been dying to try out the infinity pool.

I heard movement in the water and then a splash.

"Wow! It's heated, too!" Briana chirped. She swam to the far edge and propped her arms up on the ledge, looking out over the Atlantic Ocean.

We were all having fun, but I wasn't. Tomorrow was approaching and I couldn't have been more anxious about leaving. I poured myself another shot and downed it.

Hours passed. I was buzzed to the point where my situation seemed a little less dismal. I was lying on my back on one of the lounge chairs, staring into the night. Large and fluffy cumulus clouds hung low in the sky. It almost looked like I could reach up and touch them. There was only a handful of stars that I could see. Everything else was eclipsed by the city lights.

The weather had cooled down, but it was still in the low seventies. I was in a pair of board shorts, and I had been meaning to swim…but the alcohol kept me seated. Briana was inside with Vinny and Luke cooking something. They walked to a local market and bought a ton of food. I was sure I would be hungry soon too when the drunk munchies kicked in. Rachel was leaning against the railing of the far side of the terrace, just gazing out at the ocean. Her hair flowed at the edges from the steady ocean breeze. She had removed her disguise long ago and now wore a peach-colored sundress. Grey was to my right, in the opposite corner of the terrace, typing away on his laptop. I saw his ticket lying on the oversized beige ottoman that was in front of the L-shaped couch he was sitting on. He had drunk a little, but it was a sip compared to what we have drunk. He was so focused and had been for quite some time. The moment we all settled in, he began working.

I took another swig of whatever I was drinking. I had lost track. With every breath I took of the moist, warm air—reality continued crushing in around me. My rent was due next week, my bike was probably confiscated by the FBI, Alexis and the others were probably wondering if I was all right back at the office. I wondered if my dad was okay. Was he still being detained? Would I get to talk to him before I left? Probably not. His home and cell phones were almost certainly tapped. My old life felt like a memory, a dream I could revisit…but only when I closed my eyes. It was pointless for me to think of the mundane tasks that used to be a part of my routine. It was all *gone.* The Convergence Party was on a downhill slide, and I was the reason why. My dream of celebrating on election night was but a fantasy. With Cole gone, it wouldn't be the same. Nothing would *ever* be the same…

I swallowed and closed my eyes. I tried to hold back the urge to cry, and it worked. When I opened them, I saw Grey typing away. His focus and dedication to our plan was visible in his incessant efforts, and it gave me an idea. It was something I knew for certain he would be able to carry out when the time came.

Penthouse – Miami Beach, FL
22:59 10-19-2016

Owen was leaving tomorrow. I tried to hold myself steady against the railing, but my world was still spinning. Part of me just wanted to yak over the edge and laugh as it fell forty stories down. I wasn't sick from the alcohol…it was just all of this. I've had a knot in my gut since the day I met him. That was the day I realized that the only way I would be able to keep him safe was to get him out of the country before it was too late…before *they* got him.

My eyes began watering, and I inhaled deeply to stop from crying. My breath shuddered as it came out. I let out a cough, and I glanced over my shoulder to see if Grey or Owen had noticed—I hoped they hadn't. I wouldn't want Owen seeing me all choked up. He would be concerned. Was it selfish to want him to stay? Was it hypocritical that my heart ached from the realization that *my* plan was going to take place tomorrow? The only person I had to blame was myself. I created it. I was the one who took the leap of faith and approached him that day at the coffee shop. It was me. Who knows where he would have wound up if we wouldn't have met? Maybe he wouldn't have even made it out of Raleigh. I didn't know. It was grueling just imagining that tomorrow I would walk out of the airport alone. Sure, I would have my cousins, Briana, and Grey…but not *him*. Beneath his sarcastic shell was a guy that I wanted to get to know better. We had only known each other for days. Just shy of a week. Half of that time was spent planning, every word spoke and action took revolved around *my* idea.

I didn't have the heart to tell him, nor the courage to admit it. I couldn't put that burden on him. It would have been foolish to give into my desires. I was the definition of a hopeless romantic, and I knew that the words I wished to say so desperately would only hurt him. I didn't want to leave him with that. I could have just imagined him on an eleven-hour flight with those words swimming around his head. I fantasized about what his reaction would be like when I said it. What would I wear? How would it sound when the words left my lips?

Lately, I had caught myself rehearsing the moment. When I was alone, away from all of them, I would practice in front of the bathroom mirror saying those three words.

I…love…you. I love you. I *love* you.

Even in the wide array of tones I had said it in, it didn't make any difference. I was in a mental tug-of-war between my desire to say it before he left and my guilt of not wanting him to know…in light of the fact he may never see me again. My gut wrenched from the thought. My breath was shuddering with every inhale, and I tried to steady it.

Why was I getting so worked up over nothing? In reality, it didn't even matter. Regardless of if I uttered those three words or not, he would still be gone. I didn't even know if he would say it back, or if he even felt the same way. Maybe I was just another one of his flings. He could have just used me to get off that night on the train. My mother always told me I was too naïve for this dog-eat-dog world.

No—that wasn't it. That didn't sound right. I knew it was completely idiotic for me to expect anything from a man I met just days ago, but when I gazed into the depths of his turquoise-blue eyes, I *felt* something. Inside, I knew he felt it too. He asked me to be his *'Bonnie'*. He wanted me to be his partner in crime, and I had, willingly. I seized the moment from the very get-go.

I just prayed that everything worked out. I wished every night that perhaps one day we might be able to see each other again when all of this was over. Given my profession, I knew the chances were slim to none. It reminded me of the movie *Jaws*. Owen was the Great White and the town sheriff was after him. Except it wasn't just the town sheriff…it was the behemoth of an entity we referred to as the federal government.

I turned around to look at them. Owen was sitting in front of Grey, talking animatedly. He moved his hands around as if he was cooking an invisible meal, and the look on his face was intense. Although every hair on his face and head was so blond that he was unrecognizable to a stranger, I saw the same Owen. His strong jawline and wide smile—his features were so handsome, but that wasn't the only reason I stared. I couldn't turn away because I was getting a glimpse of something I had only seen a few times since I had met him. There was *passion* in his eyes, a restlessness about his body language. I tried to take a mental image of that moment. I felt as if I were looking at a ghost. Here today. Gone tomorrow.

Grey nodded multiple times to Owen, and I noticed his ticket and computer were beside him. I wondered what they were talking about…

He turned and my heart fluttered. His blue eyes were barely visible in the glow of the city lights, and he revealed a broad smile. I wondered if he could tell how flustered I became every time I saw him.

"Rachel, come here," he said.

Penthouse – Miami Beach, FL
23:47 10-19-2016

I quietly opened the terrace door and gingerly placed my bare foot on the smooth sandstone floor. It was cool against my skin. With the door fully opened, I slid out. Briana, Vinny, and Luke had drunk enough to pass out. Grey chose a room around an hour ago, and he had been in there since. Rachel was at the end of the infinity pool with her forearms propped on the ledge. Her brown hair was wet. It flowed down past her shoulders like a lion's mane. I carefully dipped my foot beneath the water and onto the first step, trying to keep silent. When my body submerged, it created a small splash, but she didn't turn around. I was almost certain she heard me. Gently, I swam over to the edge and propped my arms up beside hers. A smile tugged at the corners of her lips.

"You'll have to work a little harder next time you try to sneak up on me."

I chuckled. "Who said I was trying?

"I heard you *trying* to be quiet. Good try, though." She laughed with me.

"I'll do better next time," I said.

"There won't *be* a next time," she mumbled in a low voice. The words were practically forced out of her mouth. I turned to her, and I already felt the creases in my forehead form. I caught something in her expression…it was pain. Something was bothering her. I stopped drinking over an hour ago and had a meal. It helped me sober up a little. I had been dwelling on all the negatives. Maybe she was doing the same.

"Rachel, what's on your mind?"

I heard her choke on a cry and she rested her chin on her right arm, facing away from me. I slid off the ledge and grabbed her shoulders. I smoothly turned her body around to face mine.

"No," she resisted and pulled back. "I don't want you to see me like this."

"Like what? You are human just like the rest of us. People cry."

"But still," she sniffled.

I shook her lightly, trying to rouse her out of her reticent sadness.

"*Rachel*, what is it?"

She finally turned to me with tears streaming down her face.

"Is it wrong that I want you to *stay?*"

My gut panged from her words. I broke away from her stare and glanced down at the pool. I could see the distorted reflection of Downtown Miami in the rippling water. It felt like there was a rock in my throat as I swallowed, fighting back the tears. I couldn't let her know that I didn't want to go. We *had* to stick to her plan. We had come too far for me to stay here. Hiding wasn't the answer, it never was to begin with.

"No, it's not," I answered. "I understand."

I held her face gently with a cupped hand. Her hiccupped sobs only increased.

"Please," I pleaded. "Don't cry."

Her breath shuddered and they slightly lessened.

"I'm sorry. It was my plan, and now I can barely face that tomorrow you will be gone."

"For now," I said.

"You don't know that…"

"You're right. I don't," I admitted, "but I believe it. Our time apart is only temporary."

"I hope…"

"Rachel, I *need* you to stay strong. You're right, this was your plan. So when tomorrow comes, I want you to be ready to say goodbye. Don't you think for a second it won't hurt me too, because it scares me shitless that I'm leaving my old life behind."

"How can I be ready to say goodbye when we have barely just met?"

Her question was valid. We were at most, well-acquainted strangers.

"Well, while we still have time, what do you want to know? Ask me something."

She looked up at me.

"What is your favorite color?"

"Red," I answered. "Yours?"

"Purple," she answered softly.

"Atta girl! Representing my party, eh?"

She let out a chuckle.

"I always did like the Convergence's colors. Good choice."

"Thank you. See what we just did? We can do that until we pass out. Sleep with me tonight."

"I couldn't imagine sleeping anywhere else..."

A smile tugged at her lips, but there was still sadness hidden behind her expression. It was something I knew I couldn't fix. We were both reluctant to separate because we were just barely getting to know each other. I wanted to cherish our last little bit of time together. I wrapped my arms beneath hers and pulled her into an embrace. Our faces were inches apart. She stared up at me. Her brown eyes appeared black in the darkness, and her skin was an even richer bronze.

"You know..." I began. "The day we first met, when we were driving away from Raleigh, you told me the only reason you approached me was for the sake of the story."

"Back then, yes," she interjected. "Now, there are other forces in play."

Her eyes darted across my face, and her voice was smooth and seductive. I tightened my fingers around her back and pulled her closer to my body.

"I know, I feel them too. I can't wait to get to know you better, Rachel. You are great. I promise when this is all over we will have time—"

"Don't make me a promise you can't keep. For my sake, Owen—don't do that."

"Now you're the one telling me not to make any promises."

"I know, I said the same thing last night. I'm being a hypocrite, yes...but when we are talking about you, it's hard to make any *real* promises. Whether they are from you, or me.

"I am confident your plan will work. I'm not taking back what I said, but I need you to do me a favor."

"What might that be?"

"Please, no matter what happens…*don't* forget the reason why you approached me in the first place, that day. You knew I was framed, and you saw an opportunity to figure out the real story. You wanted the truth. Whatever happens to me, don't give up. Find out who did this and use your connection with Ian to get it out there. Like your father told you, 'Justice is like fire; if you cover it with a veil—'"

"It still burns…" She whispered, cupping my face with her hands.

"*You* are the fire, Rachel. Remember that."

She nodded with glistening eyes, and we began to kiss.

—

Avalon North Point – Cambridge, MA
06:57 10-20-2016

You almost here? I touched the screen to send the message. I paced around the living room, waiting for a response.

My phone vibrated.

Yes.

I walked over to my home phone and picked it up. With my free hand, I placed my index finger over my lips to ensure my three friends stayed quiet while I called. I knew *they* were listening. I dialed zero for the concierge.

"Front desk, this is Joseph."

"Joseph," I said in the lowest possible tone. "Let up my guest when they come in, please."

I hung up. My friends sat quietly while we waited. After a few minutes, I heard a knock at the door. I walked over to the peephole and saw my good friend, Tyler, so I opened it. He nodded and revealed an awkward smile. He must have been curious as to why I asked him to come here. I was sure the other three were wondering the same thing.

I grabbed the small remote that laid on the coffee table and pressed the on button. My surround-sound system came to life, and it was playing techno music. I turned the volume up loud. I motioned with my hand for my friends to follow me to my room. I prayed that with the noisy synths and the deep wobbles our voices would be lost in the sound.

Once in my room, I led them to the walk-in closet and opened it.

"Can we talk now?" my other friend Henry asked.

I nodded.

"You said it was urgent," Tyler said. "What's up? I have work in an hour."

"Guys, I'm being watched by the FBI."

"What?!" my other friend Evan asked over the music.

Our voices were so muffled by the music it was almost like we were reading lips.

"There's no time for questions. I just need your help. Our very freedom might depend on it."

Their eyes grew wide.

"I'll explain everything once I am able to talk about it again. Take off your jackets and leave them here at my place for a few days."

"What? Why?" Tyler pressed.

"You can keep these instead."

I began pulling my many pea coats off the hangers. I had at least five of a similar shade. One blue, one gray, and two black. I gave one to each of them, and they hesitantly began to put them on.

"We need to hurry. If they hear this music, they could be up here any minute. Traffic is thick."

"Where are they?" my other friend Richard questioned.

"Outside. They sit at that gas station across the street."

"No shit…" Tyler mumbled.

"Exactly. Put these on, let's go."

I pulled a handful of flat caps off the shelves and they fell to the floor. I picked four different shades of gray and handed them one each. They began to button up.

"Turn around," I instructed. They all four turned around in my bedroom, and each one looked identical from behind. This was all a part of the plan.

"Okay, it's time to go. When we get down to the lobby, we will go out the back exit, the one that faces the opposite side of the gas station. We will each wave down a taxi and get in."

"Where do we go?" Henry asked as we neared my apartment door.

"No specific place. In the general direction of Boston."

"Will you text us when you're safe?" Evan asked.

"Yes, but that might be a while. I think the only thing that kept me safe from texting you to come here was the fact we were all supposed to go eat breakfast together."

Once we exited my apartment, I locked the door. We began walking at a hasty pace towards the elevator. When we reached the lobby, I didn't see anyone—a good sign. We all walked side-by-side to the back entrance and made it to the street. It felt like I hadn't seen the sunshine in days.

"You guys may end up being heroes for doing this. Trust me when I say the matter really *is* that serious."

"Good luck, with whatever it is," Tyler said.

We spread a few feet apart and raised our hands to signal the taxis. Within a minute, we had each flagged one down.

"Thanks. I know most of you work in Boston, so at a certain point just tell the driver where you *really* need to go."

They all nodded.

I sat down in the back seat of the cab.

"Where to, boss?" the driver asked.

"The Greyhound station off of Atlantic. Step on it."

I glanced down at my watch—it was 7:05. I had twenty-five minutes to make it to the station. Hopefully, the FBI wouldn't follow…and if they did, I prayed they lost me in the mix of traffic.

610 5th Ave – New York, NY
12:17 10-20-2016

I had made it. Wherever the FBI was, they weren't nearby. The weather differed very little from what it was like back in Boston. The air was dry and crisp. My breath fumed out trails of moisture with every exhale. The sidewalks of Fifth Avenue were full of people, and a horn honked every other second. All the memories rushed back to me.

Sometimes it was hard to imagine that I actually grew up here. Most people dreamed of living in New York, but by the time I went to college I was more than ready to get out. Far too hectic for me. Boston was similar, but the size difference was of no comparison. Eight *million* people. It always amazed me to think of that many people in one city.

I climbed up the stone steps of the post office and inside. It was massive. There were dozens more here in Manhattan. This one almost looked like a courthouse in its design. The ceilings were high and the floors were marble. I walked toward one of the attendants. She was an older lady of African descent, and her hair was speckled with gray. She revealed a small smile.

"How can I help you today?"

"I need to access my P.O. Box," I replied, jingling the gold key in the air.

"Sure thing, right this way. Push the door open when you hear the buzzer."

I went around the corner to a metal door. I heard the buzz and pushed it open. Walking towards the far end of the hallway, I began to feel anxious. Emily was a perfectionist, and she was trustworthy. In the lab, when the FBI agents slammed us against the lab station, I confirmed with her if she had done what I asked. She nodded yes. I was so worried. Maybe the feds were getting stricter on the mail. What if they intercepted it?

I scanned the numbers engraved on the metal boxes as I passed. It had been over two years since I sent something here. Living four hours away, it was pretty useless. I was glad having the spare key came in handy in a situation like this. The reason I had to go through the locked door was because of how large these PO boxes were, and if I recalled correctly, his was the biggest one they had. Passing the eight-thousands, I found it.

PO Box 9000. I exhaled slowly to ease my stress, and I closed my eyes as I stuck the key inside and turned it. When I pulled the door ajar, I opened my eyes.

There it was. I gasped and a shuddered laugh slipped out. I glanced around to check if anyone heard me. The last thing I wanted was to draw attention to myself. It was a one-by-one box, and I knew what was inside. Our data and an extra sample.

I carefully slid it out of the PO box and held it in my hands. There was an envelope stuck to the top, and I ripped it off, setting the box down momentarily to read it. I tore the envelope and pulled out the letter.

You're welcome…

Get to your dad.

♥ — *Em*

She signed her name *Em*. I cracked a smile at the thought. She always insisted that I call her Emily. Maybe she was warming up to me saying it. I shoved the letter in my jacket pocket and hoisted the box in my arms. With my free hand, I locked the PO box and exited the building. I felt a rush of energy surging through my body. My pulse quickened. I wasn't in handcuffs. I didn't see the black Denali anywhere in traffic, and I had the data I needed in my hands. Their lie couldn't hold up forever. The country needed to know the *truth* about Black Monday.

"Taxi!" I shouted. One pulled up in front of me in seconds. I sat inside and set my box of evidence beside me. "Where to?" the driver asked, looking at me in the rearview.

"Corner of 8th and 41st."

Fifteen blocks. When I stood up out of the taxi, I leaned back, staring up at the forty-story skyscraper that towered above me. On one of the buildings to the right, there were two huge posters that hung off of the roof with Owen's and Rachel's faces on them. At the top in bold, black letters was the word **WANTED**. I paused for a moment, staring at Rachel's face. She looked familiar...*too* familiar...and I couldn't figure out why. I had never seen her a day in my life, but for some reason it felt like I knew her at one point. Interesting.

With my box tightly grasped in my hands, I strode up the steps and into the revolving door. The warmth surrounded me as I made it inside. I didn't stop at reception, I didn't ask where I needed to go...because I already knew.

The stainless steel elevator doors opened, and once inside I pushed the button for the 37th floor. My stomach momentarily dropped as the elevator sped up. I used to run all around this building when I was a kid. I knew it like the back of my hand. When it opened, I was in front of a massive office space. A hundred people plus were all in their cubicles typing away or on their phones. I maneuvered through the maze of cubicles towards my dad's office. When I reached the corner of the room, I saw his door was closed. I was so tempted just to pull it open and barge in, but who knows who could have been in there. Reluctantly, I turned to the left to face my dad's assistant. She peered through her glasses that balanced at the very tip of her nose, and she glanced at my box, questionable as to why I was even here.

"Hi, Stefan."

"Hello, Sharon," I said.

"What can I help you with today?"

"I need to see my dad."

She pushed the glasses up the bridge of her nose.

"Do you have an appointment?"

There it was. That fucking word I had heard my entire young-adult life—*appointment.* I bit my lower lip to keep myself from flipping out on her. Normally, I did whatever she said, but today…today was different.

"Look, is anyone in his office or not? I am running out of time. It can't wait."

"Well, you know how he is…"

I turned and grabbed the doorknob.

"Stefan, just wait!" she called from behind me.

I pushed it open to see my dad sitting in his office chair with a pen and paper in his hands. His forehead creased in confusion.

"Stefan, what are you doing here?"

Sharon popped her head through the crack in the door. Her blonde hair was so big you could barely see her face. Someone needed to tell her that she should have left Aqua Net back in the eighties where it belonged.

"I'm sorry, Ian. I tried," she said.

"Don't worry about it. Close the door, please."

I sighed with relief. He must have been in a good mood today. I slid out a seat and did the same to another to set my box down. Now that I was closer, it appeared as if my father had aged a little more since the last time I had seen him, which was only a few months ago. It was a shame he hadn't retired yet. He had enough money to last him a few lifetimes over. I'd watched it since I was a child. Of course, the progression of aging went conjointly with time, but with everything my dad had seen, it sped the process up. Sometimes I wished he would just leave his position and give it to someone else, but I knew he dreaded the thought of retiring. He had been in this position for almost twenty years and with the company for well over thirty.

"Son, what are you doing here? Are you okay?"

His question had a complex answer.

"Uh, I'm okay, for now."

"What do you mean, *for now?*" he shot me an accusing glare.

"I don't have much time to explain."

He glanced down at his watch. "I have plenty. So you better get to it."

"You have no idea how hard it was to get this here," I informed him. My voice was shaky, and I began opening up the box. I handed him the manila envelope filled with data.

"What is this?" he asked. "I am so lost. You didn't even text me to tell me you were coming."

"There are reasons behind everything I did. It was all carefully planned to get that folder in your hands."

He opened it and began flipping through the different papers and diagrams.

"Whose research is this?"

"Mine," I answered flatly.

His eyes met mine and his expression was alarmed. He continued flipping through, and then I watched his eyes grow wide.

"Is this…is this what I *think* it is?"

"Yes," I said. "It's proof."

His mouth hung open and almost all the papers were spread out on his desk.

"*You* did this research?"

"Yes, Dad. Well, I had the help of one of my colleagues, too."

"Cats from the Danger Zone. Who would have thought you'd be lucky enough to find not one, but two, that were still alive? Does your professor know you were conducting these experiments?"

"So, yeah, when you asked me if I was okay, that's the reason I said '*for now*'…"

He gave me an accusing glare that only a worried parent could produce.

"Please, don't tell me you're in any kind of trouble."

"Like I said, *for now,* I'm okay. My ex-girlfriend who works at the EPA squealed on us about the experiments we were conducting."

"You had a girlfriend recently? Why didn't you introduce me to her?"

"It was a short-term thing. If I didn't have to make an appointment to see my own father, maybe I would have, but that's a whole other conversation."

He sighed and pressed his lips together. I thought I caught guilt in his expression.

"I have a cell phone, you know."

"That you rarely answer," I added.

He huffed. "For Christ's sake, Stefan! Call the office if you want to talk."

"It's all right. I know you're busy."

"So, what happened when she squealed? And to whom did she rat you out?"

"The FBI."

He dropped his pen on his desk. I thought his eyes were going to pop out.

"Please, please tell me you're joking."

"Unfortunately, I'm not, Dad. That is why I'm here."

"Have you been followed?!" his tone of voice jumped around in fright.

"Not that I know of. I escaped in an intelligent way."

"Escaped?!" I thought he was going to turn blue in the face. "From where?!"

"I guess I used the wrong wording. My apartment was being watched by an FBI agent. I used four friends and dressed them in the same thing I was wearing. We left and took taxis all in the same direction."

"Did you not think twice about the fact that they might assume you would come here first?"

"Of course, Dad. I'm not stupid, but I *had* to get you this. If I didn't get you this information all of my research would have been in vain. The day before we got busted, my colleague Emily sent the research, along with a sample, to your PO box."

He was still fuming. Angry and confused…but as my words settled in, I saw a smug smile begin to emerge.

"That's a pretty damn good plan, actually," he admitted.

"Hey, I guess you taught me a thing or two, old man."

"Smartass," he mumbled and let out a throaty laugh.

"Dad, in all seriousness, what do you think?"

He glanced down at all the papers in front of him and shuffled through them again before looking back up at me.

"I think you have irrefutable evidence of something the government has used all of their effort to keep under wraps. I'm impressed, Son."

I tried to suppress my growing smile, but I couldn't. A sweltering warmth flushed throughout my body, and I felt proud. No matter what I did, I always was in my father's shadow. I remembered career day in elementary school. Some of my classmates' parents were cops, doctors, and firefighters. When my dad came in, it was like a free-for-all. Editor in Chief of the New York Times. The kids would surround him and ask questions. I was always left in the background. They looked up to him like he was the President or something. My classmates knew the neighborhood I lived in. Some people in this city grew up dirt poor, they had nothing. As odd as it sounded, sometimes I wished I had less. I dreaded my birthdays. My friends would pay more attention to my massive house than me. Just like that. Always in the shadows…

I was never good with words like my dad. Science was the language in which I was most fluent. Now, maybe I could be in his spotlight.

"Thanks, Dad. I tried to be thorough. I even brought one of the samples." I tapped on the box beside me.

"Seriously?"

"Yes. Everything Emily and I worked for is in this box. I came here on the Greyhound. I left my phone at home—everything. They told me if I spoke to you or our lawyer that I would be locked up indefinitely and charged with treason. They threatened to take away my citizenship."

His forehead creased and his eyes turned angry.

"Those fucking cowards," he growled.

"I know. I'm still pissed about the whole thing. I was just doing independent research. It only affirms the fact that they are trying to cover up a lie."

He rubbed his forehead and let out a long exhale. He stood up and walked to the edge of his office, looking down at the city streets below.

"*Find the other pieces to the puzzle…*" He muttered under his breath.

"What did you just say?" I asked.

"Find the other pieces to the puzzle," he repeated.

"What puzzle?"

"Their lie. That's the puzzle. Rachel was right. It's not just *one* lie—it's a string of lies. They have spread themselves too thin because the lies are not just in one place."

"Yeah, and my lie was the first one. The radioactive material found on Black Monday was not Strontium. It was something else. Russia wasn't involved. *They* did it."

My dad began pacing around his office. His hand was covering his mouth.

"Wait, did you just say Rachel? Rachel who?"

He turned to me and approached his desk.

"Rachel Flores. The one on that gigantic banner hanging from the building next door."

"Why would you talk to her? How do you even know her?"

His forehead creased and his jaw dropped.

"Stefan, do you not remember her?"

"Hell no! Why would I remember her? I've never met her!"

"My God. I shouldn't have kept you two apart for so long. She was just so far away."

The image of her face on the banner reappeared in my mind. Her dark-brown hair and eyes, her tan skin and youthful complexion.

"When I saw the banner…" I mumbled. "She looked familiar."

My dad snorted and began his pacing again.

"Oh, she's familiar all right. She's my goddaughter. You met her once, as a child."

"What?!" I shouted. "You're joking, right?"

"No, Son, I'm not. Do you remember the photographs on the mantle at our house?"

"Yes. If they haven't changed, then yes."

"Do you remember the one of the Hispanic guy in the suit holding a little girl in his arms outside of this very building?"

I tried to recall the image…and it worked. It was blurry in my head.

"Vaguely," I admitted.

"That's Emilio," he said, and turned around a picture on his desk to face me. "Emilio, my best friend who died when you were just a child. Rachel is his daughter. That banner outside is her, she's just grown up."

A chill raced up my spine as I realized the connection. A memory began to fade in. I was swinging in a park, and beside me was a little, dark-headed girl swinging along with me.

"Why didn't you talk about Rachel like you did Emilio? Why keep her from me? I was the youngest of three brothers, Dad, and I always wanted a sister."

"I know you did, Stefan. I am sorry. She lived in Miami with her mother at the time. You had school, she had school. You grew up fourteen hundred miles apart. I thought it would be easier on you both. I only saw her for birthdays and other special occasions. She did grow up without her father, you know."

I almost felt insulted. Like I had missed out on something, perhaps a friendship, or a bond I could have had. I realized, though, he was right. It would have complicated things.

"When did I meet her?" I asked.

"Remember that vacation we took when you were eight?"

"To Miami, then Disneyworld..." I mumbled. "Yes," he replied. "We flew to Miami first to visit her and her mother. We spent a few days there, but you and Rachel liked playing in the city park the most."

"I remember," I said. I accepted knowing someone I had no idea about. It didn't feel right, but it was the truth.

"She called me here, the other day," he said.

"What did she have to say?"

"Exactly what I told you. She wanted me to find the other pieces of the puzzle, of the lie. She is with Owen. Her line was secure, but she couldn't tell me anything else, just in case anybody was listening to my office lines."

My dad glanced down at his watch and paced around the perimeter of his office. He seemed to be searching the streets below.

"You can't stay here," he announced. "You have to leave, soon."

"Seriously?!"

"Son, you were the one who told me the FBI threatened you. If you stay here, it will risk all of this." He walked over and grabbed my box of information.

"I don't even know when the next bus leaves back to Boston."

"That doesn't matter," he said. I saw sweat beading on his forehead. "My driver will take you back to Boston. It will be safer, and a lot quicker."

"Dad, you realize I've already fucked up by coming here, right? They could be barging into your office door any second. They are smart enough to know I would come here."

"That's exactly my point!" he gasped, rubbing his forehead.

"What are you going to do with my data? How will you keep everything safe? Do you know when you will talk to Rachel next?"

"No, I've secured a line for her when she calls, but I don't know when that will be. I have people. Intelligent people. People who could put up walls high enough to keep them out…but for now, you must leave. Get up, Son."

I stood up out of the office chair with my mouth agape. What a quick visit.

"But Dad, I want to be with you when you're figuring all of this out. I can't even go within one mile of the campus. I am trapped up there. They didn't say I couldn't come visit you…"

He paused as if he was contemplating something.

"Do you still have the keys to the house?"

"Of course," I answered.

"Okay, my driver will take you there."

"Can't I stay a little longer? So we can discuss the plan?" I knew how dumb my question sounded when it came out.

"*They* could be listening, you know that."

"I know…" I mumbled.

He ushered me to his door and pulled my shoulder back before I could grab the door handle.

"Stefan, you've done your part. You are one of the pieces of the puzzle that Rachel spoke of. If they come to the house, play dumb. I will do the same if they come here. I doubt they will."

"How can you be so sure?"

He laughed. "Think about it. If they shut down the biggest newspaper in the country, people would know something is wrong. They most likely don't want to draw any attention to what they are doing before the election. They would want everything to remain transparent. If they take me, I will shut everything down, and I will make sure they are aware of that."

"Damn, good fucking point," I admitted.

"Watch that sailor's mouth of yours," he said with a chuckle.

"Like father like son," I said, smugly.

"I have to say, excellent job, Stefan. I am proud of you. With your evidence, this thing may actually have a shot at being a real story. Now we just have to wait."

"For what?"

"For Rachel's phone call."

Miami Int'l Airport – Miami, FL
14:38 10-20-2016

This was it. *Today* was the day. We pulled up to the departures drop-off and the car stopped. My stomach dropped as it did so.

"Well, Owen. It's been a pleasure having you…and hiding you. Yeah, that's a little more accurate," Vinny chuckled. I snorted at his humor but appreciated the sentiment.

"Thank you, both of you. I mean it."

"Anytime, man. Rachel is *familia*. You came with her, so you are *familia* too," Luke said.

Rachel and I were in the third row of the Tahoe, and Briana and Grey were in front of us. Briana grabbed the handle to the door and craned backward to face us.

"Let's go over the plan one more time," she said. "I want to hear you say it."

No one answered.

"Owen is going to go through TSA and board his flight. Grey is going to do what he needs to do, whatever that may be, and I am going to wait outside for him. When he comes out, we will get a cab back to the location Vinny has chosen," Rachel spoke up.

Briana nodded. "Good, now let's get the show on the road." She popped the door open and held it there like she was our chauffeur. Grey got out first, then Rachel was next. I shook the open hands of Vinny and Luke. They were saying goodbye…

"You'll fit in in Russia just fine, *gringo*," Vinny said with a grin.

"I know man, I'm white as hell," I laughed. Their throaty guffaws filled the air.

"You got that right!" Luke added. "Take care, man. Be safe out there."

"I'll try."

"We'll take care of Rachel, don't you worry," Vinny said.

They better…

I stepped out of the Tahoe. Immediately, I was swathed in the Florida heat and humidity. I was wearing a pair of khaki pants and a polo t-shirt. Although it was almost eighty degrees, my final destination was Moscow. I assumed that Russia in late October wouldn't have been the most pleasant weather.

Briana looked me up and down. "You look like a Swede if I've ever seen one." She pulled a clutch bag out of her purse and popped it open. From out of it she pulled a small, red booklet. On the bottom left corner were the words, *Europeiska Unionen Sverige.* I touched the edge of the book.

"Don't open it," she placed her hand on mine. "It's photosensitive, remember? Don't want to risk it not working when you're this close to boarding."

"Got it," I said. Her onyx-colored eyes scanned me up and down, and she revealed an affectionate smile.

"I know we haven't known each other long, but…I'll miss you, Owen."

"You too, Briana. Please, don't let anything happen to Rachel," I whispered.

She nodded firmly. "I would never." We gave each other a quick hug and she stepped to the side. Behind her was Grey, and he was still in his fancy button-up from last night at the hotel. His eyes sank as they met mine. He was always some version of reserved. Seeing him stand there before me made me emotional. I quickly pushed those feelings deep inside so that they wouldn't surface. Grey was the only reason we had even made it this far. He was the first person to go out on a limb for me. Everything else that followed was secondary. If he wouldn't have stolen the money and helped me rob the bank, I wouldn't have met Rachel. I wouldn't be leaving the country…and I would most likely be in handcuffs, or worse, dead.

"I hate that I have to leave, man..." I mumbled as I approached him. He could barely look me in the eyes.

"I know, dude. It's rough."

"Grey, come on man. What's wrong? Are you all right?"

"Yeah, just anxious to get this over with."

It hit me what he was referring to. His plan—everything he had worked so hard for.

"Do you think it will work?"

He finally glanced up at me, and there was a smugness behind his eyes.

"Yes," he muttered.

"Okay. Bring it in, brother," I said and embraced him in a bear hug. "I love you, man. Thank you for everything."

"Love you too, man."

When I released him, Rachel was standing a few feet ahead of us. Briana handed me my carry-on bag, and I had a brand new backpack on. She had gone shopping for some warm clothes and belongings I would need.

"Are you not going to say goodbye?" I joked with Rachel as I reached her.

"I'm going to walk you in," she said.

There was an uneasiness about her disposition. Her face wasn't glowing, and she seemed extremely nervous. I knew the feeling.

A plane was taking off overhead, and the loud drone of the turbines caught me off guard. The thought that I would be onboard in less than thirty minutes scared the living shit out of me. I had to go, but I wasn't ready. I would *never* have been ready.

The automatic doors slid open, and the chill of the ice-cold AC hit me. Inside, the airport was bustling—hundreds of people walking in either direction. My steps were measured, and I felt myself begin to tremble. Rachel grasped my hand and interlaced her fingers with mine.

"Relax," she restrained the volume of her voice.

I nodded nervously. I reached into my right pocket and unfolded my boarding pass.

Gate 31 – Terminal A

I glanced up and saw a few hundred feet away was the TSA checkpoint. Rachel tugged at my hand and ushered me forward. I was wearing sunglasses, just as I had at the hotel, but I was nonetheless petrified to approach the agents. I wondered if there was still a bounty out for my capture. Back in Raleigh, Larry had said it was fifty-thousand. What was it up to now?

My stomach was in knots. As we neared closer, I stopped and turned around to say my goodbyes to Rachel.

Miami Int'l Airport – Miami, FL
14:45 10-20-2016

I squeezed his hand as he stood there in front of me. I wanted to hold onto the sensation of his touch, his skin…

"So…" He mumbled.

Don't cry. Don't cry, Rachel. Hold it together.

"So," I managed to get out.

He revealed a halfhearted smile, with teeth so white they gleamed in the sunlight that poured in from the floor-to-ceiling glass.

"I'm sorry we didn't have more time together, Rachel…and I'm sorry we didn't meet under better circumstances."

I thought I was going to lose it.

"If it weren't for those circumstances, we wouldn't have met."

He shrugged. "You're right."

I looked him up and down, trying to soak in this moment, to remember every little detail. It was killing me, knowing that I had no idea when I would see him again. I kept adjusting my fingers that were interlaced with his, caressing them gently. His skin was warm and rougher than mine. I dreaded the moment we separated. The moment I had to walk out of here *alone.*

"Are you ready?" the words awkwardly slipped out. I wanted to smack myself for asking that question. Would he think I was trying to rush him? Ugh.

"Ready as I'll ever be," he chuckled.

I let go of his hand and reached into my purse. I scrambled around until I found it.

"I have something for you," I said.

"What may that be?" he asked.

"It's nothing big, really. Open your hand." He opened his hand. I placed a pack of gum in his palm. "You know, for when your ears start to pop."

He smiled warmly and put it in his pocket.

"That will come in handy I'm sure. Thank you. Not just for this, though. For everything."

Oh God. Don't get emotional.

"It's no problem. It was an honor, really, to get to hear your story and to meet you."

He let out a laugh and shook his head side to side.

"You didn't seem so star-struck when we first met."

"I hid it well," I admitted, blushing.

"**Transaero flight 887 to Moscow is now boarding at Gate 31. Last call for boarding in thirty minutes.**"

My stomach sank as the intercom faded out.

The planes of his face hardened. I could feel his breath as he let out a long exhale.

"Damn," he muttered. "So I guess this is it."

I swallowed and nodded. I knew what I wanted to say, but I couldn't find the words. They were stuck in my throat.

"Whatever happens, Rachel, remember what I said last night. Don't forget the reason why you approached me in the first place. Get your story and get it out there. It will all work out like you said to Ian. The other pieces are out there. You just have to find them."

I shook my head yes, and I felt my eyes beginning to glisten.

"I will. I promise."

Rachel—the paper. Don't forget the paper.

"Shit…" I mumbled and scrambled around my pockets to find it.

"What?"

"Here," I pushed it towards him.

"What is it?"

"It's my office number back in Raleigh, my email, my address. Maybe, if I don't end up in a jail cell when all this is over—you can find a way to contact me."

"Of course," he said, and put the paper in his wallet. "We will see each other again."

I nodded, struggling to hold back the tears. He wrapped his arms around me and pulled me against him.

"Well, Bonnie, it's been one hell of an adventure. Until next time…" He leaned in, and his eyes darted across my face. We met lips and he tightened his grasp around my waist as we kissed. He didn't break away, and part of me wanted to stay in that moment forever.

He broke away, and I lovingly gazed back into his blue eyes.

"Until next time, Clyde."

Our hands slipped apart, and he nodded, revealing a gentle smile. Part of me was gone when he turned away. He took a piece of my heart as he left. I would never be the same. I had fallen in love with the idea of him, because I knew from the beginning he was temporary. Now, as he walked farther away, I wished I could have had the strength, the courage, to push the words out.

"I love you."

He didn't hear me. He didn't turn back. He was *gone.*

Miami Int'l Airport – Miami, FL
14:59 10-20-2016

I wondered if she knew how hard it was for me to walk away from her. I was miserable inside. Having to say goodbye to the realest woman I'd met since I was with Megan was torturous. We didn't have time…

As I approached the TSA checkpoint, I took a deep breath.

Stay Calm. Everything will be fine.

I fell in line between a woman and a man. Every second that passed, we got closer and closer.

"Shoes off and in the basket, please," the agent announced in an assertive tone.

I slipped off my boat shoes and placed them in the basket.

"I always hate doing this," the older woman mumbled to me with a smile. I returned it, awkwardly. "Me too." I didn't want to draw attention to myself by not answering. What was I getting myself into? I took my cheap pre-paid phone out of my pocket and placed it in the basket also. I slung my carry-on bag on the rollers and watched it disappear into the scanner. I didn't have many belongings that would set off the metal detector. Nervously, I followed the lady through the detector, and nothing went off.

Thank God.

We put our shoes back on, retrieved our belongings, and at the end of the line was another agent who sat at a podium. He was checking everybody's IDs. My stomach trembled at the thought of it. I felt around my pocket for my passport and pulled it out. My clenched hand was beginning to sweat on the hard cover of the passport. *Relax.*

"Thank you very much," the lady said to the man as he handed back her identification.

"Good afternoon, sir," the agent's deep voice echoed.

"Good afternoon," I replied. *Don't act nervous. Act natural. Stay calm.*

"Boarding pass and passport, please."

I handed them to him quickly, in hopes that he wouldn't notice my shakiness. He flipped it open and waved a light over the inside. Then, he glanced up at me.

Fuck. He knows who I am.

He stamped the inside of my passport, still staring at me sternly.

"Have a good day, Mr. Arregan. Your gate is down the hall and around the corner to the left. You better hurry up."

"Thank you."

I left the checkpoint and didn't turn back. I was so thankful I had made it through. Now, the hardest part was behind me and I could board my plane. I listened to his advice and hurried through the terminal. I saw a sign for Gates 30-40 at the corner and took a left and saw Gate 31. I maneuvered around the people walking in the opposite direction of me and saw the gate had very few people left to board.

"**Transaero flight 887 to Moscow, last call for boarding at Gate 31. Last call for boarding.**"

The intercom shut off right as I made it to the gate. I was breathing heavily and handed the lady my boarding pass. She ripped it in half and handed the other back to me.

"Enjoy your flight, sir."

"Thank you," I said and walked up the long, inclined slope that led into the cabin of the plane. The plane was already full. There were only a few open seats left. I glanced at my boarding pass. Seat 25D. I had an aisle seat. *Why would Grey choose an aisle seat? I'm trying to hide.* Maybe it was the only seat left. I heard the crackly cough of the lady beside me, and I glanced over at her as I sat down.

"Excuse me," she said as she covered her mouth and coughed again. Her smile was sweet, and her thin white hair was evidence of her old age. She smelled of baby powder and a hint of overly strong perfume. White Diamonds most likely. It always floored me how it seemed to be the quintessential perfume for older women, and it smelled God awful.

"We've got a long flight ahead of us, don't we? I guess I should at least introduce myself since we will be sitting together for the next eleven hours," she chuckled and placed her bulky purse beneath her legs in front of her seat.

No, you don't have to. I don't even know my first name for crying out loud.

"I'm Millie, pleasure to meet you."

Fuck. Fuck. Fuck! Think of a Swedish name…

"Milo," I replied in an accent. "Nice to meet you, Millie."

Milo?! What the fuck was I thinking? Millie. Milo and Otis? I'm not a damn cat.

"Milo, huh?" she gently touched my arm. I tried to smile and not react. Was Grannie Millie trying to flirt with me? Please, dear God, no. "You're not from the States, are you?"

I nodded no. "I'm from Sweden."

"Oh, how nice," she patted my forearm like I was a house cat. "I should have known by the hair!" she chuckled. I smiled and nodded awkwardly.

"So, what is bringing you to Moscow?" she asked, keeping the conversation going.

If only you knew…

"Visiting my sister. She lives in Moscow with her husband and two sons. I was here on business," I answered in my accent. Perhaps Briana had rubbed off on me. I was pulling this information out of my ass and it was working just fine.

"Well, aren't you a busy-body!" she chuckled. "I bet you enjoyed the weather down here."

"Yes," I said. "Very nice."

"I'm going to visit Moscow and the Baltics. After Russia is Estonia, Latvia, and Lithuania. My granddaughter is an exchange student in Berlin, and she is meeting us there for her fall break. This is my daughter, Pamela."

A blonde woman with blue eyes popped her head out from behind Millie.

Fuck. My. Life. Her whole family is probably in the row behind us, and I will have to meet them too. Just my luck.

"Hi!" she extended her hand out to shake mine. "Pamela, nice to meet you."

"Milo," I said. "Nice to meet you. You and your mother are very friendly."

Too friendly…

"The apple doesn't fall far from the tree," she laughed. "I promise, we won't bother you the whole time."

I'm sure…

"Oh, no worries. It's a long flight. Good to be around such nice people." I was praying that my accent hadn't slipped. Millie was still grinning for no reason, but her daughter suddenly looked at me *differently*. Her smile diminished and was replaced with pursed lips. Her eyes darted over me like she was trying to analyze something. My heart sped up, and my instinct was to turn away, but I couldn't be that obvious.

"Yes," she began with the tiniest hint of nervousness in her voice. "It is. If my mom starts to snore, just tell me and I'll wake her up."

Great. She snores.

I laughed. "It's fine," I said and turned back to face the seat in front of me. The way Pamela looked at me was still in the forefront of my mind. It was almost like she *knew* who I was. I let out a long exhale. I couldn't worry about that now. We were all seated, and I had made it. There was nothing to worry about anymore. Even if she *thought* it was me, what could she do at this point? Maybe her Chatty Cathy of a mother would keep her occupied.

"**Attention, passengers. My name is Eddie Larkins, and I am your Captain. We are third in line for takeoff. Everything is on schedule, and we should arrive at 10 a.m. Moscow time. Please listen to the flight attendants for further instructions.**"

The intercom switched off. I glanced down at my watch—it was just shy of three o'clock. If my math was right, Moscow was seven hours ahead of us. I shook my head at the time gap. I would most likely be exhausted tomorrow, especially with Millie sitting next to me. We had detached from the jet bridge. This was it. In a few minutes, we would be over the Atlantic Ocean.

I saw the flat, tan-colored phone attached to the back of the seat in front of me. I felt the hard plastic of the pre-paid phone in my pocket, and I knew Rachel's number was programmed in there.

Part of me wanted to call, just so I could tell her that I loved her.

Miami Int'l Airport – Miami, FL
15:10 10-20-2016

I nervously tapped my foot against the concrete. I wiped a line of sweat off my brow. The heat was getting to me, but I knew it couldn't be too much longer. I stared at the ticket in my hand and realized for the hundredth time that the success of this plan was entirely in my hands. I steadied my exhale in an attempt to calm myself down. I had to keep focused.

There was a nonstop ruckus around me. The shuttlebuses coming and going. Taxis honking their horns and people being dropped off by their family members. Hundreds of people around me, but I had quieted my mind. It *had* to be quiet, because we couldn't fail.

I couldn't fail. Where in the world was she? I hoped everything was all right.

"Hey," Rachel's voice comforted my worry as she sat down next to me. Her eyes were sullen and she looked like she had just watched something tragic. She didn't look like her normal, happy self. Perhaps, she really *was* attached to Owen.

"Did he make it through?"

"I think so," she nodded.

The knot in my gut lessened. Owen making it through TSA was half the battle. The other half was mine.

"Good. Briana will be happy to hear that her passport worked. Do you think they made it to the safe spot yet?"

"It's only fifteen minutes away. They should be arriving there any minute. My cousins know what to do, their jobs are done. You can get the money Owen promised Briana and my cousins, right?"

"Of course I can," I answered.

"Okay, I'll wait for you here," she said, adjusting her Dolphins cap she wore yesterday. "Good luck, Grey."

"Thank you. Keep your head down and don't look anyone in the eye."

"I know," she nodded.

I glanced down at my watch. It was 3:15.

"It's 3:15. If I don't come out in thirty minutes, assume I have been caught and get the hell out of here. Save yourself."

"What?! Grey, don't talk like that. You will be fine. Everything will work out."

Her confidence in my abilities helped ease my anxiety, but my request was firm. She had to adhere to it because I knew what the consequences would be if she was caught. Owen wouldn't want that.

"I know, but still. I'm leaving now. If I don't come back by 3:45, leave without me. I will get my own cab. I'll call you and get the address. It's for your own safety, trust me."

She blinked, and her big brown eyes showed uncertainty, but she nodded anyway.

"Okay. See you soon."

"Yes, twenty-nine minutes from now," I said and walked into the terminal. The AC hit me like an icy breeze and it was relieving from the heat outside. My pulse quickened and I headed for the ticket kiosks. I turned instinctually. I knew this airport like the back of my hand.

I was still wearing the Armani suit I wore last night, and I thought it was fitting. I looked just like any other businessman. Except, I didn't have a briefcase. Just a ticket, a flash drive, and a plastic baggy in my left pocket that contained a crucial element of my plan. Every person I passed created wind that made my ticket crinkle and flap around in my hand. The code I constructed was delicate, and I hoped it wouldn't mess it up. I was surprised the CIA hadn't swarmed the building yet. *Someone* had to have been watching.

I found an open ticket kiosk and sat down. I let out a shuddering exhale and tried to balance my breath before I did the deed. My ticket wasn't even a ticket, really. It was similar to a QR code, which would be scanned by the machine and print out my boarding pass. *But*, I designed my ticket to execute an SQL injection. It would never print out a ticket, just execute an action within the system, instead of query my flight information in the database.

My eyes scanned over the tiny black lines and squares that comprised the code, and I nervously pressed the button on the touch-screen that said **Scan Confirmation Code**.

I stuck the paper in the scanner. I heard a beep, and nothing happened. *Nothing*.

That was what I wanted, though. I wanted it to appear like nothing had happened to their system on the outside and to all the passengers. The beep made me tremble…for that small noise was an indication to me that my code was read. The system *scanned* it. Step one was done.

I stood up and hurriedly headed away from the ticket kiosks. I darted down a side hall that I had already walked through many times over. I had been in every bathroom in this airport, and there were dozens. This place was fucking massive. That was what Owen, Rachel, and her cousins *didn't* know. It was the information I was so terrified of jinxing. During mine and Briana's many trips around Miami in the previous days, we came here. We scoped this place out in depth. If we hadn't, I wouldn't have been able to attempt step two of my plan. I clenched the plastic baggy in my pocket with a sweaty palm and felt the latex glove beneath it. I grabbed the latex glove between my index and middle fingers, pulling it out.

As I approached the men's restroom, I slipped the glove on my right hand. Stuck to the chrome door of the bathroom hung a sign that read, **This restroom is currently being serviced. Please use one of the others nearby. We are sorry for the inconvenience.**

Perfect. The timing couldn't have been any better. I forcefully swung open the door and saw a Haitian man mopping the floor. My heart was in my throat as his eyes met mine.

"This bathroom out of service, use other one please," he said in his accent.

"I can't hold it, I really have to go." I walked towards him.

"No sir, chemicals on seats. You can't."

With my gloved hand, I grabbed the cloth within the baggy, clutching it tight.

"I have to, I'm sorry," I walked around his cleaning cart.

"Sir," he put down the mop and turned to me. I shoved the cloth in his face and used my free hand to grasp the back of his head, forcing him to breathe it in. His eyes closed, and his body went limp. I set him down gently and began to undress him.

Chloroform.

CIA Headquarters – Langley, VA
15:22 10-20-2016

I slept in the living facilities last night. I hadn't seen the sun in forty-eight hours. I was working what they called a double, but it felt like a triple. Since we were approaching the one-week mark of Owen and Rachel's disappearance, Veronica had us searching day and night for them. Sure, she wasn't here all the time. She'd leave sometime after midnight and return around noon. I was *supposed* to be home with my wife and kids right now. Ha. What a joke, because when I *was* home, I was sleeping. I hadn't been home in almost three days. My wife was probably convincing my kids that they still had a father. I missed most of their fall break, and now they were back in school. Such bullshit. Yeah, it was overtime, but this was almost like forced labor. We couldn't leave until she said we could.

She sat in her desk at the front of the room, just as she always did. The wall-to-wall projection screens surrounded her. Each with different camera feeds from different locations in Florida. They changed every few seconds. She had her hands over her forehead and her fingers dug into her hair. She probably had one of her migraines, which were frequent.

I would switch the feed on my computer every minute or so. I wasn't eager to help her catch innocent people. What I desired was quite the opposite. Most of my colleagues were doing the same, but a few had that blind determination most young government employees had. You could see it, like a fervor bubbling within, they wanted to catch the bad guys. If only they would have woken the fuck up and realized the bad guy was in the same room as them.

"Ma'am…" A voice on the far side of the room spoke up. My stomach sank. Veronica's head barely moved upwards to acknowledge him. "Facial recognition found a match at the Miami International Airport."

The entire room went silent. Not even a click from the keyboards. Veronica slowly stood to her feet and shook her hair out of her eyes. "Blow it up on the big screen."

The image appeared and my stomach wrenched. There he was. A bleach-blond Owen Marina stood frozen mid-stride as he approached the TSA security screening. My rational mind knew, this was game over for Owen.

"It's him…" Veronica's voice trembled with a frightening excitement. "And the girl?"

"She is with him. She is seen walking away from him a few frames before this one."

"My God…" She uttered. "Why the *fuck* is Owen in an airport?! What is the time-stamp on this image?"

"Twenty minutes ago, ma'am."

"Goddamn it!" she shouted at the top of her lungs. "Let's get our shit in gear! Call the airport now, have them stop all outbound flights before it's too late!"

"I'm on it," the same, gung-ho newbie who found Owen responded to her. I glanced over at my colleague Kyle, who I'd worked with for years, and he shook his head in disapproval.

"You!" she pointed to some guy towards the front. "I want you on the phone with Miami PD and our offices in Miami, now!"

"Got it," the man said.

"Ma'am," the newbie began, "I've called five different lines to the airport—they're all dead."

"What do you mean, dead?"

"Uh, every line I call is busy. I can't dial in."

I thought Veronica's head was going to explode.

"You can't be fucking kidding me!" she screamed and slammed her fists against the metal desk. She must have had permanent bruises because she did that so damn often. She reminded me of a spoiled brat who wasn't getting her way.

"I want all law enforcement to go to the airport. Get SWAT down there, get every last agent we have down there! We are going to come down so hard and so fast on them Owen and Rachel will be in handcuffs before they can even fucking blink."

A small smile began to emerge as I processed the newbie's words. *Every* line he called was busy. There wasn't a chance in Hell that was mere coincidence. I relished Veronica's frustration, and although I struggled to find a way to revolt against her, I was pleased to know there were people out there working towards the same goal. Whoever was helping Owen and Rachel, they were good at what they did—great, actually. My smile turned into a grin, knowing that Owen and company were valiantly fighting against us. If only they knew, that someone on the inside was right there with them.

Miami Int'l Airport – Miami, FL
15:29 10-20-2016

My excitement was practically overflowing, and I suppressed the urge to smile. I had prepared for a moment like this since I was fourteen. I dreamed of performing a hack this grand, and now I was a football field away from walking through the door where I could execute it.

That was what most people didn't realize. The best hackers were experts in what we referred to as social engineering. Of course, we knew what we were doing, but the majority of our successes were dependent on whether or not we fooled the people we were trying to hack. The most famous hackers I have read about always worked their way from the inside out, and that was *exactly* what I did to prepare for this.

The laminated nametag clipped to my breast-pocket bounced around with every step. The uniform I was wearing was a little baggy, but I used my belt to tighten everything up. During mine and Briana's excursions here, I discovered the janitorial staff and the maintenance staff wore identical uniforms. Navy khakis and a white polo tucked in. It was a fatal mistake on their part because I called the airport's customer service line to complain.

I told them I had missed my five o'clock flight to JFK because two of the bathrooms nearest to my gate were being serviced by the janitors, and I had to walk to one far away. Of course, I made sure my flight information was accurate, and I gave the lady on the phone a hard time. She directed me to the manager. I let her know my fake title, then proceeded to tell her I frequented the airport often, and that I didn't want it to happen again.

She made the mistake of giving me the hours the bathrooms were serviced daily, and that was *all* I needed. I knew someone would walk in on the janitor sooner or later, but by that time, I would be long gone. I neared the door to the security room that read **Employees Only**. On our second visit, Briana flirted with a maintenance man and got close enough to him to cut his ID tag that hung from his belt. When we got back to the loft, Briana implanted my picture on the ID and re-laminated it. All of this was what I was hiding from Owen and Rachel. They didn't need to know the process, it just had to work. This was the final and most difficult step of my plan—step three.

I held the ID up to the wall scanner and the door clicked open. I quietly opened it and saw how much darker it was in here. Carefully, I closed the door behind me, trying not to draw any attention to myself. There were twenty or so employees sitting in front of a line of computers, facing away from me. On the back wall was a projected image from someone's computer screen, which they were all staring at. I slipped in behind the crowd and looked at the script that was being displayed, the script that *I* created.

"We just don't know where it came from," a female adjacent to me announced. "What do you guys think?"

I had my arms crossed, just feeling things out before I made my move.

"I've never seen anything like this before." A man standing a few feet beside me answered. I didn't even see him there. "Pedro, can you tell where this came from?" he asked another man beside him.

"No way man, I have no idea. It almost seems like this code came from within, like maybe it's a glitch or something."

"Hell of a glitch," the woman said, scratching the back of her head. I could only see her profile, but from what I could tell she was beautiful. Tan skin and long, black hair. I liked it. "No one can call out, and no calls can get in. Whatever it is, we have to get it fixed—soon."

This was my chance.

"I think you're right," I spoke up. The sound of my own voice scared me. "It looks like a glitch, but, if you look at that piece of code right there," I pointed toward the bottom of the screen. "The execution looks like it was directed through the mainframe."

The Hispanic girl's eyes were on me, as were many others. Her colleague who sat beside her wasn't bad looking either. The man and his counterpart, Pedro, huffed in frustration.

"You've got to be kidding me…" Pedro groaned.

"Who is that guy?" one of the employees spoke up.

My gut clenched from his words. Who *was* I? I was the hacker posing as an employee who had just screwed up their system. Fuck.

"He's the new guy," the Hispanic girl replied. I was shocked. What a lifesaver.

"He's cute," the girl beside her murmured. I couldn't help but crack a smile.

"Well," Pedro and his counterpart walked behind me, roughly patting me on the back. "We can let the *new guy* fix it. Have fun with the mainframe."

"Good luck," his counterpart muttered.

I don't need it.

"Yeah, you're doing us a favor," Pedro said and threw me a set of keys. "Let's go for a smoke, Carlos."

I turned awkwardly to face the crowd of employees that lined the computers. I glanced at the attractive face of the Hispanic woman and hoped that my question wouldn't reveal I wasn't an employee.

"They haven't shown me where the mainframe is yet…" I admitted.

She pointed to a door in the far corner. "Down the hall, last door on the right. Get us up and running—fast."

"Got it," I nodded and headed for the door. Getting them up and running was the *last* thing I was going to do, but what they didn't know, didn't hurt them. I hurried down the long white hallway lit by bright fluorescent bulbs. I glanced at my watch—3:35. I had ten minutes. When I reached the door I saw that it needed a key to access. I became overwhelmed as I searched through the many keys on Pedro's key-ring. *What if someone saw me struggling to find it? They would know I'm not a real worker…*

I painstakingly tried every key, rushing as quickly as I could. Finally, one of them slid all the way in. *Thank God.* I opened the door and was engulfed in darkness. The resonating hum of computer towers filled my ears, and when my eyes adjusted, the sheer size of the room was hard to take in. Rows upon rows of computer towers filled it, with only small walkways between for an employee to walk through. I could feel the heat emanating from them while simultaneously feeling the ice-cold AC blowing to keep the room at the ideal temperature. I walked down one of the aisles, grinning like a child in a candy store. Ah—pure power.

At the far end of the room, I found the main server. It had a large, flat-screen monitor, and three massive towers that formed a triangle. I moved the mouse, and the Windows home screen came alive. Immediately, I went to the command prompt. I grabbed the flash drive out of my pocket, found the USB slot on the mainframe, and shoved it in. The Windows desktop disappeared and was replaced by a black screen with green scripts racing downward.

"Yes!" I shouted and nervously checked behind me to make sure I was still alone. Suddenly, the script stopped, and the computer emitted a loud warning sound. I knew that sound. Something didn't work. My heart pounded in my chest as I glanced at the spacebar, flashing every second on the screen. I leaned in to see what it read.

/permission parameter invalid

My eyes grew wide and I controlled a trembling exhale. I was *so* close to finishing the job. Step three *had* to work. Trial and error was my only option.

/authorize

/denied

/reroute

/denied

"Fuck!" I suppressed the volume of my voice. I glanced down at my watch in the dim lighting. 3:40. *Damn it!* I only had five minutes left.

Miami Int'l Airport – Miami, FL
15:44 10-20-2016

"Come on, Grey…" I whispered as I looked down at the time on the phone Briana bought me. Frustrated, I flipped it closed. Where *was* he? He was very stern in his intentions. 3:45 on the dot, then he wanted me to go without him.

Did they catch him? Did his plan work? He was so mysterious about the whole thing. I wished I knew what was going on. I chewed on my lower lip, giving into my anxiety. My eyes roamed over the patterns in the concrete because I was too afraid to look up. The last thing I desired was for someone to recognize me as Owen's accomplice. I did glance to my left every minute or so, in hopes of spotting Grey coming out of the terminal.

My nerves were wrecked. I wouldn't feel better until Grey was safe, but it gave me some relief knowing Owen was on his flight, somewhere over the Atlantic Ocean. It had been less than half an hour, and I already missed him more than I ever had another man. The closest comparison would be the emptiness I felt when I lost my father…but this was different, it was fresher, it stung like an open wound.

I flipped open the phone again. 3:46—I shook my head, contemplating my decision. I wanted to wait, but Grey's request was non-negotiable. He knew what was best for the plan.

I stood up and waved my hand in the air. "Taxi!"

Miami Int'l Airport – Miami, FL
15:46 10-20-2016

/administrator
/no access
/bypass
/unauthorized

Fuck, fuck, fuck! I was sweating from the heat of the computer towers. I knew it was moments before someone would barge in. I knew Rachel had left, it was past the time I gave her. I was debating on just running away while I still had the chance. I already accomplished what I wanted. No one could contact the airport and vice-versa, but, it just…didn't feel right. I didn't feel safe knowing that Owen's flight could still be contacted through the control tower. *That* was something I couldn't change, but what I could change would make it extremely difficult for the CIA and FBI to intervene. *Come on, think.*

"Holy shit." I muttered. Why didn't I think of that sooner? It was elementary hacking for God's sake. Nervously, I placed my fingers on the keyboard. My code had done nine-tenths of the work for me, I just had to manually correct what the main server was blocking.

/back door

…

…

…

/

"Yes!" I laughed in rapture. "Fuck yeah!"

/settings

/1. Systems 2. Server 3. Mainframe 4. SQL Database 5. Terminal Security 6. Administrative

/6

/1. Firewall 2. Software 3. Air Traffic Control 4. Communications 5. Master Permissions

Finally, just what I wanted.

/5

/1. Internal (default setting) 2. External (emergency)

/2

/1. Local 2. State 3. Federal 4. Commander in Chief (wartime)

That was more than I was ever dreaming of.

/4

/updated

I was about to pull my flash drive out of the mainframe, but an idea came to me. I was going to add another thorn in their side. *They* deserved it. I quickly went back to the main settings.

/1. Systems 2. Server 3. Mainframe 4. SQL Database 5. Terminal Security 6. Administrative

/5

/1. Entrances 2. Alarms 3. Emergency Functions 4. Security Cameras

/4

/1. Status 2. Feeds 3. Functions 4. Archive

/3

/1. Positioning 2. Individual Operations 3. Master Functions

/3

/1. Record 2. System on 3. System off

I took a deep breath, and entered in the last piece of my plan.

/3

I pulled my flash drive out and turned around, scanning the walls for an exit sign. I found it in the far corner, and I ran out the door. The sunlight blinded me momentarily and before they even adjusted I started walking away from the room I was just in. I saw two workers walking in my direction. They were amidst conversation and seemed to be very casual with the fact I was in this alleyway with them. Now that I had my vision, I saw a metal gate a few hundred feet away. As I neared the men I grew nervous, but I tried to keep calm. I was wearing a uniform. Hopefully, they wouldn't take a second glance at me.

They didn't. A euphoria settled in throughout my body as I reached the gate and pushed it open. I looked around, trying to regain my sense of direction. To my right, I saw the arrivals and departures lane, and I power-walked towards the main terminal entrance. My heart was beating out of my chest from pure exuberance, and I couldn't stop grinning. I was so proud of myself. This was the ultimate hack, and it worked—it fucking *worked.* I reached the crowd of people and stuck my hand up. "Taxi!" I called out. A yellow Crowne Victoria swooped in to pick me up before I could take a breath, and I sat in the back seat.

"Where to?"

"Just go, I have plenty of money. Step on it!" I urged him.

"Okay, okay!" the driver replied in his Arabic accent, and we pulled away from the airport.

I was grinning so wide it was starting to hurt. I could have cried I was so happy.

"Yes!" I screamed, laughing at the same time. "I did it! I fucking did it!"

The driver glanced at me in the rearview mirror with concern. Suddenly I heard sirens, and I looked through all the windows with wide-eyes, searching for the source. Adrenaline pumped through my veins at the thought of being caught after getting away with this much. The driver began to slow down.

"Don't slow down!" I demanded. "Hurry up!"

"Mister, I do not block the cops way. I slow down."

As I processed his words, a line of twenty-something cop cars of all types raced into the entrance of the airport we were trying to leave. One by one they passed. Chargers, Tahoes, and Crowne Vics—they must have finally been alerted.

Too little, too late. My grin was replaced by a smug smile. They weren't after me. They were after Owen, and he was already gone. I was the last of us, and after the line ended, the taxi driver pulled onto the main road outside of the airport. There was no trace left. We were gone. All of our efforts paid off. I opened my flip phone and called Rachel.

Ring…Ring... "Hello?"

"It worked," I laughed in happiness. "Our plan worked!"

Boeing 777 – Int'l Waters
15:57 10-20-2016

Millie and her daughter were looking out the window at the Atlantic Ocean. The plane had just finished climbing, and the whole cabin finally leveled out. Every few seconds my ears popped. They hadn't yet adjusted. I realized what was in my pocket and pulled it out.

I slipped out a piece and began chomping on the minty gum. My ears started popping more frequently, and I smiled at the thought behind Rachel's gift. It did come in handy, even though it was small. The fact that *she* gave it to me made all the difference. I glanced down at my watch and realized we had already been flying for forty-five minutes. Our plane took off at 3:15. There were touchscreen monitors behind the headrests of every seat. I had been using my finger to scan through the available movies. There were over eighty in total. I noticed a few people already plugging in their headphones

The air smelled clean and filtered. Millie must have been hot because she turned on the little air vent above our heads. The cool stream of air blew partially on me, too. I didn't mind, but that *smell*—it almost reminded me of a hospital. My mind flashed to the morning I woke up in the ICU. The endless beeping of the heartrate monitor, the icy air, and the sanitized smell. The plane smelled similar.

That was the same morning I found out I was a wanted terrorist. *That* morning, was where it all began. I buried my old life that day, and every day since, I had been digging the hole deeper.

Owen Marina was gone. Now, I was Milo Arregan. At least I was on this flight. Who knew what my real first name was on the passport. If only I could have turned back time and not went to the debate…but, would that have changed the outcome? Perhaps, I would have been T-boned by a car? Maybe, I would have been murdered outside of my apartment?

After everything I had been through, it was apparent that someone wanted me gone. The question, though, was *who?*

I met eyes with a man sitting in the first few rows. He turned away from me. His quick, jerky movements made me nervous. Why would he have turned around that far? I was one-hundred and eighty degrees behind him. It seemed intentional…

Stop worrying. No one knows who I am.

I glanced over at my seatmates. Millie was playing Angry Birds on a tablet and Pamela was reading on an e-reader. They were preoccupied on their devices. Whatever suspicions Pamela had of me, she must have tossed them aside. I had the feeling that I was being watched. I turned in the direction of the man.

He was staring straight at me *again.* My heart started pounding in my chest because this time he didn't look away. He stared for close to ten seconds before turning away. I craned my neck around to see the row behind me and the people beside me. Was he looking at someone else? It didn't appear that way. I kept my eyes on him even after he faced the front again. *Something* didn't feel right. My stomach was in knots.

Suddenly, he picked up the phone in front of his seat and began to dial a number.

My heart was in my throat. When he put the phone to his ear, I saw his jaw begin to move, and over the drone of the turbines it was impossible to make out what he was saying. He turned over his shoulder and glanced at me again. This time with an intimidating expression, then he turned back around.

I wiped my sweaty hands against my pants. My heart was going so fast I felt like I would black out if I stood up. The man was nodding and remained on the call. As horrifying as the thought was, I knew it was true.

This man knew who I was. *What do I do?*

I nervously reached for the flip phone in my pocket and turned it on. *Come on, come on. Hurry up.* I went to the contacts and found Rachel's number. My eyes darted to the man. He was looking at me again. *Fuck.*

I picked up the phone and read how to dial out. The plastic of the phone slipped around in my sweaty palms. I dialed Rachel's number and prayed she would pick up.

Taxi – Miami, FL
16:02 10-20-2016

Ring…Ring…

The flip phone vibrated in my pocket. I pulled it out and saw that a weird number was calling. It wasn't a 305 area code like all of our phones were. It probably wasn't safe to answer. I began to put it away, and I halted, staring at the number.

What if it is an emergency?

I opened it and answered the call.

"Hello," the sound of my voice was drowned out by the traffic that surrounded the taxi.

"Rachel," he whispered, and his tone was shaky.

"Owen? What's wrong? Are you calling from the plane?"

"Yes. I don't have much time. Listen."

"What's going on?" my heart began to bounce around in my chest.

"There's a man who keeps watching me. He has turned around almost ten times and he is on the phone with someone. I think he *knows*."

The certainty in his voice made me want to puke. He had been on the plane for close to an hour, what could anyone do on a plane? Maybe it was the—*oh my God…*

"Is it the air marshal?"

"Could be. He just looked over again, he's grabbing something from his pockets."

He was talking in such a low tone I had to press my finger over the opposite ear to block out the noise of the expressway.

"Stay calm," I comforted him. "You might just be overthinking it. Everything will be fine." Now, it was *my* voice that was shaky.

"No, Rachel. It won't. I can feel it—he knows. It's over. It's *all* over…"

"You don't know that." I trembled with every word.

"He's standing up. You were right, he must be the air marshal. You better get out of Florida, fast. They will be looking for you."

"Fuck! Oh my God, I can't believe this is happening. What do I do, Owen?"

"Keep yourself safe, don't worry about me. I love you."

The phone call ended. I stared at the screen, numb to the news I received. Reality settled in like a blanket of fire around my chest. I felt hot, like my skin was burning. The taxi driver hadn't even acknowledged that I was on the phone. *'It's over. It's all over…'* Owen's words echoed in my mind and a rage percolated through my veins. My chest heaved with my rapid breath, and I chewed on my lower lip, feeling helpless as to what to do.

No—it was *not* over. We had come this far. I wasn't going to let us go down without a fight. I began to tear up as emotion bubbled up within me. He said it. I didn't have to say it, he said what I wanted to say so badly, but couldn't. *'I love you…'*

I loved him, too. I wouldn't let them take him away from me. Anger and the love I felt for Owen swirled around inside me like a powerful current, and it made me feel like I was invincible. *Fuck them. They won't win.* I opened the contacts and dialed my cousin.

Please, please answer…

"*Bueno*," Vinny's voice came on the speaker.

"Vicenzo," I breathed into the phone. My anger distorted my normal speech.

"What? *Que pasó, prima?!*" he shouted. He *knew* something was terribly wrong.

"It's Owen. The air marshal got him."

"Shit! No fucking way! What the hell are we gonna do?"

My lower lip trembled, and I felt my eye begin to twitch from the rage deep inside me.

"Get the Hummer."

Boeing 777 – Int'l Waters
16:07 10-20-2016

"Everybody *stay calm!*" the booming voice of the air marshal resonated throughout the cabin as he pressed his knee into my spine. My cheek was squished into the floor, and my body barely fit in the narrow walkway. The cuffs clicked tighter around my wrists. It was hard to breathe.

I thought it would be more dramatic. Maybe a chase, maybe a struggle, a fight…but no—*none* of that. Jamie Lee Curtis begged for her life when Michael Myer's cornered her, but I didn't. I had nowhere to run, being tens of thousands of feet above the ocean. The stony-faced agent walked towards me and yanked me out of my seat to where I was now. The most disturbing part were the faces of the passengers. They all looked at me as if I were a killer, and I guess in their mind, I was. Millie's gasps and cries were getting old quick.

"I had no idea, officer. I swear," she mumbled every few seconds.

"Don't worry, ma'am, just stay seated," he instructed.

That was the thing that made me the most miserable. I *wasn't* a killer. I was innocent, and a plane full of people believed otherwise. Oh, what damage the media had done.

"Attention passengers, thank you for your patience. Please stay calm. We have a wanted fugitive aboard, and we are turning around. We will be back in Miami in the next half-hour. I am deeply sorry for the inconvenience, and for the safety of all our passengers, the flight will take off again after our dangerous cargo is removed by the air marshal. I assure you, you are all safe."

Dangerous cargo…I snorted at the captain's snarky reference. The air marshal dragged me to my feet and pushed me forward. With my hands behind my back and my goatee slipping off my face from having been ground into the floor, I was forced to face the passengers. Many of them glowered at me, shaking their heads, and whispering to one another. Half of the people on this plane would have loved just to shake my hand before a week ago. That was how I was treated in public. Now, I was infamous…not famous. *Why should I suffer in silence?*

"I'm innocent!" I shouted. "I was framed!"

"Shut your mouth," he shoved me forward. The handcuffs dug into my wrists as he pushed me around. We reached his seat, and the person who was sitting next to him had already moved. I sat in the middle, beside his aisle seat, and I tried to find a comfortable way to sit with my arms contorted behind my back. There wasn't any. There was a freckle-faced, redheaded man who sat beside me on the left, and the moment I met eyes with him, he glanced away in fear. The air marshal joined us, picked up the airplane phone, and dialed out.

"We've got him," he said and hung up. I knew it was over from the moment he turned around and we met eyes the first time, but his words solidified it. Hearing them made the reality even harder to face. They've *got* me, and there wasn't a thing I could do about it.

CIA Headquarters – Langley, VA
16:10 10-20-2016

"Ma'am, one of our agents in Miami just got off the phone with the air marshal. We've got him! Owen is in handcuffs!"

Half of the room erupted in cheers. The other half didn't even flinch. I was one of those. One of the ones who dreaded the moment we caught Owen. Just another person added to the list of people who had been mistakenly made a target by the government…but, I knew that this was *far* from a mistake.

Veronica was gasping with laughter. She clenched her fists and shook them. "Yes!" she shouted and turned around to face all of us. The victory had changed her demeanor quickly. Her piercing blue eyes were no longer cold. They shimmered like there were jewels behind them, and her maniacal grin made her wrinkles more apparent. They were subtle because she always hid them with makeup.

"We did it!" she threw her hands up and started a round of applause. When the clapping subsided she opened her mouth to speak. "I just wanted to say thank you, to everyone, for all your hard work. We wouldn't have been able to do it without you."

No shit. The government would be nothing without all of its worker bees.

"She caught an innocent man because of us," I leaned in and said to my colleague Kyle.

"What was that?" Veronica snapped. My pulse quickened and I turned to meet her accusing glare. This was the first time she had addressed me, or even spoke to me for that matter. I avoided her at all costs. I knew it was in my best interest to keep my mouth shut, but the urge was so difficult to ward off. The fifty-something workers around me all stared, awaiting my response. The room was so silent you could have heard a pin drop.

"I *said*, you caught an innocent man because of us. You wouldn't have been able to do it by yourself."

Mumbles from my colleagues spread around the room. Veronica's eyes turned to slits, and her jaw tightened from my words. She slowly walked out from behind her metal desk and strode towards me. The clacks from her heels were unnerving. My body heated up from the stress of the moment, and I could practically feel her anger washing over as she glowered at me. I had told myself many times that I would be prepared for the consequences of my rebellion against Veronica, but was I? My heart pounded in my chest as she reached me. I had my arms crossed and stared back at her sternly.

"So, you think a man who helped kill seventeen and injure nearly a hundred is innocent?"

"Yes," I spat, "because I think he was never supposed to make it out of that debate alive."

I thought her eyes were going to pop out of their sockets they grew so wide, and her nostrils flared. She didn't yell. She didn't scream. She just leaned down to where her mouth was inches away from my ear, and I could feel her hot breath on my neck.

"If you even *think* of those words you just said again, you will be considered a threat to National Security and a traitor of the United States. You and your family will be deported to some foreign country where you will have no way to support them because we will wipe your slate clean. You will have nothing."

I clenched my jaw, trying to suppress my anger. I could have done it right now. I could have broken her neck as close as she was. I was trained to kill someone with my hands—she wouldn't have had a chance. Then I saw an image of my wife and kids in my head. I *couldn't*…if I killed Veronica, we really would have nothing. We'd be toast.

She leaned up for a second and glanced at my last name embroidered on my pullover, and returned beside my ear.

"Mr. Bolden, I suggest you stop being so unabashed and return to just doing your job. If you prefer the contrary, you can hand me your badge and ID card now."

She stood up and stared down at me. She had told me all of that in the quietest of whispers. I didn't respond. I was still mulling over that bitch's words. She threatened my family—not just me. That was the final straw. When she mentioned turning in my badge, it gave me an idea. I wouldn't lose my cool now. It wasn't worth it. If I blew up, she won, and that was the *last* thing I wanted. I had to stay calm and do as she said because I needed my badge. She might have had the power to keep me quiet temporarily, but the patriot in me couldn't be tamed. I watched my brothers sacrifice their lives to a pointless war, the same war I served in. I had been a marionette for far too long, and people like Veronica were the ones pulling the strings. Obeying blindly was easy, so easy that I could have continued drawing my government checks forever and kept my eyes closed…but I couldn't. My eyes were open, and I could finally *see*.

620 8th Ave. – New York, NY
16:21 10-20-2016

My office door swung open. Sharon stood in the opening with a crazed look on her face.

"Ian! Come look at the news! It's Owen. The air marshal arrested him on a flight headed to Moscow."

I almost spilled my coffee as I bolted out of my desk chair. *Moscow. Russia doesn't extradite to the US. Smart choice.* When I entered the main office space, all the employees were crowded around the sixty inch flat screen we kept for news purposes. The station was set to CBS and a male reporter sat in front of a glass table.

"Miami PD has the entrance of the Miami International Airport surrounded. He will be escorted to Dade County Correctional Department, where he will be held temporarily until he is transported to the District of Columbia."

My stomach sank at the thought of Rachel in handcuffs. I wondered if she was with him, and whether or not she was safe. So *this* was why she couldn't tell me where she was at on the phone. They were planning to get Owen out of the country. What a shame, he was already *on* the plane when he got caught.

"We will be bringing you an aerial view of the transport via our CBS affiliate in Miami."

The chatter began when the newscast went to commercial.

Sharon ran her fingers through her poufy hair, brushing the curls over her shoulder.

"They're in big trouble, aren't they?"

I nodded and pressed my lips together.

"Yes, they are in *very* big trouble…"

Le Jeune Rd. – Miami, FL
16:24 10-20-2016

I felt numb…like this was all some horrible nightmare. The last time I felt this trapped was the night I was taken to the Confinement Camp. This time, though, was worse. It would have been different if I had been caught back in Midlothian, or Raleigh…but this was torture. We had made it so far. I was just short of home plate. I could have only imagined what was going through Rachel's head. Maybe if I had a window seat I would have been a fourth of the way to Moscow by now.

It was too late for what-ifs. My road was a dead end. I had nowhere to run, nowhere to hide. The whole time I was on the run, I had imagined what it would feel like if I was caught, but I wasn't prepared for the reality. Whoever created this lie had won. It was like a sick game of hide-and-go-seek, and they found me. My party's hopes of winning the election were shot. Last night in the penthouse, out of curiosity, I turned on the news when Rachel fell asleep. The democrats had taken the lead in the election. It crushed me, seeing that. I imagined that if Cole were watching, somewhere up above, that he might have slammed a glass filled with whiskey and yell as it shattered on the ground. He would have known what to do to get me out of the trouble I was in. He knew people. He probably knew the person who orchestrated this atrocious lie. The past swirled around in my mind like a long lost dream, but reality was sharp as a knife. It was a little too late to wonder what *could* have been.

I adjusted my hands in the cuffs which were beginning to irritate my skin. They dug deep into my wrists from the air marshal putting them on too tight. When we turned a corner I would slide slightly on the leather seats. There were two men sitting in the front, completely silent. I was being escorted in a black Tahoe. At this point, I knew I was royally screwed. Now, all I was concerned about was the welfare of Rachel and the others.

The deep, grumbling sound of an engine filled my ears. In my peripheral, I saw a yellow Hummer about to T-bone us. Glass everywhere. The noise was deafening. My body jerked in different directions as we rolled. Over and over, crash after crash. I hung by the seatbelt at my waist as I was flung around like a ragdoll. I felt warm blood run down from my nose. Shots from automatic weapons filled the air, and behind the earsplitting sounds of crushing glass and metal, I heard something I was *very* familiar with.

Street bikes.

620 8th Ave. – New York, NY
16:27 10-20-2016

I stared at the TV screen with my mouth agape. No one spoke—just gasps as the black Tahoe transporting Owen slowly screeched to a halt. The Hummer had a massive metal guard along its grill, and it backed up and began plowing into the nearby cop cars that were firing shots out of the windows. The men on street bikes were wearing head-to-toe black, and they were shooting at any of the cops brave enough to step out of their vehicles. Who *were* these people?

There were probably a dozen street bikes. Four of them used what looked to be AK-47s to keep the surrounding cops at bay. The other eight or so bikes converged on the Tahoe. Their movements almost seemed coordinated.

Whoever these rogue men were—they were Owen's last hope.

Le Jeune Rd. – Miami, FL
16:29 10-20-2016

Someone grabbed my shoulders and pulled me through the shattered window of the Tahoe. Before I could process the chaos around me, the man who pulled me out took out a pair of bolt-cutters from his backpack and cut the chain connecting my handcuffs. He put a black jacket on me, and a black helmet. I now looked like him. I glanced down and saw the jacket had concealed the metal of the cuffs. I felt the blood smear on the helmet padding when I adjusted it, and I could tell I had a massive headache. I hadn't looked to see if I was cut anywhere else. But for the most part, I felt all right. He dropped the backpack and the bolt cutters.

"Get on," he waved his hand toward the street bike. I glanced down and saw the emblem immediately—Yamaha R1. Adrenaline shot through my veins at the thought of riding again. Regardless of what this guy may have believed, *I* was the better rider.

"Trust me," I said. "Pull my arms which direction I need to go."

"No man, get on behind me!"

A bullet whizzed past us and we both ducked.

"*Listen* to me," I growled. "If you drive we will get caught. Trust me."

I glanced up as I heard the loud whirr of helicopter blades above us. A news cameraman was recording the scene from the side opening.

The man nodded.

I hopped on the bike, and the man jumped on behind me. "Go! Go! Go! More cops are coming!" I slammed my weight down and sped up in first gear. The moment I began to drive off the other bikes followed. We were all together, weaving around traffic. I could have sworn there were more bikes…but now, there were two people on each bike.

"Crisscross! You have to crisscross!"

I weaved around and between the other bikes, and they did the same thing. All the bikes were the same color, and we were all wearing black. We all looked the same…*fucking genius.* We were crisscrossing so the news and the cops lost track of which bike I was on. We were approaching an intersection, and the guy tugged on the sleeve of my right arm. I cut right and sped up, and the other bikes followed suit. We merged onto an expressway, not to the liking of other drivers because we were met with blaring horns. We continued to weave and crisscross between each other, and I could still hear the chopper blades slicing through the air above me.

I had no idea our destination, but with another tug on my sleeve, all the bikes exited off the off-ramp. We slalomed through the stopped cars and turned into an intersection. I heard scraping from behind and saw in the mirrors someone had lost control in the turn and was sliding across the pavement. We came to a busy intersection and the man pulled my left sleeve. I whipped left and barely missed being clipped by a car. I saw in the rearview that the bikes did not follow this time. They went in other directions…

I didn't hear the chopper blades anymore. We must have been close.

"Hurry!" the man shouted over the rushing air. I shifted into the highest gear and sped up easily into the hundreds. The man began tugging at my right sleeve.

"There! That driveway!" he pointed. I clamped on the back brakes and decelerated quickly, and in a driveway on my right, Luke was waving his hands, directing me into an open garage. I slid in, and my back tire fishtailed as I zipped up the driveway and into the garage.

My passenger slid off the bike before I even came to a complete stop. There was a white Dodge Charger with its engine idling beside us. Luke had a panicked look on his face, and I had no idea whose house we were at. A crack of lightning struck outside, immediately followed by thunder that shook the ground.

"Get in the back!" Luke shouted. "They know what to do!"

"Where's Vinny?" I asked. I noticed he was the only one missing.

"He was the one driving the Hummer…"

I choked on my breath from the realization of what that meant. Vinny was probably in handcuffs by now. He let himself get caught. All in efforts to keep me out of *their* hands…and for us to find the truth before it was too late.

I scrambled around to the opposite side of the car and popped open the back-right door. Luke hurried me by pushing me down into the seat. He held open the door for a second. "Get the fuck out of Florida and don't look back! Don't worry about us, Rachel. Okay?"

He slammed the door closed. Briana backed out of the driveway and turned into the street. Grey was in the front seat, and he stared straight ahead. He didn't say a word. We were going the opposite direction I had come from on the bike. It began to downpour. Briana slowed to assist her vision, and it was like a monsoon. Everything was gray, and the fat raindrops sounded like they were marbles.

"How far are we from the turnpike?" I asked.

"Not far," Briana answered. Her voice was solemn.

I licked my lips and tasted blood. I leaned over and glanced at myself in the rearview mirror. I had tiny pieces of glass along my hairline, and everything beneath my nose was stained in dried blood. The pain was slowly starting to settle in. I hadn't felt anything until now. I heard Rachel rustling around in her purse, and she pulled out some wipes.

"Turn around," she said lightly. Her satiny voice was different. There was sadness in her tone. She gently wiped around my mouth and nose, the wet wipes being stained a pale red. My eyes darted across her face as she cleaned me. I stayed quiet, not wanting to break the silence. Sometimes I wished I could hear her thoughts, even if it be just for a moment. Maybe then I would know what was going on in that beautiful mind of hers. She noticed me staring, and a half-hearted smile tugged at her lips. I tried to return it, but it probably looked more doleful than hers.

Last night we were literally on top of the world. Forty stories above Miami Beach, looking out at the city as if we were kings. Now, after all of this, we were back to square one. Our plan failed. We merged onto the turnpike, heading north. I had no idea where we were going, nor did it matter. The energy in the car was nonexistent. Our morale was crushed, and no one would dare discuss the reality of the situation. We all knew the truth…that time was running out. There was a little over two weeks before the election, and we weren't any closer to finding out who was behind this lie. Mine and Rachel's futures didn't look so bright, and without any conversation in the car, it was difficult to ignore. My pains amplified, as did my anxiety. No matter which direction my mind wandered, I couldn't think of any ways to get myself out of this dilemma.

It felt like the car was crushing in around me. This degree of misery was the same as the night Cole passed away—I felt hopeless…

CIA Headquarters – Langley, VA
16:58 10-20-2016

"Ma'am, we've lost him…" The man's words slipped out just above a mumble. We *all* knew what was to come. Veronica's chest rose and fell rapidly with her uneven breath. I caught one of her eyes begin to twitch and her hands slowly clenched into fists.

Veronica let out a piercing, guttural scream. She slammed her fists against the desk multiple times and kept screaming until she was out of air. The whole room stared. Most of us had furrowed brows and scornful looks on our faces. She stomped and one of her heels broke in two. She let out the same childish scream again.

"We had him!" she pouted. "We fucking had him in handcuffs!"

No one said a word.

"Oh, they are going down if it's the last goddamn thing I do!" she growled and ran her fingers through her scalp. Her eyes were wide and her teeth were clenched. She was livid—beyond livid, actually.

"Ms. Hall, they followed the paths of as many bikes as they could. Four riders were arrested, and the guy who drove the Hummer is already in the slammer. They tried."

That poor soul just shot himself in the foot. Veronica scowled at him. I thought she might have ripped his head off if she could.

"I don't want to hear it! Shut your goddamn mouth! Yeah, they arrested everyone *except* Owen! The President doesn't want to catch the people who helped him, he fucking wants *Owen!*"

Her voice trembled with rage.

"No, no! This shit does *not* fly with me. We are done fucking around trying to *catch* Owen." She whipped around, and with an outstretched index finger she pointed at all of us. "Effective immediately, we want him brought in dead or alive."

I felt the blood leave my face. Her words struck me like a dagger in the heart. All the freedoms I served to protect during my tours overseas were being tossed aside casually. No right to a trial. No lawyer. She wanted him *dead.* I cringed at the thought. The saddest notion was that the American People would never know what *really* happened. In their eyes, he *was* a terrorist, and if he died, his death would be perceived as justice. The punishment would fit the crime.

It was the furthest from justice you could possibly get.

"All the double shifters, you are relieved! Go home, now!"

I stood up and slung my briefcase over my shoulder. She didn't have to tell me twice. I could barely stand being in the same room as the wretched bitch. I would finally be able to see my wife and kids. I glanced down at my watch. Ahh, I would get to see the sunset. It had been almost three days since I saw the sun. I hurried for the elevator and pressed the button for the lobby. The elevator shot up ten floors and a ding sounded. As the doors slid open, the daylight that spilled through was blinding. I walked out slowly to let my eyes adjust. When they finally did, I made my way through the lobby and headed for the main entrance. The receptionist gave me a warm smile as I neared the revolving door.

"Get some rest, Lucas."

"I plan on it," I replied and let out a laugh. The October air was nippy, and as I walked across the street to the parking garage, I noticed I could breathe easier. I wasn't as tense. The stress of working under that evil woman was killing me. I smiled, because I had decided my fate in the moments after mine and Veronica's exchange of words. She threatened me, and I kept my cool. I *still* had my badge and my ID. I knew I would never step foot in that building again. I was done with the CIA forever.

I would use my power for the greater good. I was finished sitting on the sidelines, helplessly watching this great country crumble before me. It was time to join the resistance. Owen was not alone in his endeavor. I, Lucas Bolden, was plus one in the fight to save us all.

620 8th Ave. – New York, NY
17:14 10-20-2016

I put on my pea coat and gathered my belongings. The writing staff would be here late tonight. After the pandemonium in Miami, it had to be the cover story. The footage of the Hummer slamming into the Tahoe replayed in my mind over and over. Owen got away by the skin of his teeth. If those bikes wouldn't have weaved around each other, he would have been caught again. Even those watching like myself lost track of which bike he was on.

It was a relief, because I knew when I saw Owen being transported from the airport that they would go after Rachel next. When he was still at large, he was the first target. Not her. I doubted I would be able to get any real sleep tonight worrying about them. I promised Emilio when Rachel was born that if anything were ever to happen to him, I would take care of her like she was my own child. I couldn't fall back on my promise. A glare caught my eye.

I turned back around to see the sun dipping below the horizon, obscured by the towering buildings of Manhattan. The rays of light were fragmented and illuminated the office in spots.

"Everyone," I began in an assertive tone. "I told you once, but I'll tell you again. *Any* calls, faxes, emails—anything regarding Owen—gets directed to my office. I'll see you in the morning."

I headed towards the elevator and pressed the button to go down. My stomach fluttered as it sped thirty-eight stories down to the P1 parking level.

My phone vibrated. It was ringing.

Home

I picked it up. "Hello?"

"Hey, Dad."

"Hey, Son. Is everything all right?"

"Yes, are you on your way home?"

"About to be," I answered and unlocked my car.

"I can't believe he got away..."

"Shit, you're telling me."

There was a pause.

"Has you-know-who called?"

"No, she hasn't. I just hope she's safe..."

A1A North – Cocoa Beach, FL 19:59 10-20-2016

Grey stretched his arms out, emitting a drawn-out yawn. We cruised slowly down the coastal highway, and I gazed out at the ocean on my right. I wished I could have held on to that feeling of peace it gave me. Worry always crept back into my mind.

We had been driving for a little over three hours, and so far we hadn't run into any problems. Briana was smart for renting the Charger, it looked like an undercover cop car. I wasn't sure if that was the motive, because none of us had talked the entire time besides Rachel. She spoke up to direct us from time to time. My body ached all over. While she was cleaning me, Rachel had expressed concern that I might have a concussion, but my head felt fine. Most of my pain was elsewhere. I didn't know which hurt worse, my physical pain, or the pain I felt inside. In times like these I wished I could have just talked to my mother again. Her advice was always golden. Although, in a situation like this, it might not have helped—but it still would have comforted me.

Twenty minutes ago, Rachel made us stop in Melbourne Beach. She intended on staying the night at her moms, but as we neared the street she lived on, we saw a suspicious looking SUV outside of her house. It looked like a cop. We drove past at a steady speed, acting nonchalant. Luckily, whoever it was, didn't follow.

Rachel's aunt, or *tía,* as she called her, lived in an oceanfront house in Cocoa Beach. She was certain that the FBI would not be able to trace her mother to her aunt because she wasn't related by blood. Her aunt married into the family, and she had divorced Rachel's blood-uncle years ago.

"Right here," Rachel said, pointing to a coral-colored house on the ocean. It had the same, clay-tiled roof I had seen all over Florida. We pulled into the driveway and Briana shut off the car. No one opened the doors. Rachel glanced around at everyone.

"What are you waiting for?"

"You," Grey answered dryly.

"Come on, my *tía* is cool."

We stepped out, and everybody began the awkward stretching. We didn't take any pit-stops along the way, and my muscles were cramped. The night was cool and temperate. The breeze tickled the cuts along my hairline, soothing the heat of the healing wounds. Grey and Briana were still wearing the garb of *Rose* and *Gregory*, and Rachel and I were wearing our disguises. Sadly, I had begun to get used to the bleach-blond. I was tired of trying to be someone other than myself. I spotted an aloe plant growing beside the path of large stone tiles that led to the front door. Palm trees dotted the yard. Rachel rang the doorbell. We hung around behind her. I heard some movement from inside, and the door swung opened. A pudgy woman with shoulder-length black hair answered. Her eyes bulged as she stared at Rachel. Then, she glanced at me.

"Rachel, *ay Dios mio*, come in!" she waved her hands and ushered us in, mumbling things in Spanish. "*Marta, vengase!*" the moment Rachel heard the name Marta, her eyes began to water.

"*Ma!*" she shouted. Her voice echoed. I tilted my head back to take in the vaulted ceilings. Rachel's family was well-off. Maybe Emilio wasn't the only successful one in the family. A woman came barreling around the corner, skidding on the tile in a pair of fuzzy slippers. She ran into Rachel with open arms. They both began to bawl.

"*Ay, mi hija, mi amor, gracias á Dios!*" She smoothed the back of Rachel's hair with her hand, holding her daughter tight. "I was so worried about you, *mija*! *Te amo, te amo para siempre.*" Her hiccupping cries almost made *me* tear up. I wished I could have held my mother again. If only…

"I love you too, Mom. I love you so much." Rachel pulled her mother tighter. From my angle, Rachel's mom was facing me. Her hair was long and the same, walnut-brown color as Rachel's, except hers was partially gray. She was attractive, too. She let go of Rachel but still held her hands. She rubbed them lovingly with her thumbs and looked her up and down. There were subtle wrinkles around her eyes and mouth, but regardless, I now knew where Rachel got her looks. Her eyes darted and met mine. Her nostrils flared, and she scowled.

"Is *he* the reason you're in so much trouble? Why would you go along with him, *mija?* What in the hell got into you?"

I felt my face turn red. Even though I was a few years older than Rachel, I was still just as embarrassed to meet her mom, especially under these circumstances. It was not every day a girl brought home the most wanted criminal in the United States. What a great impression.

"Mom, I can explain everything. Just sit down somewhere. We will explain everything."

I ran my fingers through my hair, trying to look somewhat groomed. It wasn't like I'd have any luck after the kind of day I had. I stretched my hand out in an effort to introduce myself.

"Owen Marina," I said. "Nice to meet you, Mrs. Flores."

She hesitantly held out her hand, but drew it back at the last second. She grimaced from my presence. "Mom, Owen is innocent. I will explain everything, I promise." Her mom cocked her head to the side, staring at Rachel as if she was insane. She then turned back to me and revealed a forced smile. She gently placed her hand in mine, and I shook it.

"I'm not Mrs. Flores anymore, but you can still call me that. I will always be a Flores because of my daughter."

"She's the only reason I made it this far. I owe your daughter my life."

She nodded, not knowing how to respond. She hadn't the slightest clue of our struggle.

She looked me up and down, turned to Rachel, and held a cupped hand beside her mouth. "*Que guapo, no?*" Rachel giggled and nodded.

Guapo—wasn't that handsome? Did Mrs. Flores just call me handsome?

Marta turned back to face the group. "*Hola, Briana. Cômo estás*?" She embraced Briana in a hug. "I've been better…" She answered. The reserved reply from Briana seemed to alarm her mom. Her facial expression changed.

"So, who is this well-dressed *hombre* in the back?" she asked. Grey stepped forward.

"Grey Maxwell, pleasure to meet you."

Her mother nodded. "Nice to meet you too. All right, come to the kitchen. I'm going to pour myself a glass of wine because I have a feeling I will need it. Rachel has some explaining to do."

I couldn't help but chuckle, and we followed her into the kitchen.

Rachel told her everything—all the way from the beginning. She left out some extraneous information, like the night on the train. Mrs. Flores was right, she did need a glass of wine…or three. The media had scared her all on their own, but hearing it from her daughter's mouth, *that* was different. Once she heard the whole story, her demeanor had changed. It was visible. The reality of the situation burdened her, just as it did us. Rachel was curious as to why she wasn't at her house when her car was still there. Her mom explained that she knew she was being watched, and she waited until the sun set one night to leave. She left the TV on and slipped out the back door. She walked the fifteen miles up the coast to Cocoa Beach. She knew it would be safer there because her sister-in-law had divorced her brother years ago.

Briana was in the shower, and Rachel and her mom went to the bedroom to talk. I saw the look in Mrs. Flores' eyes before she asked her to talk in private. It was the look of pure fear. She was afraid for her daughter, and with good reason. Rachel's aunt sat in the living room watching TV. I sat in a bar chair with my arms propped up on the eat-in kitchen. I repeatedly rubbed the smooth granite countertop out of boredom. Grey was in the dining room just through the arched opening. The tile floor in the kitchen was a beige-coral. I glanced around, taking in the design. The cabinets were wooden, stained with a deep cherry-wood finish. Grey's plate sat across the table. He finished his meal over an hour ago. Rachel's aunt had ordered two pizzas, and we were all but stuffed. On the wall, there was the same Puerto Rican flag that was in Briana's kitchen back in Orlando, except this one was painted and framed. I could tell the air conditioning was on because the coolness was dry, not like the moist air outside. It was refreshing. There was a soft yellow glow from the living room. Rachel's aunt had the lights dimmed. There were so many decorations; the burgundy curtains that draped the windows, the granite marbled counters, and the tiled floors made me feel like I was in a mansion. I imagined the typical Florida home a beach theme, with ocean blues and teals, but none of that was here. This was what I pictured an Italian home that overlooked the Mediterranean would look like. It felt cozy. It made me feel *safe*.

I bashed myself for being so naïve. *They* were still out there. I escaped by the skin of my teeth today. We were only three hours north of Miami…

"*Ay Dios mio!*" Rachel's aunt squealed from the living room. Out of concern, I walked around the corner to see what made her say that. The news was on. I covered my mouth in shock.

"…Vicenzo Flores was arrested on two counts of vehicular manslaughter. Authorities have now informed us he was driving the Hummer that assisted Owen Marina is his escape. Three of the five bikers have been arrested, and his brother, Luciano Flores, was turned in by one of the bikers. Now that the FBI has apprehended almost everyone involved, the pressing matter is finding their cousin, Rachel. Owen and she are still on the run. Please, if anyone knows of their whereabouts, please call the FBI's anonymous tip line. There is a hundred-thousand dollar reward for their capture…"

The footage of Vinny's Hummer plowing into the side of the Tahoe replayed over and over. Glass exploded and scattered on the asphalt. The Tahoe rolled three times from the impact. I rubbed the scrapes on my forearms, wondering why I wasn't in the hospital. Maybe it hadn't hit me yet. I couldn't comprehend that I even survived such an impact.

I felt someone beside me, and I looked over my shoulder to see Grey standing a few feet behind me watching the same thing. His dark, beady eyes were cold. Sometimes I wondered what was going on in his head. He was so quiet, and he always had been. Actions spoke louder than words for him. His intellect did all the talking. I was still curious to what he did in the airport.

"…Once again, there is a hundred-thousand dollar reward for Owen and Rachel's capture. Please contact the FBI's anonymous tip line at 1-888…" The words faded out. They made my stomach flop. How predictable, the government enticing the American People with money to turn me in. All the odds were against me, against us. A fog hung over my brain; it felt fuzzy. I was enveloped in it. Being *here* was the cause. It was a temporary escape from reality. Nausea overtook me every time I thought of where we would go tomorrow and what we could do. My road was becoming shorter by the day…but where would it *end?*

"Shit, they got Vinny *and* Luke?" Briana asked from the other side of the living room. She stood beneath the arched opening which led to a hall and the master bedroom. Her hair was wrapped up in a towel.

"*Si,*" Rachel's aunt answered.

She turned around and went back down the hall. I heard muffled voices. She was probably telling Rachel and her mom. I looked over my shoulder again. Grey had sat back down at the dining room table. I walked over and pulled out a chair to join him. He looked at me, blinking. His lips pressed into a line, and I couldn't tell if he was zoning out or just waiting for me to say something.

"So, I was curious…" I began. "What did you do at the airport?"

A childlike grin emerged. He actually started to chuckle.

"I used my ticket to execute a code in the existing system. All calls in and out of the airport wouldn't work. Then, I posed as an employee and hacked into the mainframe. I turned off all the security cameras and set their override clearance to wartime status. Only the President could intervene."

He was so casual about it.

"No shit!" I coughed, patting him on his back. "Fucking incredible, you're unreal man."

He smirked. "It was pretty badass, I'm not gonna lie." We laughed and continued for quite some time. It was empowering, reliving our day. Grey's plan worked, Briana's passport worked, it was just that goddamn air marshal. We were so close it made me sick. I was in the fucking plane for crying out loud. How much closer could I have gotten? I would never know.

"No wonder you didn't want to tell us. I wouldn't have wanted to jinx that shit either!"

"Yeah, you're telling me…" He said. "I knew how important it was that it worked. I wanted you to be safe, man." His statement was heartfelt. I could feel it, and it was good to know I had a friend like Grey, who had risked his life from the beginning to keep me safe. I would have never made it out of Virginia if it wasn't for him.

"Thank you, man. You have no idea how much it means to me that you've helped me from the start."

He shook his head. "What else was I gonna do? You were framed for a crime you didn't commit. It's right and wrong, man—black and white. There is no other way to see it in my eyes. I knew I had to do what is right, and that was helping you. I wouldn't change a thing."

I nodded. "Thanks, man."

"No, don't thank me," he countered.

My eyebrows quirked. "Why not?"

"Because man, I know we go way back to before you had your title, but still, I never thanked you for what you have done for this country."

My breath shuddered. He almost made me tear up. Not because I hadn't been thanked before, because I had, many times. It was because it was from him. The longest friend I had in life.

"If Cole wouldn't have badgered me for weeks on end back in our Camp, we wouldn't even be having this conversation right now. He managed to convince me."

"How?" Grey asked. I didn't expect him to question me further. I drew the memory from the recesses of my mind…and it was painful. *Very* painful. It was the question that changed my life forever.

"He said, 'The real question for you is, once you've left this world…how do you want to be *remembered?*'"

Aunt's House – Cocoa Beach, FL
23:57 10-20-2016

I stirred from my sleep and let out an obnoxiously loud yawn. I stretched out my arms and legs, accidently kicking a throw pillow off the sofa. I pushed myself backward to slide up in a sitting position, and I rubbed my eyes. Mrs. Flores was sitting in a recliner, staring at me with a warm smile. I jumped in shock. She hadn't been sitting there when I dozed off, or at least I didn't think she was. I pulled the blanket over my body more because I felt exposed, even though I wasn't. I glanced around the dimly lit living room. No one was with us. Was everyone asleep?

"Why are you looking at me like that?" she asked.

"Like what?"

"Like I'm disturbing you," she chuckled. Her voice was a tad raspy, but it had that silky tone that Rachel's did, and I couldn't handle the similarity. It was too weird.

"Sorry…" I mumbled. She held the remote in her hand, but she wasn't changing the channels. The TV was turned to a reality show from what I could tell, and the volume was muted.

"You know…" She began. My heart sped up. Where was everyone? I was afraid of where this was going. I had watched way too much porn in my life to not know what happens next in situations like these. The hot, middle-aged woman was away from her husband and couldn't resist but to watch the young stud toss and turn in his sleep…

What the fuck am I even thinking? What is wrong with me? Where is Rachel?

"My daughter really likes you…a lot."

I didn't know what to say. I just nodded in acknowledgment.

"She has always been naïve with men and her relationships."

"She told me," I responded.

"Did she?"

I nodded.

"I guess she just picked the wrong ones, for the wrong reasons. She's only twenty-three, you know."

I knew she was a few years younger than me, but I had never discussed Rachel's age with her before. Hearing it out loud made me realize she was probably only a year or so out of college. I was pushing twenty-eight. Her maturity masked her youth.

I nodded. I didn't know what Mrs. Flores was getting at. I got the sense that she was trying to feel me out, like any good mother would of a new man interested in their daughter.

"She tells me you are one of the best guys she has ever had the honor of meeting."

I couldn't help but smile. I heard Rachel's voice in my head telling her mom what she thought of me.

"The honor is all mine, Mrs. Flores. Like I said when I met you earlier, she has helped me get this far. Her connection to Ian was the reason she approached me in the first place. It is the only hope I have left. There isn't much anymore."

My words felt cold—empty. It was a difficult truth to acknowledge.

"Thank you, Owen, for your kind words. She is the brightest star in the sky…and the last one that I have remaining, in an all but dark world."

I stayed quiet.

"Seeing my daughter on the news with you was indescribably painful. I don't think you'll ever understand the feeling until you have children of your own. I haven't been eating much because I have been worried sick about her."

"I'm sorry…" I mumbled.

Mrs. Flores pressed her lips together and sighed. She adjusted her legs and turned more in my direction.

"Don't be," she said flatly. "From what she explained to me, you didn't ask for this to happen to you. You were just trying to do something good."

"I was, and I still am."

"Also," she continued, "Rachel always looked up to her father so much, and when he died, it only made her emulate him more. She was a great writer all throughout school. After high school, naturally she pursued journalism. I knew it was because she wanted to follow in his footsteps."

I stayed silent. I had a soft-spot for Rachel, and hearing her mother tell me these things was just what I wanted. I wasn't on a plane to Moscow anymore. Every bit of Rachel I could get was precious to me. Whether it be from her or Rachel.

"The way she talked tonight, it was different. She had this determination in her eyes that I have never seen before."

My eyes locked with hers. I knew exactly what she was talking about.

"I have seen it, too. When I first met her."

"Well, apparently, it's all because of you. She said that this was her chance to do a real story. One that *mattered*."

"I know she will…" I muttered. "Regardless of what happens."

Mrs. Flores tossed her hair over one shoulder, just as Rachel did. They were more alike than I thought. Her eyes met mine again, and this time, they were cold.

"Can I ask a favor of you, Owen?"

"Yes, anything."

"Regardless of what happens, *please*, keep my daughter safe. She is the most important person in my life, and I couldn't imagine losing her. The last thing I would want is to know she died chasing some story, just as her father did. I can't bear to go through that twice."

The reality of what she said hit me. Her father died covering a story, and her mother was afraid of Rachel having the same fate.

"I would give my own life for her."

Beachside – Cocoa Beach, FL
00:11 10-21-2016

The sound of the waves lapping against the shore was all I heard. It surrounded me, enveloped me. A constant, soft breeze blew over my body, and it was magical. I smiled from the sensation, and the crashing of the waves was so resonant, I began to lose touch with what was real. Was I even here? Had I escaped reality?

Yes. Even if it was only for a moment, I had escaped. The sound of the ocean was my guardian, saving me from my thoughts. The thoughts I fought so hard to avoid. My plan had failed. He was no longer safe. Tomorrow was uncertain, and that uncertainty ate away at me.

Stop. Breathe. Listen to the ocean…

I let out a long, exaggerated exhale. I let my eyes roam across the night sky. The larger stars were visible, but there weren't many out altogether. It was a familiar sky. As a child, in New York, I couldn't see any. In Miami, there were only a few. When I moved to North Carolina to go to school at Chapel Hill, I was amazed at how many more stars there were. This was nothing compared to that. The ocean made up for it, though. There was no way I could wear shorts and a tank top back home at this time of year.

Why? The question kept resurfacing in my mind. *Why* hadn't my plan worked? Why did the air marshal have to recognize Owen? The events of the day continued to replay like a film reel behind my eyelids every time they closed. What if I would have done this differently? What if Owen had been in another seat? Would he have made it then?

The endless spiral of possibilities swam around in my head. It worried me because I was all out of ideas. I couldn't come up with one thing that might be able to help Owen. Time was against us, and our running could only go on for so long. What would happen when our time ran out?

The thought made me queasy.

Stop. Breathe in, breathe out. Listen to the ocean.

I focused on the sound. The natural rhythm of the crashing was beautiful, and it was the one thing I missed about Florida the most. My eyes were closed, and I felt the presence of someone beside me. I turned to my right and saw Owen.

"Why hello there," he said. His pearly white teeth stuck out in the night so visibly. He grabbed my hand and interlaced my fingers with his. Warmth flushed from my head to my toes. Every moment I spent with Owen, I felt infinite. It was almost like time had stopped.

"Hi, handsome."

We chuckled, and I inched closer to him. His scent was intoxicating. It smelled like faint cologne, but I knew he had none. It was natural, and with every inhale, I knew he was with me and not on some plane. It wasn't that simple, though. That desire I had, to keep him here, came with repercussions. It came with the knowledge that I had no idea how long I would have him by my side.

Time was against us, and I cherished every moment.

"Why are you out here all alone?"

"Needed to clear my thoughts," I said.

"Did it work?" he asked, and pulled our clutched hands to his stomach.

"No," I chuckled. "I'm much better now, though."

"Oh really?" he teased.

"Yes, really." I squeezed his fingers tighter. I rolled on my side and threw my leg over his. His face was inches away from mine, and as I stared into his blue eyes, I knew what we had was real. We hadn't known each other for very long, but the journey had brought us closer together. If someone would have told me I would have fallen for the cocky politician sitting across the coffee shop, I would have told them to fuck off. When I approached him, it was only for the story. Now, it was *much* more than that. I loved him, and not only did I want to tell him, I wanted to *show* him.

I threw my other leg over and straddled his waist. I grabbed my hair tie and slid it off. My hair fell around my head, and the ends dangled down, just barely touching him. My palms were planted firmly in the sand beside his shoulders. It took all of my strength just not to pounce on him. I missed his touch, his kiss.

"I could get used to this," he said with a smug smile.

"You're not the only one…"

I slid down farther, teasing him. He began to open his mouth to speak, and I pressed my finger to his lips.

"Remember what you told me today when you called from the plane?"

He nodded and delicately kissed my finger.

"I love you, *too*." The words felt like a drug as I said them. It was the purest love I had ever felt. I leaned down and met his lips. They were so smooth. Our gentle kisses became passionate and fierce, and our tongues danced. I sucked on his lower lip, feeling it fill with pressure. His cock began to grow in his shorts, and I pressed down on it. I kissed my way down his chin and neck. I sucked and kissed all the way to the ridge of his collarbone. I reached down to the edge of his shirt and helped him pull it off. He ran his fingers through my hair and pulled me in for another long, passionate kiss. When we released, I kissed his pecks and down the middle of his sternum. His body was so warm—I could feel the heat emanating off of him.

He began to unbutton his pants, and I slid down my panties. We both wanted this *so* badly. The last I looked, the beach was deserted. I didn't even bother to check. It didn't matter at this point. What did we have to lose? It was so liberating, not having to think about hiding just for this instant. As long as we were together, I couldn't have cared less. Nothing else mattered. He bit my lower lip and caressed my breasts. His touch made me tremble. I slid down on top of him, and I thought I was going to melt into a puddle. I oozed affection for him. Every kiss, every thrust, I put all of my love into it. I wanted to give him a night he would never forget. Regardless of the future, we had this night together. It was ours. He cupped my ass with his hands, and with every thrust I gyrated harder.

I lost track of time. We were covered in sweat, and my hair was dripping wet. We had switched positions, and our necks were probably covered in hickeys. He hadn't came—he was trying to hold it back for me. My back was covered in sand. We were in missionary, and looking at his toned body above me was enough to get me off. The moon wasn't out, and all we were to each other were the dim outlines of bodies.

"I love you," I panted.

"I love you too," he grunted and thrust deeper. I was so close. I had never had a guy make me orgasm, but I knew we were both about to go over the edge. He leaned down, and we locked lips. We breathed through our noses as we sucked and held each other locked in the kiss. His body was crouched up, and I wrapped my legs around his ass to pull him closer. I arched my back upwards as my body began to tremble. My mouth opened from the pleasure, and I began to moan. His breath shuddered, and he gave one final thrust. My body and mind exploded with ecstasy. He panted and collapsed on top of me, kissing my face and breasts. I ran my fingers through the back of his sweaty hair, and gently kissed his lips, his nose, and his forehead. I pulled his head to my breasts and let him rest there.

"That was amazing," he said for the second time.

"I know," I replied, staring up at the sky with his arm wrapped around me. My head was resting in the nook between his chest and shoulder.

"I have to be honest…" He began. "That was different than all the times in the past."

"Different as in, bad?" I teased. I knew that wasn't the case.

"No, not at all. It was the best."

"Did you feel it?"

"Yes, I did."

"It was the love," I said. "I felt it too."

I delicately traced a figure-eight on the skin of his stomach with my index finger. The soft ocean breeze cooled off our hot skin. Owen had put his jeans back on but was still shirtless. I had redressed already. I slid my head closer to his chest, and he pulled me tight. I could hear the steady beating of his heart. My mind was finally at ease. I wasn't worried about what tomorrow would bring. Owen was here, with me—in the flesh. That was all I needed.

"Maybe we can do this again someday," he said.

"What? The sex?"

"Well, that too," he laughed. "I meant this, lying on the beach together."

Images flashed through my head. Owen and I running on some white-sand beach, looking out on turquoise waters. I could practically feel the sun on my skin. It made me smile.

"That would be nice," I admitted.

"Where do you want to go?"

"Well, I've been to the Caribbean and Hawaii. I've always wanted to go to France."

"Where, to Paris?"

"Maybe just to visit," I said. "I was thinking more like the French Riviera. Nice, Cannes, maybe spend a night playing blackjack at a casino in Monaco. I can see it now, waking up and having coffee at an outdoor café, basking in the sun on the beach, and finishing the day off with some French Cuisine and a glass of wine."

He was grinning ear to ear and let out a laugh.

"I like your taste. You know, it's kind of ironic you said France."

"Why?"

He turned to me before answering.

"Because before I was born, my mom and dad took trips to France. She was obsessed with antique French furniture and design. I remember her teaching me how to count to ten in French as a child, and she would show me so many pictures. Ever since then I have wanted to visit. I miss her a lot. I wish I could just hear her voice again."

"I know the feeling…" I murmured. Hearing him say that about his mother only made me realize further that we have both been through the same thing, just with a different parent.

"I know you do," he consoled.

Could he have been any more perfect? He understood my pain. That was something not many people could do. He was handsome, intelligent, and caring. He used every bit of his political influence to try to change this country for the better. He was just in the wrong place at the right time. I wouldn't even have been here if it weren't for what happened to him. I would still be in Raleigh, putting my articles on a desk to be approved…and they probably would have been the same garbage we have seen on the news. He strengthened his grasp around my back and lovingly rubbed it. If this were a dream, I would have been perfectly content with never waking up. I wanted to stay in this moment forever. I couldn't let reality settle in, not just yet. I had to hold it off any way I could.

"I can see us now, looking out at the sea from a rooftop terrace, without a worry in the world. Just you and me, and whatever comes next."

"That sounds like the closest thing to heaven I'll ever find."

I laughed and kissed the underside of his neck. "It does, doesn't it?"

"I'll make you my girlfriend, and then take you on a *real* date. This time, without the FBI chasing us." His soft-spoken, yet masculine tone carrying those words made my stomach flutter. Everything about him left me so enamored.

"A real date?" I egged him on.

"Yes," he answered confidently. "I will bring you flowers, we can have a candlelit dinner, and we can make love until the sun comes up."

My heart swelled in happiness. He had hit a soft-spot.

"You know, I've never had a guy give me flowers."

I could barely see his forehead scrunch up in the darkness.

"What? You're kidding me."

"Not at all. I'm dead serious. The funny thing is my last name means flowers in Spanish."

"Really? So Flores means flowers."

"Yes, and I still never got any."

"As beautiful as you are, that's such a shame…" He muttered.

"I know, I dated assholes," I said flatly.

"Don't worry, Rachel. One day."

"One day?"

"One day you'll get flowers."

"They better be from you," I said, pulling him in for a kiss.

"Of course."

"Propaganda is to a democracy what the bludgeon is to a totalitarian state."

– Noam Chomsky

The Whitney – Bethesda, MD
02:02 01-15-2015

The blaring fire alarm echoed throughout my apartment. I jolted out of bed, disoriented from the earsplitting drone of the alarm. My clock read 2:03 a.m.—what the hell was happening? I hopped around my room on one foot as I struggled to slip on my shoes. I threw on a jacket and headed for the door.

I heard voices from the hallway. I sniffed deeply as I neared the door. I didn't smell smoke…had someone pulled the alarm? I opened the door to see two-dozen of my neighbors being herded through the hall towards the stairwell by men in full military gear. They all had automatic weapons strapped to their backs. My pulse quickened from the sight. One of the soldiers saw me standing still and pushed me forward with the rest of them.

"What the hell is going on?" I shouted in reaction to his shove.

"Everything is fine. Stay calm and exit the building."

He must have been a couple years younger than me, and his unwavering tone was a telltale sign of a mind that had been molded by his superiors. Had there been another riot? Who would have given orders to evacuate a building this late at night? I tried to resist but was met with another shove against my back. We piled into the stairwell and began descending.

I lived on the top floor. We had nine more stories to go down.

"Keep it moving," the soldiers behind us said. Their voices echoed.

I had to look down in order not to step on the heels of the person in front of me. We were packed like cattle. Suddenly, the line in front of me slowed. I leaned over the railing to see the circular opening that allowed a visual of the ground floor. The rest of the floors were being evacuated also. The many voices talking at the same time was dizzying. As the floors beneath us began to exit on the ground floor, the line moved forward again.

I was pissed. I had to go to work tomorrow. With everything that happened on Black Monday, the EPA was one of the only sectors of the workforce that were actually needed. The whole country was being laid off en masse. It was tragic, but I had to try and keep mine. We were still trying to figure out what was used to create the dirty bombs.

"Daaad," a child groaned from below. The voices of the children stuck out more than the adults.

We reached the ground floor, and through the windows I saw the hundreds of people that had evacuated the building.

"All right everyone, keep it moving! Outside, now!" another soldier called out. I shuffled across the marble floor and zipped my jacket tighter as we exited the building. The January air was frigid, and my breath trailed from my mouth. I turned around three-hundred and sixty degrees to take in the chaos that was unfolding around me.

There were massive flatbed trucks with Army emblems on the sides of their camouflaged bodies. Half of them were already loaded up with people. My eyes bulged from what I saw. This was like something out of a war movie.

I began hearing shouts from the others.

"No! You can't take us like this!" a man yelled. I turned around, trying to find his location. There was a soldier in front of him pointing to the flatbed truck.

"Sir, I don't want to have to tell you again. Get on the truck!"

I shuffled backward, trying to watch the encounter. I bumped into a mother and her two boys.

"I'm sorry," I mumbled to them. I glanced back, and the man had an enraged look in his eyes.

"I'm not going anywhere!" he screamed.

The soldier tried to pull him forward, but the man slipped out of his grasp.

"Get the hell on the truck! I'm not going to ask you again!"

"What are you gonna do about it?" the man yelled and reached for the soldier's gun. The soldier threw him on the ground with brutal force. As he slammed against the ground I heard the wind get knocked out of him. The soldier swung his weapon off of his shoulder and my heart raced as I watched in horror.

"No!" I screamed. The gunfire rang throughout the air. Behind the painful ringing in my ears I heard the high-pitched cries of the children. The man who had resisted clutched his chest as blood began to seep through his clothes and drip from his mouth. He coughed and looked around at the crowd with teary eyes. Anyone who wanted to resist now knew what would happen to them. I felt like I was going to throw up, but I held it back. I was deaf. In the utter chaos around me, everything was muffled. I felt numb.

An American soldier just *killed* a citizen.

A soldier in the bed of the truck tugged at my arm. I turned to him disoriented, and my survival instincts told me to yank my arm out of his grasp and run away. I would just take my chances of them shooting me as I attempted to escape…but I didn't. I didn't want to end up like the man who was lying on the asphalt, just a few feet in front of me—dead.

He pulled me into the truck bed, where I was crowded in with dozens of other people. We all sat elbow to elbow, knee to knee. We were packed in tight. There were two soldiers sitting in the middle, holding their weapons. Clearly we outnumbered them, but no one dared to resist. They made an example of that man, and it *worked*. We were in fear, and they had control. I was tempted just to pull out my EPA ID with the government seal. Would they realize we worked for the same people? Then, I realized that half of my building worked for the government. What the fuck was going on here?

I stared into the eyes of one of the soldiers, and the gaze that he returned was cold. It was as if he was a robot. I tried to search for the smallest bit of remorse, or guilt…but I couldn't sense any. He broke our stare and looked around at the other people.

My hearing faded back in, and the only thing I could hear was the shrill, whining cries of the woman's two sons who sat across from me. The mom held them close, one arm wrapped around each to comfort them, but it wasn't working. She removed her jacket and used it as a makeshift blanket, but it was only big enough to fully cover one of them. I took off mine and tossed it to her.

"Here," I said. The engine of the truck was so loud she probably didn't hear me. She nodded and smiled, putting my jacket over her other son to keep him warm.

The children's cries were bloodcurdling. Their mouths were wide open, and their small faces covered in tears. They both stared at the soldiers with the most undiluted fear I had ever seen. They had just watched a man die, and they probably were sleeping soundly just ten minutes ago.

The soldiers ignored the children. They didn't even look at them. It must have bothered them. I mean, what kind of person wanted to scare a child? To make them cry? I couldn't help but wonder where the hell we were all going. After watching the man get shot, the possibilities were endless. This was probably the first time in my adult life that I wanted *fewer* possibilities and not more. I looked around as we turned onto the main road. Wisconsin Avenue was filled with flatbed military trucks all heading in the same direction. It horrified me to see more people being removed from their homes. This felt like a modern-day Holocaust. I glanced at the faces around me, and every one of them was terrified, half of which were quietly tearing up. The endless whine of the children's cries was an indicator of what was to come. It reminded me of when a child misbehaves, and they are sent to timeout. Except, from what I just saw, we weren't the ones misbehaving, but we were *still* being sent to timeout.

This was martial law in action. It all made sense. We were being punished for the riots that had been happening since Black Monday. Two questions spawned from that thought.

Where were we going? And how long would we be there?

The answer to that question laid in the children's cries. They knew this would be a *long* timeout.

Beachside – Cocoa Beach, FL
06:07 10-21-2016

"Owen, wake up! Please! You're scaring me!"

I was being shook violently. I jolted awake, gasping for air. I coughed and choked, trying to catch my breath. Rachel's hand rested on my leg, and she combed her hair behind her ear with her fingers. The ocean breeze was blustery. It felt cool against my bare chest. Her forehead was creased, and her eyes were wide. She looked petrified.

"What the hell was that?!"

"What the hell was what?" I asked, still panting.

"You were cussing in your sleep, tossing and turning. It looked like you were struggling against someone. Did you have a bad dream?"

The children's whining cries were still present in my mind, but they were quickly fading. The image of the man clutching his chest and coughing up blood flashed before my eyes. My breathing was shallow, and my lower lip began to tremble. I nodded yes to her, and I was suddenly blindsided by overwhelming emotion. My eyes began to glisten, and I could barely see her reaction through the blurriness. She wrapped her arms around me and pulled my head to her chest. She ran her fingers through my hair, and I started to bawl. I couldn't help it. I let it all out. She rubbed my back lovingly, and the tears streamed down my face, running past my nose and mouth.

"Owen, you're awake now. You're fine. It was just a dream."

"It wasn't just a dream," I groaned. "It was a memory."

"What was it?" she pulled me closer. "Let it out, babe."

She called me babe. I could feel her love for me, and it was beautiful.

"It was…the night…the night they took us away," I struggled to compose myself. "The beginning of the Confinement."

"Oh no," she muttered. "The fifteenth…"

She remembered. We all did. That night was engraved in the minds of every American. January 15th, 2015—just ten days after the bombs on Black Monday. We were all ripped out of the comfort of our sleep and thrown into a nightmare.

"These two kids beside me watched a man get shot. They saw him die, Rachel! They were so young! He bled out right in front of us…" My voice was distorted from the sobs. "He was the first of many to die. All the ones who resisted didn't have a fighting chance."

"I know, Owen. I know. I remember," she consoled, rubbing the back of my hair. "I'm sorry you had a nightmare of that night."

My forehead began to crease in anger.

"We can't let them win, Rachel!" I sobbed. "We can't let whoever did this, win. Please, I don't want it to happen again. A child should never have to see murder. This is the United States of America!" I exasperatedly shouted. "We are better than that. We can't let them win, Rachel. Please, we have to get your story. We have to…" I mumbled over and over again. I felt Rachel's tears hit the side of my neck.

"We will, Owen, we will. The truth will be their demise. I promise."

Rachel opened the patio door, and I quietly followed. I used my shirt to make sure my eyes were dry. I didn't want anyone knowing I had cried. The cooler, dryer air from the air conditioned house hit me. Rachel's mom and aunt were cooking breakfast. The sizzles and pops of bacon in a pan were all I heard. The scent of the scrambled eggs, sausage, and bacon were mouthwatering. I could barely remember my last real meal.

Briana and Grey stared up at us. Briana was trying to swallow her food, and Grey had a forkful of eggs that slipped off and landed on his plate.

"Where did you two sleep?" Briana asked. Her hair was finally back to normal. She wore her typical, slicked-back ponytail, with her blonde ringlet curls falling to her shoulders. Grey looked like Grey; he had just changed into something other than the suit.

"The beach," Rachel answered nonchalantly.

"You're lucky no one recognized you," she muttered.

"No joke," Grey added.

I glanced at Mrs. Flores, and she was staring at the food she was cooking. From my angle, I could almost see she had a worried look on her face. I checked my watch—it was barely 6:15. Why was everyone awake so early?

Rachel's aunt approached the table with two plates full of steaming food.

"*El desayuno*," she said.

"Breakfast," Rachel translated and gave me a flirty smirk.

"*Gracias*," I said. The aunt and Mrs. Flores laughed. Briana even let out a chuckle.

"It's your accent," Rachel explained. "Don't worry, you said it right."

"At least I tried," I laughed with them.

I sat in front of my plate filled with eggs, bacon, and sausage. It was so nice for her mom and aunt to make this, but I felt kind of guilty. We had disappeared all night. I wondered if Rachel had told her mom that she was going to the beach. Her mom was the last one to sit down at the table. Our eyes locked. I got the sense she was trying to tell me something without words.

"Remember what I said…"

Perhaps, it was just my conscience. She had asked me to keep her daughter safe, to protect her. I hadn't forgotten. Rachel's safety was my number one priority. What she didn't know, didn't hurt her…like the fact we had sex all night. I respected her mother. I didn't have mine anymore, so it only added to the weight of her words.

"This is really good, thank you," I spoke up.

"It's no problem," Mrs. Flores answered. "I wanted you all to get a good meal before you leave."

I froze. *Leave?* Who said we were leaving?

Rachel glanced over at me, but she didn't say anything. No one did. I kept eating, but her mom's statement bothered me. Did she know something that I didn't? I finished most of the food on my plate, and it was delicious. Grey and Briana had finished minutes ago, but they didn't leave the table.

"Owen, can I talk to you alone?" Grey asked.

I set down my fork. His question confused me, but I returned it with a nod and stood up with him. We walked into the foyer, away from everyone else—far enough to where no one would hear. It had only been two days, and Grey's five o'clock shadow had grown into quite a stubble.

"What's up, man?" I asked.

His face was serious, but there was something restrained in his expression. Whatever it was, he was ready to tell me.

"I have an idea," he said.

"Okay, shoot."

"Don't freak out, okay?"

I studied his face. I had no clue where he was going with this, but it was Grey. If anyone in the group had a good idea, it would be him. He was smarter than all of us combined.

"I won't. I swear, man."

"We are going to Atlanta."

"What?" my voice sounded harsh. "Why?"

"Because, I have a plan."

I let out a long exhale. I respected Grey's intellect. As pointless as Atlanta sounded, I was sure he had a reason behind it.

"What is it?"

"Okay, so last night when I was lying in bed, I couldn't fall asleep. I felt down in the dumps, and I'm sure you have too with everything that happened at the airport."

"Yes…" I mumbled. "I have. I just didn't want to say anything on the drive here."

"I know," he said. "Me neither. Anyway, as bleak as it sounds, I couldn't think of a better option than this. There isn't much left we can do."

I swallowed hard as Grey said those words. It was something I had thought about all day yesterday, but I didn't want to acknowledge it as true. It took Grey saying it for it to *really* sink in.

"You're right…" My words were barely audible.

"There's a little over two weeks until the election," he began. "We have no idea if Rachel will get her story in time. This would shake things up a bit. I'm going for shock value with this plan."

"So, why Atlanta?"

Grey's lips pressed into a hard line, and I could see his nervousness in telling me.

"CNN."

"CNN?" My forehead creased.

"I'm going for shock value, remember?"

I nodded.

"After what I did at the airport, I know I could do the same thing in Atlanta. The CNN building is there. I could hack into their wireless, watch the cameras, and find out what floor the newsroom is on. You can barge in and tell the world the truth—that you were framed."

I opened my mouth to tell him he was crazy, but I stopped myself. In actuality, he wasn't crazy, he was right. I had nothing to lose. It was just a matter of time before they caught me, so at least I could go out with a bang.

"Okay," I said. "When do we leave?"

"When Rachel's done eating. I've already packed all of our things. Remember what Luke said? We need to get out of this state. We've already stayed here far too long for my liking."

I nodded, and I walked back to the table and sat down. I ate the rest of my lukewarm food. Rachel's eyes met mine, and it was as if I heard her voice in my head asking, *'What was that about?'*. The thought of telling her frightened me. Not because I didn't want her knowing, but because I knew she wouldn't be thrilled about the idea. With her plan, I would have been safe. I would have been in Moscow right now, trying to figure out what I would do with my future. With Grey's plan, I was anything but safe. If I went on live TV, *they* would swarm me like an angry bee colony.

Then again, she knew just as well as I did. We couldn't run forever. The longer Rachel and I stayed together, the greater likelihood of them catching us together. I didn't want her to get caught, regardless of what *she* wanted. Her story was the most important thing to me now, not my safety. With the election being so close, this might turn things around. At least long enough for Rachel and Ian to find the other pieces of the puzzle.

Grey and Briana stood up.

"Thank you for breakfast, Marta," Briana said as she grabbed the used plates. "Yeah, it was delicious," Grey added. Rachel glanced between them, confused.

"Where are you guys going?" she asked.

"To pack up the car," Grey answered.

"Why are we leaving so soon?" her voice wavered, and she stood up too.

"You remember what Luke said, Rachel. He said to get the hell out of this state. Although we feel safe here, we aren't. It's just a matter of time."

"Where are we going?!"

My stomach sank from the thought of him saying Atlanta. I had no desire to be a part of the discussion that would follow. I *knew* Rachel would not approve of Grey's idea, for one simple reason. She wanted me *safe*.

"We'll talk about it in the car," he replied.

Whew. Good save, Grey.

Rachel gave her aunt a hug and then said her goodbyes to her mother.

"I love you, Mom—so much."

"Be careful, okay?" she said, squeezing her daughter in a bear hug.

"I will. I will call you once all of this is over."

"I love you, Rachel. *Para siempre*."

Briana and Grey were already in the car. Rachel released her mom and went to get in. I followed her.

"Owen," Mrs. Flores called from behind me. I turned around and approached her. She opened her arms, suggesting that we hug. I lightly hugged her and patted her back.

"*Remember* what I said…" She whispered into my ear.

I released her, and we stared at each other. Her face was stone cold. She had meant what she asked of me. I nodded in understanding. I planned on honoring her request. I would keep Rachel safe at all costs. We broke our stare, and I turned toward the rental car. I got in the back seat and immediately felt Rachel's eyes digging into the side of my face. The door thudded shut.

"Owen, *where* are we going?" she asked in an irritated tone.

I looked at her and felt my gut swimming around in fear of her reaction.

"Atlanta," I said.

CIA Headquarters – Langley, VA
09:54 10-21-2016

How had this gone so far? He had been on the run for over a week. That was seven days too long for my liking. This was a thousand times worse than when Viktor went missing. When he left New York, it was like he had disappeared into thin air. It was forgotten about in a matter of weeks. Owen's chase had been televised daily. His reappearance in Miami only caused more coverage, and the news had fulfilled their role excellently. We were leading in the polls. The Convergence Party's chance of winning was nonexistent. Although, the longer he remained out of our grasp, the more risk was involved. The last thing I wanted was for him to surprise us, to surprise the country. That would impede the work we have already done. It was counterproductive, and I was under strict orders to neutralize the threat Owen Marina posed to the existing establishment.

I had been chewing on my lower lip so frequently that I thought I tasted blood. I was unbelievably stressed. Angry, too—I was *very* angry. After what happened yesterday, I had to get out of that control room. I was so livid when I watched him escape from the Tahoe that I could have killed someone. I needed some alone time to think. What was our next move? Seven Miami officers were dead, and now the entire country was on edge. A week ago, I would have been content with Owen in handcuffs. A televised trial and then his certain prosecution. It was not like the trial mattered anyway because the election would have already been won. Now though, after what everyone *saw* on the news, would they want that?

The American People weren't compassionate towards terrorists. They wanted justice, and in my experience, they saw justice as an eye for an eye. The old Owen was dead to them. He was no longer a hero, or even a citizen. He was a *traitor*. He didn't deserve a right to a trial. So perhaps, we should give them what they wanted. An *eye* for an *eye*.

Three soft knocks came from my door. My head hurt too much to get up.

"Come in."

Marc entered and sat down in the leather stationary chair. This wasn't even my office. I hadn't a clue whose it was. The President knew how badly me and Marc didn't want to lose control of the White House, so he temporarily put us in charge of this operation. He knew what was at stake in this election. *Someone* had to do the dirty work behind closed doors, and I was happy to oblige. Marc let out a long exhale, and the bags under his eyes were more pronounced. His hair was a mess, and he just looked disheveled. I wondered how I looked...probably worse.

"Veronica," he began, "We need to talk."

If it were *anyone* other than Marc, I would have thrown something at them and told them to get the hell out of here. This was my quiet time. I only had two hours until I went to the control room.

"Well then, let's talk."

I sat more upright and interlaced my fingers, resting them on my lap. I had been in politics for over twenty years, and I still loathed how uncomfortable business clothes were.

"I overheard the Intel guys saying you gave them orders that we want Owen brought in *dead* or alive? Have you lost your mind?"

My nostrils flared, and I felt my face contort before I had the chance to answer.

"Not yet," I spat. "Have you?"

His forehead creased, and his eyes were wide.

"Veronica, are you kidding me?"

"No," I replied flatly.

"The election is in the bag. Your party has taken the lead, and mine and Owen's are trailing more and more every day. You did what the President asked of you, and now that you *can* sit back and relax, you choose to do the exact opposite. Why?"

"He is still out there, Marc!" I raised my voice. "A terrorist is still out there."

He snorted and shook his head in disapproval.

"Listen to yourself!" he huffed. "We both know that is a lie, and it always has been. We created it."

Anger began to bubble up inside me. Whose side was Marc on?

"We have seven dead cops on our hands! Do you want to just sit around and wait for Owen to pull his next stunt? Is that what you want?"

"Damn it, Veronica!" he shouted and slammed his fist on the desk. I pressed my lips together and stared at him, stunned. "I do realize that you are in charge here, but you need to remember that you were in diapers when I was in law school. I want you to get a grip of yourself! Seven dead is a drop in the hat. It makes me sick to think you have so easily forgotten about the seventeen lives that *we* took the night of the debate. The only reason I haven't left Washington yet is because I need to collect my salary for a few more years before I can get the hell out of Dodge."

I couldn't have cared less about the people we killed at the debate. All that mattered to me was the fact that Owen wasn't one of those seventeen. Cole *and* Owen were supposed to die—not just Cole. A sharp pain in my head made me wince.

"You're giving me a headache," I announced. He stood up angrily.

"You're gonna have one hell of a headache if this shit backfires on us! Getting away with murder is one thing, but doing it twice? You are pushing it, Veronica. I've seen people twice as cunning as you dig their own grave."

"Bite me," I spat.

"Have you been fishing before?" he asked with his eyebrows quirked.

"Why? Where the hell did that come from?"

"Just answer the damn question!" he retorted.

I chewed my lower lip. He was beginning to tick me off. Perhaps he had forgotten *I* was the one in charge, not him. But for the time being, I would give him the satisfaction of going along with his advice.

"Yes, when I was young."

"Well, perhaps your memory is foggy. I'm going to spell it out loud and clear for you. Let's say you're fishing at the end of a dock, and you've baited the hook."

"Are you serious right now?" I sneered, interrupting him.

He rolled his eyes at me and pushed back his graying hair.

"Just listen. You cast your line, and the bait sinks beneath the water. You feel a tug and pull back. You can feel the weight of the fish as you hook it, and you get excited, so you yank it up harder, reeling it in as fast as you can. Then, you lose the fish. You broke the line."

I was completely lost where he was going with this. So I stared at him like he was an idiot.

"Wow," he snorted. "You really don't get it, do you?"

"No."

"We have the election in the bag, Veronica. Owen is still out there, but we can consider him hooked. It is just a matter of time before you are reeling him in, and if you do it slow and steady, it will work. Giving the Intel guys those orders was mistake—a huge one. Your line is fraying, Veronica, and if you keep it up…it's going to break."

He turned around and headed for the door. He looked at me once more and shook his head with a sigh. He closed it behind him, and I was left alone…*finally*. His statement had me fuming. Who the fuck did he think he was? Talking to me like he was my father, and explaining his God awful parallel that was completely unrelated. Owen wasn't a fish. He was bright, charming, and intelligent. I could admit it. I had met him. He was the *last* obstacle preventing resuscitation of our plan. The plan that was cut short. No, Marc was wrong. My line wouldn't break. It couldn't, because I had the entire federal government helping me reel him in. I would have been a liar if I said I was content with Owen being brought in in handcuffs. I wanted more. I cringed at the thought of how much of a fool he made out of me at the airport. The older Intel guys who knew this was all a sham sure were cheeky after he escaped. I would show them what I was capable of. Veronica Hall was the wrong person to fuck with. I was ruthless, and I knew it. It had gotten me this far, so why would I change now?

If Owen was a fish…I planned on turning him into a goddamn fillet.

I-75 North – Atlanta, GA
15:03 10-21-2016

The ride was long—eight hours. We only stopped once for gas, snacks, and to use the bathroom. I pissed in a bottle. Going inside wasn't worth the risk of getting caught. Rachel had bundled herself in so many layers she was unrecognizable. Thankfully she wasn't given a second glance from what Briana and Grey said.

Much of the drive had been silent. My fear of telling Rachel where we were going was palpable, because she wasn't pleased in the least bit. She knew what me going on live TV meant, that there would be no escape plan this time. *They* would finally get the satisfaction of putting me behind bars. She worried for my safety, more so than I did myself. I tried to convince her it was an ambitious last effort, to tell the world on CNN that I was innocent, and I had been framed…but by *who?*

That was the million dollar question. It was a question I feared I would never have the answer to. Rachel wasn't having it, though. She couldn't yet bear the reality that I was slowly beginning to accept. The reality that there was no way I was getting out of this a free man. Although we hadn't talked much, she still held my hand. Our bond had strengthened since last night. One might presume it was the sex, but I was inclined to believe it was what we *felt* during it. Oh, how I wished our dreaming would come true. Rachel and I running off to the French Riviera, sipping wine under a foreign sun. Maybe one day, in a different life. Not this one. My fate was already sealed the moment the air marshal recognized me. It was that moment I knew wholeheartedly that I would never leave this country. The only thing saving me from life in prison was the hope that Rachel and Ian could compile a solid story in time. A story with irrevocable evidence.

Our time *was* running out.

The skyline of Downtown Atlanta came into view. It brought back memories of the time I had been interviewed in the CNN building. I told Grey I remembered it vaguely, but I couldn't remember what floor it was on. I was treated like a hero that day. I was escorted by my personal driver, and the interview went well. It still bewildered me how quickly it had all changed. Hell, if none of this would have happened, maybe I would have been interviewed again after we won the election. My stomach twisted just thinking about the past. The alternate reality I could never revisit. One where Cole was still alive.

Now, I couldn't show my face anywhere. What a change…

"It makes me nervous being in a city," Rachel mumbled. "So many people."

"Easier to hide, right?" I said, pointing out the positive.

"More people that could recognize you, and more cops."

I shrugged. She was right. Briana was navigating through the thickening traffic, and Grey was messing around on his laptop. There was a mobile hotspot sitting on his lap. I wondered what he was looking at.

"The Omni," Grey spoke up. "I've booked a room. It's also connected to the CNN building."

"Nice," I said.

Rachel let out a long, drawn-out exhale. This whole plan had her upset. She turned and looked out the window, facing away from all of us. There was nothing I could do to comfort her. My decision was made, and we would *all* have to live with it.

"We need to stop somewhere and get Owen and Rachel some new hair dye. Blond isn't going to cut it any longer for you, and Rachel's natural hair has to go. I'm thinking black."

"Black?" I questioned.

"We are running out of colors, Owen. We need to get you a scarf, and a big jacket. You can't just go walking into the hotel looking like you did in Miami. It won't work."

"You're right," I agreed.

We were in the heart of downtown.

"Oh…my…God," Grey practically exhaled the words. "Look at that billboard." He pointed out of his window to the right. I peered out of it, and my mouth dropped.

WITH ONE LIE

OUR FREEDOM DIES

It was written in red spray paint. The letters dripped down the white canvas. I glanced out at the street and saw a crowd of people pointing their smartphones at it, taking pictures. There was also a news crew filming. One of the cameras was pointed up at a steep angle to capture the footage. My mind darted to one name—Viktor Ivankov.

Was this his doing? It was so similar to the first message he left in the cabin for the FBI nearly six months ago. If it was Viktor, what was he doing in Atlanta?

"Do you think it's—"

"Him?" Briana finished Rachel's question.

"Yes," I answered. "I think it's him."

"His timing couldn't have been worse…" Grey huffed. "If Viktor is here, the feds are going to swarm this city. Now that you're in the spotlight, he is in the background, but they want him just as badly as they do you."

"Shit." I said.

"What are we going to do?" Rachel asked.

Grey glanced around at all the traffic nervously.

"We're going to lie low."

EPA HQ – Washington, D.C.
15:21 10-21-2016

I stood at the crosswalk, waiting for the pedestrian light to change. Ten seconds. Five. I hurried across with the others and made my turn to walk alongside the back of a building. I was at the federal triangle and moments away from walking into the EPA building. The front entrance was too busy, but I remembered the one time I was here, there was a side entrance. I hadn't the slightest idea of where to go, but given my clearance, I could get in anywhere.

Veronica should have taken away my badge. Her mistake would turn out to be a grave one. Even with my title, my mind was racing, playing out all the possible scenarios of what could happen. Would an employee try to stop me? Question me further than needed? I already had it in my head from the moment Veronica threatened me back at the CIA—I would *not* give up on securing the information I needed. The words echoed around in my head, and I held them there for reference. I felt like I was trying to solve a puzzle. Black Monday, the EPA, and the animals the students at MIT were testing were all a part of it. It was all connected. I just had to find the pieces that formed the big picture. Sure, there must have been a ton of false evidence circulating the country, but there was *always* an original. There had to be some form of documentation for the original cleanup on Wall Street, and wherever it was inside this building, I *would* find it.

There were days on the battlefield in Iraq where I felt calmer than this. The change in pulse was noticeable, and I tried to quell it. The last thing I wanted was to walk in sweating bullets and looking like I was up to something. I walked through the revolving door and immediately surveyed my surroundings. The military training always kicked in, regardless of if I wanted it to. It was instinctual. There was a moderate number of people in the lobby. That was ideal because I didn't want to stick out too much. I made my way across the marble floor and stopped at the reception desk. The woman behind the counter was young with a short bob haircut. Her red layers flared out at the ends by her ears. She smiled in greeting me.

"How can I help you today?"

I returned her smile and pulled out my badge.

"Lucas Bolden, CIA. I need to access your archives. It's a matter of National Security."

Her eyes grew wide and she nodded.

"Second floor, the elevator is right around the corner. In the first office on the left, there will be a woman who can help you. She is head of the archives."

"Thank you, miss."

I walked away with a grin, shaking my head at the thought of how easy that was. The badge sure did do the trick. It was a step above the FBI and a step below those snakes over at the NSA. I rode the elevator to the second floor and stepped out. I immediately felt how much warmer this floor was kept compared to the lobby. The carpet had an outdated look to it. The faint scent of printer paper filled the air. It was a typical office. This building was like a maze, though, so I knew there had to be a lot more than meets the eye.

There was what looked to be a break room in front of me, and I wandered a bit to my left. I found an office which I presumed was the first one. The door was open, but I still gave it a few gentle knocks.

"Hello?" a woman's voice called from inside. I opened the door a little more. For a moment, I thought I had lost my mind. She looked far too young to be working at the EPA. Her youthful appearance was more similar to an intern. She had platinum-blonde hair that flowed down past her shoulders. It was straight and sleek without a hair out of place. I couldn't help but notice her looks and well-built figure. She looked more like a model than a government worker.

"What are you doing up here?" she asked with a tone. She treated me as if I were an intruder. I guess I could have understood why.

"I need access to your archives, miss."

"Sorry, that is off limits to the public, sir. It is property of the federal government. Are you on the wrong floor?""

"Nope," I answered and handed her my badge. "I'm with the CIA, specifically Intel. I need to go through your archives. It is imperative that I do so."

She began to squint and studied me. I watched her eyes dart across my badge, over and over. I caught the sense she didn't trust me at all. She handed me back my badge. I heard her exhale, and she pushed herself out of the desk chair. "Follow me," she said. She wore a business skirt and heels. My eyes immediately went down to her ass, and it was quite nice might I add. That was my teenage mind trapped in an almost-forty-year-old body talking. My wife would have hit me so hard for looking.

"Why haven't I had anyone from the CIA come here before?" she questioned as she led me into another room. It was massive, with rows upon rows of file cabinets.

"Because my colleagues are too busy kissing ass to do any real work."

She shot me a hesitant glare and crossed her arms.

"It's all sorted chronologically. I'll be in my office if you need me." Her voice was short, and she wasn't very pleasant. I made a face behind her back. More teenage boy coming out in me. I hadn't grown up yet, so why try now?

I went to a random cabinet and opened it. I skimmed through some of the folders and saw the dates were in the early 2000s. I went one cabinet over and discovered it was from 1999. I went in the opposite direction and the year changed to 2001. With certain years, I quickly figured out that one year might have filled five to ten file cabinets. This room was gargantuan. I tried to skip around and hopefully in the process jump some years. I found 2014. *Okay, now I'm getting warmer.* Two cabinets over, I found 2015. I began to pull out the rows beside of that one also.

Skimming through, I saw many of those cabinets were dedicated to 2015. I knew it had been a busy year for the EPA. With the bombs on Black Monday, the cargo containers from the Port of New York, and the Confinement—there was a ton of environmental impact.

I began to pull out individual folders and investigate the contents. It took me a few minutes to find the ones containing information on Black Monday, but what I found only angered me further.

It was the same garbage they had spewed on the media. Strontium-90 was found at the scene. Viktor Ivankov this, Russia that. It felt like it was all planted here. These were the only records they wanted to be read. Of course, there was *nothing* about the stray animals affected by the radiation, and it didn't even mention that they executed them all. Something was missing.

"Do you mind if I ask you what you came here to find?"

I turned around to see the blonde woman standing in the doorway with her arms crossed.

"It's confidential, miss…but I will say, it is very dire that I find what I am looking for."

"Have you found it?" she asked. The snarky tone in her voice irritated me. I studied her facial expression in the fluorescent lighting, and there was almost a smugness about her. Like she knew something that I didn't. My eye began to twitch in realization of what her question affirmed. She *knew* I hadn't found what I was looking for because she *knew* it wasn't here to begin with. I slowly approached her with one of the folders in my hand.

"What is your name, might I ask?"

"Ms. Walling," she answered. Her smug smile diminished and was replaced with fear.

"Ms. Walling," I said her name slowly and intensely. "I haven't found anything besides this garbage. Whatever it is you know about what I *haven't* found, I suggest you help me find it."

She opened her mouth to speak.

"But wait," I cut her off. "That's no good, either, because I would never find what I needed in here. Am I right?"

She stayed silent and glowered at me.

"My question doesn't need to be answered. We both know the *real* evidence isn't here."

"What is it you want to find so badly?"

She was testing me. She knew that I knew, but she wanted me to say it. If she wanted to play this game, I could play it better. I was the one with the clearance. *She* should have been answering my questions—not the other way around.

"It is something I believe will help preserve the freedom and livelihood of every person in this country."

Her forehead creased. "How so?"

I set the papers down. "The fact that you are even questioning me shows that you have been lied to so well that you are beginning to believe them, even though you know the truth about what happened on Black Monday."

Her eyes grew wide.

"I don't know what you're talking about."

My steps were measured, and I neared her until I was a foot away.

"You know *exactly* what I am talking about."

She stared back at me with a blank expression. She blinked, and I noticed her chest rose and fell quickly. Her breath was rapid—she was nervous.

"I—I'm sorry I bothered you," she stammered and shook her head. "I need to make a phone call." She turned back around. She made it two steps.

"I wouldn't do that if I were you," I warned.

She whipped back around, glaring at me…but behind her distrust, there was curiosity gleaming in her eyes. At this point, I was going on my first whim. I just hoped my statements would lead me in the right direction with this woman.

"Why?" she spat with a quirked brow.

"Because, you will get yourself in more trouble than you would ever want to be in."

"How do you know this stuff? Like who the fuck are you?" She rolled her eyes and threw her hands up in the air. She was frustrated with my sudden appearance. It was obvious. She was having a normal day, then I came and screwed it up.

"I know this stuff because I work with the same people who are lying to you."

Her eyelid twitched and lower lip trembled. Her chest still heaved with her rapid breath.

"How do you know you're not being lied to, too?" she countered.

I snorted. "Ms. Walling, I came here to get evidence of the truth. Evidence that might help reverse the lie that's being told on the news. Like I said, I am an agent from the CIA, and I work in Intel. I know what's *really* going on, just like you do…but now, I need proof. I'm done sitting on the sidelines while our country is imploding before our very eyes."

I didn't want to reveal my true desires…to stop Veronica Hall in her tracks.

"You can call me Megan. So, this is about Owen? How certain are you that it's a lie?"

I laughed in her face. "You've got to be kidding me!"

She pressed her lips together. Her face was deadpan.

"Megan, it's all a sham. My department in the CIA is ten levels below the ground. I could be expatriated because of what I just told you, but I couldn't care less at this point. I don't plan on going back to work because I am done being a part of the lie. The bombs were planted to frame Owen. Their party was leading the polls by a landslide, and now look at them. Their plan worked. The democrats are in the lead. The traditional parties will stay in control. The Convergence Party is dead. Owen is innocent and always has been. I will never go back to work for them. She threatened me and my family…"

Megan's blue eyes darted across the floor, and she gently held her hand over her mouth. For the first time since I had walked into her office, she didn't seem so rigid. Her defensive glare was gone.

"Veronica…" The name was uttered so softly, I thought I had heard my own thoughts. I stared at her with wide eyes.

"*What* did you just say?"

"Veronica Hall," she replied, looking up from the floor to meet my gaze. "Did she threaten you too?"

My jaw dropped. Anger and sadness welled up inside of me because the memory of Veronica's threat was still fresh in my mind. I remembered how it felt. I remembered the fear and the pain it caused. Megan's lip quivered, and her eyes began to glisten. I could only imagine what she felt like. She had to be in her late twenties. Far too young to be sworn to secrecy and threatened by a higher up.

I nodded slowly. "She is my boss."

Megan coughed so hard I thought she was choking.

"Your boss?" she asked, and the tears began to fall. "I don't know how you do it. I could barely stand to be in the same room as her. The look in her eyes haunts me to this day."

"*Did* it," I corrected. "I quit, although she doesn't know that. I wouldn't be talking to you right now if she would have taken my badge. I needed it to get in here."

"How could you work around that vile woman?" she groaned and rubbed her forehead.

"I had no choice. It looks like you didn't, either."

"She came here with two NSA agents one day, over a year ago. She told me I would never see my family again. She put all the responsibility on my shoulders. It's too much pressure…too much stress. I've had it all bottled up…"

Her cries were guttural. She sat down in one of the office chairs and buried her face in her palms. *Over a year ago. That was after the Confinement, long before she was my boss.*

"Do you know what it's like to lie every day? Every *fucking* day I get calls, requests for appointments. All about the bombs on Black Monday. Black Monday this, Black Monday that. I smile, I go through the motions, and I give them the same paperwork you just had in your hands. They make copies, they shake my hand, and they go on their way. It's killing me, Mr. Bolden. It's *killing* me inside."

"You can call me Lucas."

She glanced up at me with tears streaming down her face.

"I know what it is like to go to work knowing that every second I spend there is contributing to more lies. The guilt keeps you up at night. It makes you want to disappear. I served overseas, Megan, and my work in the last three months has revolved entirely around the election. It was like I had a gun pointed at lady liberty, but I wasn't the one pulling the trigger. The constitution I swore to protect under oath, I was breaking for a paycheck. I couldn't live with myself."

"I know…" She groaned, hiccupping violently. "I feel so guilty. A guy I was seeing recently, he goes to MIT, and he called me to tell me he knew the *truth*. I was so scared for my own safety I told, Lucas, I ratted him out. To the same people you work for. I—I feel like such a coward. I feel like such a fucking coward…"

Her bawling was so raw. It was hard for me to watch. I had dealt with Veronica for three months. She had dealt with her for much longer.

"That was you..." I mumbled. "I was working the night the tip came in."

"Yes..." She groaned. "That was me, and I'm so ashamed to say it."

I stayed quiet and let her emotions run their course. There was nothing I could do to console her. Our decisions were in the past. The only thing we could control now was the future, but this was a battle that couldn't be won alone. I would need help, and Megan had the information I needed. After a few minutes her crying ceased.

"I used to date him," she said, with her voice raspy from crying.

"Who?"

"Owen."

I practically lost my breath.

"Are you serious?"

"Yes. We were in love. Well, at least, it was the closest thing to love I'd ever felt."

There was a pause.

"If you don't mind me asking," I began, "What happened?"

She shook her head and snorted, letting out a laugh.

"I made him choose between his party and me, and I regret it every day."

I didn't know quite what to say. I felt deeply for Megan's situation because mine was very similar. We both had been threatened by Veronica. I still had only one thing on my mind—to get the evidence.

"Well, help him, by giving him the justice he deserves."

She looked up at me and pursed her lips.

"Let's give Veronica a dose of her own medicine," I said, and held my hand out to help her up.

"Do you promise I'll be safe? I don't want her to do the things she said, Lucas. I am *afraid* of her."

"I am not afraid of her, I am afraid of what she is capable of doing. I can't promise you safety, but what I will say, is that the longer we wait to take action, the less of a chance we will have of stopping her."

Her breathing shuddered, and she turned away from me, letting out a few cries.

"I'm...so scared..." She blubbered. "It scares me that I've been lying so long that I've begun to believe the lie. It's been my entire existence since Black Monday."

"It doesn't have to be anymore." I encouraged her softly.

"She threatened to *kill* me," she hiccupped. Her blubbering continued. I bit down on my bottom lip to help ease my anger. Only someone as evil as Veronica could threaten a fellow citizen's life. All because she wanted to ensure the continuity of her agenda.

"She needs to be held accountable for the damage she has done. Will you help me?"

Megan looked up at me and wiped tears across her face.

"How long will it take to bring her down?" she asked.

"I can't say, but it's a whole lot better than helping *them* any longer."

She composed herself and stared up at me silently.

"When all of this is over, Megan, what side do you want to remember being on?"

The look in her eyes was priceless. It was the confidence that came along with making a decision to take back control. I imagined that was how I looked when I was walking out of the CIA building yesterday.

"Yes," she said. "Follow me."

We walked past the elevator and down a long hall. At the end of it, we reached a stainless-steel door. There was no doorknob, and the way the door appeared I couldn't tell if it was automatic or traditional. Megan stepped to the right and placed her eye in front of what looked to be a peephole. I heard a scanning sound, and the door slid open. She walked through the opening, and I stayed put.

"Can I come in?" I asked nervously.

"Yes," she answered. "Surprisingly enough, there are no cameras in here. The only people who can get in are me and Veronica."

"Who installed the retina scanner?"

"The NSA. Oh, and just wait—that was just the beginning."

The room was far too large to be this barren. Everything was stark white. The faded, peach-colored carpet from the hallway was replaced with white tile. Fluorescent lights illuminated the room to the point where it bothered my eyes. Against the back wall was a black file cabinet. The closer we became, the more apparent it was that it wasn't just *any* file cabinet. There were no handles, and it wasn't made of the typical, thin sheet-metal. It looked to be some type of iron. On the wall beside of it was a device around the size of a human head. It was chest level with Megan.

She placed her hand on the touch screen, and a line of light flashed from the top to the bottom. It beeped when it finished scanning. She then put her eye close to the top of the device. Another scanning sound was heard.

"Please enter nine digit security code now," a robotic voice said.

Megan used her index finger to press a series of numbers on the same screen that scanned her palm. A chime noise sounded.

"Identify confirmed—Megan Jeanine Walling."

I heard something click, and the top drawer of the file cabinet slid out. It was amazing that before it opened it appeared to have no crevices. It looked like a solid object that couldn't be opened. She pulled it out farther and handed me a file.

"This is what you will need," she said. "Everything is in there."

"Thank you, Megan. Thank you for helping me."

She nodded with pursed lips. Her anxiety was apparent. She *knew* what Veronica could do if she found out.

"You're welcome. I want to do what is right, for once."

"It feels great, doesn't it?"

"It feels better than living a lie," she admitted. "Hide that and get out of here. Go do what you need to do. Please, for the sake of my own safety, take Veronica down."

"I will," I said. I extended my hand. A small smile tugged at the corners of her lips, and she placed her smooth hand in mine, gently shaking it.

"Be safe out there," she said.

"You do the same. Skip town if anything bad happens, okay? Wait till this is all over."

She nodded. "Go, I have to do the security procedure again to lock up."

I turned away from Megan and exited the white room. My heart began to bounce around in my chest at the thought of what I was holding. There was a black stamp on the front.

CONFIDENTIAL

This was it. This was what I needed. I stuck the folder inside of my jacket and hit the down arrow on the elevator. *Ding*—I stepped in. I couldn't believe I had gotten through to Megan, but I was glad that I did. She had bottled up ten times the amount of stress I had, and she finally let it all out in front of me.

I walked out on the ground floor and headed for the nearest exit. The cold, mid-Atlantic air hit me with refreshing relief. I continued north on 14th street. I left my car and phone at home. I wasn't stupid. I wouldn't allow them to track me. I bought a pre-paid phone, and my destination was already determined days ago. I had to do it out in the public, a place where I could be sure that no one was listening. I saw the twelve-story white-marble building come into view on the corner of Pennsylvania Avenue and 14th. I nervously waited for a crosswalk light to change and made my way across. I walked up the stone steps and through the revolving door. I had been in The Willard before—it was one of my favorite InterContinental hotels. The inside resembled a palace. Low lighting and deep hues filled the lobby. The floors were so shiny you could partly see your reflection. There were four people at reception, but I didn't need their help. I already knew where the business center was. I walked toward it and saw that no one was inside. There were four computers, all with flat-screen monitors. On the far side of the counter was a copy machine. I sat down at the computer and began typing.

The New York Times Building.

The number appeared, and I punched it in my pre-paid phone. My hands were sweaty, and I became nervous. I had no idea if he would remember me, or if he was even there. Ten years ago, when I came back from Iraq, I was interviewed by one of his employees, but I had the chance of meeting him. I couldn't forget that day because he did mention if I ever needed anything not to hesitate to contact him. I wasn't the type that asked for help, but I thought in this situation it would be fitting. There was no one else I could give this information to. I worked for the CIA, and our system was so broken, there was no one that would dare try to get this information out to the public. My hope in Washington was dead. Now, it all boiled down to this one phone call.

Ring…Ring…Ring…Ring…

"New York Times, how may I direct your call?"

My heart was beating out of my chest I was so nervous. This *had* to work.

"Uh…hi, could I speak with Mr. Westlake? It is extremely urgent."

"Mr. Westlake has been in meetings all day, I can send you to his voicemail."

"Ma'am, please, don't transfer me. I have to talk to him."

"I am just a receptionist, sir. If Mr. Westlake happens to be in his office, I'd recommend talking to his assistant first. Hold one moment."

"Ma—" the line began to ring again. *What a bitch.*

"This is Sharon, how may I help you?"

Thank God, she sounded a *little* friendlier.

"Hello, Sharon, I need to speak to Mr. Westlake. It is extremely urgent."

"Hold one moment," she said shortly.

The hold music reminded me of riding in an elevator. I heard the line snap back on.

"In what regards is this call?" she asked curiously. "And if you don't mind, may I ask who is calling?"

In what regards is this call? I took a deep breath and let it out.

"It has to do with Black Monday, with Owen, with everything. My name is Lucas Bolden and I am an agent with the CIA."

I heard her faint gasp in my ear.

"I'll transfer you now," she said in a shaky voice.

Ring…

"Ian Westlake," a stern, familiar voice picked up.

"Hello, Mr. Westlake…I—uh, I know this is going to sound bizarre, but I needed to speak with you right away. One of your journalists interviewed me when I got back from my tours in the Middle East, and I met you that day. I saved one of my fellow soldiers, a wounded brother, and that's why you guys did the story. Do you happen to remember me?"

There were a pause and a crackling in the background.

"Yes, actually. They gave you a medal, correct?"

"Yes, they did, Mr. Westlake."

"You can call me Ian," he corrected. "So, agent Bolden. What is it that you have to tell me? Don't worry. This is on a secure line. I just hope no one is listening on your end."

"No," I assured him. "I am at a hotel using a pre-paid phone. I am actually sitting in front of a fax machine, and I need your direct fax number. I have to send you some documents."

For a moment, I thought he had hung up.

"Ian? Are you there?"

"Yes, I'm here. Are these documents what I think they are?"

"Indeed, they are, and I'm sorry to throw this on you all of a sudden, but I had nowhere else to turn. My sector of the government is an absolute nightmare. This country is turning to shit before my own eyes. So please, when the time comes, use what I am about to send you for the right reasons. There are very good people involved that are depending on me not to let them down."

"I understand. Don't be sorry, Lucas. It is a miracle you called me. You just made me the happiest I have been in my entire career."

I couldn't help but smile.

"Oh," I chuckled. "If you think you are happy now, just wait until you see what is about to come through your fax. What is the number?"

My breathing began to steady. My work had paid off. My mind darted in a hundred different directions, imagining what would take place over the next few days. I wished with every cell in my body that Veronica's plan would come to a screeching halt. I had fought for this country once, and I would continue fighting for it in whatever manner I was able to. That was the oath I swore to uphold, and my rebellion was needed at a time like this. Maybe one day, kids would read in the history books about the people who helped dismantle this house of cards, built from the lies of the wicked.

Omni Hotel – Atlanta, GA
22:38 10-21-2016

Grey and Briana had taken the rental car, and apparently they were going to crack the wireless of CNN. He told us he would bring back some dinner. That was over two hours ago. Our room was just the standard. It had two queen beds. It was a closet compared to the penthouse suite we were in the night before last, but it was no less comfy. It was well decorated. Rachel was flipping through the channels for the hundredth time. She stopped for a moment on one of the local news stations.

"…Authorities warn that Viktor Ivankov may be in Downtown Atlanta. Analysts say the graffiti on the billboard is similar to his first message. Please call the police if you have any information…" Rachel changed the channel.

"I wonder what he is doing here," she said.

"Who knows," I responded. "I just hope he doesn't interfere with tomorrow."

Her lips pressed into a hard line, and her cheek muscles flexed. She was clenching her jaw and didn't even respond. I knew why, but nothing needed to be said. She had already expressed her disapproval of Grey's plan.

My stomach growled violently. It was pushing eleven o'clock, and I was starving. I knew we weren't supposed to go anywhere. It would be risky and plain dumb, but something inside me was pushing me to go. Perhaps, it was my primal instinct of wanting a meal, or wanting to rebel against the fact I was trapped everywhere I went. Hostage to my infamy.

"Let's go get some street food," I said.

Rachel cocked her head towards me.

"You're joking, right?"

"No, I'm not. Put your hair up, get your hat on, and change clothes. Let's go eat."

I grabbed a toboggan lying on the bed and pulled it over my blond hair. I put on my sunglasses even though it was dark outside. Grey had left a scarf that I wrapped around my neck, and I zipped my jacket tight.

"What has gotten into you?" Rachel threw her hands up.

"Hunger," I answered flatly. "You have to be hungry too."

"I am, but I can wait until Briana and Grey bring us something back. They were going to pick up stuff for our new disguises too, remember?"

"I do. It's been three hours. It shouldn't take that long, and I'm tired of being cooped up in this hotel room anyway."

She was still in the bed. She hadn't moved at all.

"Are you coming or not?" I asked.

She stared at me so intently, as if she was trying to speak to me through her mind. Her whole expression radiated defiance. Maybe she was trying to tell me without words, *'This is your punishment for agreeing to Grey's plan. I'm not going anywhere with you.'*

"Come on, babe…" I pouted softly. "I want to spend as much time with you as I can."

She exhaled sharply through her nose and bit her bottom lip. She turned away from me, but I could see her roll her eyes.

"Okay, fine. You win."

She used her hair tie to wrap her hair up in a tight bun, and she dug around her backpack for the Dolphins cap. She borrowed one of Briana's jackets. The weather was freezing compared to Florida.

"Where do you have in mind?" she asked. "It's not like we can just walk up in a restaurant and ask for a table for two."

I laughed. "No shit, I wish we could. I saw a hotdog stand around the block. It's close, and it will hold us over until they get back."

"All right," she obliged.

Once our disguises were on, I walked to the door and peered out the peephole. No one was in the hall. I signaled to Rachel that the coast was clear. I opened the door and immediately headed for the exit, with Rachel at my heels. Briana and Grey checked us in again as *Rose* and *Gregory*. She lied, telling the front desk her sickly mother was with us, and we needed the ground floor. We needed the ground floor because it was a quick in and out. We didn't have any elevator rides, and we had fewer chances of someone recognizing us. It was only fifteen feet before we walked out the exit door, and the chilly autumn air hit us. I made sure my scarf and toboggan covered the majority of my face, and Rachel was bundled up pretty well herself.

The exit nearest to our room put us out on the back side of the hotel, almost in somewhat of an alleyway. There were no cars, just one wide sidewalk. I was glad. No cars meant fewer people that could potentially recognize us. We wrapped around to the *real* street, and I saw the hotdog stand a block away. A few people passed us, but none gave us a second glance. I was extremely happy we were blending in. I stopped and leaned in to nudge Rachel before we reached the stand.

"How do you like your hotdogs?" I asked.

"All the way," she mumbled.

"I could have made a really dirty joke with that answer," I chuckled.

She slapped the backside of my coat and revealed a small smile. I approached the hot dog stand. There was no one else in line.

"What can I get you two?" the man asked.

"Two hot dogs all the way, please."

"That will be 4.14, sir."

I pulled out my billfold and handed him a ten. He handed me the change, and Rachel grabbed the two hotdogs wrapped in foil.

"Thank you," she said.

The moment I turned around, I unwrapped it and devoured it in a matter of bites. The warm chili and chopped onions were perfect. It was sad to say, but that hotdog might have been the best meal I had in days, probably because I hadn't eaten in so long.

"Slow down there, cowboy," Rachel giggled.

My mouth was so full I couldn't even answer.

We passed more people in the street. I tried to keep my head down, but I had slid my scarf down so I could eat. We neared the alleyway we had come from, and I quickly turned down it. The back entrance door was made of all glass and well-lit. I saw many people walking through our hall. They were kids, actually. They all wore basketball uniforms. I saw many parents with the children, too. It was a commotion. A commotion that made it far too risky to go right back in our hotel room. We would have to wait until it cleared out.

I stopped Rachel just a few feet shy of the entrance.

"What?" she asked. I pointed through the door. She leaned over to glance in.

"Oh. I see," she said. I nodded. "We can just wait a few minutes out here," I suggested. "You still have to finish your hotdog, anyway."

She shrugged her shoulders and took another bite. I shoved my hands in my pockets and just stared at the glass door, waiting for the crowd in the hallway to thin.

Something was pulled over my head, and I couldn't see. I heard Rachel's hotdog splat on the ground. I was in a headlock, with a forearm pressing onto my face, covering my mouth. I could hear Rachel's muffled screams as her mouth was covered too. I struggled to breathe. I fought and kicked, but just as quickly I was thrown chest-first onto the hood of a car. That same forearm was now pressed down into my back, to the point where I couldn't even try to lift my body. It had to have been a man behind me. I could tell by the physical strength, but also, his body was pinned against mine. He was using every part of his body to keep me pushed against the car…and it *definitely* wasn't the body of a female. My hands were pulled behind my back, and a moment later I felt fisherman's rope being tied so tightly around my wrists I thought it would cut off the circulation. Rachel's whimpers and cries continued, so I knew she was still with me. My heart pounded in my chest. Were we being arrested? What kind of cops would put a bag over the suspects' heads? Two car doors popped open, and I was pushed inside. My body slammed into Rachel's, but luckily we didn't bump heads. I felt suffocated. Every breath I took felt struggled, and the air that filled the sack was already muggy and moist.

The car was moving. I had no idea where we were going.

"Did anyone see?" a male voice asked in a low tone.

"No," a female voice muttered.

I was sitting in a chair with my arms wrapped around the back of it. I couldn't tell where, but I knew Rachel was beside me. I could hear her breathing. The black material of the sack barely let in any light, and I still couldn't see our kidnappers. I was angry, and my body was sore. The car ride was less than five minutes long. I tried to memorize which way we turned, like I had seen in some movies, but it didn't work. I lost track of our direction. Too many lane changes, and too many turns. When we got out of the car, we were dragged down some steps. The only thing I could think of was a basement of some sorts. My imagination was running wild. The grimmest possibilities of what could happen to us bombarded my mind. Did some overly-patriotic serial killer kidnap us? Had they been stalking us since we arrived in Atlanta? Maybe they really *did* think we were terrorists and wanted to serve their own form of justice. I shuddered at the thought.

The sack was pulled off of my head. I glanced to my left to see Rachel looking at me in fear. The smoothness of her face was replaced with hard lines and teary eyes. I had never seen her this frightened since I met her. I quickly whipped my head around to examine where we were being held for any clues of its location. The floor was wooden and worn. I remembered hearing its creakiness when we were brought in. The concrete walls were windowless. There was a row of twin beds along the back wall, a sofa with the leather peeling off, and an old TV in the corner. I heard voices and footsteps above us. I couldn't help but assume we were underneath some backstreet bar. The whole room had a musty smell to it. I tugged at the ropes around my wrists, but they wouldn't budge.

"What do you want with us?" Rachel asked, her voice trembling.

I turned to face forward, and I was finally able to see our kidnappers. The man faced away from us, and there looked to be some sort of cart in front of him. The closest thing I could compare it to would be the cart a waitress delivers room service on. There was a laptop open atop it, and to the right of his body was a projector. The woman faced us. It looked like she was chewing on bubble gum, but in the dim lighting of the room, I couldn't tell if it was that or her lip. She had black, voluminous hair that was put up in a complex-looking bun. There were long strands that hung by her ears and down to her shoulders. There was something different about her features, they weren't like the typical American girl. She had high cheekbones, and her makeup was dark. She had a borderline gothic look.

"Natasha," the man said. "The lights, please."

I could have sworn I heard the faintest accent in the man's voice. She hit the light switch, and the faint yellow lighting was replaced by the white glow of the projector. The man turned around to face us. He didn't say a word, just glanced back and forth between me and Rachel. There was something oddly familiar about him, and it caused me to squint. His hair was jet black, just like Natasha's, but his features were strong. His jawline was twice as manly as my own, and the look in his eyes just screamed that he had been angry for a *very* long time. Something told me I had seen his face before, but I couldn't put my finger on where.

"Do you know who I am?" he asked.

In my peripheral, Rachel was shaking her head no. I had zoned out, still studying why his face looked so familiar to me. Suddenly, I realized he had asked us a question.

"No," I answered.

He laughed and shook his head side to side. He snorted, exhaling out of his nose as he continued to chuckle.

"Good," he said flatly. "See Natasha, your disguises have worked very well."

She winked at him and gave him a nod. I couldn't help but notice that incredibly faint accent every time he spoke.

"So, you don't recognize me at all?" he asked us again.

"You look very familiar," I blurted.

"Aha," he said, and began to clap slowly. "Bravo, Owen."

I was about to ask him how he knew my name. Then, I realized how stupid that question was. *Everyone* knew me.

"Did either one of you happen to see the billboard when you came into downtown?"

My stomach flopped. There was *no way* this was who I thought it was.

"Yes," Rachel mumbled. "We all did."

"What did it say?" he pressed. His tone became tenser. It was like he was trying to coax us into saying what he already knew.

"With one lie our freedom dies," I repeated the dripping red words that were on the billboard earlier today. The man revealed a twisted smile.

"With *one* lie our freedom dies. All it took was *one* lie to send this country spiraling down into an oblivion so abysmal we would never be able to escape it."

"What…what are you talking about?" Rachel asked with her breath catching.

He huffed, rolling his eyes. "You two know *exactly* what I'm talking about. You are fucking living it!" he shouted and walked over to me. He leaned over and propped his hands on his knees. His face was a mere foot away from mine. "The lie they created about *you*, Owen, was like giving oxygen to a dying flame. Now, they have a raging fire, one that will consume this whole country!"

"You know I was framed?" I muttered, with my mouth agape.

"Of course I do!" he shouted, his accent thickening with every word. "I know because I was framed, too!"

I felt the blood leave my face. I stared into his dark eyes, and his lower lip quivered.

"You've been on the run for a week and a half. Try two years."

"Viktor…" The words slid out of my mouth like I was in a trance. I saw Rachel's brown locks swing in my peripheral as she whipped her head around.

"Viktor? Are you really?" Rachel questioned. I could hear the panic in her voice.

"*Yes,*" he glanced between us. "Viktor Ivankov."

Then, it hit me. I was sitting in front of the most elusive man the country had ever tried to catch. I struggled to loosen the ropes around my wrists, and my eyes darted around the room for an exit. Viktor and Natasha hadn't killed us, so *why* were we still alive? What did they want? My logical mind was trying to figure it out. How did they find us? Were they watching us from the moment we got in Atlanta? So many questions. The most important of which, spawned from Viktor's statement. He had been framed also.

Now that I knew who he was, his identity was more recognizable in his features. The face I had seen on the news for so many months. Viktor Ivankov in the flesh—right in front of me.

"Why did you kidnap us like this?" Rachel croaked. Her face was still contorted with glistening eyes.

"Because," he began, turning back around to the laptop. "I needed to show Owen something."

My forehead creased. "And this is how you had to bring us here?" I shouted, and shook the wooden chair by pulling at the ropes.

"I had no choice," he replied. "It's not like you two would have willingly hopped in the car with a terrorist and a stranger. We saw you in traffic and followed you the rest of the day. You deserve to know the truth."

The words pierced my mind with such clarity it was indescribable.

The *truth*. My heart sped up just from the thought. I turned left to see Rachel staring at me with the same expression. She knew just as well as I did, those two words meant more to our struggle than anything else. The truth meant Rachel had a story to write. If Ian published the story, we might be able to save the election in time.

"Natasha, untie them, please."

Without missing a beat, she walked over to us and knelt behind our chairs. After a few moments, I felt the ropes slide off my wrists. It immediately alleviated so much discomfort. I stretched my arms out, and I heard Viktor doing something on the laptop. He held out a remote, and an image projected onto the wall. He stood away from the projector so we could see. The image was in black and white, but there was something peculiar about it. It looked like a gigantic rectangle, filled with other items. In the corner, there was a timestamp.

09:54 – 01/02/2015

Viktor began clicking the remote and flipping through more images. It looked as if it were an x-ray. I noticed the timestamps became later and later in the day.

"Do you know what this is?" he asked, crossing his arms. Rachel stayed quiet. Then, the realization of what it was hit me.

"It's a shipping container…" I mumbled.

He snorted and grimaced.

"Bingo!" he shouted, and gave us an unenthused, slow clap.

"How…how did you get those images?" Rachel asked, her voice detached.

"Ten years…" He growled. "Ten years I worked there before this shit happened. So, before the New Year, I noticed something I had never seen before. I saw my bosses walking around with a few people dressed differently than our inspectors normally would. They wore suits and asked our employees questions. They talked to me, asking me questions about my position and how long I had been there."

My pulse quickened with every word. I was getting to hear what really happened at the Port of New York before the Wall Street dirty bomb.

"I found it odd that I had never been asked these things before. I had a feeling something wasn't right. Our inspectors usually didn't come until the end of the first quarter, and these people were *different*. They gave me a bad vibe. So, I began copying the daily archive of everything I x-rayed onto this jump drive. Although, I came to find out they didn't know this. It wasn't until after I was framed when they conducted the fake investigation, that they realized what I had done. That was why they wanted to find me so badly. They knew I had proof that I had nothing to do with the bombs."

"Why didn't you put the proof on the internet or something?" I interjected.

He glared at me. "Don't you think I've already thought of that? Owen, you know just as well as I do, if I were to leak those images, they would be wiped clean off of the internet in an instant. It would be immediately labeled as a conspiracy. We are two people, and they have an entire army against us."

I nodded, looking down at the floor. He was right.

"Were you two in the Confinement?"

"Yes," Rachel answered. I said the same.

"I wasn't," he said. "I was outside of the boundaries. There was rumor around town that the National Guard said it wouldn't be long until everyone was rounded up and put into Camps. Natasha intercepted emails from two higher-ups in Washington while we were passing through, trying to get information. Within those emails, it stated that the Supreme Court had sabotaged their plan, and in order to revive it they had to do something *new*."

"We were never meant to get out…" I mumbled. The statement I made to Cole that fateful day in the bunkers during the Confinement was right.

"Correct," Viktor said. "The Confinement was the first step towards a totalitarian regime. Then, you and Mr. Pavich came along and screwed things up for them even further. The Convergence Party. I have to admit, I admired what you two did. I still do to this day, and when your party took the polls by a landslide, it immediately put a massive target on both of your backs. It was just a matter of time. *You* were the target they chose in order to revive their plan. They framed you so that they wouldn't lose their power."

I felt sick to my stomach.

"The images in my jump drive prove two things. One—that I had nothing to do with the Wall Street dirty bomb, and two—that the radioactive material used to create the bomb came from right here. *They* just involved Russia because I am Russian. When in actuality, they created the bomb. It was made on American soil."

Viktor aimed the remote toward the projector. An image appeared. Anger flooded my body.

"Do you know who—"

"Alexei Malchikov," I interjected. Saying the name made me cringe.

"Alexei Malchikov…" Viktor repeated. "He was innocent, like you. His family owned massive textile plants all over the US, and they owed the IRS tens of millions of dollars. They were funneling most of their money into a Swiss bank account. Alexei made a deal with them in order to give his family amnesty. He knew it could possibly cost him his life, but he did it anyway. The media didn't mention anything about his family background, though. It was all orchestrated by the same people."

I rubbed my sore wrists. They itched from where the ropes had scraped them. I felt numb to all of this information. Deep down, I had always known that it was a sham, so that the people in power wouldn't have to give up their reign. But hearing it, though, hearing it was *different.* It was nauseating to hear that our elected officials were trying to take away the very thing our nation was founded on…*freedom.*

"Why are you telling us all of this?" Rachel asked. She sounded exasperated.

"Better yet, how do you know all of this?" I added.

"Natasha was the one who got the information we needed," he said. I glanced over at her, and she was still acting like she wasn't listening to any of this, chewing her gum and twirling a long strand that fell out of her bun. She must have been a hacker—a female Grey.

"Also," Viktor's voice pulled me from my thoughts. "We need your help."

"With what?" I jeered.

"To help expose the person behind all of this."

The person behind all of this. The words resounded in my mind over and over again. It was something I had thought about since the morning I discovered my predicament at the coffee shop. *Who* was behind framing me?

"What?" Rachel snapped. "Look, Owen is in enough trouble as it is. He has already heard enough wild ideas for one day—"

"Show them," Natasha said from her dark corner, without any inflection in her tone.

Viktor stood in front of the laptop again, and I heard the fast clicking of the keyboard. An image appeared. My jaw dropped, and I lost my breath.

"Veronica…" I mumbled. The words weren't even audible. I could hear Rachel's confused questioning in the background, but it was distorted and hazy. I felt lightheaded and nauseous. I stood up and inhaled deeply, trying to ground myself. Her ice blue, cat-like eyes gave me a chill down my spine, just as they had the day I met her. My chest felt tight. I walked over to the projected image on the wall and studied it again. Her hair was shorter in this picture—it must have been from the internet. I remembered how cold her hand was when I shook it and that uneasy feeling her presence gave me.

She was behind all of this. I thought I was going to be sick.

"Owen!" Viktor shouted. "Are you all right? Sit down." He grabbed my shoulders, and I shook him off. "I'm all right, I'm fine!" I insisted, and he let me go.

"Who the hell is she?" Rachel asked frantically. "You look like you just saw a ghost!"

"She's the Chairwoman of the Democratic Party. I've met her before."

"What? When?" Rachel pressed further.

"The night of the final debate. I remember her snarky comments towards me, and it pissed me off. She told me with as much as I had accomplished at such a young age, I would surely have a bright future ahead of me in Washington."

"She knew what was going to happen to you before you ever stepped foot in the debate." Rachel mumbled.

"Owen was never supposed to make it out of the debate alive. The only thing that saved his life was the fact he stood up and left his seat just before the bombs went off. The rows Owen and Cole were sitting in received the most causalities. That was no coincidence."

My suspicions were correct. I was supposed to die that night. Veronica wanted both of us dead…but, I was still here. For some unknown reason, I noticed Alexei's peculiar behavior and stood up. That was the only reason I was still alive. Maybe I would have been better off dead. *No, that doesn't sound right.*

"He thought the same thing, too," Rachel said, pulling me from my thoughts. "Earlier, I heard you say that you needed our help. With what?"

Viktor's lips pressed together in a hard line.

"Natasha looked into Rachel's background and saw she was a journalist. I have hard evidence right here in this flash drive that could help take her down. All we need is a way to get it out there."

Rachel glanced at me and Viktor. "I know someone…" She began. "Someone who could get it out to everyone. I told him to find the other pieces of the puzzle, to figure out what other evidence was out there, and this is a huge step closer to solving it."

Natasha walked towards us from her corner, and Viktor's eyes grew wide.

"Do you really?" he asked.

"Yes," she answered. "My godfather is the Editor in Chief of the New York Times."

His jaw dropped. "No fucking way."

She nodded in confirmation.

"How do we get in contact with him?"

Viktor's eyes were bulging in excitement.

"He has a secured line I can call him on…but first, we need to go back to the hotel and get Briana and Grey. They are probably back by now and more than likely worried about us. Grey has similar skills as Natasha, he can help her out with whatever we decide to do."

"I don't need any help," she spat. Her tone irritated me.

"Now why is that?" I shot back. She pursed her lips and cocked her head to the side.

"Because I know what I am doing. I'm just as capable as he is, or more so."

"Have you ever hacked into the mainframe of an international airport?"

She huffed and turned to Viktor, mumbling something. There was excitement in Rachel's eyes. Her story was beginning to come together right in front of her, but there was an unsettling feeling growing in my gut. She was forgetting about the task at hand. Grey was going to help me get into the CNN building and interrupt the newscast. I was going to tell the world the truth.

"Have you forgotten about our *other* plan?" I asked Rachel. She turned from Viktor to me, and in her stare, I could almost hear her pleading, *'Please, don't bring it up.'* Her face was deadpan.

"*No*," she replied coldly.

"What is he talking about?" Viktor asked.

When I turned to Viktor I could feel Rachel's eyes practically burning into the side of my face.

"Tomorrow, with the help of Grey, I am going to barge in on a newscast at the CNN building."

"What!?" Viktor snapped, with a quirked brow. "You've got to be kidding me!"

"No, I'm not. The election is just too close to forfeit everything I have worked for. The world *needs* to know."

In my peripheral, Rachel crossed her arms, and Viktor stared back at me, shaking his head.

"Owen, take it from someone who has been on the run for almost two years. You *will not* walk out of that building a free man."

"I am aware of the risk," I said, raising my voice, "but I know what I need to do."

"Actually, I don't think you do. You see, an article is just as powerful as the television. The New York Times is everywhere. It's not like every single person will be watching CNN the moment you come on," he countered.

I bit the inside of my lower lip. His persistence was adamant, but so was mine.

"It doesn't matter!" I yelled. "Rachel already knows my story, she has everything she needs from me. The longer I stay with her, the longer she is at risk. You and I *both* know, Viktor, that the longer she is with me, the more likely it is she won't be able to get her story out. She is the link to her godfather, Ian. Without her, we have nothing."

Natasha shook her head and turned back around to head to the corner of the room. Viktor was clearly still heated, but I could tell in his expression he was processing what I had just said.

"Why don't I have a say in any of this?" Rachel interjected and stood up. "Grey just comes up with this grand idea, and yet you don't even take my opinion into consideration? It is pathetic that I am thinking more about your well-being than you are. Grey's plan is a dead end. Sure, it has shock-and-awe, but that's it. It doesn't keep you safe like Russia would have."

Frustration bubbled up within me.

"Well guess what? That plan didn't work. It's over, and I didn't take your opinion into consideration because I know your decision-making process is currently clouded with emotion. You don't want anything to happen to me because you love me, and it hurts too badly to admit that you *are* safer without me. You know it's true! So stop trying to protect me and start thinking of one thing and one thing only—the compilation of your story."

I was breathing heavy, and Rachel's reaction made me realize very quickly that I had fucked up. Her lower lip trembled, and her eyes began to glisten. She shook her head and exhaled sharply out of her nose. She stood up, walked to the other side of the room, and sat on the couch.

"I can't run forever, Rachel!"

"You'd be surprised…" Viktor mumbled.

I turned to him, and at this point, I felt like everyone was making me out to be the bad guy. If only Grey were here to defend me. My cheeks flushed.

"You aren't much help, are you?" I sneered.

He snorted. "Clearly, you are blinded by your idea. You are ignoring all the information I have just told you and focusing on one tiny detail, that Rachel *might* be a little safer without you around. Did you process anything I said?"

"Obviously not," Natasha chimed in.

"I did, I get it—"

"No, you *don't*," Viktor cut me off, and he pressed his index finger against my chest. "I told you, Owen, you are like fresh air to a dying flame. *You* are who they chose to revive their plan. *I* was the beginning, and *you* are the end. We aren't that different after all."

"We are different," I countered. "Because I am not afraid to show my face to the world and tell them the truth. I could never hide for as long as you have."

"What you want to do tomorrow, it's not courageous. Can't you see? If you show your face on that newscast you will be walking straight into the lion's den. They will win! You will be giving them *exactly* what they want!"

"Fuck you, Viktor! If I am going to be in handcuffs one way or another, I want to keep my dignity. I don't want everything I did with

Cole for our party to be in vain! I *want* the world to know I am innocent! If Rachel doesn't get her story, then there won't be any proof. There will be no way for me to speak up then, when I am rotting away in some maximum security prison."

His eyes were practically popping out of their sockets, and his face was beet red.

"Don't you see what I am trying to say to you, Owen? All you are is a gambit to them! You are a fucking *sacrifice!* You are just a pawn and Veronica is the queen. If you go through with your plan, I promise you, *they* will win. Don't be their gambit. Don't give yourself up so easily."

My eye twitched, and I chewed on the inside of my bottom lip to keep calm as I digested his words. He said I was a *sacrifice*…and *that* word, gave me a chill that ran up the entire length of my spine. I wasn't an idiot. I knew what he said was true, but I also knew my points were valid, regardless of the risk. Rachel could write a story whether or not I was with her or in a jail cell. Perhaps then, she would be out of the spotlight. Something in my gut told me that I *had* to go with Grey's plan. I wanted to keep my integrity intact.

I thought I heard Rachel crying. I took a deep breath and exhaled slowly.

"Thank you, Viktor, for spelling it out so clearly to me. I understand what you are saying, but I need to stick with Grey's plan. You all can focus on the story. I will do what I need to do to preserve my party. I have to wake people up enough before it's too late."

Viktor shook his head side to side in disappointment.

"Fine," he said flatly. "You stay here. Rachel, Natasha, and I will go get Grey and whatever her name is from the hotel. When we get back, Rachel, can you call your godfather?"

West Village – New York, NY
23:24 10-21-2016

My phone vibrated violently, skidding across the nightstand. Groggy and disoriented, I slapped my hand blindly to grab it. I squinted as my eyes adjusted to the light of my iPhone screen.

Restricted

I glanced over at my alarm clock—11:25. Was it *her?*

"Hello," I answered in a whisper.

"Hey. It's me."

I sat up in my bed wide awake and alert. We hadn't talked in days. I had been waiting to hear from her, and I thought about it every minute of the day.

"Thank God you finally called. I was getting worried."

"I could imagine…" She mumbled.

"I can't believe he escaped. In my thirty years in this industry, I have never seen anything like it."

"I believe it."

There was a pause.

"So, what made you call?" I asked.

"I found another piece of the puzzle."

My pulse quickened from her words.

"I found two," I added.

"Really?" her voice jumped up in pitch.

"Yes, one was from my son. Do you remember him?"

"Stefan, right?"

I smiled at how keen her memory was.

"Yes. I am surprised you remember."

"Women remember everything. You should know that by now," she teased.

"Indeed, I do," I chuckled.

"So, what was it he figured out?"

"I can't talk about it." I mumbled. "You know, just in case."

"Mhmm."

"Just know it is a very important piece. What about yours?"

"It is a massive piece. Something that will contribute to at least half of the story. The situation I was just thrown into is hard to believe that it even happened. It feels surreal."

For a moment, she sounded distant…almost detached.

"Are you okay?" I asked.

"Yeah. I'm okay, I guess."

"You *guess?*"

"You-know-who is being stubborn, and there is nothing I can do about it."

"What do you mean?"

"I can't say exactly, but be sure to have the news on. I know it's a Saturday, so if you're not at work, at least put it on at home. Tell your journalists on the floor to have it on in the office."

Her statement intrigued me. I hadn't a clue what she was hinting at.

"They always do. I make sure they do."

"Good," she said. "So, how do I go about getting you this information?"

"Wait until tomorrow. Then, call the office. They will get you transferred to the secure line, and I'll give you what you need to fax it to me."

"Sounds good," she said. There was a somber note in her voice that I couldn't put my finger on. It probably wasn't worth bringing up.

"Please be careful out there," I said.

"I will try my best," she responded flatly, and the call ended.

Hideout – Atlanta, GA
23:48 10-21-2016

Grey and Briana were finally up to speed. I tried to imagine their reactions when Rachel, Viktor Ivankov, and his unnervingly quiet counterpart, Natasha, showed up to the hotel room. Grey was sitting in the corner of the room with Natasha, chatting away. I guess she was more comfortable talking to someone who knew her line of work. Briana was passed out on the sofa. She had driven all day and immediately went off to assist Grey upon our arrival in Atlanta.

Rachel wasn't even in the room. She wouldn't make eye contact with me, and it was driving me absolutely crazy. I knew I had said touchy words. I shouldn't have let them come out. Unfortunately, I couldn't reverse time. If I had that ability, I wouldn't have been in the situation I was in right now. I would be with Cole at some bar, discussing our plans for election night.

No—all of that was gone. False memories that *could* have been reality. Now, they were solely wistful thoughts. Viktor told me that there was a bar above us. We were in the basement. The owner was in on it with Viktor and gave him a place to hide out whenever he was in town. Rachel couldn't show her face, just like me. I wondered where she went. She couldn't have gone into the bar. I stood up and walked to the steps that led out of the basement.

"Where are you going?" Viktor called from behind me.

"To get some fresh air," I answered.

He stared at me quizzically.

"Be careful," he advised, and I walked out of the basement. The air was frigid, and I bundled up tight in my jacket. I glanced around the alleyway—nothing. Where had she gone? I did a three-sixty to search for any signs of where she might have been.

Then, I found it. It was a metal emergency ladder that ran up the side of the bar. Maybe she really did want to be alone. The roof would have been ideal for that. I placed a shaky foot on the rusty rung and began to climb—it was at least fifteen to twenty feet I had to scale. When I reached the top, I threw my leg over the edge and saw Rachel standing against the opposite side of the roof. She had her arms against her sides, with her hands tucked in her jacket pockets. The chilly Georgia weather was the complete opposite of what we were prepared for. Rachel's short-shorts, t-shirt, and Dolphins ball cap weren't going to cut it. Briana purchased her a pea coat and some pants. I slowly walked up beside her. She didn't even acknowledge that I was there. She just shivered and looked out at the Atlanta skyline.

"I'm sorry," I murmured.

I heard her exhale. She didn't respond.

"I didn't mean to sound so harsh, Rachel. I promise."

My words were met with silence. She wasn't budging.

I backed off for a moment and pondered my next statement.

"Rachel—"

"I don't want an apology," she snapped, spinning around to face me. "I want to know *why?* Why did you just use the fact that I am in love with you against me?"

I opened my mouth to speak.

"In front of everyone! Owen, do you know how badly that hurt? Do you know how hard it was to stop myself from bursting into tears down there? Is that my punishment for caring about you? I wanted you to stay, and now I got what I wanted, and it's more than I could ever swallow. I'm going to lose you again, this time in handcuffs! Please, Owen, don't go along with Grey's plan. I have a bad feeling, and I just want you to be safe. I want to be by your side, so don't push me away! You told me you *love* me—"

I wrapped my arms around her and pulled her into a firm embrace. She started sobbing with her head on my chest.

"I do love you…I do," I consoled, rubbing her back. "I am sorry, Rachel."

"I j—just want you to be safe," she sputtered as she cried.

"I know. I promise everything will be fine."

She continued to let out all of her tears. Her groaning caused me to well up because Rachel's emotions were now linked to my own. After last night on the beach and all of the events leading up to it, I *loved* her, and it was real.

I ran my hand down her long hair, smoothing it. The feeling of her chest heaving against mine as she cried tore me apart. Then, it hit me. Despite all the chaos that had transpired since my framing, I found her. The extent of her knowing me would have been limited to the TV screen. I would never have met Briana, her cousins, and her mother. This moment existed only because I chose to be her copilot that fateful morning at the coffee shop. For a moment, I imagined never being framed, sitting next to Cole on election night, jubilant of our victory over the traditional parties and having some whiskey on the rocks. I tried to remember the *feeling*, though, of going home every night to my apartment alone. Or, if I did bring home a woman, the feeling I felt after she left, lying on my back staring at the ceiling wondering what did I ever do to become such a loner, was terrible. I was famous. I had money…but inside, I was miserable. I craved the day of the elections so that I could take a deep breath for the first time in years. The glamor of my title had long faded, and even then, sometimes I wished I was just normal again.

Although, I wouldn't have said this situation was normal, or even remotely close to ideal…but when I was with her, everything was all right. Yesterday was gone, and tomorrow didn't matter. All that existed was the present moment, and in that moment, we had each other.

Would I have traded her to be able to go back to my old life?

No. The answer was *no*.

"Please, Owen, stop with all these promises," she pleaded. "You have no idea what will happen if you step out on camera."

"I know I don't…but I promise you, I know I'll be fine."

"There you go again with the promises. *You* might be fine, but what about me? What am I supposed to do while you are locked up?"

I tilted my head down to where my chin rested on my chest, and I stared into her amber-brown eyes. Hers darted across mine, and within them I saw pain and uncertainty. I held my grasp on her with one arm and let go with the other, using it to cup her face gently.

"Write. You're supposed to write," I answered softly. "I heard your conversation with Ian, and I can tell the story is coming together. Now you have Viktor's piece, mine, and whatever he said he has. No matter *what* happens, Rachel, you have to write your story. Veronica needs to be exposed to the world as a traitor. Justice needs to be served."

She nodded, and her lower lip quivered.

"I know," the words barely came out. "I will."

"You want to know something else?

She shrugged and nodded yes.

"You are the best thing that has ever happened to me."

The amount of joy in her expression was practically overflowing. Her lower lip quivered, and the tears began to flow once more.

"You mean that?" she asked in her silky-smooth voice.

"More than anything I have ever said. I love you, Rachel, with all of my heart. Please don't stop loving me if I get locked up tomorrow. I want to get to know you better once all of this is over, and it *will* be over. Don't doubt it for a second."

"I love you too, Owen. This feeling is so empowering. Yet at the same time, it is overwhelming. I have so many mixed emotions running through my head about Grey's plan. If you love me like you say you do, and I know that you do, please, sleep on it before you decide what you're going to do tomorrow. If you can't do it for yourself, do it for me."

I paused before answering, and that caused her happiness to fade.

"Owen. Please."

"Of course," I submitted. "I'll sleep on it."

Oakengate Lane – Midlothian, VA
16:06 09-07-1998

I quietly opened the back door and stepped inside. Mom always locked the front one when she was home alone. She did it on purpose, so that I had to pass by her to get to the stairs and to my room. I peered to my right. There was no one sitting at the dining room table.

Whew, thank God.

I could sneak through the dining room and walk through the living room to avoid the kitchen. I wanted some chocolate milk so bad, but I would wait. I didn't have a good day, and I knew Mom would notice. I would just play Super Nintendo until she went to the grocery store. I stepped on the stairs.

"Owen! Is that you?" my mom called from the kitchen.

I closed my eyes and let out an aggravated exhale.

"Yes," I huffed.

"Can you bring me your hamper? I'm doing laundry."

I rolled my eyes. Mom was *always* doing laundry. I tried to avoid her, but it didn't work. I trudged up the stairs and walked to my room. I grabbed the hamper and dragged it downstairs. It clunked against every step. I slid it across the hallway.

"I can hear you, you know! Pick up that hamper, Owen. It'll scratch the wood floor."

I grabbed it with both hands and awkwardly carried it into the kitchen. I set it down to get my grip again, and I carried it the rest of the way to her. She was facing the washing machine.

Smile. Smile and act normal.

She popped her head out from behind the doorway that separated the kitchen from the utility room.

"How was your day, honey?"

"Good."

I relaxed my face from the smiling. Did I sound like I was *good?* I hoped she didn't notice. Crap. Her forehead and nose scrunched up like she was smelling stinky feet.

"Is something wrong?" she asked the question I was afraid of the most.

"No," I said meekly.

Her lips tightened, and she shook her head side to side.

"*Something* happened today, didn't it?"

I stared at her and blinked. I shook my head no. She chuckled and tossed the towel she was holding into the machine. She knelt down so that she was eye level with me. Her blonde hair fell past her neck, and her blue eyes were like mine. I had a pretty mom. That was what my friends would say.

"Owen, how about this," she began in a whisper. "You are going to tell me what happened today at school. I won't get mad. I promise."

"How did you know?" I asked. "I tried my best to hide it."

"Because I am your mother. I gave birth to you, Owen. I can tell when you are upset. Something is bothering you. Now spit it out."

I felt like there was a rock in my throat. I didn't want to retell the story at all.

"Owen, don't make me take away your Nintendo," she warned.

"There was a fight today at school."

I felt so much better just from getting that little bit off my chest.

"Were you involved?" Her tone was accusing.

"No. I wasn't."

She stood up from her squatting position.

"Then what is wrong?"

"I feel bad," I mumbled.

"What do you feel bad about, honey?"

I kicked at the tile floor and jammed my hands in my pockets.

"*Owen,*" she pressed. "I'm going to need to hear the whole story."

I was looking down at my feet, and I played with my hands nervously.

"Ricky called Josh a loser when they ran into each other in the bathroom. Josh gets picked on a lot. He wears these glasses that have white tape wrapped around the part that sits on your nose. Josh just tried to wash his hands and ignore him, but Ricky didn't let him."

"How old is Ricky?"

"I don't know. He's in sixth grade. Josh is in my class. Ricky is a lot bigger than us."

"Go on," she said.

"Ricky grabbed Josh by his shirt and pushed him up against the wall. He called him a pussy for not fighting back. He wanted him to fight back, but Josh wouldn't. So he brought him to the stall and gave him a swirly. I could hear Josh choking on the water and trying to push back. I felt so bad, Mom."

"Where were you during all of this?"

"In the stall next to them."

"What did you do?"

"I tried to stay quiet, but once Josh left the bathroom, he heard me. He threatened to beat me up if I didn't come out, and when I did, he told me that if I told on him he would do something to me way worse than what happened to Josh."

"Owen, did you tell your teachers?"

"No," I muttered. "That's why I feel guilty."

She shook her head and let out a long sigh.

"Come sit down with me at the dining room table."

My stomach hurt from hearing that. I knew I was probably in trouble.

I sat in the wooden chair diagonally to my mom's. She placed her hand on top of mine.

"Owen, honey, why didn't you do anything?"

I swallowed hard.

"Because I was afraid."

"Because you were afraid…" She repeated the words. "Giving into fear is almost always easier than showing your courage. Doing what is easy isn't always right, and doing what is right isn't always easy."

I cocked my head at her saying.

"Were you friends with Josh?"

"Not really," I said. "I've only talked to him a few times."

"Well, what if it was one of your friends? Or, what if it was someone you loved? Like me—what if Ricky put *my* head in the toilet?"

"I'd be angry."

"Would you do anything, then? Would you stand up against him for me?"

"Yes, I would."

"Then, what you're telling me is, that the only reasons you didn't help Josh were because one, you were afraid, and two, you didn't really care about him."

"But I—"

"No buts," she cut me off. "Owen, your fear should never be stronger than your courage because when that happens, you live life afraid of everything, and bad things will happen all around you and you will feel worse and worse for not doing something about it. Just because there weren't any people who cared about Josh enough to help, doesn't mean you shouldn't. What happened today honey, was practice for life—and you failed."

I felt my lip tug into a pout.

"People like Josh need someone to fight for them, so that one day they can fight their own battles. As your mother, I don't care if you come home with a black eye, or if you told the teacher and then got a black eye. I would be less mad at you then, than I am right now because you did what was *right.* You stood up to the bully and showed him that he can't just do whatever he wants. There are so many bullies in this world, Owen. When you're older, you're going to have to have the courage to do what is right. You might have to defend your wife, your job, or maybe even your country."

I nodded as I continued to listen.

"That's what Dad does, you know. He stops the bullies around here in town from doing bad things. If he were afraid of them, they would do whatever they wanted. Just like what will happen if no one were to stand up to Ricky, he will just continue bullying other kids and giving them swirlies, too. Do you want that?"

"No," I said.

"Imagine if you were in Josh's shoes. Wouldn't you want someone to stand up for you?"

"Yes."

She rubbed my hand with her thumb lovingly and leaned in closer to me, looking at me in the eyes.

"There are a lot of bullies in this world, Owen…and unless you want to live your life afraid, you have to gather up the courage and stand up to them. You have to take that courage and face them head on. Remember my advice because *one day* you will need it. Keep it in your head at all times, and if you do, the world you leave behind will be a lot better of a place than the one you came into…"

Hideout – Atlanta, GA
10:24 10-22-2016

"Wow. I don't know if I can get used to this."

Rachel angled her head and blow-dried her hair. She used her fingers to comb through it and isolate its sections.

"Me neither," I said, staring back at my reflection in the tiny excuse of a mirror in the bathroom of our hideout. I was crammed in with Rachel in a space the size of a linen closet. I rustled my fingers through my jet-black hair, and every time I glanced at Rachel it was like I was looking at a different person. The black accentuated even more of her Hispanic side, but it was fitting. Her new hair color looked natural. Mine made me look like more of a goth with my paler skin.

Every other second I was having flashbacks of the dream I awoke from. I hadn't dreamed of my mother in over six months…and it was *so* vivid. Rachel said I was shaking in my sleep, and that I was very distressed. She said I kept muttering 'I will' over and over again. I didn't tell her the details of the dream, only that it was about my mom. It startled me that I would have a dream like that the same night Rachel had asked me to sleep on my decision. I woke up breathing heavily, and I announced my decision before I even became coherent. I *had* to stick to Grey's plan. I felt like the dream was my mom subconsciously screaming at me to stand up for myself and what was right. It was hard to shake off the feeling it gave me from having talked to my mom in the dream because it wasn't just a dream, it was a memory.

Rachel was disheartened, but she soon let it go. Perhaps, it was because she was the one who helped me break out of the dream. She saw how much it affected me. I didn't remember muttering anything, and I didn't remember shaking…but *she* did. Whatever the reason, she had finally cooled off from last night, and I was glad. The last thing I wanted was for her to hold something against me. If I did get locked up, I didn't want to have that weight on my mind, knowing that she was angry with me.

We met eyes in the mirror, and a smile tugged at her lips. I returned it with a playful smirk.

"You know, we look like international spies or something."

I chuckled.

"Bonnie and Clyde turned secret agents?" I played along with her.

"I can roll with that," she said.

Natasha and Grey were on their computers, and Briana was sitting by Viktor, but they weren't making much conversation. Besides talking about his framing, I couldn't imagine it being easy trying to make small talk with someone who had been alone for two years. I walked out into the room, and Grey shook his head at my darkened hair.

"You could pass as my brother," he said.

"Sure could," I agreed.

"So, Owen," Viktor began. "Are you ready?"

I nodded yes.

If only I would have known what was to come. Then, I would have answered no. There was no way I could have *ever* been ready for that.

Marietta St. – Atlanta, GA
11:17 10-22-2016

The clicking of Grey's computer keys was the only sound in the car. They were such soft sounds in the silence that it was unnerving. Nervousness began to settle in. Viktor had parallel parked into a spot, and we were sitting across from the CNN building. I was staring at it out of my window.

Natasha and Briana stayed back at the hideout. The car only fit five, and Viktor didn't want Briana staying there alone, just in case the owner came downstairs. Rachel sat beside me, and she was holding my hand, delicately rubbing her thumb across my skin. It was so cool against mine, and the sensation was refreshing. I tried to imagine that this might be the last bit of time I got to spend with her. I would almost certainly be in handcuffs by the time all of this was over. I recalled the feeling of saying goodbye to her at the airport, and this was ten times worse. In Miami, I was escaping to gain freedom. Now, I was telling the world the truth to *lose* my freedom.

Losing mine was worth saving theirs. My dream was a sign that I should follow through with Grey's plan. I had to stand up for what was right, even if I got a little roughed around in the process.

"All right, I am in their security system. Over fifty cameras—that's a lot to keep up with."

"After what you did in Miami, it should be a piece of cake," I encouraged.

"Should be," he said. "*Should* being the key word."

"I don't doubt you for a second."

"Why thank you, Owen. Viktor, can you hand him the stuff?"

Viktor turned around and handed me a plastic baggy with a white cloth inside, and with his other hand he gave me a latex glove.

"What's this?" I asked.

"Chloroform," Grey answered. "And I suggest wearing that glove unless you want to accidently knock yourself out with the chemical."

"What? Who am I going to use it on?"

"Well, the newsroom is on the fifteenth floor. From what I can tell from the security cameras, the elevator opens right up to a hallway beside the newsroom. You would be visible from offices and such that encircle it. Now, on the other hand, it looks like right now on the first floor there is a maintenance man taking his break in a mechanical closet."

"Grey, do I *really?*"

"Yes, really," he replied. His beard was already filling in. It amazed me how fast it grew compared to my own. "You will take his keys and his uniform, if you'd like, and then, those keys will have access to the service elevator for the maintenance staff. According to the blueprint we found in the public records, there is a storage closet just behind the newsroom.

On the security feed, it seems like there is a set of double doors that connects the newsroom to the storage closet.

"I see…" I mumbled.

"You don't have to do this," Rachel whispered.

'There are a lot of bullies in this world, Owen…and unless you want to live your life afraid, you have to gather up the courage and stand up to them.' My mom's voice echoed in my head.

"I do," I said flatly.

"Why? What happened to sleeping on it?"

"I *did* sleep on it, and I had a very vivid dream of my mother."

She clutched my hand tighter.

"What happened in the dream, Owen? Why were you so shaken up when I woke you?"

"I dreamed of a memory of when I was ten, when my mom was still alive. She reminded me of why I have to do this. I have to do what is right."

"I just fear this isn't the right thing to do…" Her voice trailed off. Viktor and Grey minded their own business. I leaned in and stopped beside Rachel's ear.

"If your dad gave you advice in a dream, I know you would take it."

I pulled back away and she stared into my eyes. Even behind her disheartened expression, she nodded. She knew what I said was true.

"Sorry to interrupt," Grey said, "but I have to make a phone call before you go, Owen."

"Got it," I said.

"I've been skimming through what I can through their wireless, and I found the name of the company who services their technology. That, my friends, is a hacker's jackpot."

We all chuckled.

He had the phone to his ear.

"Hello, my name is Chad Elliott and I am with Georgia Systems Management. I need to do some routine maintenance on the server."

Rachel and I were smiling, and I shook my head. Grey was such a badass.

"Oh, no, no, you don't need to transfer me at all. My access ID is C-H-Elliot-182. Actually, if you want to save us all some time, I can just request the access right through your computer?"

There was a pause.

"Why yes, ma'am. It really is that easy. Just accept the access request and I can download the system update wirelessly. No need to talk to anyone else."

Another pause.

"Thank you, Renée. You are too kind. They need to give you a raise, you sound like an angel on the phone."

Viktor and Grey were both grinning, and I couldn't help but be in awe of Grey's abilities.

"Oh no, it was my pleasure. Have a good day off tomorrow."

He closed the flip-phone.

"Well damn," Rachel dragged out the words. "You going to take Renée out to dinner and a movie while you're at it?"

We all cracked up from her comment.

"Eh, maybe, if I knew what she looked like," Grey teased. "You see what I just did? That is half of hacking. You have to know enough about what you're doing to convince people you are legitimate. I sweet-talked her a little, and she just opened the gates for me to come right in. Now, I can access any part of their system."

"I guess Natasha wasn't lying this morning when she told me how good you were," Viktor complimented him with a smirk.

"Ah, I'll remain humble on that note. She is highly skilled herself, Viktor. She is definitely a good asset to have on your side."

"I know," he responded. "She is the only reason I have made it this long without getting caught."

There was a solemn tone in his words. For a brief second, I thought of Grey as a parallel to Natasha. If he wouldn't have taken the risk to help me, we would never have even got out of Virginia. I wouldn't have met Rachel. We wouldn't have been *here*.

And now it all boiled down to this.

"Owen, the midday news will start in twenty minutes. It's time to go."

My stomach sank. Rachel's hand slid away from mine, and feeling her touch disappear made me further realize that I was *sticking* to my decision. If I wanted to turn back, now was my chance. No—I couldn't just give up. I had to stand up for everything my party has fought so hard to change in this country.

I clutched the plastic baggy in my hand and looked around at everyone.

"If they arrest me, which I'm sure they will, just know that I am very thankful for everything you have done for me. Please tell Briana the same thing, Rachel."

Her eyes were glistening. It looked like she was trying to hold back tears.

"I will," she said.

"It's been one hell of a ride, Owen." Grey said, reaching around the back seat to grab my forearm. I grabbed his and patted him on the back. "It has, my friend."

"Now listen," he began. "When you go in there, make a left, and then an immediate right. It will be a long hallway. Count the doors you pass. When you get to the third door on the right, that is where the maintenance office is. He is still eating his lunch on camera, so hurry."

I nodded and turned to Rachel. She looked into my eyes like hers would never meet mine again. It killed me inside to see how much pain she was in, and I just hoped she knew she wasn't alone in that pain. I felt it too. Her eyes darted across me, and she didn't say a word. It was like she was trying to take a mental picture of me, trying to hold on to this moment as long as she could.

"Rachel, thank you for everything."

She nodded, and her bottom lip quivered, but she pressed them together to hide it.

"Like I said, it was an honor to get to know you and to hear your story. I promise I will write it well."

"I know you will," I said with confidence. "I can't wait to read it, even if I am behind bars."

I gave her a wink. She cracked a smile.

"I love you," she said softly. The words made my heart swell.

"I love you too. Don't forget it, either."

She nodded, and I pulled her into a hug. I squeezed her back and rubbed it lovingly. I tried to remember the feeling of her arms around mine, the scent of her hair, and how affectionate her beautiful brown eyes were as they gazed into my own. I had no idea how long it would be until I got to be with her again. I wanted something to remember, something to hold on to. I pulled back and cupped her face. She waited, and I went in to kiss her. We held it for as long as we could, and I wished I could have stayed there forever. I saw flashes of the beach, of how magical that night was. I planned on having many more with her once all of this was over.

When we separated, she embraced me again and put her mouth beside my ear.

"When will I get those flowers?" she whispered, her voice like velvet.

I leaned into her ear.

"*One day*," I whispered back.

She looked at me with watery eyes, and a smile tugged at her lips.

"Until next time, Bonnie."

I popped open the car door.

"Until next time, Clyde," she said, wiping tears from the corners of her eyes.

"Good luck," Viktor called out from the driver's seat.

"Thank you. Take care of her, okay?"

Viktor nodded.

"Hurry, Owen. It's now or never," Grey said.

"Okay."

I closed the door. They drove off. I looked both ways and weaved my way across the street. My heart began to race, and I jammed my hands in my pockets, just to double check I hadn't forgotten the baggy. It was there. Anxiety began to course through my body. I neared the entrance of the CNN building, and it didn't look as big as I remembered it to be. It was a faded beige, and there were bright red letters with CNN at the top corner.

I was ten feet from the revolving door. I made sure to keep my eyes down, and I zipped my jacket up tight, all the way to my chin. Today was the day I would finally be noticed, but I didn't want to ruin my chances of that by being recognized on the way in. The whole *country* would notice who I was in less than half an hour. Suddenly, another thought entered my mind.

What would I *say?*

I had a feeling that I would know *exactly* what to say when the time came.

I slipped into the revolving door, and the warm air of inside hit me. I quickly scanned my surroundings. The reception area was diagonal to my right, and there were many people walking around. I recalled Grey's instructions and turned left. A few feet down that hall was a dead end, and the only way I could turn was right.

He was correct in his description. It was a *very* long hall, with many doors lining the right side. The left side was floor to ceiling glass windows. I passed the first door to my right. *One.* I saw the second one coming up. *Two.* Farther away was the third. I passed people and did my best not to make eye-contact with them. I prayed my jet-black hair was enough to make them not notice me.

Then, I reached it. *Three.*

The door read:

EMPLOYEES ONLY

I let out a shuddering exhale as I turned the handle of the door and pulled it open. The lighting was so dim I could barely see what I was looking at. There was a Hispanic maintenance man, mid-bite in his sandwich, staring up at me in shock. I tried to smile and act confused. My main goal was to seem trustworthy enough for him to stand up. I needed him to think I was just an innocent stranger who was lost. The man swallowed his food and wiped his mouth with a napkin.

"Can I help you, sir?"

"Uh, yeah, I think I'm lost." I pulled out my flip phone and opened it. "I'm sorry, I have to find the name of the person's office. Do you mind pointing me in the right direction?"

"Yeah, I can," he said in a faint accent and stood up. My heart pounded, and I acted like I was scratching the side of my leg, but I gently opened the baggy instead. I had no time to use the glove. I would just hold my breath.

"Here it is," I exclaimed, and turned my phone to him.

"Did you click off of it? I don't see any—"

I jammed the cloth in his face, and he struggled to push my arm away. With one inhale, his eyes rolled to the back of his head, and he passed out. I began to undress myself, and I locked the door to the room. I saw the key ring on his side and knew I was in good shape to execute the rest of Grey's plan.

Once dressed, I left my old clothes in the room and headed out the door. I walked with confidence, like I had nothing to worry about. I wanted to appear like I *belonged.* I continued down the long hall, and then I realized—Grey never told me where the service elevator was.

Fuck. I walked aimlessly, roaming the different halls. At the far end of the one I was walking down, I saw a man in a similar uniform open a door and disappear. I figured it was worth a shot. As I neared it, I saw that it had some sort of locking mechanism attached to it. I reached for my key ring to get in as quickly as possible. With people passing by every few seconds, I didn't want them to see me struggle. I was an *employee* here, not someone trying to break in. Upon closer investigation, there wasn't a keyhole at all. It was a card slot, similar to a hotel door. I reached for his ID card and slid it in the slot. The light turned green, and I was in. My breath was rapid, and I tried my best to calm it. The hall was long. Its floor was concrete, and the sound of my feet scraping across it made me feel too vulnerable. I saw no one, but that didn't mean there wasn't anyone around. The fluorescent lighting felt brighter than the lights outside, and the walls were stark white. I glanced to my left and right constantly, in an attempt to find what I needed.

I turned a corner and saw another maintenance man. It took every bit of control I had in my body not to jump, or to let the shock I felt show in my face. He glanced at me a little funny but kept walking. An idea popped in my head. It was risky, but it reminded me of what Grey did in the car. I didn't want to walk circles in this place forever. The midday news had probably already begun. I spun around.

"Excuse me," I said. My voice echoed down the hall. My heart fluttered in fear.

He stopped and turned around.

"What?" he asked, confused.

"I'm the new guy. Someone told me to meet them by the service elevator. Is it around here?"

I struggled to keep my voice from trembling. His eyes darted up and down the length of my body quickly. He didn't answer right away, almost untrusting in his body language. His questionable expression returned to normal.

"It's around the corner. Halfway down the hall on your right."

"Thanks," I muttered and quickly turned around.

I followed his directions and found it. I pushed the arrow to go up and tapped my foot impatiently for it to reach the ground floor. The longer I was here, the more I risked my ultimate goal. I *had* to get on TV.

The doors slid open. I stepped inside

'The newsroom is on the fifteenth floor,' Grey's voice echoed in my mind.

I hit the button, and the elevator accelerated. There it was again—the sound I used to cherish. The smooth hum of the elevator. No, this elevator wasn't taking me to my apartment. It wasn't taking me to see Cole in the hospital, or to a penthouse suite in Miami. It was taking me to fate's doorstep…and *today* I decided I would knock.

I took a deep breath and tried to calm my pounding heart.

The doors slid open. It was another plain hallway. It must have been disconnected from the main newsroom in its own secret corridor. I tried remembering Grey's instructions.

'According to the blueprint we found in the public records, there is a storage closet just behind the newsroom. On the security feed it seems like there is a set of double doors that connects the newsroom to the storage closet.'

The hallway wasn't straight. It bent, almost like if I were to keep walking, it would form a hexagon. I meandered farther down and saw a doorknob jutting out of a wall. I hurried to it, and as I reached it, I saw black lettering towards the top.

STORAGE

So, *this* was it. *This* was what it felt like to have nowhere to run once I made my move. I was trapped. All by the work of my own hands. The fear I felt had never been this real, this raw. It ran through my blood hot, and almost burned. I tried to harness it and use it to my advantage. When I was ready, I would burst through the doors in front of me and tell the world the *truth*. My heart was beating out of my chest, and another wave of fear percolated through me. But this time, I held onto it. I transformed it into something different. Now, it almost felt like electricity, tickling my skin. The hairs on the back of my neck stood up, and I felt so alive. It was courage. Courage was building up within, slowly replacing the fear.

What did I have to lose? Everything I had worked for was gone. My best friend was dead. My party was dying like a wilting flower. At this point, as long as Rachel was safe, I could live with whatever happened next. The repercussions didn't matter anymore. My public image was trashed to the point where I couldn't even show my face. I was a wanted man. *They* wanted to wipe out my mark and destroy all the good I had done in this country.

No. Not today. Today, right now, was the moment I would fight back. It was the moment I would show them that they should have never picked me. Someone else might have given up. They might have quit after the cat and mouse chase across the country wore them down, but not me. Cole and I had a vision for what this country could be, and I wasn't going to let them take that away. I wasn't going to just so willingly hand over our country to the people who had fought so hard to run it into the ground. *They* were sick people. *They* were frauds, corrupt, and above all else—evil.

Freedom. It was the word they threw around so carelessly, acting like patriots, and trying to further convince the public that they had their best interests in mind. No, that wasn't the truth at all. I knew the truth, and it was time for the rest of the country to find out. Our government was behind Black Monday. *They* caused the bombs and the stock market crash. The attacks at the debate were premeditated by Veronica.

Most importantly, the Confinement was never supposed to end. It was just the beginning. A chill raced up my spine at the thought, and my teeth clenched with anger. My breath shuddered, and I gently held the cold metal push bar of the double doors. My palms were sweaty, as was I. Darkness engulfed the storage closet, and from behind the doors I could hear the muffled voices of the news anchors. They were probably only ten feet away. Oh, were they all in for a big surprise.

If someone would have told me a week and a half ago, on the evening of the debate, that I would be the most wanted criminal in the United States, I would have told them they were crazy. I would have never believed that any of this was possible. I was blinded from the Convergence's success, and I was living in that bubble. If I would have only known that behind the scenes, the very people responsible for Black Monday and the Confinement were plotting something new. This new plan would allow them to stay in power, it would allow control of our country for another four years, and that would be enough to revive what the Supreme Court snuffed out. Like Viktor said, I was the oxygen to their dying flame. *They* chose *me*. I was the sacrifice they needed in order to regain what they had lost from the emergence of my party.

I was the gambit—just a pawn in their grand plan.

My chest heaved up and down rapidly, with realization of what I was about to do. Images of my journey flashed through my mind, and looking back, it felt much longer than a week and a half. So much had changed in such a small amount of time. My breath shuddered as I prepared my hands to push the double doors open, and my heartbeat was so rapid I could feel it pulsing in my throat. *They* thought I would go down without a fight, but they were so far from being right. I was raised to stand up for myself, and today was that day. I had to fight to regain what I had lost. My party had the chance to save this country from the destiny Veronica fought so hard to make everlasting. I would not go down in history as a terrorist. I would not go down in history as a coward. They had used the media to destroy my influence, and now, it was time to give them a dose of their own medicine.

The words of Laura came back to my mind suddenly.

'What they say on the news. That is shallow water. If someone were to shine a light, they would see under the surface is lies. Their water not deep enough to hide truth for long.'

Veronica hid her lies in shallow water, and now, it was time for me to shine a *light.*

428 Valley Dr. – Allentown, PA
12:03 10-22-2016

I held the remote and began flipping through the channels. I was glad Mom let me skip karate practice. All I had to do was act like my cough was worse and rub my forehead to make it warm. I hated how on Saturdays I missed my favorite shows.

None of my friends took karate. They liked to skateboard, and I did too.

I thought that my mom just wanted me to be involved in something. She thought I liked it, but I really didn't. I just didn't want to hurt her feelings.

"Brody!" my mom called from the kitchen. "I heated up some chicken soup. Come get it!"

"I'm coming," I answered but didn't move. I wasn't even really sick, so I didn't want chicken soup. If she ever left the kitchen I could have just thrown something in the microwave. I kept flipping through the channels.

"I am innocent!" a voice screamed from the TV. My face scrunched up as the image faded in. My mouth dropped—it was that guy they were all looking for. Owen, I think his name was. He was the one who created the party, and then he bombed the debate and ruined everything. At least, that was what my friends said about him.

"My name is Owen Lee Marina, and I am innocent!" His face was beet red, and his chest heaved up and down from screaming so loud.

"Holy crap!" I shouted. "Mom, come look at this! Owen Marina is on the news!"

"What was that, honey? The faucet is running, I can't hear you! I'll be there in a second."

"Come on, Mom!"

If the news cut off, no one would believe me. I pulled out my cell phone and opened the camera app. I switched it to video and hit record.

"I, Owen Lee Marina was framed for the bombs at Georgetown University. This was all orchestrated by *our* federal government! The bombs on Black Monday, the Confinement, the bombs at the debate—it was *all* planned!"

My face went blank. I could feel my stomach flopping around.

The Confinement was *planned?* It almost made me want to cry, thinking about that. Those were the worst three months of my entire life, and I was only thirteen. Why would our government have done that? It just didn't make sense.

Owen's black hair was dripping with sweat, and there was something in his eyes that was frightening. Maybe what he knew was so scary that it made him look that way. Was he telling the truth? Was he really innocent?

"Viktor Ivankov is innocent! He was chosen, just like I was, to keep their plan alive! There is evidence! Loads of evidence, which proves exactly what I am saying! The evidence we have been given is false! They *lied* to us! Do not fall for their trap, America! Wake up before it's too late! Do not let them stay in power! If you vote democratic or republican, your freedom will *die!* It'll be gone forever!" His voice was becoming hoarse from all the shouting.

"Mom, hurry up!" I yelled. "Come look at this!"

"Coming!" she replied.

I heard other voices besides Owen's in the background of the news.

"…Shut it off!" a woman's voice said. It sounded like she was behind the scenes or something.

"…I can't! Our system is completely frozen. It just keeps rolling. Go for the main power!" a man yelled.

"…No!" another voice called. "Screw 'em, our ratings are sky high. Call security instead..."

Owen was still center screen. These side conversations were distracting.

"Veronica Hall, Chairwoman of the Democratic Party, is behind this! *She* is singlehandedly destroying this country. Don't let her! Don't let the government turn this great country into a nightmare!"

Who is Veronica? Hmm…

"Our ancestors fought for this land in the Revolutionary War, and now we have to fight too! If we don't, we are going to lose everything! We will wake up one day and we will find ourselves in a Confinement that never ends!"

"*What* did he just say?" my mother asked with wide eyes. She stood underneath the archway to the dining room.

"He said he was framed. Don't worry, I filmed it all."

His words made me nauseous. I honestly would rather die than be in Confinement forever. Now, when I went to the zoo, I looked at the animals in the cages differently. The zoo wasn't fun to me anymore. I felt like those animals in the cages, during the Confinement. I still had nightmares about it. I prayed that my little sister was too young to remember what happened inside. Maybe I could ask her when she got a little older.

"Good," my mother said. "What he is saying sounds very important."

She was right. It did sound important. The energy he put into his words was overwhelming. It scared me to wonder if they were really true. I was going to have to put this on my YouTube channel.

CIA Headquarters – Langley, VA
12:08 10-22-2016

"He said *my name…*" The words slipped out of my mouth and were met with silence. The entire control room was so quiet you could have heard a pin drop. I stared at the projected video of the newscast, streaming live on CNN. I was numb. I felt all the eyes in the room on me, but I didn't want to turn around and face them—not yet.

"Rewind it back thirty seconds," I instructed.

It played again.

"Veronica Hall, Chairwoman of the Democratic Party is behind this! She is singlehandedly destroying this country. Don't let her! Don't let the government turn this great country into a nightmare!"

The video stopped. I pressed my lips together, and my heart began to pound in my chest. The intensity in Owen's face was disturbing, and it made me even angrier than I already was. I tried to control my breathing. I didn't want anyone to see how this affected me. The reality of what had just happened, hit me. Owen just exposed my involvement on national TV. Everything he mentioned was kept so tightly under wraps, that if I didn't eliminate him and all he had done to threaten the existing establishment, it would be me that paid the ultimate price.

For the first time in ages, I felt *embarrassed.*

My eye began to twitch, and as I breathed I felt my nostrils flare. I harnessed all the fear and embarrassment I felt and turned it into anger. Pure, undiluted anger. I would be damned if I let a sniveling little shit half my age ruin my career and everything I have worked for in my life. I let out a small chuckle, and I admit, it sounded like I was going crazy. It brought me so much pleasure to imagine the moment we won. Owen was the most talked-about political figure of the twenty-first century, but he wouldn't go down in history as the victor. He would be famous, but not for anything good. His label as a terrorist would stick. We had enough false evidence to brainwash the millions of people who were glued to their TVs. He might have leaked the real truth, but with every spill, there were always people willing to clean it up.

We had plenty of people to clean it up. Our guys would erase this so quickly people wouldn't even have the chance to let it sink in. Owen would have just wasted his breath, and in the end, still be remembered as the terrorist who helped kill innocent people. *That* was what we wanted, and *that* was what we would get. Nothing would change. This was in actuality less of a ruckus than what happened in Miami. We didn't have him in handcuffs, but he was in the CNN building. He couldn't go far this time.

I turned around and felt the rage bubbling up within me.

"I want *every* FBI agent and police officer in a ten-mile radius to converge on that building! If we have to fucking shut down Atlanta, then that's what we will do! Now!"

The man who I was looking at stared back at me with a glare in his eyes that was disturbing. I could sense in his expression that he didn't want to listen. After hearing what Owen said, he wanted to rebel.

"Did I fucking *stutter*?!" I shouted. "Now!"

He glowered at me with such disgust. "Yes, ma'am."

I turned back around to the screen.

"Today is the day that Owen Marina goes down!"

The maniacal high I felt was addicting. My power extended over everyone in this room, and I would use it to finish what I started. Owen might have thought this was like David and Goliath, but he would soon find out his rebellion was futile. He was but an insect to us, and he would be squashed like one *very* soon.

620 8th Ave. – New York, NY
12:11 10-22-2016

"Ian! Ian, come in here!" Sharon called from outside my office. I shot out of my desk chair and ran towards the door. I tried to imagine what I was going to see, but I had no idea. I should have been home right now, but Rachel told me to keep the news on at work. Sure, I could have stayed home and just sent out a mass email, but that wasn't my style. If something was going to happen that my journalists needed to write about, I wanted to be there with them.

I swung open the door, and the moment I laid eyes on the many flat screens, I saw Owen standing in front of the anchor's desk, and he was center screen.

"Someone turn up the volume!" I shouted.

All of my journalists were crowded around the TVs. I stood at the back of the group and watched bewildered as Owen yelled at the camera on national TV.

"I hope you heard everything I said loud and clear, America! Because if you didn't, and if you believe these lies you've been given, we might go to a Confinement that never ends!"

I couldn't help but smile. He did it. He fucking did it. He was trying to revive his party just before the election. I was no fool, but it worried me because so much damage had already been done. It would take a lot more than that to sway public opinion back to the way it was before the bombs at Georgetown.

"All right, everyone," I began. "I want all of you writing. They will take this off the air any moment. There will be nothing to write about once they get ahold of it. We are watching history being made here, and everything else we have written about in the past week and a half, disregard it. As of now, we are going to push a new thought on the American People."

"What's that?" one of the younger, female journalists asked.

"That Owen Marina might be innocent."

Newsroom – Atlanta, GA
12:13 10-22-2016

"Get him!" a security guard yelled from the far corner of the studio. There was another behind him with what looked to be a Taser outstretched towards me.

"Oh shit!" I yelled and ran back into the storage closet. I darted through blindly, nearly tripping over some boxes. I still had the maintenance keys I stole, and I tried to slam the door behind me to slow the guards down. Sweat dripped down my forehead as I sprinted through the hallway. I barreled toward the service elevator and began jamming the button over and over again. It was coming up from the ground floor. The guards rounded the corner, and I bolted farther down the hall until I found the stairwell.

"Put your hands up!" I heard one of them yell.

I have to hurry. They are right behind me.

I practically slid down the steps I descended them so quickly, and I began looping around the flights of stairs with incredible speed. Adrenaline surged through my body. The energy I felt from having revealed every lie I knew on TV was unlike anything I had ever felt in my life. For the first time since my framing, I felt like I had *control* again. I had a choice over what I did next, and it was liberating. I wished I could have felt this forever, but deep down, I knew my freedom would be short-lived.

I glanced up through the opening in the stairwell, and I saw them two flights above me. I kept my speed as constant as I could. I had an advantage over the guards because they were not in as good shape as me.

Suddenly, I hit the ground floor and swung open the exit door. The refreshing lobby air hit me in the face as I sprinted across the marble floor.

"Move, move, move!" I shouted and waved my hands as I ran for the revolving door.

"Everybody get down!" the guards behind me demanded. As I neared the exit a bullet whizzed past me and barely missed. It shattered the glass, and the noise was earsplitting. I made it through the revolving door, and I gave it an extra shove as I exited. Whatever I could do to slow them down. Running down fifteen flights had me completely out of breath, and the chilly autumn air surrounded me. I didn't stop. I continued to run down the street, but where did I have to go?

There were buildings lining the street to my right, and I saw a park to my left. I heard cop sirens echoing from every direction, and before I made my move into the park, they all began to converge on me.

Tahoes, Chargers, and Crowne Vics surrounded from every angle. Their tires screeched as they stopped, and I could smell the burnt rubber in the air. I turned around in a complete three-sixty and realized I was trapped. My heart pounded against my chest at an unbearable speed, and the midday sun beamed down on me, creating slight shadows between the buildings. I could only see blue sky for miles. The sirens were dizzying, and every which way I turned, I couldn't avoid the sounds or lights. More and more cops pulled into the area, forming a large circle around me. They made a barrier I couldn't escape.

Dozens of the officers stepped out of their cars, all with their guns raised. I very slowly began to raise my hands.

"Put your hands up!" the officer facing me shouted at the top of his lungs. I continued to raise them higher. Some of them were kneeling beside their patrol cars with automatic weapons against their shoulders. My hands were now above my shoulders, and I struggled to catch my breath. The liberation I felt from barging into the newscast was fading away, and was being replaced by a sinking feeling in my stomach. Had my mom's message in my dream steered me down the wrong path? Should I have kept running forever, like Viktor?

I would never know. It was too late now. I had already made my choice, and there was no turning back. I hoped my mother was proud, and wherever my pops was, I hoped he felt the same.

"Get on the ground, now!" the same cop hollered even louder this time.

So, *this* was what it felt like. I was cornered and had nowhere to run. This was how Jamie Lee Curtis felt with Michael Myers only a few feet away. Except, there were a few dozen Michael Myers after me, and they all had weapons pointing in my direction. I had tried so hard to do what was right for this country, and this was what I got in return for all my effort. I could only wish that my stunt in the newscast was enough to bring our support back up. The Convergence Party *had* to win, or else, we will have lost everything as a nation. There would be no hope, no light left in the darkness to guide us out of the abyss. As nauseous as I felt, I had a sudden clarity of mind. I realized that this situation wasn't just isolated to me. If *anyone* were to threaten the existing establishment, the same thing would have happened to them. If you give someone enough power, what will stop them from wanting *more?*

"Owen Marina! Get on the *fucking* ground! Now!"

I wanted to fight, but I knew this was where my road would end if I did. That nagging feeling I have had since I met Rachel—that my road would be a short one, made sense now. It *all* made sense now. I loved her so much, and if I wanted to be with her again one day, I would have to submit. I would have to surrender. Rachel would write her story regardless. I hoped she would keep herself safe and not do anything stupid just for me.

Our story didn't end here. It was far from over, but today, *today* was the end of mine.

Marietta St. – Atlanta, GA
12:18 10-22-2016

The sirens were so loud I was beginning to go mad. We were parked along the road in front of Centennial Olympic Park. Grey was nervously tapping his fingers against the plastic interior of the car, just beneath the window. The taps were keeping pace with my racing heart, and it was unnerving. The air inside was too warm. I felt like I couldn't breathe. Each breath was deeper than the one before it. My hands were moist, and my stomach was in knots. Viktor was staring at the many people who were walking away from the park, trying to see what all the commotion was about in the street.

None of this felt right. He shouldn't have to be behind bars. He did *nothing* wrong. I wanted to be with him so badly, even if that meant behind bars.

'No matter what happens, Rachel, you have to write your story.'

Owen's voice echoed in my mind. I knew I had to write the story, and I would. Right now though, I wanted to be there for Owen, even if he didn't know I was. If he was going to be arrested, maybe his reaction would be an added touch to bring out emotion in those who would read the story. I had to see these kinds of things to document them. I glanced around the car and saw a Nikon camera bag sitting near the stick shift. Without asking, I grabbed it and popped open the door.

"Hey, that's mine!" Viktor called from the front seat.

"Rachel, what the hell do you think you're doing?" Grey raised his voice angrily. "Are you out of your mind?"

I slammed the door closed before they even had a chance to say anything else. I hurriedly walked with the crowd, and it grew denser with every step. I fumbled with the zipper, and I yanked on it to open the slit just enough to pull the camera out. I took off the lens and hung the strap around my neck.

I must have been nearing the center because I bumped into people left and right.

"Excuse me," I said meekly, keeping my head down. I wore a scarf high around my neck, and my dyed, jet-black locks concealed most of my face.

"Get down I said!" a man's voice echoed loudly.

"I am innocent!" the voice placated the uneasiness in my stomach because I knew he was okay. I pushed past more and more people, readying the camera above the heads to get a good shot of Owen. In reality, I just wanted to see him. I wanted a photo I could hold onto while he was locked up.

"Watch it, lady!" an old man sneered as I slid past him. I was now less than ten feet away from the cops, and through the many heads, I was almost certain I saw Owen in the center of it all. It *had* to be. He was still wearing the maintenance uniform he stole.

"Everyone, everybody back!" Another line of cops stood back to back with the ones facing Owen. I held my camera up and started snapping.

"Owen, get down on the ground now!" the cop screamed, his voice hoarse. "If you don't put down your weapon, we will have no choice but to—"

The camera dropped, jolting my neck from the weight. I couldn't hear the screams of the people around me, and I didn't feel them as they ran away, pushing past. Another gunshot split the air, and I felt it pierce my soul. A sickening chill ran up my spine, and it raced past my scalp and face like lightning. My chest heaved up and down, and the ringing in my ears was so loud I could barely process what was going on. Everybody fought to go backward, but I didn't. I pushed forward. Cops were in front of me, and I tried to jump up and push my body weight against them. I couldn't hear their shouts, but they were trying to stop me.

He is fine, Rachel. He is fine. He is fine. Those were just warning shots.

My heart pounded as I fought against the burly police officers to get a better view. I knew I was risking it all. They could have recognized me, but it didn't matter. I had to *know.* I didn't even notice that I was screaming.

"What did you *do* to him?!" I screamed a guttural, helpless cry.

The cops broke for just a moment, and what I saw made me freeze.

It was him. Owen. He lay on the street face down, and I caught a glimpse of his black hair identical to mine. I was pushed back violently by the cops, and I fell hard against the asphalt. I was probably scraped up, maybe even bleeding, but I pulled myself up to my feet. The image I just saw burned into my mind as if it were being branded there.

I could have sworn I saw *blood.* It was pooling up beside him. I couldn't breathe, and I began to cough and choke. I now walked the same direction as everyone else, but I couldn't feel my feet. I didn't know where I was going. Heat flushed over the length of my body, my lower lip trembled, and a rock formed in my throat. To everyone around me, I was just a stranger. They had no idea I was his partner in crime. They had no idea I was his *Bonnie.*

The thought made me burst into tears. I covered my mouth in an attempt to silence my cries. I grabbed my gut with my other hand because I was almost certain I was going to vomit. The streets were wide and open, but I felt them narrowing. Everything was closing in. Hot tears blurred my vision, and I kept bumping into people. In those first steps, even after what I had saw, it almost felt like it wasn't real. No, that wasn't him. That wasn't Owen. It *couldn't* have been real. He was supposed to be in the back of a police car, going to some jail cell. The tears fell, but it hadn't hit me. Then, like a freight train, it *did*.

Owen was dead. I saw it with my own eyes. He was bleeding out on the street. I collapsed to my knees and covered my face with my scarf. I sobbed, yet tried to conceal it. Someone reached down to grab my forearm and tried to help me to my feet. I pulled myself up by their grasp and shook them off. The tears dripped down every part of my face.

Owen Marina was dead. My Clyde was dead. The man I loved was dead. The thoughts attacked my mind like a ruthless parasite, and I could barely function. Where was I?

Suddenly, I felt a pair of hands on my shoulders, and through blurred vision I thought I saw the scruff of Grey's chin. He guided me somewhere, and I heard a door open. I was pushed into the back seat, and I realized I was back in the car. I felt the camera get ripped from my neck.

"What happened? What just happened?" Grey's voice asked behind the sound of the engine accelerating.

My lower lip trembled, and I sobbed so hard I could barely keep my mouth open. My forehead was so scrunched up it hurt.

"He's dead!" I screamed, followed by guttural moans. "He—he's dead! I saw it, he is dead, lying on the street. They shot him! He—he is gone…" My voice stretched out and was distorted from the choking tears.

I could hear Grey coughing, but he didn't respond.

"Hold on tight," Viktor's steady voice instructed. "We have to get out of here, fast. They are going to block off these streets so quickly we will be dead meat if we aren't quick enough."

I didn't remember the car ride. It was a blur. Just as soon as I was pushed in, I was pulled back out just as fast. I couldn't process much, but I went down some steps. They looked like the steps that led to the basement—Viktor's hideout. I heard him fiddling with keys, and then he swung open the door. Grey had one arm of mine around his shoulder, and he was supporting me walking. I heard him cry the entire way back. He didn't say a word. He just cried.

"No—no! Don't let her in here!" Briana shouted; her voice was frantic.

"What do you mean?" Viktor shot back.

"Natasha, turn it off! Turn it off, now!"

"I'm trying, the button doesn't work, and I can't find the remote!"

"What the hell is going on here?" Viktor raised his voice.

"She can't see this right now, Viktor, please! Natasha, unplug it!"

She…

Was she talking about me? I shook myself out of Grey's grasp and stumbled forward past the worn couch. The old TV set was behind Briana. She pressed her backside against the screen so I couldn't see it.

"What don't you want me to see?" I asked, disoriented.

"*Amiga*, after what you just saw out there, you *can't* see this. Trust me!" I pushed her out of the way. "Please, Rachel! Don't do this to yourself right now! Trust me!"

I could barely hear the muffled voices of the news anchors behind all of our shouting. I wiped the tears out of my eyes and pointed a finger at Natasha as she neared the outlet.

"Don't even *think* about it." I warned her. She stopped in her tracks and pressed her lips together, turning around. Then, I noticed Briana *and* Natasha's faces were wet from tears. Briana began bawling and walked over to the couch. The sound pulled me back into reality a bit because I had never heard her cry like that. I had helped her through dozens of break-ups, but she never cried like *that.*

"I'm begging you, Rachel! Just wait!" she shouted again between groaning tears.

"Shh!"

I neared the faded image of the old TV set and bent down to hear better.

"…We are covering both stories simultaneously. We will go back to the scene outside of the CNN building in Downtown Atlanta in just a moment, but back to our other breaking news out Melbourne Beach, Florida…"

"No!" Briana shrieked. Her voice was raspy from yelling.

I stared at the TV screen numb, afraid of what was to come next.

"…Marta Cruz, the mother of Rachel Flores, was found dead this morning in her beachside home. Emergency responders found a suicide note vaguely stating her daughter's involvement with a terrorist was just too much to bear. She said she had failed her family and her daughter…"

The words became garbled. I heard Briana's violent cries behind me, followed by the muffled voices of Viktor and Grey. My breathing was shallow and rapid, and I could feel my stomach churning. I began to dry heave and retched everything that was in my stomach onto the carpet floor. I felt the clammy hands of someone around my arms, and they dragged me away. The room was closing in, and I felt so hot the sweat must have been dripping from my skin. I dry heaved on an empty stomach, but I didn't stop. I didn't listen. I couldn't hear anybody.

A tremor arose within me, and it was so painful it made all the muscles from my stomach to my forehead contract, and I let out the longest, rawest cry I had ever experienced. Drool slipped out of my mouth which was stuck open, and I groaned and sobbed. I was too numb to feel anger. I was too hurt to feel anything else but pain. I hiccupped and cried violently, and my vision began to turn fuzzy. The room turned yellow, then black. I hit the floor.

I remembered one thought.

They killed my mother.

620 8th Ave. – New York, NY
12:39 10-22-2016

I locked the door behind me and walked to the far corner of my office, cupping my mouth in order to silence my cries. I hadn't cried in years…but this, *this* was something tragic. Rachel's mother was dead.

I sobbed harder and slammed my fist against the Plexiglas that encircled my office. It bounced and recoiled away, but I ignored the throbbing pain. Even nine-hundred miles away, I could feel Rachel's anguish. It singed the edges of my soul. I had watched her grow up without her father, and now, her mother was gone. Both of her parents were dead at the age of twenty-three. She didn't deserve this kind of misery so young.

I walked over to my desk and wiped the tears from my eyes. I grabbed the picture frame and stared at the photo. It only crushed my heart further. To this day, it was my favorite. It was of our families' picture at one of the Christmas parties here at work. My wife held Stefan, with her poufy brown curls and a brilliant white smile. My two oldest sons clung to my legs, being camera shy as always. Emilio and Marta held Rachel in their arms. She was just a year old in the picture. I had lost my best friend, but my goddaughter had now lost it all.

"Why?!" I screamed, sobbing harder. I needed to compose myself. My entire staff was just beyond the door, and I couldn't stay in here forever. I had to remind myself that the anguish I felt was only a fraction of what Rachel was going through. I wished I could have just given her a hug and told her that I loved her. *Deep breaths,* I told myself. *Deep breaths.*

Marta was a good woman. She would have never done something like the news suggested she did. Rachel was her only child. The fact that they were even allowing such lies on the air was abhorrent. I was absolutely certain the same people who took down Owen were the ones who killed Marta. *They* were also the ones who staged the bombs at the final debate and outside of Wall Street on Black Monday. They were the same people who arrested my son for conducting research and framed Viktor Ivankov for letting the radioactive material through the Port of New York.

Like my son proved, the isotopes came from here. Russia was never involved. It was all one monstrous lie. It seemed like it consumed anyone that tried to uncover the truth, and now, my greatest fear was that Rachel would end up like Owen. *That*, was a possibility I couldn't let come true.

I turned around, glancing at all the papers strewn about my desk. I had *so* much information that could take them down, but something was missing. If we had everything we needed, why did this happen? What if I had made Rachel write her article sooner?

Maybe then, Owen would have still been alive. I felt so lost, and I didn't know where to turn next. I only hoped that the magic piece of the puzzle fell into place soon because we were running out of time. The election was two weeks away, and if we didn't find a way to reveal the truth to the rest of the country, *all* of our time would be up. *They* would win.

CIA Headquarters – Langley, VA
18:16 10-22-2016

This was the happiest I had been in over two years. I could barely recall when that was—it must have been back when we came up with the idea. I still remembered the dimly lit boardroom where it all began. It was a big deal. The President was there in secret. A few volunteered to lead the pack, but I think I was chosen because of my fervor. The President knew I had a cutthroat attitude, and that was exactly the kind of person he wanted. Time had been slipping by far too fast for my liking, and yet I had reaped just a tiny portion of what I sewed. Years of time and effort…for what? Was I better off than when I was just starting off as a paralegal for some chauvinist lawyer here in Washington? No. Men still ran this country, and I was determined to absorb as much power as I possibly could.

When I began my job as the assistant director of finances for the Democratic Party, I was still Ms. Goody two-shoes. I was trying to climb the ladder just like everyone else was, the right way, but it wasn't getting me anywhere. I dressed nice, was poised, and kept myself knowledgeable in the areas I needed to be, but it was never enough. Sometimes, I watched how the chairman would talk to some of his right-hand men, the ones just beneath him. When they didn't do what he wanted, he would get rid of them, replacing them with people who did. He talked down to me many times, but his public image was quite the opposite of how he acted in the office. He was kind, charming, and a social butterfly. I studied him for years. All while I was rubbing elbows with the *right* people.

One day, he stepped down. Ironically enough, it was just shy of a month before the plan began. Sometimes I wondered if he was a kinder person than he made himself out to be, because I would never forget the look on his face when he came back from that half-day meeting. His color was gone, and he immediately stepped down. We never heard of him in Washington again.

I was nominated for the title by a few of my well-connected colleagues. My predecessor must have had a cleaner conscience than me because when I was briefed on the plan, I was all for it. The amount of wealth would be unimaginable. I had few friends. I was a widow with no children. Life had sucked the happiness out of me. If there *were* people I wanted to include in our safety net, I was sure that I'd be able to.

Being a doormat gets old. I was fast approaching fifty, and that opportunity was the chance I always dreamed of. Why should I be forced to live in the shadows of my counterparts' successes? I was *done* being the nice girl because in forty-something odd years it had gotten me nowhere. It was my turn to call the shots.

It became the drug I was still addicted to, and there wasn't a sweeter high than what I felt right now.

Owen was dead. The chase was finally over. I knew from the very beginning we would win, and I was overjoyed to know that I had succeeded. I had carried out the duties I was given—to eliminate the threat the Convergence Party posed to our plan. It was supposed to have been much easier than this, but I am one to know, there were always bumps in the road. If Cole *and* Owen would have died at the debate, we would have had no struggle. The public would have just accepted that their favorite political hero was actually a terrorist, and the polls would plummet like we predicted. That happened naturally, even when Owen made it out of the debate alive. Now, we would have to clean up the mess he made. We would have to wipe that video clean off the internet, and the news could never replay it. CNN would regret their decision of not pulling the plug in time just to keep their ratings high. It was embarrassing to be called out like that on national TV, but I would have the last laugh. When the election was behind us, we could finally proceed. This time the Supreme Court would be useless. Our legislative branch would dissolve in a matter of days. The American People would be powerless to change the future we envisioned so long ago. We knew how it needed to be done. Quick and sharp. So fast that they wouldn't know what happened to them.

Our vision would come true—a totalitarian society. Half of our armed forces could possibly rebel, but the other half were just dumb grunts. They would do whatever they were told. We would quadruple their pay if we had to, to keep them on our side. Once the people were in the Camps again, there would be no getting out. Eventually, we would convert the holding camps into their own little cities. Everyone would be assigned a role. They would have to work if they wanted to be fed.

See, the thing was, we wouldn't have been hurting ourselves compared to any other countries. They would have followed suit in time. We would pave the way for the others. That was the reason all of this came to be—*knowledge*. The people were finally waking up and realizing what was *really* going on in government. The internet was the main contributor to that awakening. With that endless wealth of information, a citizen could essentially find out whatever he or she would like to find. Or rather, they could share it with the world in a single click. That was why the video of Owen spilling the truth had to vanish quickly. With such a global connection, it could be seen around the planet in a matter of hours. Luckily, we had the best of the best working for us. In just a few months, the internet, free and open, would be a thing of the past. We would determine what people could read, watch, and learn. Ten years ago I would have been appalled at the idea, but now it was quite alluring. I had power, but I wanted *more*.

A few years prior, once I became the chairwoman of the party, I finally saw what went on behind closed doors. The exchanges of large amounts of money, the ridiculous bills written late at night, and the shady deals made in five-star hotels paid by our tax dollars. The longer I was involved, the more I realized the people that surrounded me were hypocrites. They would cut funding to this or that, and yet give themselves pay raises, all while convincing the voters to give them their support.

It made me sick. Hard to believe, I know…but it did. Our government was both a plutocracy and an oligarchy. A small group of individuals with an exorbitant amount of money controlled almost everything that went on in the government. Many in the country, like Owen and Cole, recognized this and grew their following from people who understood what was really going on.

I knew it was going on long before they did. Their vision was noble, in all honestly, but sometimes the good people in this world got suffocated by the ones who played dirty. I was just like Owen at one point, when I was his age, and then this world made me bitter. Everything I saw going on in Washington made me want to strangle the people committing these heinous acts.

No. I was patient. I took the time needed to climb the ladder, and once I learned how to play their game, I played it better. I played it so well that when I took this position, and when I was briefed on the beginnings of the Confinement, I realized I couldn't turn back. Fuck doing what was right. I would have ended up just like them—dead.

I couldn't beat them, so I joined them. Not only did I join them, I led them. To be given temporary control over the CIA was entirely unheard of. It wasn't like I was going to contest. I will never forget the day the parked van blew up outside of Wall Street. It happened exactly as we had planned, few casualties, and a lot of contamination. FEMA and the EPA started the cleanup, but a few people in both agencies knew what to do with the information that was recorded. It was taken and false evidence was produced instead. It worked seamlessly. All I had to do was wait. Then, the riots began. First it was Los Angeles, then Miami, Chicago, Atlanta, Philadelphia. The list went on and on. Lines of people trying to withdraw their money. When they couldn't, they set buildings afire, torched cars—it was like an all-out war.

Then, Obama stepped in and signed an executive order to initiate the Confinement. None of it was televised. The citizens were blindsided, but that was exactly what we wanted. January 15th when the clock struck midnight, it began. The people living within a twenty-mile radius of the two-hundred cities with the greatest populations were rounded up like animals and put into the makeshift camps. Then, the fences were erected. The National Guard and the Army helped facilitate the process, and amazingly, it was all done within twenty-four hours. Everything was going as planned until the third party resistance groups began to show up in thousands at their state and local government buildings. Although, many times those cities were smaller, it didn't matter. The nine Supreme Court justices took notice, and Ruth Bader Ginsburg, along with a few others heard the voices of the people on the outside of the boundaries. Unfortunately for us, the Supreme Court was the one entity that wasn't in on the plan. They were the law of the land, and many of them couldn't be bribed. After three months from the date, they overturned Obama's order. Everyone was released. It was a blow to our morale.

Our country was stagnant. No one had been in their homes, went to work, driven in their cars. Bills weren't sent out. People didn't even know what to do when they were taken back home. They were lost. The government who imprisoned them, suddenly released them, and were things just going to go back to normal overnight?

Not at all. Once Congress was back in session, bills were passed to jump start the economy. Prices on domestic goods were deflated to a twenty-year low. It was like going to the store back in the nineties. On imported goods, the same thing was implemented, but the government took the tab for the difference. Our dollar was worthless in the global economy, but we had to encourage spending here. Cheap gas, cheap food, and then finally people began to go back to work. The federal minimum wage was raised. All of these an effort to get things back to normal.

That's not what we wanted.

Then, the Convergence Party blossomed out of nowhere. They had a candidate. All throughout D.C. there were flyers for meetings being held, billboards, and a headquarters was rented out in a building down the street from ours. Where was all of that money coming from? Cole Pavich, ex-congressman and lobbyist, funded all of it. He was the co-founder, along with a strikingly handsome young man. His name was Owen Marina.

He had lived in D.C. for almost a decade and was as green as they come. The only information I could gather on him was that he was a field chemist for the EPA. What was he doing trying to be a politician? The answer was change. He and Cole were trying to *change* the system.

The media caught wind of Owen, and once they did, the Convergence Party blew up overnight. Cole was smart. Owen had the looks, charm, and public speaking skills that every figurehead needed. I remembered watching interview after interview, and with each one the party's popularity grew. Cole had enough money to get them on the fast-track to being on the ballot, and they were. They paid their dues.

That was when we had to come up with another plan. Our analysts in the first quarter estimated that within six months, at the current rate, they would take the lead in the polls…and they did.

In August, we had a meeting. We designed a way to shift the polls back in our favor. There had never been a final debate in D.C., so we decided to keep it here. Even more reason for Owen to attend. He was an alumni of Georgetown University, and we could make a connection to that. Soon, the plan was underway.

That was all it took to take out our biggest threat, and it worked. He was one less worry on my mind. For the first time in a week, I didn't have a migraine, and it was enough to make me smile. I leaned back in my office chair, staring out at the sunset. It was a cloudless sky, and a deep orange met the soft blue of twilight on the horizon. I felt at peace, but there was the tiniest thought that crept into the back of my mind, and it made me uneasy.

Viktor Ivankov was still out there, somewhere…

I shook my head and shrugged the thought off. He didn't matter anymore. Owen was dead, and the battle was over. Now, the real fun began.

Hideout – Atlanta, GA
15:35 10-25-2016

I stared at the stucco of the basement wall just inches away from my face. I had the blanket wrapped around my body, trying to keep myself warm. It didn't help much. The coldness, the emptiness I felt inside was unbearable. It radiated outwards, as if there was an invisible, gaping hole in the center of my chest. Agony was the only sensation left I could feel. The icy sensation had taken its grip over my body, and I didn't move. I had no motivation to do anything at all. Physically, I was numb, and growing weaker by the day.

I hadn't eaten in three days. *Since*…I couldn't bring myself to replay it in my mind anymore. That was all I had done. The image of Owen's body lying on the street flashed into my mind every time I closed my eyes. When I finally was able to sleep, I would dream of him. In my dreams, he was still alive. I could still hear his voice, savor his scent, and feel his firm embrace around me. He was just a memory now, nothing more. I remembered the night at the penthouse when I was watching him talk to Grey across the terrace. I felt like I was looking at a ghost, and that feeling only amplified every time his face popped in my head. *Here today, gone tomorrow*. Now that he *was* gone, I didn't know what to do. I was completely alone and left with my thoughts. I wondered if I would have pushed him harder not to go through with Grey's plan, would he have been lying next to me right now? Would I have been able to hear his masculine tone whisper in my ear?

I would never know. He was *gone*, and so was my mother.

A choking, hiccupped cry came out as I thought of that. I tried so hard not to imagine what they did to her, but in between the thoughts of Owen, it was hard not to picture what transpired. I could see the fear in my mother's face, knowing her death was imminent. I just prayed she didn't have to suffer.

It was all because of me. My mother wouldn't have died if it wasn't for me meeting Owen. I saw a chance of a lifetime, and I took it. This was the end result. If I would have known this would be the outcome, would I still have approached him at that coffee shop? I didn't have the answer to that question. Not now. My thoughts spiraled around my head uncontrollably, and I was in a dark abyss of misery. I couldn't bear to face reality. Just shy of twenty-four years old, both of my parents were dead. I had no siblings. There was no one left but my aunt and uncle, and Ian. My stomach was in knots at the notion that *they* could have even gotten away with something like this. How was any sort of authority given to such diabolical people? How could the American People believe this just because it was on the news?

I was appalled at how naïve they all were. Could they not see the connection between the two? The government had the money to control the media. It was that simple. Now, the last remaining founder of the Convergence Party was dead. The hype would fade away in a few weeks, and by that time, the elections would be lost to a traditional party. It was everything they wanted and more. There wouldn't have to be a trial. You couldn't give a trial to a dead man.

Owen was dead. My mother was dead. In what kind of sick world could this be reality?

It made me sob even harder. My face had been perpetually wet since it happened. I couldn't muster the strength to turn around. I knew they were all behind me. I could hear Natasha and Viktor mumble in their conversations. Briana wasn't quite as bad as I was, but she was torn up over this too. Grey hadn't said much since that day. I heard the basement door open every so often. I think it was because Grey didn't want us to see him cry. He had lost someone very dear to him, just as I had, but Grey had known him since they were children. I had only known him for a week and a half.

That was the roughest part of it all. I fell in love with a man who I knew from the beginning was temporary, but I didn't know *this* was what that meant. I thought he would have been locked up at most. If only I could have gone back in time just to spend one more moment with him. Maybe then, I could have expressed my love a little stronger, or a little clearer. I hoped he would tell my mother how sorry I was for all of this, wherever they were now.

I was raised Catholic, but my faith lessened as I got older.

Still, though, I believed there was something after this life. There had to be. A piece of me wished I was with them, wished I would have pushed just a little harder against the cops. Maybe they would have shot me, too.

The TV clicked on, and I began to sob harder. I did it on purpose. They would turn it off because of my reaction. When I fell asleep, they would turn it back on. They thought I didn't know, but sometimes I just acted like I was asleep. I lay awake—prisoner to my misery. I knew they were just trying to stay current with the news, but I didn't want to hear. I saw it with my own eyes, in the flesh. I didn't need to see it again.

It was not like it mattered. I would have to carry that memory for the rest of my life.

I felt someone behind me, and then I smelled some kind of sandwich, maybe a sub, nearby. I heard a plate cling against the wooden coffee table.

"You need to eat, Rachel," Briana said softly.

I didn't respond. My body knew it was hungry, but the nausea I felt was unrelenting. Eventually, I would have no choice. I would either eat or slowly die. Now, my restless night I had was catching up to me, and I yawned. Drowsiness overtook me, and I felt the pit in my gut ease slightly because I knew where I would go when I slept. A tear rolled down my cheek, but the thought was enough to make me smile.

I would be with *him*, back when he was still alive.

"Rachel," a familiar voice drew me from my sleep. "Rachel."

They gently shook my back.

"Rachel, please wake up," the voice a little firmer.

I groaned, griping at whoever was trying to wake me.

"I have to talk to you," the man gingerly pulled my shoulder over.

I opened my eyes. It was Grey. There were dark circles beneath his brown eyes. In the dim light, they almost looked black. He must have had trouble sleeping too. There was no light coming in from the two tiny openings in the basement walls. It was night, and I guess I had slept longer than it felt like I did. I wished he hadn't woken me. I was having dinner with Owen, and we visited my mom's house.

I burst into tears and buried my face in the pillow. Grey rubbed my back gently for a few minutes until it ceased.

"I know," he consoled. "I've done a lot of crying, too."

I glanced up at him and saw tears pooling in his eyes. The basement was dead silent, and I swiveled my head around to see what was going on. There was no one but us.

"Where is everyone?" I asked. The sound of my own voice took me by surprise. I hadn't heard it in three days.

"Out to get food. I told them I needed to talk to you alone."

I swallowed.

"I hope they know I'm not hungry."

Grey pressed his lips together and glanced over my body as if I were an emaciated stray puppy.

"You're going to have to eat sometime," he said.

"I can't."

He stood up and walked across the room. He returned with a mirror. I could see the reflection of the underside of his chin as he held it in his lap.

"Take a look at yourself." He handed me the mirror. I cautiously moved it in front of me, and I didn't even recognize the person looking back. My glowing tan was gone. My skin was a pasty yellow. My face was soaked in tears, and there were bags under my eyes, just like Grey's. I ran my hands down my neck and felt how cold I was. I could tell in the mirror that I had lost weight just from how much tighter the skin on my neck was, and I could see my cheekbones more predominantly. I looked sick, like I was on the road to death.

Above all else, in my eyes I saw pain. A deep, burdensome pain.

"Here," I pushed the mirror towards him. "I can't see that any longer."

He grabbed it and set it beside the bed.

"So, will you eat something when they get back?"

"I'll try," I said.

He nodded, revealing the smallest beginnings of a smile, but it soon faded. He looked down at his feet and let out a long sigh. My arms began to shake from trying to hold myself upright. I was *so* weak. I scooted up against the basement wall to support myself.

"Was that all you wanted to talk about?" I asked. My suspicions told me no.

He turned to me and almost looked thankful that I brought it up first.

"About that..." He mumbled. "Look, I know you are going through a lot right now."

He paused, and I just stared at him with a blank face. *A lot* didn't even come close to what I was going through.

"We *all* are going through a lot right now," he reiterated, "and I know you're weak, so you've got to get some food in you. Once you've got a little more energy again, we need you to call Ian."

I think he expected me to respond, but I had no urge to. My mother and Owen got ripped out of my life, and he wanted me to revert back to how I was before they died? It was not that easy. I didn't even think I would be able to go to my own mother's funeral because I was wanted by the feds.

My chest heaved up and down, and I felt a rock in my throat. I began to sob again. The shuddering cries were violent. Grey scooted closer to me and rubbed my shoulder. It didn't help ease the despair that crept through my veins. I could see my whole family now, blaming her death on me. They would curse my name for helping a *'terrorist'*. If only they knew the truth.

"Rachel," he said as he rubbed the top of my back in a circular motion. "You and I both know what he would have wanted..."

I wiped my eyes and stared back at him, dumbfounded he would bring that up so soon. I knew exactly what he was talking about.

"Oh yea?" I coughed. "Did he tell you too?"

"Yes, he did," Grey began. "He asked me to make sure that no matter what happened to him, that you would still write your story."

I only cried harder, and I heard his voice in the back of my mind.

"Write. You're supposed to write."

"I know, and I will. I'm just not ready yet. How can I write about something so personal to me? I have to write it as an article, not a memoir. Journalists aren't supposed to help their subjects, and I broke that golden rule when I approached Owen."

"I don't know what to say," Grey admitted. "I'm good with computers…and not so much people."

A smile tugged at my lips, but I didn't feel like adding anything.

"*But*," he continued, "I do know a few things for certain. Tomorrow will come, and it will probably feel just as awful as today. There is nothing we can do now to change what happened, the only way we can look is forward, to the future. The election is two weeks from today."

I could hardly believe it was so soon. I counted the days in my head, and he was right.

"*That* might be something we can still change, Rachel."

"With my story…" I mumbled.

He nodded. "You are going to eat something when they come back. You are going to rest some more, and then you are going to do what Owen would have wanted."

I dried the tears on my face with the cuff of my sleeve.

"Okay."

"Good," Grey sighed with relief, scratching the scruff of his chin. "I was worried you might not have ever willed yourself to get out of this bed."

"Part of me still doesn't want to," I admitted, "but that's not what Owen would have wanted. He made me promise I would write the story."

Grey took his hand off of my back. His eyes grew wider as if he had just remembered something important.

"Anyway, Viktor needs to talk to you before you call Ian. He said something about an idea he wanted to run by you, but he wouldn't tell me what it is. I've tried to get it out of Natasha, but she swears she doesn't know."

"An idea?"

Hideout – Atlanta, GA
10:17 10-27-2016

I grabbed the cold metal rung and placed one foot securely on the first step. Vapor trailed from my mouth—the morning was unusually cold for October. I pulled myself up and put my other foot on the second step. My muscles quivered slightly. They were still weak, but they were much better than when Grey and I had our talk. I had been eating at every meal and slowly regaining my energy. I still have cried…a lot. Then again, I would probably cry for the next year, and there wasn't a thing I could do to change that. Much of what Grey said resonated with me. I knew it was true, but in that kind of despair, it helped to have someone remind me again.

This was what Owen wanted.

I climbed higher and higher until I was almost at the ledge. Viktor wanted to talk to me alone, and this was about the only place that was suitable. The basement was far from private—even the bathroom didn't have a door. A breeze blew by, and it tousled the ends of my black hair past my face. I was still getting used to the color, and part of me wanted to keep it that way. It reminded me of mine and Owen's final morning together.

I threw my leg over the ledge and stepped onto the rooftop. Viktor was standing on the far side, facing the Atlanta skyline. It was the exact place I was standing when Owen came to talk to me that last night. I couldn't believe in two days it would be a week since he had been gone. I knew it was real, but it just didn't *feel* that way. I approached the ledge and rested my arms against it as I stood next to Viktor silently. To my surprise, when he saw me, he didn't say anything.

"So you wanted to talk?" I asked meekly.

He snorted and drew in a long inhalation.

"I did," he replied. I was surprised he was being so short with me. I had waited two days to call Ian for this?

"About?"

He paused, and the muscle along his jaw twitched from clenching his teeth. He had very strong features, and his skin was pale white. It stood out against his hair the same shade as mine.

"You know, my parents came to this country a few months before I was born. My mother got pregnant unexpectedly, and she and my father found a way to get here. They wanted their children to have a better life, a better opportunity to thrive…and we did. We came to New York, and my father worked in a factory. My mother worked as a teller. They had a hard time learning English, and my dad still struggles with it. My sister and I both spoke well because we learned it in school."

"My parents were immigrants, too," I added. Hearing myself use *were* instead of *are* made the aching pit in my stomach return.

"From where?"

"Puerto Rico. They came to New York just like yours did. I think it's something common among immigrants. They see the New York skyline on TV and in films and want to go there. The United States embodies opportunity to them."

He chuckled. "You're right. My parents did exactly that. I'm sure our parents had similar difficulties adjusting to life in the States."

"I suppose," I said. It hurt too much to talk about them, and I knew he had more to say.

"I always saw life in this country as limitless. As I got older, I started seeing it differently. What they portrayed in movies and on TV, was much more fantasy than it was reality. The media plants the idea in your mind that you can only be happy if you have it all. A big house, a nice car, and a happy family—the American Dream."

I stayed quiet.

"I wanted to be a director growing up. My Dad would take me and my sister to the movies every Sunday after church. That is still my fondest childhood memory. I had a plan. I was going to move out west to Los Angeles and work in the production world. That was until my mother got sick. She was diagnosed in 2000 with Leukemia. My dad had insurance through his job at the factory, but it wasn't enough. The cancer bills began to pile up. My mom lost her job at the bank, and the lack of income put a lot of stress on our household. My sister was sixteen, and she worked at a grocery store to help with the bills. I was nineteen at the time, and although I wanted to move out west, I had an obligation to my family. She received treatment off and on for three years, and once she was cured, luckily, it never returned. My dad never told me the exact amount, but I knew he had accumulated at least a hundred thousand dollars of debt from the hospital bills. They would be paying that off for the rest of their lives. Prisoners to their debt."

"That is half of the reason I support the Convergence Party," I said.

"Exactly," he huffed. "I thought this is the land of the *free?* Sure, my life in Russia would have been dismal compared to here, but I never understood that many of these freedoms came with a price tag. Without me knowing it, the cycle began to repeat. I didn't go to college, and in 2005 I took a job at the Port of New York operating a forklift. I stayed in Brooklyn to help my parents with the bills and so did my sister. That's another thing I never understood about Americans."

"What's that?" I asked.

"Their lack of family bonds. My parents would come home from work, and we would all eat dinner together every night at the table. My parents told us stories of how some of their work friends talked about their own parents. Saying that they 'found their mom or dad a nice home'. That is unheard of in Russia, and you would be looked down upon for doing such a thing. Family is everything where my parents come from. As I worked at the Port, I began to see why this was so common in the States. You must sacrifice something. Here, it is either your time or your money. You can't have both. You must choose one."

I snorted and nodded my head in agreement. What he was saying was so true. I couldn't have said it better myself.

"Americans can't sacrifice their time because it takes time to make money. So, they spend their money to have someone else take care of their parents because it saves them time. It's all a chain-reaction."

"The Latino people are the same. *Familia* is everything."

He turned to me, smiling. "I'm glad you understand."

"I do," I nodded.

"Have you ever seen *The Green Mile?*"

My eyebrows furrowed from his question.

"Yes, I have. Why?"

"My dad and I saw it alone when it first came out in 1999. It was around six months before my mom was diagnosed when I still had hopes of moving to LA. It was the first movie I really, truly cried in. I thought about it for weeks after. It moved me emotionally, and I was inspired. I wanted to make films like that, films that touch people. Before I knew it though, I was a slave to my paycheck. I did what I felt was right as a man and that was to take care of my family."

"It was an honorable decision," I encouraged him.

"I'd like to think so…" He mumbled. "You know, the irony of my situation is that it's similar to *The Green Mile*. In the blink of an eye, I was accused of something I didn't do. My bosses turned on me, my coworkers turned on me, and I hadn't a clue what to do next. I worked my ass off for ten years, working my way up to the head Radiograph X-Ray Operator, and that was how I was repaid for all my effort? I had just started dating Natasha in the months before I was framed. She had a degree in software design at NYU, and she helped me get out of New York without getting caught."

I bit my lower lip, and my eyes welled up. The similarities between Viktor's and Owen's stories caused me to become emotional. Natasha helped Viktor get out of New York. I helped Owen get out of Raleigh. Viktor took notice and turned to me.

"Are you all right?"

"Yes. I—I'm fine," I assured him.

"I abandoned my family, Rachel. Sometimes, I feel guilty for leaving…but I didn't have a choice. If I stayed, I would have been caught."

"You shouldn't feel guilty," I said.

"I don't," he replied matter-of-factly. "Not anymore. Now, all I feel is *anger*."

He turned to me, looking deep into my eyes as he emphasized the word.

"I know I told you the other night, but I still remember when she first came into my work, right before the New Year. She slithered around the Port like the snake she is with her clipboard, writing down notes. The clacking of her heels always signaled her entrance, and the sound of them gave me chills. When she shook my hand, it felt like ice. I had never met someone that gave me such a cold feeling inside my body, and her face still haunts me. The face of the woman who ruined my life, who took *Owen's* life…"

My nostrils flared from him mentioning that. I felt the anger he spoke of. The agony I felt inside was, for a moment—gone. The anger was almost *soothing*. Viktor's jaw muscles flexed again, and he stared back out at Downtown Atlanta, letting out a long sigh.

"Being on the run for two years wears you down," he announced. "It makes you exhausted to the point where sleep no longer helps. I'm tired of running, Rachel."

I turned to him, curious to what he was getting at. My eyebrows quirked.

"There's nothing to run from anymore," he began. "The feds left Atlanta days ago. Yes, we are still wanted, but because of what happened to Owen, we are out of the spotlight."

I trembled just hearing the words *'what happened to Owen.'*

"Grey told me you had an idea," I blurted.

He stared at me blank-faced, and his lips pressed into a hard line.

"I know I just met you, but I am no dummy. I can tell you loved Owen."

Loved…

I choked on a cry just from hearing the word. It wasn't in the past tense in my mind. Not one bit.

"I still do," I corrected him and wiped the tears from my eyes.

"Like I said, I am tired of running. I am sure you are too. My idea would take us back to where this all began, in Washington. Where the criminals who created this lie are still roaming free. There is one person behind all of this, and she ruined my life and took Owen's and your mother's."

"Veronica…" I shivered from a passing breeze as I said her name.

He nodded.

"I have watched her destroy enough in the past two years, and I am finished with running. I want to bring the battle to her, where she has no way to run, and nowhere to hide."

"Are you suggesting?"

A fire burned behind his eyes.

"Yes," he said. "We are going to kill her."

My initial reaction was shocked, but it was only for a fraction of a second. Hearing his idea caused that anger to bubble up within me again, with pain and resentment fanning the flames inside of me.

"You and I both know the importance of family," he began, "and she stole yours from you."

My breathing grew heavy, and my pulse began to quicken.

"Rachel, you have no idea how long I've wanted to see her taken down. I've fantasized about it since Black Monday, but in light of what happened, I thought I'd let you do the honors."

"Me?"

"Yes, you. Trust me, I would love to do it myself."

"I am going to kill Veronica Hall."

Hearing myself say it out loud made it sound that much more appealing.

"Yes. We have nothing to lose. We have all the information we need to take her down, but you know what? I say we take matters into our own hands. If Owen didn't get a trial, neither does she. They say an eye for an eye makes the whole world blind. I've tried to live my life by that philosophy, but our situation is different."

"How so?" I asked.

"Veronica has taken everyone's eyes, and now they can't see. If we take hers, perhaps we can restore the country's vision. People's memory of Owen will fade, and they will forget about him. We need to make people *remember* why all of this happened, and we will time it perfectly before you write your article."

A smile slid over my face, and for the first time in days I didn't feel hopeless.

"Let's do it."

620 8th Ave. – New York, NY
11:01 10-27-2016

I stared down at the copy of tomorrow's paper I had to sign for approval. The government would shut us down if I would have just let the journalists blatantly assert that Owen was innocent, so I had taken the only possible route. We were weighing in both sides, trying our best to remain neutral. I couldn't risk being able to publish Rachel's article when she hadn't written it yet.

The past few days had been really rough. I visited Emilio's grave twice. I needed to get some stuff off my chest and to ask him to watch over his daughter now that her mother was gone. I had planned on making arrangements to attend Marta's funeral, but given that Rachel was still out there somewhere, I figured I would wait until I heard from her to book my flight.

There was a week and a half until the election. We were running out of time.

I saw the button for my assistant's line flash red. I picked it up.

"Yes, Sharon?"

"There's a call waiting for you on your secure line," she said.

My heart fluttered in my chest. It was *her*.

"Send it through."

I walked over to a small table where a separate phone sat. This was the secure line my IT guys rigged. I picked it up.

"Hello," I said.

"Hey, Ian. It's me."

Her voice wasn't nearly as brittle as I expected it to be. It almost sounded rejuvenated.

"I'm so sorry, Rachel…I have no words."

I heard her whimper, as if she was about to cry, and it was followed by a sharp inhale. She steadied her breath.

"I know. I have done a lot of crying."

"I could imagine. I have too, you know. Just know I love you, and my wife and I will always be here for you."

"Thank you, Ian. You mean the world to me," she said, pausing to take a deep breath. "I am actually surprised I am calling you this soon."

"I am too."

"Owen's…good friend helped me regain my strength. Before what happened, Owen made me promise to write my story no matter what. I have all the information you need."

"Then fax it to me," I said.

There was silence.

"Rachel?" I checked to see if she was still there.

"It's not that simple anymore. I need to settle the score with someone. She is responsible for all of this."

"Who?" I asked.

"Veronica Hall."

"Are you kidding me?"

"No, I'm not kidding. The same person who provided this massive piece of the puzzle knows everything, and she is the one behind it. Behind Owen's death and my mother's. If we don't keep what happened to Owen in the spotlight, she will be behind the death of this country. She needs to be stopped."

There was zero sadness in her voice, only determination. *She needs to be stopped.* I pieced together what she was trying to tell me, and once it hit, I was shocked.

"You aren't suggesting—"

"Yes," she cut me off, "and that's why I need your help."

"How could I even begin to help you with that?" I asked, raising my voice.

"Ian, you *know* people—powerful people. The last time we spoke, if I remember correctly, you said you found *two* pieces of the puzzle. One was Stefan's, and the other?"

Lucas.

"It was from a veteran, one that we interviewed years ago when he returned from the Middle East. He faxed me some very sensitive material. He works for the CIA."

"Ian," Rachel gasped. "That's it. That's the kind of person I need."

I was becoming overwhelmed with everything she was throwing at me. I had lost Emilio, and I wasn't going to sit back and watch her put herself in harm's way.

"Rachel, you realize what could happen to you if you go through with what you're thinking? You could wind up just like Owen."

It pained me to make that parallel over the phone, when I knew she was so hurt.

"I have nothing left to lose," she said flatly. "I have lost it all, Ian. I can't just turn the other cheek this time. If *they* win, then my mom's and Owen's deaths meant *nothing.* They will just be another victim in this sick, sick game…"

I paused, pondering her statement. The conviction in her tone was overflowing, and it was so apparent to me, being someone that watched her grow up. These past two weeks had transformed her as a person.

"I need the help of that person, Ian. He will help us do what we need to do, and we will time it just before you publish my article. The shock value will remind people to question what is *really* going on. What is his name?"

"Lucas," I answered. "But what if he doesn't want to help?"

She let out a trembling exhale, and I could almost *feel* her anger.

"If he even knows a smidgen of what I do about Veronica Hall, then he would be more than willing."

4118 Ridgeview Rd. – McLean, VA
11:39 10-27-2016

I felt defeated. So defeated, that I took a week of sick pay just to buy myself more time. I told myself I wouldn't go back to work ever again, and I didn't want to, but I also wanted to keep out of Veronica's radar. If I didn't show up for work, that might cause her to become suspicious of my whereabouts.

Watching Owen die on national television crushed me. It quite literally deflated my morale and left my soul aching. I knew it was *her*, and when I heard about what happened to Rachel's mother, I was even more disgusted. Oh, the things I wished I could do to that woman.

It had been six days since I faxed Mr. Westlake my files. Why hadn't I read an article about it yet? I was helpless. I had no desire to go back and work for those traitors, but I couldn't wait forever. You couldn't just *quit* the CIA. It didn't work like that. My level of clearance was one of the highest that existed. Either Veronica went down, or I would be forced to return to work.

My week off would be over the day after tomorrow. I wondered if anything had changed since I'd been gone. Perhaps, I wouldn't have to see her any longer. Would things go back to normal? That was impossible. With her in control and Owen dead, things could only get worse from here…and that was what I was most afraid of.

The kids were in school. Today was my fifth day straight of binge-watching *Game of Thrones*. I felt useless sitting around not working, but it was a nice change to be home for dinner with the family. During the chase for Owen, I wasn't home for days at a time. My wife was happy that my schedule would go back to the way it was before he went on the run.

My wife rounded the corner from the kitchen.

"Honey, that pre-paid phone you bought is ringing," she said as she scurried over to hand it to me. I glanced at the number. It was a 212 area code—Manhattan.

I picked it up.

"Hello," I answered nervously.

"Lucas," the familiar voice said. "It's Ian. Is this line secure?"

"Uh…yes, hold on a moment. Let me take a walk down the street, just in case."

I never could be too sure given my profession. They could have had my entire house tapped for all I knew.

"Luc, is everything okay, hon?" my wife asked from behind me as I walked out the door. I kept my elbows pressed to my sides because it was chilly out with a persistent breeze.

"Can you talk now?" Ian asked.

"Yes. I am glad you called."

"We'll see how glad you are after you find out *why* I called."

My forehead scrunched up.

"What do you mean?"

"I'll explain everything, I just need to ask you a few things. When was the last time you've been to work?"

"Since the day before I sent you the files."

He choked on his breath.

"You're kidding, right?"

"No, I'm not kidding," I said flatly.

"Did you quit or something?!" Panic made his voice jump around.

"I took a week of paid sick leave. Ian, why is any of this relevant?"

"Oh, thank God…" He gasped. "That would have been bad."

"You didn't answer my question," I pressed.

There was silence.

"Ian?"

"So, I'm assuming you saw everything that happened in Atlanta."

"Yes, of course I did. I recorded the whole thing."

"Good," he said. "Lucas, I have to ask you an extremely important question that I have a feeling you already know the answer to…"

My eyes squinted from his wording.

"Shoot."

"What do you know about Veronica Hall?"

I thought my head was going to explode. I quickly scanned my surroundings to make sure there were no government cars parked nearby. I knew what to look for.

"Ian, are you *sure* your line is secure? Secure in civilian talk and secure in my line of work are two entirely different things."

"He's the best guy I know. It's not like it matters anymore. You risked that when you sent the files."

He was right. If the CIA found out even the smallest portion of what I had done, I would be dead meat. I could wind up in some freak car accident or in prison for the rest of my life. I took in a deep breath to suppress my anger before I spoke.

"Let's just put it this way. The things she has done are so vile, that every single move I have made in regards to the information I gave you were to take her down. If you read through that file, just know that she was behind all of it. If we want to salvage what is left of this country, her power has to be dissolved. She has to go."

Ian didn't respond. I heard faint static through the phone. I hoped I hadn't scared him off.

"Hello?"

"Sorry," he mumbled. "I was just still in shock."

"About?"

"She was right."

His voice sounded distant again, like he was out of it.

"Who was right?"

"Rachel Flores—my goddaughter."

My jaw dropped.

"She's your *goddaughter?* My God. I'm so sorry about everything that has happened."

"Me too," he said. "Trust me."

Disgust began to settle in throughout my body. Veronica helped kill Owen and Rachel's mother in the same day. I was glad that I wasn't working that day, because if I was, I would have probably pulled out my gun and killed her in front of everyone. Her body count just grew higher each passing day. Everything she touched eventually rotted away, just like her soul had long ago.

"Lucas, Lucas, are you there?" Ian asked frantically. I had zoned out.

"Yes," I answered. "Anyway, what was your goddaughter right about?"

"How you feel about Veronica."

"How does she know who I am?"

"I told her," he responded nonchalantly.

"Are you out of your mind? You do realize I work for the most covert agency in our country, right?"

"I do."

"Then why on Earth would you tell her who I am?"

"Because she asked for my help, Lucas. Her parents are dead, and she isn't even twenty-four yet. I'm surprised she called me this soon, considering what happened to her. She has nothing left but me."

His explanation placated my temper.

"What was it she needed your help with?"

"Getting in touch with someone like you," he replied without hesitation. "In reality, she ultimately needs *your* help, not mine."

"How so?" I asked.

"I can't say it word for word right now, but it involves Veronica. She, and whoever she is with, wants her gone too. The night before Owen died she called me and said she had found a massive piece of the puzzle we have been trying to solve. So, whoever she is with, that person must know a lot, just like you."

The seeds of imagination began to take root in my mind. Was Ian referring to what I thought he was? Rachel wanted her gone like I did, and that could only mean *one* thing. I was debating on what to say. Rachel was young, and I had a family. I had children, and that changed everything. Whatever I chose to do, I had to be very careful. It was obvious that Ian wasn't going to give me any details, if he knew any at all to begin with.

"Lucas?" he butted into my thoughts.

"Yes," I answered absentmindedly.

"I had asked her, just before we got off the phone, 'what if he doesn't want to help?'. Do you want to know what her answer was to that question?"

"Yes," I said. I felt like I was in a trance.

"She said, 'If he even knows a smidgen of what I do about Veronica Hall, then he would be more than willing.'"

My stomach dropped, and my heart began to race. Rachel *knew* just like I did. She knew that Veronica was behind all of it, and that the blood of Owen and her mother was on her hands. I had taken an oath to defend this country, from enemies foreign *and* domestic, and after Owen's death, my options were limited. Sure, the information I faxed could be used in Ian's article, but that wasn't how I was trained. That wasn't my style. Just because we wrote articles about something bad that was going on, didn't mean it just disappeared overnight. We needed people like me to go in and stop it at the source. Rachel must have had a similar idea, and I knew deep down, that she was right…I would be willing to help her.

"Ian," I blurted out, jarring myself from my thoughts.

"Yes?"

"Give her my number."

Outskirts – Arlington, VA
22:49 10-27-2016

Besides two stops at the gas station and one to get food, we had been in the car for ten hours. My legs were beginning to cramp. I was sitting between Briana and Grey. Natasha was driving, and Viktor was in the passenger seat. A few times I had napped against Grey's shoulder, and Briana did the same on mine. Much of the drive was silent, and I couldn't keep the aching feeling in my stomach at bay. Someone was missing from this car…and the thought of his name almost brought me to tears. I missed the sensation of his warm hand interlaced with my own.

When I wasn't staring at the passing trees, I just closed my eyes and tried to nap. When my eyes were closed, he was with me—it was just like my dreams. I could hear his voice. I knew if he was here, he would most likely scold me for agreeing to Viktor's plan. He would tell me to write my story and to avoid the risk. I smiled at the thought, because I would tell him this was his payback for going along with Grey's plan.

But Owen *wasn't* here. That wasn't reality. The reality was that he wasn't here to see the pain I was in from him not being around. He wasn't here to ease the aching I felt in the center of my chest, which never seemed to subside. Neither my mother nor father were here to console me. I just prayed that one day this pain would dissipate, but I was doubtful.

The address we had was for McLean. Grey said that we were only a few minutes away. I was glad because I wanted to stretch out my legs. I had talked to the man named Lucas on the phone, and just from his voice I knew something that Ian could have never conveyed. Lucas *knew* Veronica, much more in depth than I did. It was evident in his tone. I could practically hear the suppressed rage behind every word.

Viktor told me to relay to Lucas that he thought a hotel would be too dangerous. Our faces had been too many places. He felt it was just a matter of time before the CIA tied Briana and Grey in with me. Although hesitant, Lucas said we could stay in his basement. He also had a three car garage that Viktor could park the car in. I was nervous about trusting this CIA agent to begin with. What if he was just deceiving Ian in an attempt to catch me? After everything I had been through with Owen, I wasn't inclined to trust anyone. The evidence Viktor showed us was concrete, and it only made me realize further how corrupt our government truly was. Lucas's voice though…*that* was something no actor could pull off. I knew he felt the same as I did about Veronica, and that was without ever having met him.

The scenery changed once we got off the highway. The streets were narrower and lined with suburban homes. All the lawns were perfectly manicured, but a few were beginning to brown. Winter was slowly creeping in. Some of the homes had entrances where part of the roof was supported by pillars—similar to what you would see in a mansion. As hard as it was for me to live with, I knew my life would have been different without the money my father left behind. I would have remained in Hialeah with Briana for far too long. I probably wouldn't have even gone to college. I would have traded it all for him.

I would have done the same for Owen and my mother, too.

"This is it," Viktor announced. "We're here."

"Which one?" Briana asked.

"That one," he pointed out of his window. I ducked down beside Briana to see out. It was a two-story house made of red brick. There were many windows facing us, and a few of the rooms on the first floor had their lights on. The walls of the house were lined with shrubs and other greenery. In the left side of the yard was a massive, old oak tree. Behind the shrubs were lights that illuminated the sides of the house. It looked like the CIA paid well.

"What did he say again?" Viktor asked, turning around in his seat to face me.

"All he asked was that we don't ring the doorbell," I said. "It might wake up his kids."

He nodded in response, mulling over my statement.

"You said he doesn't know anything about who is with you, right?"

"Yes, all he knows is that I am with four other people."

He turned around and chuckled.

"I can't wait to see his face when he finds out he just let Viktor Ivankov into his house."

Natasha let out a stifled laugh, and Viktor began to slowly accelerate into the driveway. He had a three car garage, and we parked right in front of one of the bay doors. He turned the car off and popped open his door.

"Hopefully we aren't walking into a trap," Grey said. He voiced my concerns without me having to bring them up. Natasha glanced at him as she was about to step out of the car. "I've been thinking the same thing," she admitted. Briana pressed her lips together and shook her head as she popped open our door. She must have been concerned too. I slid out from my seat in the middle and stretched out as my feet hit the pavement. I knew they were all worried. They had reason to be. Lucas was a stranger who I had just talked to on the phone once. I had second thoughts myself, but I knew Ian wouldn't have steered me in the wrong direction. Lucas gave him information. He willingly gave Ian another piece of the puzzle, turning his back on his employer. My gut said everything would be okay.

It *had* to be okay…because I didn't think my reality could get any worse than it already was. As I finished stretching out, I noticed everyone staring at me.

"What?" I asked.

"We are waiting on you to lead the way," Viktor replied. "You were the one who talked to him."

I nodded and led everyone up the entranceway. There was monkey grass lining its edges all the way to the stone steps of the porch. My heart began to pound in my chest. We walked up, and I held my clenched fist hesitantly in front of the door, and I knocked three times. I didn't knock too hard because it was almost eleven o'clock, and he mentioned having kids.

The light that spilled out from the peephole went black, and a moment later the door swung open. In the dim lighting of the foyer, many of his features were obscured. He was of average build, and his hairline was receding. The wisps of brown stuck out in the light. He wore a thermal long-sleeve shirt and pajama bottoms. He glanced around nervously at us and opened the screen door.

"Come in," he whispered. He held open the door and we filed in one after another. "Try to walk lightly, the kids are asleep."

I nodded and waited behind him as the rest of us made it inside. He closed and locked the door behind us. "Follow me," he instructed and led us down a hallway with cherry oak floors. Lucas and his wife had good taste. The farther we walked, the more we saw. We entered a kitchen with granite countertops and tiled-rock floors. It reminded me of my mom's house, but it wasn't decorated as tropical. Just the thought of her caused the ache in the center of my chest to radiate outwards. It felt like flames were searing my insides, but I had almost become accustomed to the sensation since that day. I knew I would be feeling it for a *long* time.

Lucas opened a door and led us down the stairs into a basement. He flicked on a light as he rounded a corner, and it took a few seconds to take it all in. It was fully-furnished. The carpet was off-white, and there was a massive, black leather sectional in the center of the room. A flat-screen of gargantuan size was on the wall across from the sectional. There were two love seats along the short side of the sectional of the same color. The walls were painted a deep burgundy. It almost gave it a look like this was a theater. There were two doors along opposite corners of the room. I assumed there was more than just this. Once the last of us had entered, we all stood there awkwardly. Lucas motioned to the sectional with his hand.

"Please, take a seat."

We all sat down. I saw Natasha on the other side nervously glancing around the room. Viktor and Grey kept stern dispositions, as to not show fear of this man. Briana was elbow to elbow with me. Judging by Lucas's expression, he felt just as awkward as we did.

"Are any of you hungry?" he asked. "Would you like something to drink? Tea? Lemonade?"

"Actually," Natasha blurted out, "which way is the bathroom?"

"It's that door right there," he said, pointing to the far corner.

She stood up without thanking him.

"I would love a glass of lemonade if you don't mind," Viktor added with a smile. I glanced over at him with an annoyed expression. Why were they being so rude?

Lucas nodded with a halfhearted smile and headed for the stairs.

"Sure, I'll be right back," he said.

The moment he was almost up the stairs, Viktor stood and walked away. I turned around, confused as to where he was going. He opened the door opposite to the bathroom Natasha was in. I saw a light turn on and heard his footsteps growing fainter. Within about ten seconds, he returned, turning off the light and closing the door behind him.

"The exit is through there," he breathed heavily as if he had ran throughout the rest of the basement. "I unlocked it." Natasha sat down just a moment after him. "I found these in one of the drawers," she announced, holding up a silver pair of cuticle scissors.

"You've got to be kidding me," I gasped in shock.

Natasha glared back at me with the most serious expression I had ever seen on her face. Her black eyes were empty.

"Viktor and I didn't make it two years on the run by trusting strangers."

I swallowed hard, and her words hit me in the gut. The way hers and Viktor's minds worked was not crafted by chance—it was by practice. *This* was their reality, and it had been for two years. They were always prepared for the worst, even in seemingly innocuous situations.

Lucas's footsteps sounded as he descended the staircase. I saw Natasha clutch the scissors within her palm to conceal them. He rounded the corner with a glass of lemonade, and I could hear the pieces of ice clinging around inside. He walked over and handed it to Viktor.

"Thank you," he said.

"You're very welcome."

But *were* we welcome? We were sitting defenseless in the enemy's home. I was staring at the face of a man who worked with the same people that had been chasing me and Owen across the eastern seaboard for the past two weeks. Doubt and suspicion darted around my mind.

"So, Rachel," Lucas began, sitting on the oversized ottoman in the middle of us. "I was told by your godfather that you might be in need of my assistance."

"Yes," I answered, nodding nervously. "He told me you worked for the CIA."

"I do." His voice was solemn. "I have been there for almost ten years."

"That's a long time," Viktor said. I turned to him to see the same stern face he had when he first sat down. He was distrusting of him. Lucas seemed to take notice, and his eyes squinted from being scrutinized by Viktor.

"It is," he responded calmly. "The past year, though, has felt longer than the first nine combined."

"Was that because of Veronica? Or because you couldn't handle the guilt of knowing you were helping destroy this country?" Viktor jeered. I turned to him with my mouth agape. How brash he was being. Lucas snorted and nodded his head slowly with pressed lips.

"A little bit of both, actually," he admitted. "I am ashamed that I sat on the sidelines while all of this went on, but you wouldn't understand how trapped we were. If we defected, we would be dead men—"

"Better to die with some integrity," Viktor interjected, "instead of just letting them use innocent civilians as pawns."

I saw pain in Lucas's eyes. Viktor was testing his will, and it was visibly hurting him.

"That is *exactly* why I contacted Ian," he said. His tone rose in frustration. "I served three tours in Iraq and Afghanistan, all for what? To watch the people that sent me there attempt to dissolve our freedom?"

"That was a pointless war built on *lies*," Viktor sneered.

"Viktor," Grey scolded. "Stop this."

Lucas's face contorted. He was becoming angry.

"That's not the point!" he yelled, and then tried to suppress his voice. "I didn't create the lies, did I? I thought I was doing something good. I thought I was protecting our freedom from terrorists, and then after some time in the CIA I realized it was all for profit. You don't have a clue what I have been through. I have watched my brothers die beside me in battle, and many of my friends and I suffer from PTSD. Do you know what it's like not to be able to take pictures with your family? I can't handle seeing a camera flash anymore."

Viktor's face softened from hearing his statement.

"The point is, I took an oath to protect the constitution of the United States from *all* enemies, foreign *and* domestic. The terrorists are a stone's throw away from us. Do you know how *badly* I wanted to just kill her myself? Could you imagine sitting twenty feet away from her in a control room for three months straight?"

"No," Viktor said. "I could never."

Lucas calmed down, and his heavy breathing subsided.

"If only you knew how much I am risking by having her in my house," he said to Viktor, nodding in my direction. "I am risking the safety of my wife and kids by agreeing to help you all, but I have to. I despise Veronica with every cell in my body."

"So do I," I spoke up.

"Me too," Viktor added.

Lucas nodded and looked around at all of us.

"I can tell you both do," he said, turning to look at me. "I was told by Ian that someone you were with had a massive piece to the puzzle, as he referred to it. Do you have it here with you?"

I glanced over at Viktor, and Viktor turned to Lucas.

"Yes, I do," he responded. He slid off his backpack and unzipped the laptop slit. He pulled it out and turned it on. A moment later, he put the flash drive in a USB port. I saw the images open. He stood up and handed Lucas the laptop.

"Hit the right arrow key to go through them all," he instructed.

I watched Lucas's eyes flicker as he clicked through the images of the shipping containers, and with each passing second his face scrunched up more.

"The timestamp…" Lucas muttered. "It says January 2nd, 2015…are these…shipping containers?"

"Yes," Viktor answered.

"Where did you get access to these?"

Viktor didn't answer, but Lucas continued clicking through the photos. Suddenly, he glanced up at Viktor with wide eyes and looked him up and down.

"There's no way. There's no way you are who I think you are."

"I am who you think I am," Viktor said with a smile tugging at his lips.

"Viktor Ivankov?"

His voice sounded so dazed. Viktor nodded in response.

"I can't believe this," he muttered. "You, the most elusive person in the country, are sitting right here across from me in my own house."

"Believe it," Viktor said. Lucas handed him back the laptop.

"How did you meet Rachel?"

"We kidnapped her and Owen," Natasha answered flatly.

I began to laugh, as did everyone else.

"Natasha and I saw them in traffic and followed them to the hotel they were staying at. We watched Grey and Briana leave, and we decided to be patient to see if Rachel and Owen would come out of their hotel room. Luckily for us, they walked around the corner to a hot dog stand. We snatched them at the back entrance of the hotel."

"Thanks for letting me finish my hot dog, by the way," I teased him sarcastically.

"Sorry you didn't devour it like Owen did."

Owen…hearing his name made me want to burst into tears. Speaking of the night before his death brought back so many memories. It was too fresh in my mind, and it was so difficult to accept the truth—that he wasn't coming back.

"Oh. I'm sorry, Rachel."

I turned to Viktor, wiping my eyes as they started glistening.

"It's fine. I—I'm fine," I stammered.

What a flat out lie. I wasn't fine. I wasn't anything close to being fine. Every passing moment I felt like I was falling apart, but externally, I was trying to hold the pieces together.

"We didn't even know you had these files…" Lucas mumbled.

Viktor's eyebrows quirked. "I find that kind of hard to believe. Veronica wouldn't have wanted to catch me so badly if she didn't know I had proof."

"You would be surprised at how much we *don't* know," he countered. "We are their worker bees. We do as we are told and collect the Intel. There are things that we aren't told, believe it or not. I was just beginning to piece together Veronica's involvement when the bombs went off at the debate. After that, it all became clear to me. Veronica wasn't the only one behind this. She was given temporary control over the entire CIA by the Commander in Chief himself. Obama is in on this plan, too."

Oh, how his words made the world seem so bleak. How could we possibly stop their army with an article? I didn't know for certain, but my dad instilled in me how invaluable the truth was, and I would also keep my promise to Owen—write the story.

"That doesn't surprise me," Natasha huffed.

"I walked into work every day feeling like I was drowning," he said. "I left feeling the exact same way. My hands were tied behind my back. I couldn't tell my wife, nor my children. I couldn't tell anyone. The day Owen was arrested in Miami, I stood up to her in front of the control room. I can still hear the clacking of her heels as she walked over to me and then whispered threats into my ear. She threatened my family."

"She killed the only family I had left," I spoke up. The words felt like glass as they left my mouth. It was excruciating to say it out loud.

"I know," Lucas replied with a somber expression. "I'm assuming that's half the reason you are here."

I nodded. "The other half is Owen."

His green eyes locked with my own, and in that moment, I felt the same sensation as when I talked to him on the phone earlier today. He *understood.* The volatile mix of pain and hatred, he felt it too. I took a deep breath to steady the surge of emotions coursing through me.

"Lucas," I began slowly. "The most important question I have for you is, how can you get us close enough to Veronica Hall to take her out?"

"Well, that is a very good question. When you and Owen were still on the run, her schedule was regimented. Now, from what a few of my coworkers are saying, she is just popping in here and there. That could be a problem for us.

"Why?" Grey asked. Lucas shot a confused glance back at him.

"Because, that means we would have to follow her outside of the CIA and risk being spotted. Wherever we end up deciding to do this, most likely we will need an ID to get in. My CIA clearance can get me in just about anywhere, but the problem is everything is palm or iris scanner nowadays."

We stayed quiet. No one responded. He glanced around at all of us as if we were crazy.

"What?"

"Do you think that makes it difficult or something?" Viktor questioned.

"Uh, yeah!" he exclaimed. "One wrong move in a system as sensitive as that and you could get yourself screwed. How you could possibly fool an iris scanner is beyond me."

"There are ways," Natasha said with a cocky smirk.

His forehead was still scrunched up in disbelief.

"Do you guys *really* think you are capable of pulling this off?"

"Of course," Viktor answered. "I am the muscle. I'm not afraid to do what I have to do."

I decided to chime in. "You are looking at the best of the best, Lucas. We have two hackers." I nodded in the direction of Natasha and Grey. "Briana makes fake IDs and documents that can fool even the keenest eye. That is how we have gotten this far unscathed."

Lucas's eyes met my own, and there was a seriousness about his demeanor.

"And what about you?"

My jaw clenched as he asked the question, and the answer came to me instantly.

"I'm the one that's going to pull the trigger."

"Truth is treason in an empire of lies."

— George Orwell

428 Valley Dr. – Allentown, PA
10:37 10-28-2016

Today was a teacher workday. That meant a three-day weekend for me. Halloween was Monday, too. I would get to hang out with my friends. All of us agreed it wasn't cool anymore to dress up, but we still wanted the candy. We were going to skateboard from house to house. We didn't need costumes. We would just be skaters.

I opened up a new tab on the internet and typed in YouTube. My history auto-filled it, and it went to my channel. I checked it all the time now. I finally had over two thousand subscribers. I could get ad shares from YouTube, where they paid me monthly. I liked the idea of not even being fourteen yet and having more money than my friends. Thank God for the video.

The day I filmed Owen on CNN, I uploaded it onto YouTube. It had been a week and it already had over fifty million views, and it kept going higher every day. I was blown away by all of this. I had no idea it would become so popular. All the kids at school had seen it, and they knew it was me. I felt like a celebrity.

My Dad told me he didn't think it was a good idea to put it on the internet, but my mom disagreed. She mentioned something about the greater good, and that not putting it out there for everyone to see would be a waste of our first amendment. I was just glad Mom stood up for me. Random people kept trolling in the comments saying that the video was fake. Then there were others who warned to share the video as quickly as possible because the government would take it down. I had watched it so many times in the past week I thought I finally understood why they were warning me to begin with.

If Owen really *was* innocent, even if he was dead now, they wouldn't want people finding out. Whoever Veronica was, I was sure she wouldn't want to be all over the internet. Every time I heard Owen say what he said about the Confinement in the video, the fear it gave me was unimaginable. He said they never meant to let us out to begin with. I didn't want to go *back*. Those three months gave me nightmares as it is.

For now, everything would be all right. I was going to forget about what Owen said in the video for the first time since it happened. I deserved to enjoy my time off and not worry.

I could smell the chicken tenders cooking downstairs. My mom was making me lunch. My friend Colby was coming over at twelve when he got out of his orthodontist appointment. Maybe he would bring over his new videogame too. That way we could go skateboarding while it was still warm outside and play the videogame in my room after. I scrolled through some more of the comments while I waited for my food to be ready. I kept seeing the word *conspiracy* written in every other comment.

I opened another tab and Googled **Owen Marina Conspiracy**. It pulled up millions of results in a fraction of a second. I began clicking on different articles and reading.

They all said the same thing. That not only was Owen innocent—he was *framed.*

My stomach flopped from the stuff I saw. Why would our government do such a thing? Why would they want to keep us in the Camps? Who knows? I sure didn't.

I heard the sound of doors closing outside. I stood up and walked over to the blinds and peered through. There were two men in black suits wearing matching sunglasses. I could see nothing but the reflection of the house off of their dark lenses. I wondered if they had the wrong address. Their black GMC Yukon was parked in my driveway. My heart began to race. I ran outside my room and leaned over the railing that looked out on the foyer.

"Mom!" I yelled. No one responded. I heard the sound of the vacuum downstairs. She couldn't hear me.

"*Mom!*" I put more energy into it, and the vacuum cut off.

"What, honey?"

"Someone's here!"

Whoever they were, I didn't have a good feeling about why they were coming to visit.

4118 Ridgeview Rd. – McLean, VA
23:58 10-28-2016

Lucas appeared as he made it down the last few steps of the staircase. He rounded the corner with two pizza boxes in hand. When he got closer, I saw how much more pronounced the bags under his eyes were. Maybe what he said last night was true, that every time he went to work he felt like he was drowning.

His wife had brought us down some plates of leftovers around six, but she didn't say much. She seemed uncomfortable around us. I had been anxiously waiting all day for Lucas's return. I just hoped he had some information regarding Veronica, because every day that passed, was another day closer to the election.

As difficult as it was for me to handle, I watched the news today. That was when I discovered that Owen had been right. The stunt that cost him his life actually worked. According to what I saw today, the morning Owen barged into the newscast, the Convergence Party polls were twenty-nine percent. Republicans were twenty-one percent while democrats claimed fifty. One week later, the Convergence Party had forty-one percent, equal to the democrats, and the republicans dropped three points.

If only he were here to see it.

Perhaps, after *my* little stunt, we would be able to give the Convergence Party the push it needed to defeat the democrats in the election. I prayed so, because after everything I have learned I knew the outcome would be deadly if we didn't.

"I got one cheese and one pepperoni," Lucas announced. No one got any right away, but Natasha glanced around at all of us before she stood up and grabbed a slice.

"I can never turn down pizza," she shrugged.

I wasn't hungry. I probably wouldn't be until Lucas told us how his day at work was. We were all restless—at least I was. We were cooped up in here all day watching TV and Netflix. Viktor and Grey played his PlayStation 4.

"So," I began. "How was work?"

A small smirk began to tug at his lips before he spoke. That alone was enough to ease the anxious pit in my gut.

"It went better than I expected."

"That's great," I gasped. "What went on?"

"I went in and began work like usual. I haven't been there in a week, so I had to be brought up to speed by my colleagues. Interestingly enough, although they still have you on the wanted list, Rachel, you aren't their primary concern anymore—Viktor is."

"I should be," he laughed. "What changed?"

"Veronica is pretty certain the quote on the billboard in Atlanta was your doing, and she wants you gone. I could tell just by her disposition that she was worried that you are still out there."

"Good. I want her to be worried. Serves her right after what she did to me."

"Indeed," Lucas said. "So, after working around Veronica for so long, I already know her routine. She takes her lunch break half an hour earlier than we do. I walked past the hallway where her office is, and she left her door cracked. I went to her desktop and bugged her computer."

"Nice," Grey added.

"It gets better," he continued. "Veronica typically only works for eight hours. I work for twelve. So, whenever she left, I snuck back into her office and retrieved the information I needed. I found something golden."

"Which was?" Natasha asked, nervously twirling the black strands of hair that fell from her bun.

"An email from the Chairman of the Republican Party, Marc Fleming, reminding her of the meeting Monday morning at ten on the second floor boardroom of the EPA headquarters. It is to debrief on everything that has happened up to this point, and then a brief on what the plan of action will be after the election is won."

"That's great!" Viktor exclaimed. "Now we know where she is going to be."

Lucas's smile began to fade, and he glanced around at all of us.

"There is one downside, though…"

"What?" I asked.

"My CIA ID can get me into the EPA, no problem, except it will cause attention to whoever is using it. If Veronica is in the building, I am sure security will be tight. What we really need is an EPA ID. It would allow us to slide by unnoticed."

"How do we get one?" Natasha asked.

"Well, that's the problem. I just hope the person I have in mind is willing to help. She was actually the person who gave me the information to fax Ian in the first place. It took a little coaxing, but it didn't take long to get the truth out of her. Veronica had threatened her since Black Monday if she were to tell anyone. She was sworn to secrecy. Veronica gave her sole access to the room where the actual files from the Black Monday cleanup were kept. Her office is *also* on the second floor, the same floor the meeting is being held."

"Who is this woman?" Grey asked.

"Her name is Megan Walling—"

Grey began to cough as if he was choking, and Lucas stared at him perplexed before continuing.

"When she finally told the truth, she broke down in tears. She told me she felt guilty about what they were doing to Owen, framing him for a crime he didn't commit. She said he was her ex, ironically enough."

My forehead scrunched up and my eyebrows quirked. His *ex?*

"Wait, are you serious?"

"I am," Lucas replied. "At least, that is what she told me. She said they were in love."

Grey finally composed himself enough to speak.

"He's serious. I met her when they were still in college together."

Jealousy seethed through my veins. The only thing I recalled him telling me about his ex was the day I met him, when we were driving to Briana's, before we totaled my car. He said he only had one girlfriend since he was twenty-one. He never told me how long, or that he was in love. I wondered what she looked like. Was she prettier than me?

My thoughts spiraled on.

"It's perfect," Briana spoke up, and we all turned to her. "You have to get her in on this, Lucas. I can take her ID and put Rachel's picture on it. That would get her past reception initially, right?"

"Presumably," he said.

"Then, if Megan is working the day of the meeting, she can use her own iris, or her own palm to get Rachel into wherever she needs."

Lucas nodded, and a smile began to emerge.

"You are exactly right," he said.

I pondered Briana's suggestion. I knew Owen loved me, as I did him, but the thought that at one point he *loved* Megan made me cringe. Why would I want to even be in the same room with her? *Stop*—I told myself. We needed her help to take down Veronica.

"Natasha and I can hack into the EPA's system," Grey blurted, looking around at all of us. "Just so we can keep an eye on everything."

Natasha smiled in reaction to his statement.

"That sounds like a good idea," she agreed.

"Do you know what would make the payback even sweeter?" Viktor asked Lucas.

"What?"

"If we sent all of my files to Ian from one of the fax machines at the EPA."

"That will be a blow to their gut," Natasha chuckled. "Sending the truth from the same agency that helped cover it up."

"Exactly," he said, smiling. "After everything they have put me through, I would love more than anything to be the one that pulls the trigger…but I think we all know Rachel deserves to do the honors."

I pursed my lips and gave them a nod. No words were needed.

"All right then," Lucas said. "Let's get to work. First, I have to contact Megan."

Mai Thai – Washington, D.C.
18:14 10-29-2016

I shoved my hands deeper in my jacket pockets. The wind was blowing against me. It wasn't even winter yet, and I was already ready for summer. After nearly a decade of living here, the mid-Atlantic winters had worn out their welcome. Everything felt dead. I walked between the tables outside of the restaurant that were normally filled with people in the summer, but now were vacant. I could already see the red glow from the lights inside.

This was one of Megan's favorite restaurants, apparently. It happened to be one of mine too. I opened the door, and the warmth enveloped me. There were abstract shapes of red, orange, and white placed along the walls. The whole vibe was contemporary. I was bombarded with the intoxicating smells of ginger, curry, and the brininess of soy sauce. A mix of cooked meats wafted through the air along with it. My stomach trembled at the thought, and as I rounded the hostess stand, my stomach trembled at *another* thought. Would Megan help us?

She sat in a booth by herself, nervously playing with her fingers. Her platinum-blonde hair was perfectly straightened, and it rested at her chest level. She spotted me, and I didn't know what to make of her expression. It was a mix between she had expected me, or that she was going to throw up. She nervously glanced around at all the tables around us. I sat down.

"Megan," I said, giving her a nod.

"Lucas," she replied with the same gesture.

"How have you been?" I asked. I wanted to start off casual and let her settle into the conversation. She pursed her lips and revealed a sardonic expression.

"As good as you can be knowing that you handed over the most confidential files of the twenty-first century to a CIA agent, and that at any moment you-know-who might come after me and my family."

My gut twisted from her words. *Veronica.*

"That's actually what I wanted to talk to you about."

She raised an eyebrow in curiosity and pulled her interlaced fingers closer to her side of the table.

"Before you go any further," she began, "do you mind footing the bill?"

I cocked my head in surprise.

"Well, I guess so now that you asked. Why do you seem so blasé about asking someone you've only met twice to pay the bill?"

A satisfied smirk slid across her face.

"I have a feeling that you will owe me, because you are going to ask me to help you with something. Even though I don't yet know what that is, I feel a tasty meal should suffice as payment.

"Deal."

Suddenly our waitress popped out of nowhere.

"Hi! My name is Kim, and I'll be serving you tonight," she chirped. Her oriental eyes were almost slits, and her teeth were impossibly straight. "Can I get you guys something to drink?"

"I'll have a shot of the house vodka and some sparkling water, please."

"Of course, and for you, sir?"

"I'll take a diet Coke."

The waitress smiled.

"All right, I'll bring that right out t—"

"I'm actually ready to order," Megan cut her off.

"Oh, okay!" the peppy waitress said awkwardly. "What would you like?"

"I'll have the sushi sampler. Make them all vegetable, California, and spicy tuna rolls. Ooh, actually, switch out the vegetable roll for a

Philadelphia roll. I'd also like the pad Thai chicken curry plate, extra spicy, please."

"Good choice," she said, smiling. "Are you ready to order, sir?"

I was still staring at Megan wide-eyed. Had she not eaten all day?

"I will have the same entrée she had, without the extra heat."

"Okay, sounds good! I will be back with your drinks and your sushi."

She darted off and I stared back at Megan.

"What?" she snapped. "I had a rough week."

"I can tell," I teased.

"You look like you need a shot," she cocked her head in my direction.

"I'll probably need one after I tell you why I am here."

"Aha," she chuckled. "After hearing you say that, maybe I need two more."

I rolled my eyes. The waitress reappeared.

"Here is your shot and sparkling water," she said as she set them down. "And your diet Coke, sir. Your food will be out in just a little while, is there anything else I can get you while you wait?"

Megan shook her head no before I had the chance to answer. She walked off.

"So," I began. She held her index finger up.

"Wait."

She turned the shot glass filled to the brim with vodka skyward, and her face puckered up after she downed it. "Ahh," she breathed out. I could smell the liquor from across the table. She took a sip of her sparkling water and set it back down.

"Okay, now tell me what you need my help with."

"By the way. I was going to ask you, how did you know I needed something?"

She tossed her hair over her shoulder.

"Because that's the same thing you did when you came to me the first time."

I snorted. "Well played."

She took a deep breath in and out. There was something about her that seemed tense. Our waitress walked past our table.

"Excuse me," Megan put out her hand to signal her. The waitress stopped. "Yes?"

"Can I have two more shots of vodka?"

My brow furrowed from her request. We were here to talk about something important, not to get drunk on my tab.

"Yes, I'm going to grab this table's order and I'll get that right to you."

Megan turned back to me with a vacant face. *Something* was up, but I couldn't put my finger on it. She was beyond stressed the day at her office when she had her breakdown, but before she opened up to me, she hid it quite well. Now, it was almost like whatever was going on inside of her was breaking through the surface. There were faint bags under her eyes concealed with makeup. I decided to wait and feel her out. I wouldn't throw the news on her this second.

"How was work today?" I asked.

She slanted her head and glared at me dumbfounded.

"God awful," she said. "How about yours?"

"The same. Just a little better now that Veronica isn't around as much."

"Lucky for you, because now she's back at mine more," she griped. "I'd rather gouge my eyes out than have to see her one more day."

"I know the feeling," I consoled. "When do you work next?"

She squinted quizzically.

"Why?"

"Because it has to do with what I came here for."

Her eyes darted over my face cautiously.

"Monday," she said.

Monday—the day of Veronica's meeting.

I caught myself beginning to smile.

"Here they are!" the chipper waitress announced in a singsong voice as she set down Megan's two shots. "Your food will be right out!" The moment she stepped away Megan downed the shot. She shivered after the first, and then immediately did the second. This time, she didn't chase it with anything. She just slid the shot glasses to the edge of the table and looked up to meet my eyes. Her eyes glazed over as the buzz from the alcohol began to kick in. Her face was blank, almost stoic. In her blue eyes, I saw so much pain it almost made me turn the other way.

"Megan, is everything all right?"

"Do I *look* all right to you?" she countered flatly.

"No," I said. "Not at all."

Her lower lip quivered, and I noticed her chest kept heaving up and down.

"Well, I'm not. Like I said, I had a really rough week. I've been a wreck since Owen died."

She pressed her lips together and covered her mouth with a closed fist, turning to face the window. Her forehead was scrunched together from trying to hold back the tears. If this was how Megan felt, I could have only imagined what Rachel was like that day.

"I—I'm sorry," she hiccupped and took a sip of her water.

"You're fine."

I saw tears escape the corners of her eyes.

"I just feel so guilty!" she choked, suppressing her voice. I glanced around to see if anyone noticed her worsening condition. We were in the clear. "I mean, do you blame me for thinking that? Maybe if I would have told someone sooner he would still be alive," she groaned. "I listened to *her* so I could stay safe, so nothing would happen to me. Owen wound up dead."

She choked back another cry and wiped her face off with the napkin. I prayed our waitress didn't bring out the food during this. It wouldn't look good if the pushy customer she served three shots to was already bawling.

"It should have been me," she said firmly. "It should have been *my* life, not his."

I shook my head and tried to console her.

"No, Megan. It is bad enough he is gone. It didn't need to be you. Don't blame yourself. A life is a life. Be thankful that you *are* still here."

"Why?!" she raised her voice ever so slightly and scowled at me. "Why would I want to be here? This country is fucked. I'm better off dead…and that's the thing, that's what you don't understand. I spent *five years* with Owen. I know him like the back of my hand, and you know what? *He* was the better person. He still had more to do in this world, Lucas. I was just a paper pusher at the EPA and he left it all behind to do something no one had done before, and he did it. I would have rather it been my life than his. My life *never* mattered. Now, I am left all alone and have nothing to do but wonder what I could have done differently…"

Her pain was so real that it was making my heart race. I could feel it across the table.

"Megan," I said softly. I waited for her to compose herself.

"What?" she mumbled with her head tilted away from me, wiping her eyes again.

"There is still something you can do."

She sniffled and then looked me straight in the eyes.

"Is that why you wanted to meet here? To instill me with some false hope?"

I shook my head side to side slowly.

"No, I came here to tell you a way that you can make your life *matter.*"

She squinted, studying my expression—trying to pick it apart.

"What do you mean by that?" she asked.

I motioned her to lean in with my fingers, and I was about to open my mouth when our waitress reappeared at our side. "All right, here's your food!"

"Thank you so much," I said. She disappeared a moment later. We each took a few bites of our food before I motioned to her again to lean in towards me.

"If you want your life to matter, if you want to contribute to a cause bigger than yourself, then please, hear me out."

She nodded.

"You are going to help us take down Veronica Hall."

She dropped her fork and it clung against the plate. Her eyes grew wide. Her expression frightened me because she looked so shocked. For a moment, I thought she was appalled by the idea…but suddenly, the surprised look began to fade away, and it was replaced with malice.

She nodded her head in agreement so slowly, I almost thought she was in a trance.

"Thank God," I gasped. "Because without you, we wouldn't have the capability of doing it. We have assembled a team. They are the same people that helped Owen, actually. For now, I will need to borrow your EPA ID. Come to my house late tomorrow night, I will give the ID back to you, and we will go over the details of the plan. We have one chance and one chance only to do this properly. The election is a week and two days away. Our time is running out."

Megan's eyes were still glazed from the buzz, but her face was frozen in a maniacal smile. The resentment she felt towards Veronica was all too similar to my own.

"Megan," I said, trying to jar her from her daze. "Are you sure you're okay with this?"

She finally snapped out of it and shook her head, gazing into my eyes with complete clarity of mind.

"I have never been surer of something in my entire fucking life."

"The tree of liberty must be refreshed from time to time with the blood of patriots and tyrants."

— Thomas Jefferson

4118 Ridgeview Rd. – McLean, VA
09:11 10-31-2016

I was a dead woman walking. There was no guarantee that tomorrow would ever come. All that mattered was this moment, and the events that would take place today. If I lost my life in the process, so be it. When I went to bed last night, I talked to my mother and Owen before I fell asleep. I asked them to watch over me. At this point, I was more concerned about what the outcome would be for this country if I were to fail.

No—I would *not* fail. That was not an option.

Last night Megan came over. I was in the shower for the first half of her visit, and when I walked out and saw her, I knew it was *her*. I was surprised. She looked like the exact opposite of me. Blonde hair, cream-colored skin, and blue eyes. I wondered how much time she spent dating Owen, but I kept my urge to ask her suppressed. We didn't talk much. We barely even greeted each other. I sat back and listened, because my role in the plan was the easiest—to pull the trigger. Lucas warned me what would happen after. The cops would swarm the EPA building twice as fast as they did with Owen in Atlanta. He said I might be shot at, but I made it very clear to him that I was not worried. Death was an escape from all of this. I did not fear it any longer. He instructed me exactly what to do when the time came.

Briana had been working longer than any of us. She spent all day in the basement workroom with Megan's ID, trying to make a duplicate with my picture on it. Her dark roots were getting longer, making the golden blonde in her locks disappear more by the day. Natasha and Grey worked well into the night. Lucas had to run to the department store to get her some business clothes and a flash drive. It was all a part of the plan. After seeing Grey do it twice, listening to them plan it out in front of me was nothing short of amazing. It was intriguing to hear what went on inside the mind of a hacker. They both were brilliant, and what I came to realize was that two-thirds of what they did was making their target trust them enough to let them in. All they needed to do was throw around some technical jargon and make a good impression. Once the people on the inside made the mistake of letting them in, the ball was in their court.

The only thing we didn't know was what time the meeting ended and how many people were going to be in that boardroom. We knew for certain Veronica and Marc Fleming would be there, and in all honesty, I didn't care about any of the others. Lucas and Megan both knew she was behind this, so in my mind that was the only justification I needed.

I was going to kill someone today.

We had all showered one by one early in the morning. Lucas's wife made us breakfast and brought it downstairs before she took the kids to school. From what Lucas said, she knew what was going on, but for the kids' sakes she didn't want them knowing we were here.

Briana had just gotten out of the shower, and she was getting dressed in one of the nearby bedrooms. I stood in front of the mirror, curling my hair. The steam was slowly receding from the top of the glass, and I could finally see my reflection. Looking at myself, I felt like a whole other person. Rachel Flores was dead, and this was what remained. I tried my best to embrace it, so I wouldn't focus on what had happened to the old me. I wore light makeup and some red lipstick. I felt like I spy, and I looked like one too. Lucas wanted to make sure that Natasha and me didn't blend together. She was wearing business clothes. I wore black dress pants and a white blouse. I had on a black pea coat that went down to about my knees. I was going to wear all black, but Lucas advised against it. It would only draw more attention to myself. He said that all black would make me look more suspicious, and he was right. Strapped to the outside of my right leg was a holster, where Lucas's gun was. Yesterday, when the sun set, he brought me to a vacant field. We walked near the edge of the woods, and he put up a target. I practiced point blank and went through many clips until I was confident. I knew when the time came I wouldn't miss. Not after all she had put me and my loved ones through. Viktor had our files, and he would fax them to Ian right as I made my entrance. He wore a normal button up with khaki slacks. Lucas, Grey, and Briana would remain in the car. Briana and Lucas had done their parts, and Grey would work remotely while Natasha did what she needed to do on the inside. Lucas *borrowed* some goodies from his work. We all were going to wear earpieces that were too small to be visible, and they had a range of a mile. We would be able to hear each other, which was crucial in a plan as elaborate as this.

The time was ticking. Forty minutes until the meeting began.

I set the curling iron down and stared at my reflection again. I felt numb—empty. Perhaps, what would take place today would reset me. I hoped so. I could barely get out of bed each morning like this. I had no drive. The only thing that motivated me now was the notion I could save Owen's party for him. So that all of his work wouldn't be wasted.

"Knock knock," Grey said, rapping twice on the door as he slipped in the opening.

"Hi, Grey," I tried to muster the strength to smile.

"Happy Halloween!"

"I forgot that was today," I admitted.

I saw him look my reflection up and down.

"What?" I chuckled.

"Your costume…and you, look marvelous."

A smile tugged at my lips.

"Thanks, Grey."

"Did I forget to mention deadly?" He winked.

"That's more like it," I teased.

"So…" He began hesitantly. "Are you ready for this?"

"As ready as I'll ever be."

He snorted and nodded his head.

"You know, he would have never let you do this. He wouldn't have ever gone along with this idea because he wanted you safe."

Our eyes locked in the reflection of the mirror. Grey pressed his lips together.

"I just wanted to make sure I told you before we go, how much he loved you."

Hearing those words come from Grey's mouth caused tears to pool in the corners of my eyes. "I've known him since I was six, Rachel, and I had never heard him talk about another girl the way he did you. He loved every moment he spent with you, and he told me all of this the night in the penthouse, out on the terrace…"

My mind flashed back, and I could see him again. He was leaning in across from Grey, talking animatedly with his hands. I wondered what they were talking about, and now I knew.

"Just remember, Rachel, no matter what happens, I will take care of my end of things. Briana and your cousins will get their portion of the money. I will do what is right. It's what he would have wanted."

I threw myself into Grey's arms and hugged him in a firm embrace. Tears rolled down my cheek and disappeared into his shirt. The warmth coming from his body was soothing. It reminded me of Owen. I was holding onto a piece of Owen—Grey—his childhood friend.

"Thank you, Grey, for everything. Thank you…"

EPA HQ – Washington, D.C.
10:10 10-31-2016

Natasha and I walked side by side towards the main entrance of the EPA. I tried to breathe in an attempt to steady my racing heart, but it was pointless. I had to embrace the adrenaline. The metal of the gun was now warm against my leg. With every step, it reminded me of its presence. Natasha cleaned up well. Her hair was straightened, and I was surprised at how much longer it was when it wasn't up in the chaotic bun. We both wore business heels, but nothing too flashy. I was glad that we wouldn't be together because we looked like twin assassins or something. Our jet-black hair was identical.

It felt so odd to be here in Washington. I looked around at the massive sandstone and marble-clad buildings and realized this was where it all began. Owen lived here for almost a decade, and now I was back in his turf to finish what he started.

We were maybe one-hundred feet from the entrance. I used my finger just to double check my earpiece hadn't fallen out. It was so tiny I didn't even know it was there. Natasha looked at me midstride.

"You ready?"

"Yes," I breathed the words.

"We are in position in the parking lot," Grey's voice said in my ear. "Rachel, do you have your ID?"

"Yes," I replied softly. I didn't want anyone to hear me talking to myself.

"Megan," Lucas began, "how is everything up there?"

"All is well. Still in meeting."

"Remember, only respond if you think you are being spoken to. We don't want to jumble ourselves up in a situation like this."

None of us answered Lucas's reminder. We knew what to do.

We neared the revolving door, and I split off to the right.

"Good luck," I whispered to her. She winked back at me, smiling. After hearing her and Grey plan this out together, I could tell she lived for moments like these. I walked over to a bench nearby and sat down. Now I had to wait, but more importantly, I had to listen.

The feed went silent for fifteen seconds.

"Good morning," I heard a male voice say.

"Good morning," Natasha replied. Her voice was louder than the man's in my ear, and I had never heard her speak in this tone. She almost sounded delicate.

"Empty all of your belongings into this bucket and step through the metal detector, please."

I heard nothing. No beep, just silence.

"Have a good day, officer," she said.

Good to know. It was one officer—not two.

In the background, I heard the faint clacks of her heels against the floor.

"Good morning, how may I help you?" a female asked.

"Good morning to you, too," she said politely. "I actually have an interview with Ms. Walling. She told me it was on the second floor, correct?"

There was a pause. It made my gut wrench.

"Oh, okay. My apologies, I was just a little taken aback. They haven't hired in the archives in over a year."

"Guess it's my lucky day, huh?" Natasha chirped. I smiled in reaction. She didn't miss a beat.

The receptionist laughed. "Why yes, I guess so. Let me call her line to tell her you're here. What is your name?"

"Natasha Ericsson."

"Thank you, Ms. Ericsson. Just give me one moment."

"Great, thank you so much."

"That's my girl," Viktor cheered in my ear. "Using her real name like a badass."

I restrained the urge to chuckle. Another pause.

"Hi, Megan, there is a Ms. Ericsson here to see you for an interview. Shall I send her up?"

Silence.

"I'll send her right up," the receptionist said.

"Thank you *so* much," Natasha said, and I began to hear her heels again. "Oh! I almost forgot, I need a *huge* favor if you don't mind."

"Here we go," Grey said. "It's show time."

"Pardon me?" the receptionist sounded caught off guard.

"I'm so sorry, I don't want to be a bother to you, but I wanted to see if I could print off my letters of recommendation anywhere in here?"

"Uh, not really," she answered. "There's a FedEx Kinkos down the street. That might be your best bet."

I smiled because I knew what was to come.

"Ah, I'll even pay you for the paper," Natasha pleaded. "I've just worked really, really hard to land this interview and my printer broke at home. I don't want to waste four years of school on one little mistake."

"Well…I mean."

"All I have is this flash drive, and the two letters of recommendation are the only things on there. You have a printer here. You would be the *biggest* lifesaver if you could. Literally, all you have to do is just stick this in your tower and print it. It'll only take twenty seconds."

"I was your age once," the receptionist cackled. "Sure, just hand me the drive and I'll print it for you."

"Ah! Thank you so much. What's your name?"

"Evelyn."

"Evelyn, you are a miracle worker! Whose boss do I have to sweet talk to get you a raise?"

They both began laughing together.

"You're such a good liar," Viktor complimented.

"She didn't lie," Grey said. "It will only take twenty seconds."

A moment later I heard the printer spit something out.

"Here are your letters."

"Thank you again, wish me luck!"

"Ms. Ericsson!" the woman called out. "You forgot your flash drive."

"Oh my God, I almost forgot. Thank you again, Evelyn."

"Take care and good luck," the receptionist wished her well. The clacking of her heels began again, and I could hear Natasha's breathing. She was worked up. The footfalls stopped, and I heard the ding of the elevator.

"Grey, did it work?" she asked, breathing heavily.

EPA HQ – Washington, D.C.
10:19 10-31-2016

"I'm in," I answered.

"Thank God," she sighed in relief.

"Natasha," Lucas began, "Megan's office is the first one on the left. Go there. Rachel, you're on deck, followed by Viktor."

"Roger that," Rachel said.

I began navigating the system as fast as I possibly could. We only had one real shot at this, and it would be a shame if I let it slip out of our hands because the meeting released for lunch too soon, or something of that nature. Originally, we were going to just hack into the system from Megan's computer in her office. She informed us that the receptionists' computers had access to the security feed, but hers didn't. That was beneficial to us because the closer we could get to the area we needed to be in, the better. I needed to do two things, one of which I would do after Rachel was in the building. I didn't want to alarm anyone too soon because that could be disastrous. The second, and most difficult, was to disarm the metal detector. Either that or I could get it to glitch right as she walked through. She was trying to bring a weapon into a federal building, and it was up to me to make it happen.

This was much more difficult than what I did at the airport. Being in the mainframe was like being a kid on a playground with an unlimited amount of toys to choose from. Now, I was taking shots in the dark. I found an encrypted ping in the event log from just three minutes ago. Someone walked in on camera, and it sent another. It was the metal detector. The ping Natasha's walkthrough sent was quite different from the one I was looking at. I switched tabs to the cameras and saw that the person who had walked through had to do it again. He must have walked through with something metal on him.

Damn it. In reality, I couldn't do much with these pings. Sure, they were received by the event log, but the event log didn't ping anything back to the metal detector. It was entirely one way. I began scrolling far into the history of the event log.

"Grey, how's it looking?" Natasha asked.

"Could be better, but I'll find a way."

"You will," she encouraged.

Suddenly, I found something new. It wasn't a ping at all. It was just a system status, or a setting. It was a code. It pinged the code once late at night and then early in the morning when it was reset back to normal. Then, the frequent pings of people walking through restarted.

It must have been some form of sleep mode when the public was no longer allowed in the building. That made perfect sense. I had to use that coded system setting late at night and send it to the metal detector *now*, so Rachel could get through undetected.

"Give me five minutes, and I've got this," I announced.

No one said a word. I used a program on my computer to decrypt the code. I had to make sure that what was extracted was the raw command that would turn the detector to sleep mode. I began typing faster and faster. I wiped some sweat off my brow.

Almost there…

I knew it was going to work, and excitement began to bubble up within me. It was the closest I felt to normal since Owen died. I still couldn't believe he was gone. It made me want to cry just thinking about it. All the memories growing up in Midlothian together would be just that—memories. Wherever he was, I just hoped he knew how much I admired him. As corny as it sounded, he was my hero. My best friend did so much good in this country, and I still felt honored to this day to have assisted him in his escape from the feds.

I never fully grasped the possibility that he might wind up dead. Guilt soaked into my mind all day long. I felt so horrible for having been the one to suggest to him the idea of going to Atlanta. It was me who planted that seed in his mind, and I didn't know if I'd ever be able to forgive myself. The polls went up by twelve percent. The Convergence Party was now tied with the democrats, and I smiled at the thought. I knew Owen would be smiling, too. That was the only reason he went along with my plan—to revive his dying party—and it *worked.* Even if it was just a little bit, it worked.

Since he died, I wondered sometimes if he could hear my thoughts. Well, my brother, if you could hear this right now, just know I did everything you told me to do that night. *Everything.* No matter what happens, I would keep my promise I made to you that night on the terrace. Brothers kept the bonds they made—in life, and in death.

The command code was decrypted. I found the way to input settings on the metal detector, and I typed in the code I just found. The moment I entered it in, it pinged the identical encrypted code that the detector would ping when it was set in its sleep mode.

"Rachel," I said. "It's time to go."

EPA HQ – Washington, D.C.
10:27 10-31-2016

I stood up without hesitation.

"Are you sure it will work?"

"Positive," Grey's voice eased the knot in my gut.

I swallowed hard, and it felt like there was a rock in my throat. The air outside was cold, but my body felt like it was on fire. I walked towards the revolving door, as confidently and nonchalant as I possibly could. The beige-stone building towered over me, with its gigantic pillars running down the length of its crescent shape. I guess the government needed such a formidable-looking structure to hide its deepest darkest secrets.

That all ended today.

I arranged some curls in front of my face before I walked into the door. I didn't want to be recognized before I had the chance to do what I needed to do. I took a deep breath and stepped in the revolving door. Immediately, the autumn cold was replaced with the warmth of inside. The same officer who greeted Natasha was there to greet me. He stood up from his seat behind a chrome counter and outstretched the bin to me.

"Put your belongings in here, ma'am."

He sounded docile enough. *Breathe.* There was nothing to worry about. What belongings did I even have? I placed my pre-paid phone and my EPA ID inside. I had nothing else. How embarrassing and unusual for a female in 2016. I turned to face the metal detector, and I prayed inside that Grey was right. I held my breath and walked through.

Nothing. No beep.

"Yes!" Grey shouted in my earpiece.

Next step. I walked across the marble floors, with my heels clacking just as Natasha's had. I saw the receptionist who I presumed to be Evelyn, and I began to walk past her.

"Excuse me," she called out. "Do you have an appointment?"

I smiled. "No, I work here."

She gave me a confused look.

"ID please," she stuck out her hand behind the counter.

I handed it to her, and she examined it through reading glasses that sat on the edge of her nose. I grew nervous when she didn't hand it back. She stuck it under a machine. I watched as a purple light shined down on the ID, and she looked at it again.

"All right, here you go," she turned around and handed it to me. She shot me a weird glance.

"Thank you," I said, turning around to head towards the elevator. The clacking of my heels was so noticeable it irritated me. Just another thing to draw attention to myself. When I made it to the elevator, it felt like an eternity for it to open. Once I was inside, I hit the button for the second floor and let out a huge breath. I was exasperated. Now, I understood why Natasha was breathing so heavy when she reached it. My nerves were on edge the entire time.

"I made it," I gasped.

"Bravo, Rachel," Viktor complimented.

"Briana, your ID just saved my ass. She put it under UV light and it still worked."

"That's what I'm here for, *amiga*," she chuckled.

"Grey and Natasha, thank you so much for getting me in here."

"Don't thank me," Natasha said. "It was all Grey."

"She's too kind," he added humbly.

Ding.

The elevator opened. This floor was like I had just taken a time machine back to the nineties. The carpet was a faded coral, and the wallpaper was light yellow. I remembered Lucas's instructions.

First office on your left. There were a few women on the right in their cubicles, but they weren't paying any attention to me.

I gently pushed opened the first door on the left and saw Megan and Natasha sitting across from each other.

"Long time no see," Natasha said.

"Tell me about it."

Megan sat there with her perfectly straight, white-blonde hair and remained expressionless. I wondered if she was as nervous as I was. The almost hot metal against my outer thigh was a constant reminder of what I was about to do. I didn't say a word to her. Her lips were pressed together, and she stared back at me with blue eyes that were searching my own.

She nodded her head and stood up. Natasha revealed a soft smile.

"We'll see you on the other side," she said and gave me a nod. "I know how much Viktor wanted to do this himself one day, but it wouldn't be right if it was anyone other than you."

My breathing became more pronounced as the time slipped forward. It was hard to grasp that this was even reality…but undoubtedly, it was. The pain I had endured *was* real. Owen and my mother *were* gone, and I couldn't get them back. The aching feeling in my gut returned, and I harnessed it. I controlled it and didn't let it control me. I was finished being the victim. The people I loved were ripped out of my life, and there was only one thing left to do—to make them pay the debt for what they took. Blood for blood.

I placed my hand gently on Natasha's shoulder.

"Thank you," I said, gently. "I'll see you on the other side."

Megan stood beside me and waited until I said my goodbyes to open the door. I noticed her chest rising quicker than normal. She *was* nervous.

My heels were silenced by the carpet, and I was thankful. Veronica probably thought she had won, and that she had nothing to worry about. Unfortunately for her, I was just down the hall, and in a few moments she would be face to face with *me*—the woman she stole everything from.

"Viktor," Natasha's voice sounded in my earpiece. "It is time to come."

"I'm on it," he answered.

Megan turned a corner and I followed her around it. We began down an elongated hall that seemed to stretch out forever, and there was a single, opaque glass door at the end of it.

"Is that it?" I whispered.

"Yes."

My memories of Owen began to flood my mind. The day at the café when I had the courage to first approach him with my idea, the conversation we had in the pool in Miami, and the night on the beach. There were so many others darting around, all of which were precious to me.

My steps were measured, and as we neared the door my heart began to race. I knew if Owen and my mother were here, things would be different. I wouldn't crave the revenge so ravenously, and in all my conversations with him, there was one thing I remembered above all else. What I was about to do, this wasn't for *me*. This was for *everyone*. Every life that was lost in the Confinement, and all the families that were torn apart—this was for *them*. If we didn't stand up for our freedom, who would? That was what I had realized throughout this journey, from Owen and Viktor, was that this wasn't an isolated incident. This had been going on for decades, only reaching its pinnacle in the time after the Confinement. All the elites were in on this, and they couldn't care less. They had the power and influence to keep us subdued forever. *We* were the last hope for this great country, and I would be damned if I sat back and watched our citizens get piled into Camps by the hundreds of thousands. *No*, that would never happen again. Not on my watch.

We were ten feet from the door, and I caught a whiff of Megan's perfume. Her long, blonde hair flowed side to side with her every step. She was well-built, and we had similar figures. I knew she was a big part of Owen's life, and on a personal basis, I was jealous. I wanted to say something snide. Last night, I finally had the courage to ask Grey how long she was with him. They were together for five years. I remembered on the drive to Orlando he had mentioned that he only had one girlfriend since he was twenty-one. They were together less than two years ago. It hurt to know they were an item for so long, but I also remembered Owen's words. He loved me. I felt the same way about him, and part of me wondered if I would ever feel the same way about another man again. I pulled it together as we reached the door, and I swallowed my pride. Megan had agreed to help us, and without her, I wouldn't have been standing in front of the boardroom door right now. I would still be lying in bed, wallowing in my grief. She loved Owen too, just like I did…and I knew that he was probably half, or all the reason she agreed to help us. I had to show some respect for that.

She stood in front of the palm and iris scanner and turned to face me.

"Thank you," I broke the silence.

She revealed a smile so gracious it made me feel bad that I wanted to be rude to her just a few moments ago.

"No, thank *you*," she corrected.

I nodded, and she held her hand six inches away from the scanner. She turned to me again.

"Are you ready?"

I wiped my sweaty palms on the sides of my pea coat and swallowed hard.

"Yes," I whispered, with my heart beating so fast it distorted my voice.

She scanned her hand and nothing happened. I saw an icon appear on the screen indicating for her to use the iris scanner. She began to lean forward, and I touched her forearm. She halted and turned to me with a quirked brow.

"You're lucky," the words slipped out just above a whisper.

"Why?" she asked.

"Because you got to spend more time with him than I did."

She didn't say a word, but I could see the sadness clearly in her eyes. She knew who I was talking about, and she knew it was the truth. I got that weight off my chest and managed not to say something vulgar. She slowly put her eye to the scanner, and I watched as the light zipped across her eye.

"Identity confirmed—Megan Jeanine Walling," the robotic female voice said.

I heard a lock click, and the door popped ajar. I glanced at Megan, and she nodded towards the room, telling me to *go*. She walked away and back down the hall.

My pulse was in my throat, and I could see the murky blobs behind the opaque glass crowded together. I took out the gun and made sure the safety was off. I held it with my left hand and used my right hand to pull open the door. I silently took a step in and was immersed in bright, white fluorescent light. This room was carpet too, and my heels were silent. The men on the long side of the rectangular table looked up at me with wide eyes. I had the gun outstretched with both hands clasped around it and a finger on the trigger.

I saw sandy-brown hair at the end of the table, facing me. Suddenly, she looked up.

Veronica Hall.

Her ice-blue eyes turned to slits as she saw me, and her nostrils flared.

"None of you move a fucking inch," I growled.

The men sat frozen, and I made sure to wave the gun around in everyone's direction just enough. Veronica was one of two females at the table. I counted eight people total. I had six rounds.

"Well, well, well," Veronica's sickeningly-smooth voice began, and she stood up. I straightened my arms as I neared the table. I was maybe ten feet from her.

"I recognize a pretty face when I see one," she chortled and stared at me vehemently. "Rachel Flores."

"I *said* sit down," I warned her. My upper lip curled in my utter disgust for her.

"You don't call the shots, sweetheart. I do."

She pressed her hands against the mahogany table and stood to her full height. She was a few inches taller than me in her heels, and my finger was so close to pulling down on the trigger.

"Why are you even here?" she mocked. "We won," she slit her eyes and stared at me as if I were a hard-to-kill pest. "There is nothing you can do to stop us."

"Rachel," I heard Viktor in my ear. "You're good to go. The fax is going through to Ian as we speak."

My breathing was shuddered, and a ruthless smile began to slide across my face.

"Would you bet your own life?" I snorted.

She huffed and slowly walked around the corner of the table. She crossed her arms, resting them against her blue business suit.

"Do you think I am *scared* of you?" she sneered, inching closer. "I bet my life that even if you pull that trigger, we will *still* win. It's too late—"

I pulled the trigger, and the sound was so loud I went deaf. Veronica clutched her chest with wide eyes, looking down at her wound and then back up at me.

"That was for killing Owen," I spat and waved my gun at the men who tried to stand up. I fired a shot in the ceiling above them, and crumbled drywall fell atop the table. I pointed the gun back at Veronica who began to sink down to her knees. Her thick, maroon-tinted blood dripped to the carpet. When I reached her, I pushed her back. She folded over against the floor and stared up at me with the most vileness I had ever seen in a human being. Even in her death she wouldn't let go of the notion that *they* couldn't be stopped. I held the gun a few inches above her head, and I thought about how painless it would be for her that way. No, she deserved worse than that. That was too easy. I knelt down above her as she clutched her chest. I tossed my hair over a shoulder and leaned in to where my mouth was a few inches away.

I saw someone in my peripheral move, and I jolted back up. The man was trying to come behind me. I shot him straight in his kneecap, and he collapsed. I stood up.

"Back up!" I screamed. "If you want to live, back up! Now!"

He crawled backward across the floor as he winced with the blood dripping across the carpet. The other men looked at me with their hands up as I pointed the gun at them. They remained seated. I leaned back down to Veronica. The color was fading from her face, and she had a glazed look over her eyes. I made sure I was close enough that only she would hear me.

"You lost your bet," I whispered.

"*Fuck…you…*" She snarled. Anger surged throughout my body, and I shook my head at her stubbornness. I jammed the gun against her gut and held it there.

"And *this* is for killing my mother," I said as I pulled the trigger. She gritted her teeth and gasped as it went through her, and I could feel the blood running past my knees. I knelt back down, and to my disbelief her mouth opened once more.

"You'll *never* win," she forced out. "Even with me gone."

I stared into her empty, ice-blue eyes as the life began to fade out of them, and leaned in one final time.

"Viktor Ivankov is across the hall, and he just faxed the New York Times all the documents you have kept hidden since Black Monday. Your *monstrous* lie unravels today. It's over."

Her eyes grew wide, and her mouth was agape. Veronica was seconds from death. I stood up and shot another bullet into the ceiling above the table. The men slid out their chairs to avoid debris.

The door swung open, and Viktor walked towards me with the most determination I had ever seen since meeting him. His chest heaved up and down. He glanced down at Veronica behind me and revealed a sinister grin. One that only bloodlust could produce.

"What are you doing?" I asked.

"Get out of here. I'll go out the back."

"Viktor, they might arrest—"

"Rachel. Let me have this moment. Move aside."

I pressed my lips together and nodded. He walked around me and I turned to see Veronica's skin was now a deathly shade of gray. She was still conscious, barely, but the pure, undiluted fear I saw in her eyes when she stared at Viktor caused a chill to race up my spine.

"Remember me?" he growled.

She gasped for air, choking on her own blood, and I turned away from them. My heels squished in the blood beside her body, and I walked out of the room. I began down the hall without a worry in the world. I felt *good* for the first time in a week. I didn't care what happened next, because I relieved the world of yet another psychopathic plutocrat. This one, was the one hell-bent on destroying what was left of this country. I still had my gun in hand, and I continued strolling down the hallway as if I had just come back from lunch break. I glanced down at my blouse and pants to see blood splattered on them.

I didn't care. It was my trophy.

I rounded the corner to see the ladies I saw earlier now cowering behind their cubicles as I passed. Natasha was gone. I spotted Megan in her office, and she smiled graciously when our eyes locked. I pressed the button to the elevator.

Ding.

I stepped inside and tried to calm my breathing from the adrenaline-high I was on.

"R—Rachel," the voice of Grey said, crackling through my ear piece.

"Yes?" I asked. "Can you hear me?"

"Barely. We—we are get—getting out of r—range. R—remember, put y—your hands…"

The elevator door slid open. I knew *exactly* what he meant.

Put your hands up.

Evelyn, the receptionist from earlier, let out a bloodcurdling scream as she saw me exit the elevator covered in blood. My heels clacked loudly, and I strode confidently across the marble floor with my hands held high. I dropped the gun I was carrying and walked towards the exit. The police officer who manned the metal detector was pointing his gun at me. The sounds of police sirens echoed from all directions, and I saw them swarming outside in the parking lot. I fell to my knees and kept my hands as high as I could.

The anger that filled me began to subside, and I felt just as I had before—numb—and that was perfectly fine with me. I knew killing Veronica wouldn't bring them back. The people I loved were still dead, but perhaps something greater would become of my bold act. Like Viktor said, *'Veronica has taken everyone's eyes, and now they can't see. If we take hers, perhaps we can restore the country's vision. People's memory of Owen will fade, they will forget about him.'*

That was the truth of our fast-paced society. People would *forget.* They would go about their daily lives and then latch onto whatever was dangled in front of their faces next. All of this, though, would hit home. The Confinement still haunted every American who was put behind the walls of those Camps. Owen tried to lead them out, but his efforts were cut short. People would forget about their hero…but today…today, they would *remember.*

"Down on the ground! Get on the ground, now!"

I lay flat on the ground, and the cold marble felt refreshing against my cheek. I saw the black shoes of cops surrounding me, and I felt the metal cuffs clasp around my wrists.

"Rachel Flores, you are under arrest!"

I-78 West – Williams, PA
10:51 10-31-2016

Ring…Ring…Ring…

I struggled to pull the phone out of my pocket. I held the steering wheel steady with my left hand. It was my son.

"Hello?"

"Dad! You won't believe what just happened."

My stomach sank. The worst possible scenarios crossed my mind as he said that.

"Is Rachel okay?!"

"She's alive…" He began, and I let out a huge sigh of relief. "She was just arrested at the EPA headquarters. She shot and killed Veronica Hall."

My jaw dropped, and I had to be careful to pay attention to traffic as I got off the interstate.

"No fucking way," I said. "She did it. She really did it…"

"Dad, it's all over the news. I could only imagine what's going on at your office right now."

My office…

He was right. It was probably pandemonium with a headliner like this for tomorrow.

"I bet," I said. "I'll have to call the office."

"Yeah, I'd say so."

"How is everything back at the house?" I asked.

"Good. I'll head up to the office if you want, to see what I can do until you get back. Where are you anyway?"

"Remember the video on YouTube of Owen revealing the truth that went viral?"

"Of course," Stefan answered.

"I'm about to interview him and his mother."

"Do you think they will be willing to talk?" he questioned.

"I do," I said. "They have nothing to worry about anymore. The truth will be out soon."

"You're right," he chuckled. "The world will finally know."

"Yes. Thank you for all of your contributions to that effort, Son. I love you."

"I love you too, Pops."

"I'll talk to you later. I have to go."

"All right, if I don't see you when you get back, I'll be down to visit soon. It's time for me to go back to Boston."

"Sounds good. Take care, Son."

"You too, Dad."

I ended the call and slowly navigated the suburban roads of Allentown. The son's interrogation wasn't publicized, but one of my sources informed me of the sudden removal of the video off the internet. *They* were trying to cover their tracks, and every little piece I could find would help Rachel compose a hard-hitting article. We had one week left until the election.

Images of Rachel shooting Veronica Hall point blank kept resurfacing in my mind. I knew she had a good heart, and it was hard to picture that she even did it…but it was reality. Somewhere in Washington, my goddaughter was sitting in a jail cell. I had so many phone calls to make.

Ring…Ring…

It was my office number calling.

"Hello?" I picked up.

"Ian," Sharon began, her voice trembling with excitement.

"Yes?"

"You got a fax," she breathed into the phone.

My heart pulsed from her words. Was it from them?

"From?"

"The number it was sent from is a 202 area code. It looks like it was sent from Washington. It's everything, Ian. Everything you needed to confirm Stefan's research. Everything they hid about Black Monday is there. I'm holding it in my hands right now."

I almost slammed the brakes from the news. It was difficult to listen to Sharon while simultaneously trying to find this house I was headed to.

"Sharon," I lowered my tone. "Take those files down to my storage safe in the basement and lock it up until I get back."

"Got it. I'll go now."

"Also," I said, "I'll be back in around three hours. Book me the first flight after 3 o'clock from JFK to Dulles."

"Will do, stay safe out there. Okay?"

"I will, thank you, Sharon. Take care of those files with your life."

"Absolutely. See you in a few hours. Goodbye."

"Bye."

The call ended. I navigated down a neighborhood street and stopped at a stop sign. The green street sign on the corner read **Valley Dr.** I took a right and slowly crept down the street. I read each mailbox as I passed them. 437, 435—they were counting down by odd numbers. It must have been on the other side of the street. I struggled to see the numbers on the other side, but I saw a two-story brick house on the opposite side with the address above the door in gilded numbers.

428—this was it. I pulled in the driveway and put the car in park. I hoped that someone was home. I got out of the car, stretching out after the two-hour drive from New York. I followed the pathway up to the porch. Dead leaves blew around the yard, and most of the trees had already lost their leaves. Winter was coming fast. When I reached the door, I rang the doorbell and combed through my hair with my fingers.

Twenty seconds—nothing.

I rang it again. I wasn't going to leave after driving so far to get here. I purposely wore a pastel-colored button up and a simple tie. I figured, when the feds came, they were most likely dressed in black and were intimidating. I was not in a cop car, I drove my Tesla. I hoped I appeared harmless enough for someone to open the door.

Suddenly, the door barely cracked open. I saw the eye of a woman hiding behind the door. Her reddish-brown hair slipped down beside the half of her face she revealed.

"Can I help you?" she asked. Her voice was shaky.

"Yes, actually. My name is Ian Westlake, and I am the Editor and Chief of the New York Times. I had a source tell me that he was quite certain that you and your son were interrogated by the federal government."

She shut the door in my face. I banged my fist on the door in reaction. I was surprised that she didn't even give me the time of day.

"I am not a cop!" I shouted. "I want to help you!"

Nothing.

"You know, if you don't tell your story, they will do what they did to you to someone else!"

Nothing.

"Miss, you have to understand that you are no longer in danger! The people who took that video off the internet are about to be exposed for all the treason they have committed. They are terrorists, miss! We have proof they framed Owen, and if you don't help us, the people of this country might be in danger! Please…" I pleaded.

The door swung fully open. On the other side of the storm door was a woman who looked to be in her late thirties. She pursed her lips and looked at me as if she was still distrusting. Her arms were crossed, and there were bags under her eyes.

"Why do you want to help us?" she asked.

"Because," I began, "the only way we will stop them is to show the country what happened. You are a part of that story, unfortunately, and I know you wouldn't want them to do that to anyone else. They had no right to come into your home. They had no right to scare your son. All I want to do is document what happened and let you tell your story."

Her lower lip quivered, and I saw tears pooling up in the corners of her eyes.

"Come in," she said, and opened the door for me.

620 8th Ave. – New York, NY
15:14 10-31-2016

I pressed the B5 button in the elevator. It was beneath the four floors of parking our building had, and B5 was our level for storage. I checked in with Sharon to make sure she had done what I asked of her. Like I expected, she had. I was still disturbed from Mrs. Bryant's account of the interrogation. Her son, Brody's YouTube video got over fifty-million views in less than a week. When the feds came to interrogate them, she said two men arrived in a black Yukon Denali and told her to let them in. They threatened to kill their family if they were to ever speak of the interrogation, or that they even visited them to begin with. They made Brody take down his video immediately.

She was frightened for her family. What was a mother to do but remain quiet? After what Rachel did today, I knew in just a day or two we would all be safe. The people who were behind all of this would be served justice.

Ding.

The doors opened, and I slowly meandered through the full room. There were boxes and plaques, rows of file cabinets, and in the far corner of the room I had a massive, iron safe. When I finally reached it, I took a deep breath. I began turning the large, metal dial to put in the combination. The numbers were Emilio's birthday.

It showed in the years after his death I had a hard time forgetting about what happened to him. I turned the iron bars and popped it open. Inside there were some belongings, but on the top shelf was a manila folder thick with paper. My heart fluttered as I took it down, and I opened it. I knew my son's evidence was already in here, but the papers on top were different. They were images of what looked to be shipping containers. The timestamps were from January of 2015.

This was it. Now, Rachel had everything she needed to write the article. I slid the papers from my interview with Mrs. Bryant inside. It was handwritten. I closed it shut and headed back to the elevator. I rode the elevator up to the parking garage. It was time for me to go. On the way back from Allentown, I called my lawyer and told him to start charging me effective immediately. I offered him a hefty payment if he could accompany me on the flight to Washington. It took off at five, and I had to get these papers to Rachel.

I reached my car and got inside. The Tesla's design was nothing short of incredible. It was wicked fast and a zero-emission vehicle. I circled out of the parking garage, slowly making my way up. The falling sun hung in the blue sky. There wasn't a cloud to be seen.

Something felt *different.* I smiled, because the sensation began to percolate through my body, and it was wonderful. Although Rachel was behind bars, I knew that the contents of this folder would get her out of there…and maybe, just maybe—we could save the election in time.

1901 D St. SE – Washington, D.C.
18:38 10-31-2016

Four white walls surrounded me. There was a square hole in the door I could see out of. It was a sad excuse for a window. I sat on the bed, leaning against the wall. The mattress was more like a wrestling mat and extremely uncomfortable. I could only imagine what it was like to spend a lifetime here. Sometimes, the punishment fit the crime. I wondered how many politicians should have spent time behind these bars, but were never accused of the crimes they committed. I knew why I was here.

Murder. I killed Veronica Hall, and I didn't regret it for a second. I just prayed that my mom wasn't looking down at me ashamed of my actions. I knew Owen would have been happy just at the fact that I made it out alive. I wondered if someone was coming for me. There was no clock in my cell. I had no perception of the passing time, and that was miserable. I think it had at least been six or seven hours. I looked down at my garb.

'Happy Halloween,' Grey's voice echoed in my head, and I chuckled. I had gone from assassin to prisoner in less than an hour. Now, my costume was an orange jumpsuit. The guards pushed me around as they led me to my cell and wouldn't even look me in the eyes. I guess that was how the most wanted woman in America gets treated. My counterpart was dead, and I was the only one left for them to catch.

I wondered where Grey, Briana, Viktor, and Natasha were. I hoped Viktor made it back to them without getting caught. I was glad they left me. Anything to keep them safe was what I wanted. Our plan worked. Third time's a charm, right?

Suddenly, the flap in my cell door opened.

"Ms. Flores, stick your hands through the opening."

I walked slowly and stuck them through. The handcuffs clasped tightly around my wrists. I stepped back, and the door slid open. "Follow me," he instructed in his gravelly voice. We walked down the same hall that I had come in from, and then we turned a corner. It was hard to make progress when my ankles were shackled together. The man led me to a door, and he pressed a button that opened it. When I was inside, I almost cried from who I saw.

It was Ian and another man, sitting behind a Plexiglas wall. Tears began to stream down my cheeks, and I sat down in front of them. He hadn't changed a bit. He still had his salt and pepper hair, which was a little grayer than the last time I saw him, and there were fine wrinkles around his eyes and mouth when he smiled. The man next to him was in a full suit and had a briefcase sitting on the counter. Ian picked up the phone and I did the same.

"Hello, Rachel," he said and revealed a comforting smile.

"Hi, Ian."

I tried not to cry. I missed him. He was the only *real* family I had left.

"So, I have some good news and some bad news. Which do you want to hear first?"

My heart sank from his words, but how much worse could it get?

"The bad," I answered.

He pressed his lips together before answering.

"The bad news is, that because the government views you as a threat to National Security, you haven't been granted a bond. I can't get you out of here."

I felt my lip curl up into a pout as I fought the urge to cry.

"But, the good news is that I have convinced the magistrate to give you an isolation cell and allow you to have a pen…"

I locked eyes with him and realized what he was referring to.

"This is my lawyer, Thomas Gladden—the best legal representation in the Northeast. He is your lawyer now. We are going to work on getting the judge to set you a bond, and once we do, I will pay it."

"Ian, you don't have to do that," I said, becoming emotional. This man was the father who helped guide me when I felt lost after my own died.

"I want to. You don't deserve to be locked up. Veronica should have been locked up a long time ago."

I nodded, looking through the glass at them.

Mr. Gladden opened his briefcase and pulled out a manila folder so thick with papers it bulged out from every side. He handed it to Ian, and Ian slid it underneath an opening in the glass to me. I looked down at it and stared with disbelief. My heart began to race.

"Open it," he said.

I set the phone down and felt my heart flutter before I opened it. The first paper had the logo of the EPA on it. A few more back and there were the images of Viktor's bomb-less cargo containers. I felt so overwhelmed. Ian tapped on the glass and pointed to the phone. I closed the folder and picked up the phone again.

"Is that?" I gasped.

"Yes," he said, nodding. "That is *everything* you need to write your story."

My jaw dropped. I couldn't believe this day had finally come, even if I was in handcuffs. My hand quivered as I held the phone against my ear.

"Rachel," Ian began, pulling me from my thoughts. "You have forty-eight hours to write the story. I will stay here in D.C. in the meantime and work on getting your bond set."

"Time's up," echoed the guard behind me.

"I love you," I said to him.

He placed his hand on the glass, and I placed mine against his. Mine was so much smaller.

"I love you too," he responded. I grabbed the folder and hung up the phone.

"Rachel!" I heard his muffled voice from behind the Plexiglas. I looked at him confused. He pointed down to the counter. "You're forgetting something."

It was a pen. He pushed it through the small opening, and I grabbed it. I gave him a nod goodbye out of respect. He was the *only* person fighting for me now.

The guard came behind and pushed me forward.

"Keep your hands out where I can see them," he huffed.

"Got it," I said.

He led me down a new hall, and we took a few turns before he opened a door. It was a different cell. It was newer and cleaner. The bed looked just as uncomfortable. There was a notebook sitting by the deflated-looking pillow.

"Drop the pen, and stick your hands out of the slot."

I tossed the pen on the bed, and within a moment, my hands were freed.

"You have forty-eight hours until you are returned to your original cell."

I didn't say a word. I just took a deep breath and walked to the bed. The folder was clutched to my chest. I sat down and held the folder in my lap. I let out a long, exasperated exhale. The pen was sitting next to the notebook, and I knew the moment that slot closed the time was ticking. I wouldn't sleep if that was what it took to finish in time.

My eyes started to glisten, and a tear rolled down my cheek. I choked back a laugh as I cried, and I started to smile from the memories as they resurged in my mind.

All of this began with that one morning at the coffee shop…and to think, I was debating on just going to a drive-thru instead. I couldn't imagine what my life would have been like if I *hadn't* met him. Sure, I would have been safer. I would have been free, but for how long? How long would it have been before the people who caught Owen, did the same thing to everyone else? I went in for a cappuccino and walked out with the most talked-about politician of the twenty-first century. I had no idea that he was standing behind me in line. I still remembered the feeling of when he sat down, and we first locked eyes. I was a bundle of nerves, but something inside told me to stand up and not let the moment pass me by. Opportunity had knocked, and that fateful day, I chose to open the door. I knew he was innocent, and I knew he needed my help. I wished I could have kept him safe. I wished I could have saved him. In a way, though—he saved me. He saved me from leading an average life, from just being a name in bold font at the top of an overlooked section of a local paper.

I wiped the tears as they flowed down my face. I flipped through all the papers and began reading. I glanced over at the pen, knowing that when I was done, what was to come. My dad's voice echoed in the back of my head. *'Justice is like fire; if you cover it with a veil, it still burns.'* It only made me cry harder, and I struggled to keep my vision from blurring.

I told Owen that morning it was fate that we met. Now, two weeks later, I realized the truth in my words. I wanted to document something that was being covered up by the people who had too much power, who were killing this country. That was all I wanted when I first saw him. I had no idea what I would go through. I had no idea that I would fall in love…

Owen was gone, but I got what I wanted…and so did he. Above all else, he wanted me to get the *truth* out there. And now, in *this* present moment, I was going to write the story that would save us all, in honor of the man who sacrificed his life to make it possible.

Sofra Bakery & Café – Cambridge, MA
09:22 11-01-2016

The cold air whipped around my coat, and I stood there with my hands deep in my pockets. She said she would be here at 9:15. It felt like it had been so long since we were separated that morning at the lab. People walked by without paying me any attention. They were all on their cellphones, sipping on their coffees or listening to music. They had no idea they were walking past the scientist who helped contribute research to uncovering one of the most dangerous lies in the history of the country, but they would know soon enough.

"Well hey there, stranger!" a delicate voice called from behind.

I turned around to see Emily, with her short, black hair tucked behind an ear. The rest of it whipped against her neck. A smile tugged at her lips, and I walked over and gave her a big hug. After a few seconds, she pulled her head back to look at me. Her eyes darted across my face, and she revealed a perfect grin.

"Hello, Emily,"

"*Em*," she corrected.

I let out a loud laugh, shaking my head.

"I thought you hated that nickname?"

"It's starting to grow on me," she said with a wink and pulled me closer.

"Oh, is it now?" I flirted back. I never felt this kind of chemistry between us before, but wherever it came from, I liked it.

"I believe so."

"You know what's crazy?" I asked.

"What?" Her eyebrows quirked.

"This is where you tried to talk me out of testing a second specimen, remember?"

"Oh, did I now?" she said with a wink. "Don't let that get to your head, Stefan. I ended up helping you with it anyway."

"I'm glad you did."

She rolled her eyes.

"Yeah, because with me you had a pretty girl to gawk at *and* do the dirty work in the lab."

"Aha, there's the Emily I remember—sharp as a knife."

She looked up at me smiling and let out a laugh.

"So…" She began hesitantly. "What's going on with your dad?"

"Actually, he is in D.C. with Rachel. She is his goddaughter. They had been talking to each other since the beginning when Owen was framed. She is a journalist, and she has all of our evidence. She is writing the story that will reveal the truth."

"Oh my God," she said. "You have *a lot* to tell me."

"That I do," I said, releasing her from the hug.

"Who said you could let me go?" she teased. "I've missed you."

Her voice was almost *loving*.

"I've missed you too. What happened to you while I was gone? Are you sure someone didn't kidnap the old you, and replace you with someone else?"

She laughed. "No. Maybe I just realized what was right in front of me. Our atoms never touch, but I felt something just now, when you held me close. That must mean something."

I glanced down at her with a growing smile.

"Now, is this just a hypothesis, or a theory?"

She slapped my forearm lightly.

"Funny, real funny."

Her eyes darted across my face again, and she gently bit her lower lip. I got the sense that she was waiting for something, and I leaned in and gave her a kiss. She held it longer than I expected. When we parted, her eyes were glowing.

"What was that?!" she asked, gasping from surprise.

I looked down at her slyly.

"I was testing the hypothesis."

"Very clever, Stefan," she chuckled.

"You know, we have to test it thousands of times before it's a *theory.*"

Her dimples appeared as she pursed her lips, trying to hold back a smile.

"Yes, I know. I think I'm okay with that."

I gently grabbed her hand, interlacing her fingers in my own.

"So, do you think the FBI is stalking us anymore?" she asked.

"No," I answered. "They are long gone. In a few days, everyone will know what has been going on the past two years. That's why I was so excited to see you. I wanted so badly to tell you that our research would be used in Rachel's article. Our resilience paid off, Em. It *worked.*"

"That's what two bright minds can do when they break a few laws. You saw past the lie from the beginning, Stefan. I helped because I knew science trumps any sensationalized rumor."

I gazed into her dark eyes lovingly.

"Thank you, Em," I said, clutching her hand tighter. "Let's go inside."

1901 D St. SE – Washington, D.C.
12:10 11-05-2016

I wrote the article in less than twenty-four hours. I didn't need forty-eight. I had all the information I could have ever wanted right at my fingertips. He flew back home on the second, and I knew he would take care of any editorial issues. The finishing touches were his job, not mine. I just compiled a tragic story into an eloquent article. I started all the way back at the beginning, before Black Monday, and went all the way to the end. There were many tears throughout the process…but I had never felt a more satisfying feeling than signing my name at the top when I was finished.

Rachel Flores — 11-02-2016

It was similar to the feeling you had when you finished a good book, like as if I were mentally parting with the pieces of the story that comprised it. It felt like a funeral, but I knew better. This wasn't the end of the story…it was the beginning. If my article spread like wildfire, then there would be nothing the government could do to stop it. It was our first amendment right, and I utilized it the best I could. Perhaps, it would be enough to save the election.

Ian came to pick up the article midday on the second. If what he told me was correct, then the article was published two days ago on the third. I prayed that it was being read and taken seriously. If people treated it like they did a tabloid, we wouldn't get very far. I hoped the reputation of the New York Times would help.

I wasn't granted a bond. I would be stuck here indefinitely. I passed the hours sleeping and reading. Mainly though, I thought about *him*. I talked to my mother before I fell asleep every night, and every morning when I woke. I called on their strength to get me through this dark time in my life. I was locked up for twenty-three hours a day, and that was how it would be until Ian found a way out for me, if he ever was able to.

I could rot in this prison for all I cared. As long as my article *worked*, I would be fine. That was all that mattered to me, and I realized that further when I wrote the article. Regardless of what happened, the world would remember the cover story of the New York Times on November 3rd, 2016. I authored it, I lived it. It was a part of me, a part of *my* story.

I knew it was just past noon because we were at recreation. The one hour of the day we were able to do something other than sit in our cells. Briana was right—a *'Barbie doll'* like me wouldn't do well in prison. I almost got beat up my second day out on the quad. So now, I would watch TV in the rec room. Or, I would do exercises on the far side of the quad. Anything to stay away from the larger, more muscular women. Today, I was almost finished with a puzzle in the game room. There was a foosball table, a TV, and many board games and puzzles. The older inmates hung out in here. They didn't get near the more violent ones.

Orange was all I saw nowadays. On myself, and on others. I could have never seen the color again and I would have been perfectly happy. I read two books in the past three days, but nothing seemed to pass the time well enough. I sat upright and placed the different pieces in their correct spots, and the picture began to form. It was a cheetah. Now, all I had left to do were the edges.

"Isn't that the same girl named Rachel?" I heard someone ask. My forehead scrunched up because I rarely interacted with the other inmates. I had no desire to.

"Yes, it is," an older inmate I knew as Betty replied. I didn't talk to her much, but she was kind enough to befriend me at lunch and dinner. I wasn't trying to make friends in here, but whatever protection I could get, I would take.

"Go get her!" the other voice urged. The rec-room was two rooms connected by a short hallway. The TV and couches were in one room, and all the games in the other. I saw Betty walking down the hall, and immediately my heart raced. Betty seemed harmless, but from what I had already seen in this prison, that could change in a second.

She stopped a foot away from the table and glanced down at my puzzle.

"Take a break. You need to see this."

"Why?" I asked, startled.

"Just trust me. Remember the story you told me at dinner about why you are in here?"

My eyes grew wide, and my heart fluttered. She didn't need to say more. I pushed myself up from the table and I followed her down the hall. I could hear a man's voice on the TV. When we rounded the corner, I saw three other female inmates surrounding the TV.

"Make some room," Betty demanded as we approached.

"Is that really her name?" one of them asked, glancing at me.

"Yes," Betty answered for me. "Look, Rachel…"

The anchor's voice was finally clear.

"…In remembrance of Guy Fawkes Day, every November 5th, people across the country and the globe protest political corruption. In years previous, it has primarily been in Washington, D.C., and many other capital cities around the world. Today is different. Many believe it is due to the article published by the New York Times two days ago regarding the framing of Owen Marina for the bombs at Georgetown, and Viktor Ivankov for the events that took place on Black Monday. Once again, here is an aerial view of what is going on in Times Square. Tens of thousands have shown up to protest, shutting down city streets, and we are getting reports in from Washington, Miami, Los Angeles, Chicago. These protests are nationwide…"

My mouth was agape. I covered it with my hand in disbelief of what I saw. There were *thousands* of people chanting in the streets. I saw signs that read, **Free Rachel Flores**. My eyes began to glisten, and I choked back a cry. There were others, one which read, **Viktor is a Hero. Owen is a Hero.** I saw another, **With One Lie Our Freedom Dies**.

I couldn't believe what I was seeing. The tears streamed down my face as I witnessed this moment. The passion in the voices of the people was unreal, all standing up for us at the same time. The article worked. People *knew*.

The camera zoomed in, and I saw a woman holding a huge white sign.

She Saved Us.

I couldn't silence my cries any longer. That sign was about *me*. If only they could have come along for the journey I had been on and felt the pain. Then, maybe, they would realize that I didn't save them at all. We saved ourselves. I was just like them. I just knew what I had to do, and I did it. Owen was the *real* hero of this story, and maybe now his effort wouldn't be forgotten. Maybe they would *remember*.

620 8th Ave. – New York, NY
12:21 11-05-2016

I stood at the edge of my office, looking down at the crowd of thousands in awe. Emotion welled up inside of me, and I covered my mouth in shock. The floor to ceiling glass gave our office a perfect view of the protests below. The signs were about everything that was in the article, from freeing Rachel, to hailing Viktor and Owen as heroes. It was what they deserved. After what our government put them through, it was more than necessary. Owen gave his life for his party, and this story.

We could hear the echoes of the voices below, and the photographers in my office were shooting through the windows, and using the roof access to document this moment in history. I knew when I signed my signature approving Rachel's article to be published, it would galvanize the masses into action.

Nothing had been written so truthful in decades. I read it dozens of times. It made me cry. Rachel's writing was so *raw*—it was a beautiful, yet tragic story. It not only told the series of events that led up to Owen's death, it touched the hearts of those who read it. Stefan had the same reaction. He called me up shouting in joy.

The election was in three days, and I was nervous on whether or not we could still beat the democrats. With their chairwoman exposed as the most villainous figure in Washington, I didn't see how that would be possible. Although Owen's party hadn't won yet, I felt like I could finally breathe. Rachel was still in jail, and unfortunately, there was nothing I could do at the moment about that. I just hoped she had access to a TV, so she could see what came about after her article. In all my years, I had never seen anything like *this*. Today would go down in history as the day when our country finally woke up. Owen and his party helped provide the initial push towards change, and it was somewhat like a spark. Rachel, what she did with her article, was like pouring gasoline and causing a blaze.

Veronica was dead, and the people involved would soon be held accountable for their treason. The American People wouldn't settle for anything less, and I was damn proud to have been a part of this. The people *knew*, and that truth was priceless.

Emilio would be proud. I knew he would be if he was here, to see the effect his daughter had at such a young age.

"Ian," Sharon called from behind me. Her head popped in between the crack in my office door.

"What is it?" I asked.

She made a confused face and shrugged her shoulders.

"I mean, I can send it to your voicemail if you want. She doesn't speak good English."

"What is it regarding?"

"Well, she claims to have met Owen during his journey. She said something about a picture."

Although the article was already published, this intrigued me. I figured I would give the lady a chance. Given the popularity of the article, people had been calling en masse to our office. They ranged from people who went to school with Owen, worked in his office, or knew him when he was a child. This though, made me wonder enough to want to speak to the woman.

"Send it to my line," I said.

Sharon nodded her head, and her poufy, blonde curls bounced as she did so.

I walked over to my desk and let out a long exhale. I hadn't felt this relieved since I found out Rachel was still alive and well.

Line four flashed red, and I picked it up.

"Ian Westlake," I said.

"Oh, hello, Mr. Westlake," a woman responded on the other end. Her oriental accent was extremely heavy like Sharon described.

"Hello there. You mentioned to my assistant that you had a picture of Owen during his journey?"

"Yes. Yes, I do."

"What is your name, my dear?"

"My name is Laura Vang, and I meet Owen three weeks ago."

"Tell me, Laura. How did you meet him?"

"Well, he was eating pizza across from me at hotel restaurant in Raleigh. He so handsome, you know. I couldn't not stare. We end up talking for long time, and he was so kind to me. I know the government frame him all along, and I tell him advice."

"Really? How interesting. How did this picture come about?"

I heard her chuckle, and I couldn't tell if she was just sniffling, or if she was tearing up.

"My daughter and I very poor, and Owen needed hair dye and new clothes. He offer me money to get it. He gave me twenty-two hundred dollars, and gave me twenty-eight hundred more when I came back. I bought a camera, and we took a picture together. I read article and decided to call. You know, I cry when Owen die. He asked me not to show the picture to anyone."

"Yeah…" I began, with a somber note in my voice. "I heard from a few people he was a very good guy."

Rachel…

"Yes, Mr. Westlake—very good guy. May I email you picture? Maybe, if you publish an article in future, you can use my photo. It would be an honor."

"Yes, please. My email is ian.westlake@thetimes.com."

"Okay, I send now."

"Thank you very much, Ms. Vang. It was a pleasure to hear from you."

"The pleasure is all mine," her raspy voice crackled.

The line hung up, and I opened my laptop. Within a few moments, I saw a new email in my inbox. I opened it. There was an attachment, and it took only a second to download.

When it opened, I couldn't help but grin.

It was Owen, standing with his arm around this Asian woman with a humungous grin. She had a missing tooth, and the ones that remained were yellow. She wore a green windbreaker and purple pants. He was smiling, too. The whole feeling I got from the photo was genuine. Even better, Owen's hair was still his natural color—sandy-brown.

This photo was from the beginning of Owen's struggle, and now he was no longer on this Earth. Wherever he was, I knew if he could see the *thousands* upon *thousands* of people filling the streets of every major city in the country, he would be smiling. He lost his life, but what was gained in the process was something no money could ever buy. He saved his fellow man, risking his own life, and in the end, sacrificed himself for the greater good…because of his bravery, America would not perish. Lady liberty would live on.

I smiled, and my eyes glistened. The truth was what he was fighting so hard to get out, and it worked. There was also another truth I was aware of, and that was the most important of all.

A true hero *never* dies…

Le Café – Cannes, France
10:51 03-04-2017

Today was a special day. I got a letter from Grey. It sat on the wrought iron table in front of me—unopened. I didn't dare open it at home. If I did, I risked staying in bed all day. It would have brought back too many memories. So, I forced myself out of my flat and came here. I hadn't talked to any of them since the day I killed Veronica.

I spent my twenty-fourth birthday in prison. Ian came and visited, and I appreciated that. I had no one left to celebrate it with. Those two and a half months I spent in there were a reminder of why we did this in the first place. It was like living through the Confinement twice. I couldn't stand to see the color orange anymore. It made me sick. I read probably over a hundred books while I was in there and had a lot of time to think. *Too* much time.

Sometimes, the silence was my best friend. Sometimes, it was my worst enemy. In that time in prison, it was my only companion. I grew to know it well. Now, the silence wasn't as bad. It was calming because I was free, but, deep down, I wished I had someone to talk to. My family was gone, and so were my friends. Glancing down at the American return address on the envelope and seeing the name Grey Maxwell made my stomach tremble. I missed them all terribly. It was a short and tumultuous two weeks, but during that time we made an unbreakable bond. How could one forget the things we went through? It was impossible. I was changed from the experience, and I doubted I would ever feel *normal* again. Then again, did I really want to? No. The answer was no. I would have done it all over again just to see him one more time. He still visited me in my dreams, and I savored every moment of it.

I thought in time it would get easier, but I was wrong. I couldn't think of his name anymore. It just hurt too much. The memory of him lived on in my mind forever, and I was perfectly content with that. I had no desire to *forget*. I knew if it were reversed, he would do the same thing. He wouldn't forget me. It wasn't his nature.

I sipped on my coffee and stared out at the sea. Its cerulean hue was emphasized by the light of the sun, which beamed down on me. I had a light, long-sleeve shirt on. It was cool, but not cold. This part of France stayed temperate for the majority of the year. I hadn't even been here two months, but I was slowly adjusting to the way of life. People needed less to make themselves happy. The instant gratification of life in the west was nonexistent. Stores closed at seven, and there was more time off for workers than back home in the States. Sure, there were plenty of things that were different. The language was one, and I was slowly learning. The cars were smaller, and there wasn't really any fast food. So far, though, I liked it. It reminded me of *him*.

The letter beckoned me to rip it open, but I didn't. I grabbed it and rubbed my fingers along its edges. I had to prepare for the emotions that would come with reading whatever was inside, and hearing Grey's voice as I read it would be enough to put me over the edge. I wondered whatever wound up of Viktor and Natasha, and I prayed that Briana was healthy and happy.

I tossed my hair over one shoulder and smoothed it out with my hands. It had begun to grow back out, revealing its natural brown color, and I quickly dyed it again. There was something about having black hair that made me feel whole. I clung to my former self. The reality in which *he* was still alive. It also matched my soul—black, and empty. Maybe one day I would let it grow out again, but in the meantime there wasn't a chance in Hell.

Ian called me one night shortly after I moved. After some small talk, he had asked me why I decided to live here. I didn't tell him the *real* truth because he didn't need to know. I told him it was because of the weather, and that I needed to get away. He was surprised because, after all that had changed from my article, he figured I would have stayed. He couldn't have been more wrong in that assumption. Why would I have wanted to stay in the country that *he* gave his life for? I was thankful the rest of the country would be safe, but for me, it was different. Every step I took on that ground was like walking on thorns. It caused my insides to ache after a while. I was living on the land that took the man I loved from me. I couldn't do it any longer. I knew that the moment I got out I would be gone…and I kept that promise to myself. So now, here I was in Cannes, living in a flat and taking a much-needed break. Ian had no clue why I *really* came here. It was because of him. Anything I could do to get closer to him, I did.

"I was thinking more like the French Riviera. Nice, Cannes—maybe spend a night playing blackjack at a casino in Monaco. I can see it now, waking up and having coffee at an outdoor café, basking in the sun on the beach, and finishing the day off with some French Cuisine and a glass of wine."

I heard the echo of my own voice that night on the beach. It was my suggestion, but he told me immediately after how he wanted to visit too, because his mother loved French Culture. If only he were here with me, on the vacation he would never get to go on.

I drew in a sharp inhale and steadied it as I let it out.

It took everything in my being to hold myself together.

That was why I came here. It reminded me of him. It was where we were going to go together when all of this was over, and now it was…but I was alone. That, was why I cried falling asleep at night. I fell in love with a man who I only knew for two weeks, and I would never get the chance to *have* a chance at loving him. It killed me inside.

The palm trees whipped around in the breeze, and cars beeped their horns as they drove down the road between me and the sea. I was already getting used to this stress-free way of life, but something was missing. *He* was missing, and I couldn't get him back.

On November 8th, it pained me that I couldn't cast my vote for the Convergence Party, but I knew that up above, wherever he may have been, he knew I did what I could to keep his party alive long enough to make it to the election. My article had touched every corner of the country, and that evening from jail I cried when we heard the news.

Paul Goodman was President-Elect. The Convergence Party won—*we* won. It was the happiest I had been since before he died. I smiled for an entire week it felt like. After everything we had been through, our effort paid off. I *did* what Owen wanted me to do most, and he was right, it worked. My article worked. I remembered looking up at the ceiling of my jail cell and cheering to the sky, telling him that his party had won. I cried even harder when I realized he wasn't here to celebrate, and neither was Cole. The founders of the Convergence Party were killed by the hands of a few evil people. I slept easy that night, though, knowing that the people would never have to be awoken in the middle of the night, thrown into flatbed trucks, and brought to Camps. The Confinement was a blemish in our history, and it would never be repeated. The people behind all of it were held to justice. My court date was set for June, but luckily for me, I was pardoned by President Paul Goodman on January 20th—the same day he took office. It was an amazing feeling to finally be free again, but I didn't stay long. It hurt too badly to be reminded of the things he gave his life for. Sure, I could have lived the rest of my life in the States and enjoyed the fruits of his labor, but I couldn't. Maybe I would go back someday, but not now. It was too soon. There was nothing left for me over there but pain.

I took a deep breath and let out a shuddering exhale. I used my finger to open the envelope, and I pulled out some papers. It wasn't just one. It looked like a letter, and a long one at that. I noticed some of them were photocopies of something, but I decided to start with what I saw first. I found the front page and tried to calm my racing heart before I began.

Dear Rachel,

It will probably take you a month to get this letter because you are across the pond, but I hope you do write back. I miss having you around, and I think of the days we all spent together constantly. I have a feeling you do too, and that was why you couldn't stay around after you were let out…

Grey—he was always a few steps ahead of everyone. I chuckled from his accurate assumption.

How is the French Riviera? Are you eating lots of baguettes and drinking lots of wine? Please do, for me. Briana is well. I spoke to her recently. She is back in Orlando and apparently going to college. That is, after she got back from her three-month trip around the globe with her boyfriend. She told me to please tell you that she loves you and misses you, and that she will come visit soon.

CBS did a Sixty Minutes special on Owen and all of those involved. I decided to give them some of my side of the story, and they dubbed me as the 'hacker who couldn't be stopped.' I wished Natasha would have joined me, because she is just as talented as I am. I have only spoken to Viktor once, but from what he told me he is back in New York with Natasha. He was reunited with his family for the first time in two years, and he said he has no plans on leaving them any time soon. Lucas retired from the CIA and was given an honorary ceremony for his bravery against what Veronica and company were up to. Megan left Washington altogether he told me, and I'm not sure where she went. Vinny and Luke say hello. They are making good use of their money. They are expanding the garage. I hope you are making good use of yours, too.

He was talking about the money he stole in the beginning. He promised Briana and my cousins 350K, and he kept his end of the deal. I assumed Grey kept a portion for his self, but I didn't know for sure. When I was finally let out, I returned to my apartment in Raleigh. Unfortunately, I was evicted for three months overdue on rent. During that time, I kept receiving mail. I found a letter from a Swiss Bank. It was a statement. I was surprised to find I had three-hundred and fifty thousand dollars in it. I knew it was Grey.

You thought that all Owen and I were talking about on the terrace that night was how much he loved you, but that wasn't all. He told me to make sure you got that money no matter what. So now you know…

I felt a smile tug at my lips.

That sly dog he was. I looked up at the sky and wondered if he could see me now, thanking him for all he did for me in the time we knew each other.

Our country is doing better than ever. Goodman is cleaning house in Washington and there is zero opposition. The American People support him wholeheartedly. After the Confinement and discovering the massive lie they were spoon-fed just before the elections, I am pretty sure that is the reason they are all for him. He will be a good president. The stocks are up, spending is up, and crime is down. People are finally getting back to normal again, which is hard for most to remember what that was like…

Just remember, Rach, you are always welcome to come back. I am still in Virginia for now, but I think I might be moving soon. Too many memories for me here, and I am sure you know the feeling. I want to go somewhere warm. How is the weather over there? Maybe I should join you. Well, anyway, I hope to hear from you soon. The other papers you see are photocopies of your article. I wasn't sure if you ever got to read it. It is excellent, by the way. It couldn't have been better executed. Oh, and somewhere between those papers I stuck in two pictures of Owen. One was from another article Ian published in the newspaper, and the other one you took…

I took?

It was from Viktor's Nikon—the one you took to see Owen just before he…Yeah, you know, I don't have to say it.

My stomach dropped from the thought of seeing him in a picture. Would I be able to contain the tears? I decided to skim through my article first. I picked up the paper, and two pictures fell out. I flipped them over before I could see them. I straightened the papers out and began to read.

The Gambit

By: Rachel Flores

The New Year came all too quickly for Viktor Ivankov, who was Port of New York's Chief X-Ray Radiography operator. He informed me that during the holidays, the federal government paid visits to his department on numerous occasions, but a certain woman stuck out more than the rest—Veronica Hall. Ivankov began to keep a record of the containers he x-rayed during the day and put them on a flash drive. He knew his work habits were being studied, and soon, he was framed for a crime he didn't commit…

I continued skimming, and it made me emotional reliving the hours it took to write this. It was emotional and painful. I went through everything from the beginning with Viktor, to when I decided to approach Owen at the coffee shop that fateful morning. Then, I quickly highlighted our journey, but made sure to pepper in the evidence throughout the story. I tried to finish it with something that would hit home and resonate with people.

Veronica Hall was behind the murder of Owen Marina. There are many other officials involved, which will soon come to light. As a country, we should never forget the sacrifice he made for us. Owen was a pawn on the chessboard, and the queen took him out of this world. He had the courage to fight until the end, for all of you. He went through the Confinement, just as I did, and just as you all did. That memory, that bond—it's powerful. He knew that if he let Veronica win, we would all lose. None of us would be safe, and the process would begin again. We could have been put into a Confinement that never ends. No one wants that, and he didn't either. It was an honor to assist him in his struggle and to be able to document the process. As you share this article with your loved ones, keep one thing in mind. Owen Marina died for us, and we shouldn't let his life be in vain. We can't let the people who did this win. We the people rule this country, not the governing body. Honor him, and make the decision to fight back against the people who did this to us. So, the real question is, are we going to sit back on the sidelines and watch as our country falls to pieces? Or, are we going to take action and become a part of history? The choice is ours. **11-02-2016**.

I titled it the Gambit, because that was what Viktor called him in the basement when he and Natasha kidnapped us.

'Don't you see what I am trying to say to you, Owen? All you are is a gambit to them! You are a fucking sacrifice! You are just a pawn and Veronica is the queen. If you go through with your plan, I promise you, they will win. Don't be their gambit. Don't give yourself up so easily.'

I could still see the vein in Viktor's forehead pulse as he yelled at him. Sadly, he was right. Owen *was* their sacrifice.

I turned the first picture over. It was Owen, and he had a determined stare on his face. His hands were high in the air, and his knees were just barely bent as if he were about to start kneeling. His dyed, black hair was sweaty and disheveled. I brushed my finger across the photo, and emotions swam around my insides. It was such an intense picture, with the dozens of cops surrounding him with their automatic weapons. I almost thought if I stared long enough I would be able to see his chest heave up and down in breathing. Although, this photo was the moment before his death, I had never seen him look more *alive.* It was beautiful.

I picked up the other one and immediately giggled. Owen was staring back at me with a huge grin, holding an Asian woman by his side. She was grinning equally as wide, but her teeth weren't quite as nice as his. I flipped it over on the back, and it looked like Grey had written on it with a pen.

Raleigh, North Carolina — 10-13-2016

The thirteenth. I pulled out my phone and flipped back through my calendar. That was the night before we met. I clutched the photo to my chest and wiped my eyes as tears began to form As much as it hurt, I would have to keep this photo for memory's sake. A photo was a photo, though. It wasn't the real thing.

I shuffled through more of the papers and realized that Grey had written some more on the back of one of the papers. I began reading.

Anyway, Rachel. I hope to see you again. Never forget how much he cared about you, all right? It still saddens me that he died despite the precautions me and Viktor took…

My forehead scrunched up at the word—*precautions?*

What was he referring to? How come I hadn't known about this?

Huh, interesting.

Enjoy France. Get some sun, and let time heal the wounds you have. I know you think they will never go away, but take it from someone who is dealing with the same thing you are right now, they will. Take care of yourself, Rachel.

Love, Grey. 2-15-2017

I put the letter down and wiped the tears out of the corners of my eyes. I knew Grey was right, but it was hard to accept right now. In my mind, it felt like time couldn't heal all wounds. To me, nothing could get rid of the aching hole in my chest besides him. It would have helped if I had my mom here to console me, but she was gone, too. I felt like I had been dealt the shittiest cards at the table, and I hadn't even a single chip to cash in. *We* won, but *I* lost.

My promise still haunted me to this day. I promised him everything would be all right.

'Don't worry, you'll be fine,'

'Why did you just say me? You will be fine, too. We are going to get you out of this mess. I promise.'

'Don't make a promise you can't keep, Rachel.'

He was right all along. I couldn't keep my promise, and the fact that he wasn't here made me feel even more morose. I could still hear the eerie tone in his voice as he said, *'Don't worry, you'll be fine.'* It was like he knew. He knew all along he wouldn't make it out alive, and that notion destroyed me inside. And now, it was all over, and I *was* okay. I broke my promise.

Chatter surrounded me, and there were people at the many tables nearby. All amidst conversation, except me. I sat alone with a cup of coffee, as I had for over two months now. I wondered if I would ever feel whole again. Sure, the memory of him was enough to keep me going, but part of me didn't want to move on. I didn't want to *let go*. How could I let go of someone I never got the chance to call mine?

I couldn't. That was the answer. I still wanted Owen, but he was gone.

"*Mademoiselle,*" the waiter's voice said beside me. "*Pour vous.*"

He placed a vase full of red and purple roses on the table in front of me. I glanced back up at him confused.

"*Pour moi?*" I asked, almost breathless.

"*Oui,*" he said with a smile and walked away.

No, it can't be. There is no way…

My breath was shallow as I stared at them, and they were so beautiful. My heart fluttered, and my mouth remained agape. There was a little white tag attached to the glass vase. I grabbed it and paused before opening it. I rubbed the stock paper just to ensure I wasn't dreaming. I drew in a breath and exhaled slowly. I opened it.

Bonnie,

Today*, is one day.*

— Clyde.

There was a rock in my throat as the tears began to flow. A tremor arose within me, and I struggled to compose myself in front of everyone. The words echoed in my mind as if I had just heard them yesterday.

"Don't worry, Rachel. One day."

"One day?"

"One day you'll get flowers."

Every ounce of my being felt a mix of emotions so extreme I couldn't tell if I was crying out of sadness or joy. I gently rubbed one of the purple petals between my index finger and thumb. Owen's voice resurfaced once more. This time, it was from the night in Miami.

"What is your favorite color?"

"Red," he answered. "Yours?"

"Purple."

Red and purple roses. He signed the card *Clyde.*

I choked and struggled to wipe my eyes to clear my blurred vision. I became overwhelmed with a sensation I couldn't describe. It was as if all the pain I had kept bottled up since he died dissipated into thin air. It *had* to be him. How could he have known where I was going to be? I was smiling now, streaking the tears across my face as I wiped them. I let out a laugh, and the love I felt for Owen surged throughout my body. A gentle breeze blew past, and for a moment, I could have sworn I caught his scent in the air. This feeling was too strong to be anything but real, and I *felt* him. His presence was here. I could feel it. I sobbed harder at the thought of seeing him again, but my soul told me it wasn't lying. I cleared the tears from my eyes and drew in one long, steadying inhale. I let it out and grinned as the feeling only grew stronger. He *was* here. He had to be. I wasn't afraid anymore, and for the first time since the day he left me I didn't feel *alone.* We would have our time together. This was just the beginning.

My heart was full of love, and there was only one thing left to do.

I looked up.

About the Author

Allen Longstreet is a fiction author who resides in Hickory, North Carolina. Now at 22, he is attending college for a degree in creative writing, and has also been writing since he was a child. He has a preference in post-apocalyptic and dystopian. Allen has a strong interest in contemporary issues and problems society faces in this day and age. He plans on writing across a broad-spectrum of fiction, creating characters and stories we all can become attached to. Allen is an indie author and reviews are the backbone to an indie author's career. If you have any comments or would like to leave a review of this book, please go on Amazon and Goodreads to leave your opinion.